The BEASTLY Bride

Other Anthologies by
Ellen Datlow & Terri Windling

The Adult Fairy Tale Series
Snow White, Blood Red
Black Thorn, White Rose
Ruby Slippers, Golden Tears
Black Swan, White Raven
Silver Birch, Blood Moon
Black Heart, Ivory Bones

The Green Man: Tales from the Mythic Forest
The Faery Reel: Tales from the Twilight Realm
The Coyote Road: Trickster Tales

A Wolf at the Door
Swan Sister
Troll's-Eye View

Salon Fantastique
Sirens
The Year's Best Fantasy and Horror Volumes 1 through 16

The BEASTLY *Bride*

TALES *of the* ANIMAL PEOPLE

edited *by* Ellen Datlow *&* Terri Windling

introduction by Terri Windling

selected decorations by Charles Vess

VIKING

An Imprint of Penguin Group (USA) Inc.

VIKING

Published by Penguin Group

Penguin Group (USA) Inc., 345 Hudson Street, New York, New York 10014, U.S.A.
Penguin Group (Canada), 90 Eglinton Avenue East, Suite 700, Toronto, Ontario, Canada M4P 2Y3 (a division of Pearson Penguin Canada Inc.)
Penguin Books Ltd., 80 Strand, London WC2R 0RL, England
Penguin Ireland, 25 St Stephen's Green, Dublin 2, Ireland (a division of Penguin Books Ltd.)
Penguin Group (Australia), 250 Camberwell Road, Camberwell, Victoria 3124, Australia (a division of Pearson Australia Group Pty Ltd.)
Penguin Books India Pvt Ltd., 11 Community Centre, Panchsheel Park, New Delhi—110 017, India
Penguin Group (NZ), 67 Apollo Drive, Rosedale, North Shore 0632, New Zealand (a division of Pearson New Zealand Ltd.)
Penguin Books (South Africa) (Pty) Ltd, 24 Sturdee Avenue, Rosebank, Johannesburg 2196, South Africa
Penguin Books Ltd., Registered Offices: 80 Strand, London WC2R 0RL, England

First published in 2010 by Viking, a member of Penguin Group (USA) Inc.

1   3   5   7   9   10   8   6   4   2

LIBRARY OF CONGRESS CATALOGING-IN-PUBLICATION DATA

The beastly bride : tales of the animal people / edited by Ellen Datlow and Terri Windling.

v. cm.

Summary: A collection of stories and poems relating to animal transfiguration legends from around the world, retold and reimagined by various authors. Includes brief biographies, authors' notes, and suggestions for further reading.

Contents: Island lake / by E. Catherine Tobler—The puma's daughter / by Tanith Lee—Map of seventeen / by Christopher Barzak—The selkie speaks / by Delia Sherman—Bear's bride / by Johanna Sinisalo—The abominable child's tale / by Carol Emshwiller—The *hikikomori* / by Hiromi Goto—The comeuppance of Creegus Maxin / by Gregory Frost—Ganesha / by Jeffrey Ford—The elephant's bride / by Jane Yolen—The children of Cadmus / by Ellen Kushner—The white doe: three poems / by Jeannine Hall Gailey—Coyote and Valorosa / by Terra L. Gearhart-Serna—One thin dime / by Stewart Moore—The monkey bride / by Midori Snyder—*Pishaach* / by Shweta Narayan—The salamander fire / by Marly Youmans—The margay's children / by Richard Bowes—Thimbleriggery and Fledglings / by Steve Berman—The flock / by Lucius Shepard—The children of the shark god / by Peter S. Beagle—Rosina / by Nan Fry.

ISBN 978-0-670-01145-2

1. Human-animal relationships—Literary collections. 2. Supernatural—Literary collections. [1. Human-animal relationships—Literary collections. 2. Supernatural—Literary collections.] I. Datlow, Ellen. II. Windling, Terri.

PZ5.B387 2010   810.8'0374—dc22   2009014317

Printed in U.S.A.   Set in New Aster   Book design by Nancy Brennan

*For Charles de Lint and MaryAnn Harris,
who know the Animal People better than most,
with thanks for all you do to keep magic alive.*

—E.D. & T.W.

CONTENTS

PREFACE

Ellen Datlow & Terri Windling

Werewolves, vampire bats, fox demons, the Animagi in the Harry Potter books, and Beast Boy/Changeling in the *Teen Titans* comics. What do all these characters have in common? They are shape-shifters. More specifically, they are *therianthropic* figures, capable of transforming between human and animal shape. And as such, they are part of a mythic tradition as old as storytelling itself.

Although the werewolf is undoubtedly the best-known human-to-animal shape-shifter in popular culture today, when we turn to world mythology we find that transformation legends are attached to almost every kind of animal—as well as to a wide variety of birds, fish, reptiles, and even insects. Shape-shifting can be voluntary, as in the many stories of witches who turn into hares, owls, or turkeys (yes, turkeys!). Or it can be involuntary, like the men in *The Odyssey* who are turned into swine by Circe. In some mythic traditions, the Animal People (with human and animal characteristics intermingled) were the first inhabitants of the earth, from whom all two-legged and four-legged beings have descended. In other traditions, only certain special people can claim such mixed-blood ancestry—Siberian shamans descended from swans, for example, or Irish wisewomen with seal blood in their veins, or Malaysian animist priests who honor the tiger as their ancestral spirit. The therianthropic tales of myth can thus be divided into three (overlapping) strains: stories of gods, men, and supernatural creatures who shape-shift between animal and human forms; stories of those who have been transformed from one state to another against their will; and stories of animal-human hybrids whose bodies and natures reflect both worlds.

In this book, you'll find stories inspired by animal transformation legends from around the world, retold and reimagined by some of the very best writers working today. We're defining *animal* loosely here, for in addition to stories of bears, cats, rats, deer, and other four-footed creatures we have birds, fish, seals, a fire salamander, and a yeti's child. In myth, many therianthropic tales involve the marriage of a human man or woman to an animal or animal-like monster . . . and so there are also some wonderful beastly brides (and bridegrooms) in the pages ahead.

The Beastly Bride is the fourth installment in our "mythic fiction" anthology series, each volume dedicated to a different aspect of world mythology. In previous volumes, we've explored the legends of the forest, the folklore of faeries, and trickster tales. This time, we follow deer tracks through the snow, wrapped up in cloaks of feathers and fur. As the moon starts to rise, the edges of the world start to shift and blur. . . .

Let's go.

INTRODUCTION:
SHAPE-SHIFTERS, WERE-CREATURES,
AND BEASTLY SUITORS

Terri Windling

Who among us hasn't wondered what it would be like to see the world through an animal's eyes? To lope across the landscape as a wolf, fly above the trees on the wings of a crow, leap through the waves with a porpoise's grace, snooze winter away in a bear cub's den?

Many books for young readers explore the common childhood desire to run wild with the animals, from Rudyard Kipling's *The Jungle Book* to Maurice Sendak's *Where the Wild Things Are*—but even better than dancing *with* the wolves would be to have the power to become an animal oneself. T. H. White tapped into this fantasy in his Arthurian classic, *The Once and Future King*. Here, Merlin educates the young Arthur by transforming him into a badger, a fish, an owl, an ant, et cetera; and Arthur must learn to live as they live, gaining knowledge, even wisdom, in the process. This isn't a standard part of the Arthur myth, but White hasn't made it up from whole cloth either. He's drawn on a worldwide body of tales even older than Arthur mythos: tales of shape-shifting, therianthropy (animal-human metamorphosis),* and shamanic initiation.

Animal-human transformation stories can be found in sacred texts, myths, epic romances, and folktales all around the globe, divided into three (overlapping) types. First, there are stories of immortal and mortal beings who shape-shift voluntarily, altering their physical form at will for purposes both beneficent and malign. The second kind of story involves characters (usually human) who have their shape changed *in*voluntarily—generally as the result of a curse, an enchantment, or a punishment from the gods. The third type of story concerns supernatural beings who are a blend of human and animal; they have the physical and mental attributes of both species and belong fully to neither world. Animal bride and bridegroom stories (in which a human man or woman is married to an animal, or an animal-like monster) can fall under any of these three categories: the animal spouse might be a shape-shifter, or an ordinary mortal under a curse, or a creature of mixed blood from the animal, human, and/or divine realms. There are so many beastly brides and bridegrooms in the traditional stories of cultures worldwide that we'll look at the archetype in more depth a little later on.

Right now let's start, as a number of mythic traditions do, with the gods, goddesses, and supernatural creatures who have both animal and human characteristics. Ancient Egyptian myth, for example, features several important deities with human bodies and the heads of birds or beasts. Ra, god of the sun, has the head of a hawk; Horus, the sky god, the head of a falcon; Thoth, god of wisdom, the head of a baboon; and Anubis, lord

---

* Therianthropy, referring to animal-human transformation, is a controversial term, employed by some mythic scholars and not others. Its origins have been variously dated to the sixteenth, nineteenth, and twentieth centuries.

of the afterlife, the head of a dog or jackal. The Great Mother Hathor is part woman and part cow; the pleasure-loving goddess Bastet has the visage of a cat; and, most striking of all, the river god Sobek has the head of a crocodile.

In Greek myth, the goddess Artemis has been pictured with the head of a bear in her aspect of Lady of the Beasts. Young girls in her cult pledged service to the goddess somewhere between the ages of five and ten, wearing bear-skins and living as wild as cubs before entering adulthood and marriage. Pan, the Greek god of the wilderness, has an upper body shaped like a man's, and the horns and the lower body of a goat. He is the leader of the satyrs, goatlike spirits of the forest famed for their wild and lecherous behavior. Cernunnos, the woodland god of Celtic lore, has the body of a man and the head of a stag; he is an elusive figure of the wilderness, associated with both fertility and death. Aroui, a dog-headed god, is lord of the forest in Yoruban tales, which spread from Africa to Cuba and Brazil along the old slaving routes. The Jaguar God of the Mayans can appear as a man, as a jaguar, or as a cross between the two. He is associated with the dark magic of shamans across Central and South America. In Hindu myth, the trickster god Ganesh has the head of an elephant with a single tusk and a potbellied human body with four hands. Revered as the Remover of Obstacles, he is often pictured riding on a rat. Coyote and Hare, immortal tricksters in tales told across North America, are sometimes animals, sometimes animal-human hybrids, and sometimes disguised as handsome young men. In the latter form, they seduce pretty girls and cause all manner of trouble for human beings.

Among the hundreds of Indian nations spread throughout the United States and Canada there are numerous mythic traditions in which the Animal People were the first inhabitants of Mother Earth. In some of these stories, the Animal People are divine beings shaped much like ordinary animals but possessing magical attributes and the power of human speech. In others, they are shape-shifters who can take on either animal or human form; and in still others, the precise nature of what they are is left deliberately obscure. The Animal People are credited with primary acts of world creation (placing the sun and stars in the sky, creating the mountains and rivers), and have been charged by Creator with the task of teaching human beings how to live a proper life. Similar tales are told by the Ainu of Japan, for whom all animals contain a spark of the *kamui*, or divine beings, of the mountains and the sea. Kimun Kamui is one of these immortals—a bear god who sends the deer down from the mountains to be hunted and eaten by their human kin. If the slain deer are honored with prayers and songs, their spirits rise and return to the mountains to report that they've been hospitably treated. Only then are they willing to be reborn in flesh and to be hunted once again.

In addition to deities who appear primarily in animal-human form, there are also gods and goddesses worldwide whose regular appearance is human (more or less) but who change into animal shape at will. In Norse myth, Odin, chief god of the Æsir, can transform into any bird or beast; and Loki the trickster has shape-shifting powers that he boasts are the equal of Odin's. Freya, the fiercely independent Norse goddess of love, beauty, and sensuality, shape-shifts into a bird with the aid of a magical cape made of robin feathers. Zeus, the sky god of the Greek pantheon, likes to shape-shift into animal form in his relentless pursuit of delectable young women . . . and to elude the wrath of his wife, the goddess

Hera. Zeus impregnates Leda, a princess of Sparta, while shaped as a great white swan, for example, and abducts the Phoenician princess Europa in the guise of a sacred bull. The fertility goddess Demeter, by contrast, transforms herself into a mare in order to *avoid* the amorous attentions of Poseidon, the lusty god of the sea—who promptly changes into a stallion and has his way with her all the same. Tefnut, the Egyptian goddess of water and moisture, turns into a lioness when riled. In one famous myth, the goddess argues with Shu, god of the air and dryness, and leaves Egypt for Nubia. The other gods want to persuade her to return, but Tefnut, in animal form, destroys any god or man who approaches. Julunggul, from Australian Aboriginal lore, can appear as both a woman and as a colored snake. She's the goddess of rebirth and oversees the initiation of boys into manhood. Inari, in the Shinto myths of Japan, is the god of rice, agriculture, and foxes. This god shifts from male to female form, and appears in both fox and human shape. The *kitsune* (fox spirits) of Japanese folklore are under Inari's protection. In Ireland, Edain and Flidais are shape-shifting goddesses in some old Celtic tales, turning into a mare and a deer respectively, while in others they are members of the Tuatha Dé Danann (the fairy race of the Emerald Isle) and their shape-shifting is but an illusion (a "glamour") cast over mortal eyes.

There are numerous stories like Demeter's, in which physical transformation is prompted by the desire for protection or escape. In Roman myth, a beautiful princess, Cornix, is threatened with rape by Neptune, god of the sea. Her cries are heard by the goddess Minerva, who promptly turns Cornix into a crow—preserving the young woman's honor, but at a price that is rather steep. In Greek myth, Proteus (son of Poseidon) is both a shape-shifter and a soothsayer—but he will not use the latter talent for mortals unless he is forced to do so. The king of Sparta is advised to grab hold of Proteus and to hang on tightly while the god shape-shifts in an effort to escape—for if he cannot, he'll be compelled to answer the Spartan king's questions. (It is from Proteus that we get the word *protean*, meaning "changeable in shape or form.")

Proteus's story is echoed in a classic tale from Welsh mythology: Gwion Bach, servant of the witch Ceridwen, steals three drops of wisdom from the cauldron of knowledge. As he flees the house with the witch in pursuit, he transforms into a hare. Ceridwen transforms into a hound. He turns into a fish, she turns into an otter, and on and on until he's a grain of wheat, and as a hen she gobbles him up. Nine months later, the witch gives birth to Gwion Bach in infant form. The child grows up to become Taliesin, the greatest of all Welsh bards.

A similar tale is told in the Scottish border ballad "Twa Magicians." One magician (female) is pursued by another (male) and tries a similar escape. The prize at stake is her virginity, which she is determined to keep. In another famous border ballad, "Tam Lin," the eponymous hero (a prisoner of the fairies) undergoes a series of protean transformations in the song's climactic scene: he becomes a lion, a bear, a poisonous snake, a flaming sword, a red-hot band of iron. His lover, Janet, bravely stands her ground and holds on tightly through each metamorphosis, by which means she wins Tam Lin's mortal soul back from the Faerie realm.

The fairies themselves, in the lore of the British Isles, are often shape-shifters. Indeed, some fairies change shape so often, or so dramatically, that it can be hard to ascertain their true appearance. Monstrous fairy hags can appear as lovely maidens; wizened, lumpen, ragged old fairies can appear as sweet-talking, handsome young men; and sickly fairy change-lings can look just like the human babies whose cradles they've usurped. When not attempting to pass as mortals, shape-shifting fairies most commonly borrow their appearance from elemen-tal forms (earth, air, fire, water) or from the plant and mineral kingdoms (trees, flowers, mushrooms, standing stones)—but there are, nonetheless, some species of fairies who engage in therianthropic transformation. Kelpies, for example, are mali-cious river fairies who shift between human and equine form; the hyter sprites, by contrast, are a gentle breed of fairy who shape-shift into various birds. Piskies delight in disguising themselves as hedgehogs or hares of a strange green hue. Poo-kahs turn into big black horses or dogs to play nasty tricks on mortal men, and selkies are shaped as humans when on dry land and as seals within the sea.

In Japan, we find a number of animal shape-changers among the *yōkai*, supernatural spirits that range from dead-ly demons to mischievous tricksters. The *tanuki* is a kind of shape-shifting raccoon dog, jolly and comical, often pictured with testicles so big that they are slung over his back. The *mu-jina* is a nastier, devious fellow whose primary animal form is the badger, but who also takes the form of a faceless ghost to terrify mortals. The *bakeneko* is a cat shape-shifter; the *in-ugami* is a dog spirit; and the most famous of the *yōkai* are the *kitsune*, who are shape-shifting foxes. *Kitsune* are known for disguising themselves as attractive mortals (of either sex), in which form they seduce and even sometimes marry human men and women. In most stories the *kitsune* are dangerous, and relations with them lead to madness or death—and yet some *kitsune*, the *zenko* (good foxes), are said to be wise, intelligent creatures, often poetic and scholarly by nature, who make faithful spouses and are good parents to their half-human, half-animal children.

In Africa, we find shape-shifting lion- and hyena-people with many of the same traits as the *kitsune*. In a Mbundu tale, a young lioness is dressed and groomed by her lion kin until she resembles a stately, enticing young woman. She marries a wealthy man, intending to kill him as he sleeps and steal his cattle away, but a child witnesses her nightly transformations and blows the whistle. In Native American legends, Deer Woman is a sacred being but also dangerous. In one tale from the Lakota tribe, a young man walking far from camp meets a beautiful maiden in the woods. It is (he thinks) the very woman he's been courting, who has previously rejected him—but now she's smiling flirtatiously, looking enchanting in a deer-skin robe. As they talk, he playfully loops the braided rope he carries around her waist . . . whereupon she panics and turns to flee, shifting into her true deer shape. The rope holds her fast. "Let me go!" she cries. "If you do, I'll give you magical power!" The young man releases her warily, and Deer Woman disappears through the wood. Then he vomits profusely, for he's sick with the knowledge that if he had carried on with making love, he would have gone mad—like the other young men who'd encountered Deer Woman before him. Afterward, he lives alone and is plagued by fits of wild, deerlike behavior. Deer Woman keeps her promise, however, and gives him a magical ability: his skill with horses and other four-footed creatures is unsurpassed.

The Elk Man is another dangerous, seductive shape-shifter in Native America myth, and "elk medicine" could be used as an aphrodisiac or as a charm to attract the opposite sex. In an Elk Man tale from the Pawnee tribe, a handsome young man has the ability to attract any woman he desires, and soon there are only a few women left with their reputations intact. The other men decide to be rid of him. They persuade his reluctant brother to help them, promising him riches in return. The handsome young man is duly killed, but his sister steals his head and an arm, hiding them in the forest nearby. The young man regenerates himself with these parts, and comes home to his brother's tepee. He's not angry with the brother but with the tribe, who have not yet fulfilled their side of the bargain, and he goes to the council tent to demand the wealth that his brother was promised. Fearful now, the council produces many horses, tepees, and fine blankets. The young man takes them home, and the siblings now live in luxury. After that, the narrative concludes, the young man "fascinated all the women so much there was not a single good woman left in that tribe. And then it was clear the young man was really an elk, and it was beyond their power to kill him, and neither could they put a stop to his attraction for women. They finally gave in and said no more. That is all."

When human beings have the power to shape-shift at will, it is either a sign that they're not as human as they appear (as in the stories of Deer Woman and Elk Man), or the shifter is a shaman, a healer, or a witch. The *brujos* and *brujas* of Mexico, for example, are believed to have the power to transform themselves into dogs or donkeys or turkeys, and the sorcerers of West Africa plague their enemies by assuming the shape of owls. The skin-walkers of the Navajo tribe can take on any animal shape, while the jaguar shamans of the Amazon draw magic from intense engagement with a single patron animal. Students of magic seeking to gain healing, prophetic, or shamanic powers sometimes undergo a ritual metamorphosis into one or more animal shapes in order to gain an understanding and mastery of the natural world. In Arthurian lore, Merlin goes mad after the Battle of Arderydd and flees into the forest, where he lives with the wild boars and the wolves for a long period of time. During this time of madness (a common part of shamanic initiation the world over), he learns to shape-shift into animal form, to understand animal languages, to control the elements, to foretell the future, and to perform other magical arts. The Irish tell a similar tale of Suibhne, a warrior cursed in battle and forced to flee into the wilderness. Shaped as a bird, he wanders for many years in a state of anguish and madness—but by the time he returns home again, transformed back into his own human shape, he has gained certain magical powers and a strong rapport with the beasts of the wood. Other stories in which metamorphosis comes about as the result of a curse have less positive outcomes than Suibhne's, however, for humans forced into animal shape are often tragic or horrific figures. The werewolves of European folklore, or the were-tigers of India, or the were-jackals of the Middle East rarely regain their humanity; they are outcasts, shunned and feared by other men and cursed by God.

Human shape-shifting in fairy tales is usually involuntary and calamitous, resulting from a stepparent's curse, a fairy's punishment, or some other dark enchantment. In "Brother and Sister," from the tales of the Brothers Grimm, two siblings flee their wicked stepmother through a dark and fearsome forest. The path of escape lies across three streams, and at each crossing the brother stops, intending to drink. Each time his sister warns him away, but the third time he cannot resist. He bends down to the water in the shape of a man and rises again in the shape of a stag. Thereafter, the sister and her brother-stag must live in a lonely hut in the woods . . . but eventually, with his sister's help, the young man resumes his true shape. In "The White Deer," from the French fairy tales of Madame d'Aulnoy, a princess is cursed in infancy by a fairy who had been insulted by the king and queen. Disaster will strike, says the fairy, if the princess sees the sun before her wedding day. Many years later, as she travels to her wedding, a ray of sun penetrates her carriage. The princess turns into a deer, jumps through the window, and disappears. She is then hunted and wounded by her own fiancé as she roams sadly through the forest.

There are many, many fairy tales where the hero or heroine marries an animal: a frog, a snake, a bear, a cat, a rat, or an animal-like monster. Often they've been obliged to do so by poverty, honor, or a parent's fecklessness. Among the thousands of Animal Bride and Bridegroom stories to be found in cultures all around the world, "Beauty and the Beast" is probably the one that most of us know best today. "Beauty and the Beast" is not a folktale—it was written by Madame Gabrielle-Suzanne Barbot de Villeneuve in the eighteenth century—but it draws its plot from older stories in the Animal Bride/Bridegroom tradition, including the Greek myth of "Cupid and Psyche," the "loathly lady" stories of medieval literature, and "East of the Sun, West of the Moon," a popular Scandinavian folktale. In the Scandinavian story, the heroine must actually marry her beast (a big white bear) at the *beginning* of the story. Each night, by dark, he comes to their marriage bed in what seems to be a human form—but his wife may not light the lamp to see if she is married to a man or to a monster. She breaks this taboo, and the white bear disappears from sight.

Having grown fond of him by now, she sets off on a journey that takes her "east of the sun, west of the moon," where she breaks the spell that binds him and restores his humanity.

The three motifs common to Animal Bride and Bridegroom stories are evident in "East of the Sun, West of the Moon": marriage to (or cohabitation with) an animal or animal-like figure; the breaking of a prohibition and subsequent departure of the magical spouse (or suitor, or lover); and a pilgrimage to regain the loved one and achieve a more lasting union. Most fairy tales end on this happy note, but if we look at older tales in the folk tradition, we find that many end after the second part of this cycle. These are tragic tales (or horrific ones) in which the union of lovers from human and nonhuman worlds cannot be sustained. The selkie tales of the British Isles and Scandinavia generally fall in this category:

One night a fisherman spies a group of seals emerging from the sea, shedding their skins, and turning into beautiful maidens upon dry land. As the selkies dance under the moon, the fisherman steals one of the skins. Sunrise comes, the maidens turn back into seals and depart—except for one, who is unable to transform herself without the magic of her sealskin. She begs the man to return the skin—but he refuses, insisting she be his wife. Resigned, she follows him to his cottage and learns how to live as humans live. Eventually she comes to care for her husband, and bears him seven fine sons and a moon-eyed daughter. One day, however, she finds the skin—and she swiftly returns to her life in the sea. In some versions, she departs without another thought for

the family left behind; in other versions, the children also
turn into seals and vanish along with her. And in still
other variants of this tale, she joins a large bull seal in
the waves. "I love you," she calls back to the fisherman,
"but I love my first husband more."

Similar tales are told of swan maidens in Sweden, of frog
wives in China and Tibet, of bear women in North America,
and of *aspares* (nymphs) in Hindu myth who appear in the
shape of waterfowl. In the "Crane Wife" story of Japan, the Animal Bride is happy in her marriage and works hard to please
her husband, a weaver, by making sumptuous cloth to sell—
but in his greed for more and more of this cloth, he works his
faithful wife to death. It's a tragic story, for when he realizes
that he loves his magical spouse, it is too late.

In some stories, Animal Brides and Bridegrooms are de-
cidedly less benign figures. In the English tale "Reynardine,"
for instance, a young woman pledges marriage to a handsome
red-haired stranger who is actually a fox shape-shifter. He
intends to murder and eat her in his ruined mansion in the
woods. The cat-wives in English tales, by contrast, are merely
mischievous. In one story, a young man's bride alarms his
mother by her merry, immodest ways, and the mother soon
learns that her daughter-in-law used to be the cat sitting by the
hearth. She tells her son he must chase his bride away, and the
son reluctantly agrees—but he later regrets the deed, for he
misses his charming animal wife. In a Native American story
from the Pacific Northwest, a man who is lost in the woods
meets a beautiful bear woman and marries her. She gives him
two bear cubs for sons, and the family lives in harmony—until

hunters from his tribe come upon the bear bride's cave and kill her while she sleeps, believing that they are rescuing their kinsman from captivity.

In the fairy tales of the Middle East, an Animal Bride can prove to be quite valuable. In one old Arabic story, a sultan's son makes a promise to a tortoise and must marry her. "But this you cannot do, my son!" the sultan tells him in alarm. "This tortoise is not of our village, our race, or our religion—how can such a marriage work?" His elder brothers will not attend the wedding, and their wives refuse to prepare the marriage bed. Nevertheless, the young man spends his wedding night with the tortoise, and every night thereafter. Each morning he appears looking well contented, causing tongues to wag throughout the village. The sultan falls ill and must decide which one of his sons shall inherit the throne. Deciding to choose the son with the best marriage, he devises a series of impossible tests—which the tortoise wife wins through cleverness, common sense . . . and a little magic. In the end, she discards her shell and becomes a young woman, and her husband wins the throne.

Similar tales can be found in other fairy-tale traditions—such as "The Frog Princess" from Russia and "The White Cat" from France—although they tend to avoid the frank sexual conjecture that gives the Arabic version its spice. In the French story, from the tales of Madame d'Aulnoy, the prince and his animal paramour do not marry until the end of the tale, *after* the cat turns into a woman. It's also made clear that the Animal Bride is really human underneath the fur, the victim of a fairy's curse. But in older stories, like the Arabic tale, the bride may really be an animal (or a magical shape-shifting creature), consenting in the end to give up her true form in order to live in the human world.

In his fascinating study *The Serpent and the Swan*,* folklorist Boria Sax comments: "Just as marriage between two people unites their families, so marriage between a person and an animal in myth and fairy tale joins humanity with nature." He points out that the changes in Animal Bride and Bridegroom tales as they've passed through the centuries have reflected the changing relationship between humankind and the natural world. The oldest known tales are generally those limited to the first part of the story cycle: the romance and/or marriage of human beings and animals (or other nature-bound creatures). Tales of this sort include ancestral myths such as the Chinese stories of families descended from the marriage of humans and shape-shifting dragons, or the lore of Siberian shamans who trace their power and healing gifts to marriages between men and swans. Such tales evoke an ancient worldview in which humans were part of the natural world, cousin to the animals, rather than separate from nature and placed above all other creatures.

Animal Bride and Bridegroom stories that go on to the second part of the cycle—ending with the loss of the animal lover—arise from a worldview in which sharper distinctions are made between the human sphere (civilization) and nature (the wilderness). In such tales, humans and their animal lovers come from distinctly separate worlds, and any attempt to unite the two is ultimately doomed to failure. Crane Wives always die, and selkies always return to the sea.

---

* Boria Sax, *The Serpent and the Swan: The Animal Bride in Folklore and Literature* (Blacksburg, Va.: McDonald and Woodward, 1998.)

Stories that move on to the third part of the cycle—like "East of the Sun, West of the Moon," or the Arabic tale of the tortoise wife—end with the lovers united, and the transformation of one or both partners. Such tales, notes Sax, express "an almost universal longing to reestablish a lost intimacy with the natural world." Although the tortoise might consent to the loss of her shell in order to live in the sultan's court, she brings the scent of the wild with her as she steps into civilization. She will never be an ordinary woman; she'll always be the Fantastic Bride—joining the hero to the mysteries of nature.

In the older folktales, marriage between humans and animals broke certain taboos and could be dangerous, but such relationships weren't generally portrayed as wicked or immoral. Even when the marriages were doomed to failure, often a gift was left behind: children, wealth, good fortune, or the acquisition of magical skills (such as the ability to find fish or game in plentiful supply). By the Middle Ages, however, animal-human relationships were viewed more warily, and creatures who could shift between human and animal shape were portrayed in more demonic terms.

One of the best-known Animal Bride tales of medieval Europe is the story of Melusine, written down by Gervasius of Tilbury in 1211. A count meets Melusine beside a pond and falls in love with her. She agrees to marry on one condition: he will never see her on a Saturday, which is when she takes her bath. They wed, and she bears the count nine sons—each one deformed in some fashion. Eventually the count breaks the taboo, spies on her bath, and discovers her secret. Every seventh day, his wife is a woman from the waist up and a serpent below. When the count's trespass comes to light, Melusine transforms into serpent shape and vanishes—appearing thereafter only as a spectral presence to warn of danger. In medieval tell-, ings, the monstrous sons are evidence of Melusine's demonic nature—but in older versions of her story Melusine is simply a water fairy. The emphasis of the older tales is on the husband's misdeed in breaking his promise, thereby losing his fairy wife, rather than on his discovery that he is married to a monster.

In the fifteenth century, a wandering alchemist by the name of Paracelsus wrote of magical spirits born from the elements of water, earth, air, and fire, living alongside humankind in a parallel dimension. These spirits were capable of transforming themselves into the shape of men and women, and lacked only immortal souls to make them fully human. A soul could be gained, Paracelsus wrote, through marriage to a human being, and the children of such unions were mortal (but lived unusually long lives). Several noble families, it was believed, descended from knights married to water spirits (called "undines" or "melusines") who had taken on human shape in order to win immortal souls. Paracelsus's ideas went on to inspire the German Romantics in the nineteenth century—in tales such as Goethe's "The New Melusine," E. T. A. Hoffman's "The Golden Pot," and especially Friederich de la Motte Fouqué's "Undine," the tragic story of a water nymph in pursuit of love and a human soul. Fouqué's famous tale, in turn, inspired Hans Christian Andersen's "The Little Mermaid," along with other literary, dramatic, and musical works of the Victorian era. Many folklorists consider such tales to be part of the Animal Bride tradition, depicting as they do the union of mortal men and creatures of nature.

In the years between Paracelsus and Fouqué, fairy tales came into flower as a literary art of the educated classes, popularized by Italian and French publications that eventually spread across Europe. Animal Bride and Bridegroom tales were part of this enchanting literary movement. Giambattista Basile's *Il Pentamerone*, published in Naples in the seventeenth century, included several stories of the type—such as "The Snake," about a princess who marries a snake, loses him, and then must win him back. Later in the century, the term "fairy tale" (*conte de fées*) was coined by the writers of the Paris salons, who drew inspiration for their tales from folklore, myth, medieval romance, and prior works by Italian writers. A number of the *contes* were by women who used the metaphoric language of fairy tales to critique the social systems of their day while avoiding the notice of the court censors. In particular they railed against a marriage system in which women had few legal rights: no right to choose their own husband, no right to refuse the marriage bed, no right to control their own property, and no right of divorce. Often the brides were barely out of puberty and given to men who were decades older. Unsatisfactory wives could find themselves banished to a convent or locked up in a mental institution. The fairy-tale writers of the French salons were sharply critical of such practices, promoting the idea of love, fidelity, and *civilité* between the sexes. Their Animal Bridegroom stories reflected the fears common to women of their time and class, who did not know if they'd find a beast or a lover in their marriage bed. Madame d'Aulnoy, for instance, one of the leading writers of the *contes*, had been married off at age fifteen to an abusive baron thirty years her senior. (She rid herself of him after a series of adventures as wild as any fairy story.) By contrast, the lovers in d'Aulnoy's tales are well matched in age and temperament; they enjoy books, music, intellectual pursuits, good conversation, and each other's company. D'Aulnoy penned several Animal Bride and Bridegroom tales that are still widely read and loved today, including "The Green Snake," "The White Cat," "The White Deer," and the tragic tale of "The Royal Ram."

Madame de Villeneuve, author of "Beauty and the Beast," was part of the "second wave" of French fairy tales in the following century, but arranged marriages were still the norm when she sat down to write her classic story. The original version is over one hundred pages long and is somewhat different from the story we know now. As the narrative begins, Beauty's destiny lies entirely in the hands of others, and she can do naught but obey when her father hands her over to the Beast. The Beast is a truly fearsome figure, not a gentle soul disguised by fur; he is a creature lost to the human world that had once been his by birthright. The emphasis of the tale is on the Beast's slow metamorphosis as he finds his way back to the human sphere. He is a genuine monster, eventually reclaimed by *civilité* and magic.

Sixteen years later, Madame Le Prince de Beaumont, a French woman working as a governess in England, shortened and revised Madame de Villeneuve's story; she then published her version, under the same title, in an English magazine for young women. Tailoring the story for this audience, Le Prince de Beaumont toned down its sensual imagery and its implicit critique of forced marriages. She also pared away much unnecessary fat—the twisting subplots beloved by Madame de Villeneuve—ending up with a tale that was less adult and subversive, but also more direct and memorable. In Le Prince de Beaumont's version (and subsequent retellings) the story becomes a didactic one. The emphasis shifts from the transformation of the Beast to the transformation of the *heroine*, who must learn to see beyond appearances. She must recognize the Beast as a good man *before* he regains his humanity. With this shift, we see the story alter from one of social critique and rebellion to one of moral edification. Subsequent retellings picked up this theme, aiming at younger and younger readers, as fairy tales slowly moved from adult salons to children's nurseries. By the nineteenth century, the Beast's monstrous shape is only a kind of costume that he wears—he poses no genuine danger or sexual threat to Beauty in the children's version of the tale.

In 1946, however, Beauty and her beast started to make their way out of the nursery again in Jean Cocteau's remarkable film version, *La Belle et la Bête.* Here, the Beast literally smolders with the force of his sexuality, and Beauty's adventure can be read as a metaphor for her sexual awakening. It is a motif common to a number of Animal Bride and Bridegroom tales from the mid-twentieth century onward, as an adult fairy-tale revival brought classic stories back to mature readers. One of the leaders of this revival was Angela Carter, whose adult fairy-tale collection, *The Bloody Chamber* (1979), contained two powerful, sensual riffs on the Animal Bridegroom theme: "The Courtship of Mr. Lyon" and "The Tiger's Bride." With the works of Carter and other writers of the revival (A. S. Byatt, Tanith Lee, Robert Coover, Carol Ann Duffy, etc.), we find that we have come back to a beginning. Contemporary writers are using animal-transformation themes to explore issues of gender, sexuality, race, culture, and the process of transformation . . . just as storytellers have done, all over the world, for many, many centuries past.

One distinct change marks modern retellings, however, reflecting our changed relationship to animals and nature. In a society in which most of us will never encounter true danger in the woods, the big white bear who comes knocking at the door is not such a frightening prospective husband now; instead, he's exotic, almost appealing. Where once wilderness was threatening to civilization, now it's been tamed and cultivated (or set aside and preserved); the dangers of the animal world have a nostalgic quality, removed as they are from our daily existence. This removal gives "the wild" a different kind of power; it's something we long for rather than fear. The shape-shifter, the were-creature, the stag-headed god from the heart of the woods—they come from a place we'd almost forgotten: the untracked forests of the past; the primeval forests of the mythic imagination; the forests of our childhood fantasies: untouched, unspoiled, and limitless. Likewise, tales of Beastly Brides and Bridegrooms are steeped in an ancient magic and yet powerfully relevant to our lives today. They remind us of the wild within each of us—and also within our lovers and spouses, the part of them we can never quite know. They represent the Others who live beside us—cat and mouse and coyote and owl—and the Others who live only in the dreams and nightmares of our imaginations. For thousands of years, their tales have emerged from the place where we draw the boundary lines between animals and human beings, the natural world and civilization, women and men, magic and illusion, fiction and the lives we live. Those lines, however, are drawn in sand; they shift over time; and the stories are always changing. Once upon a time a white bear knocked at the door. Today Edward Scissorhands stands on the porch. Tomorrow? There will still be Beasts. And there will still be those who transform them with love.

ISLAND LAKE

E. Catherine Tobler

Viewed from the dock, the old tree of the island appears to be a woman, branches curving down, as if she holds a child. Everyone calls it the Madonna tree, though it only looks like such from our dock. From the opposite shore of the lake, it looks like a tree caving in on itself.

Father used the Madonna tree to teach me and my sister Laura about perspective, about how something looks different from every angle; different too depending on whose eyes are doing the looking.

My sister looks at the tree and sees a jumping fish, mouth pointing north, evergreens as mad, frothy water. She calls it her Madonna fish. I look and I see the Madonna but wonder if I see her because I honestly do, or because I have been taught to.

ᛥ ᛥ ᛥ

Laura's teeth left long scores across the apple's golden flesh, juice dribbling down her chin. She wiped it away and narrowed her brown eyes upon me.

"Perhaps today, wee Lizzie," she said.

I stretched in the afternoon sun, the splintered dock beneath me warm. My feet dangled in the lake water next to Laura's. I splayed my toes and for once could not feel how small my left foot was. In the water, both feet floated weightless.

"Today," I said and stretched my arms above my head. Hands, free of cane or guide rail, reached until they found the edge of a dock board. I slid my fingers between the boards. The underside of the wood was damp and warm, fragrant as I rubbed my fingers over it. Like velveteen rubbed wrong.

It was a perfect day, with the clouds building into foamy castles in the mid-August sky above. No ordinary sky this, but one under which Father should return to us. We had not seen him for four years, but it seemed longer than that, longer since the Japanese attacked Pearl Harbor. I was ten and Laura twelve when he last scooped us into his arms.

He was missing one of those arms now, Mother told us, and would be escorting Uncle Eugene's casket home. Two brothers gone to war and only one returned to us. I closed my eyes to the castles and said silent thanks that it was our father come home. In the house behind us, our cousin did not have this luxury.

"Have you thought about what Uncle Eugene meant to you?" Laura asked.

I opened one eye to peer at her. She looked across the lake, still eating that apple. More juice dotted her chin, but she had not wiped it away.

"I don't know what he meant to me," I said.

Granny had bid us that morning to think on our uncle and what he meant to us. She wanted each of us to share this with the family at his funeral.

I could not remember his face without the aid of a photograph. There were many photographs of us prior to my illness, some taken by the pond that robbed me of my health.

What I remember of my uncle is this: large hands hidden under a dry, rough towel, the rotting smell of stagnant water, the gruff admonition to "damn well never do that again."

"Aunt Esme made peach pie," Laura said.

She had eaten the apple to its core and flung it into the lake. It landed with a plop, and I rose on my elbows to watch it bob in the water. Soon enough, a silver fish head glided up and swallowed it whole.

As children we spent summers with our aunt and uncle, so I was told. Laura could recall more than I could; remembered pie and picnics and the pond. She didn't like to talk about the pond.

In the distance, I heard the slam of a car door, followed by another. Laura turned her head to listen.

"Father!"

She leapt up, her yellow and white daisy-print skirt brushing my face. She jammed her wet feet into her sandals and was halfway up the lawn before I had even sat up. I drew my feet out of the water and reached for my shoes.

But Laura came back for me. She lifted me into her arms, an action made easier from years of practice, and carried me up the lawn when I could not run with her.

Part of me didn't want to see Father. I wanted to remember him as he was, broad shouldered and striking enough to challenge the moon to a beauty contest. I didn't want to see his sorrow at the death of his brother, or the ways the war had likely changed him.

Laura carried me up the sloping lawn, and up the thirteen

steps that brought us to the second-story back porch. There she made a grab for the towels Granny had left us on the rocking chairs. We were to come into the house dry or not at all. Laura gently deposited me into a chair, and I rubbed at my wet legs and feet.

"My shoes."

This wasn't at all how I wanted Father to see me. I cradled my withered left foot in my lap and listened to the sound of him—of Father after all these years—greeting Mother and Granny, Aunt Esme and Winnie. While they cried as my father came out of the car, I longed for my usual skirts, not these short pedal pushers, and for the thick and sturdy sole of my shoe.

"Walk or ride?" Laura asked. She offered her arms and I shook my head.

"Walk."

My cane had been left at the dock as well, but there was a spare by the back door. I took up the length of pale wood and silently praised its smooth grip. Our grandfather certainly knew how to make a fine cane. He wouldn't thank me if the fish carried off the one I had left behind.

I hobbled my way into the house after Laura, who ran with fluid strides. She burst through the open front door and hurled herself into Father's arms.

The empty left sleeve of his shirt had been rolled and neatly pinned to stay out of his way. But it was the same shirt I remembered, the pale blue that was the color of Mother's favorite vase. It was worn at the right collar and the left elbow. It would smell like Burma-Shave. It would smell like my father.

I stood in the doorway, watching Mother wipe her tears away and Laura grab cousin Winnie's hand. There should have been two men come home. I could not clearly remember the second one, but there were those who could.

My father's eyes sought me out and found me, even in shadow. He smiled and ran to me in long strides that made me think of a horse. So agile and balanced my father, even without his left arm.

"My girl," he said, and swept me up. My small foot lifted from the floor, weightless in the air as my father spun me round, round, round.

℘   ℘   ℘

Father and I were sitting on the back porch when I saw the lights on the island.

We each rocked in a rocking chair, wood planks below us making a kind of music. To and fro, back and forth, neither one of us could sit still. Laura was with us, but she sat near the porch railing, legs dangling into open air, silent all this time. While Father and I tried to fill the four-year gap we each carried, Laura looked across the dark lawn, toward the lake.

Its surface was black glass, reflecting every now and then a light from the houses on the opposite shore. But tonight, there was another light, a light that could come only from the island.

"Laura, what is that?" I asked.

But she had not noticed the light and didn't until I pointed it out to her. The light didn't look like any of the house lights or their reflections. It was golden and flickering. There was no breeze, so I imagined the flicker came each time someone crossed in front of it.

"Don't go out there," Father said, and blew a stream of pipe smoke into the night air.

The smoke plumed pale against the night, growing ever thinner until it was gone. I squinted across the lake, as if I might be able to see whoever was out there, but saw only a ripple on the glass lake, a moment's disturbance in the reflected lights. *Don't go out there*, I thought, but it was the one place I suddenly wanted to go. The expression on Laura's face said the same. What were those lights? Who was out there? We both wanted to know.

◉   ◉   ◉

Cousin Winnie couldn't abide the idea of swimming in the lake. When she learned there were fish, she was doubly repulsed.

"All those fishy mouths. This is as close as I can get," she said and sat down in the middle of the dock.

I could only get a little closer, sticking my bare feet in. It wasn't that the fish bothered me; I wouldn't have minded their fishy mouths nibbling at me. It was that I could not swim, not with my withered leg.

While Laura floated in the water up to her nose, with her hair fanning around her like seaweed, Winnie and I sat on the dock and made up stories about the island fire.

Winnie talked of young men, long limbs browned by the sun, hair glistening with lake water. She dreamed of their sodden swim trunks in colors we could not yet put a name to, and strong legs pushing off from the muddy island shore. She envisioned toe prints in the mud, not ten but twelve, each one webbed.

I dreamed up women—Dellaphina, Allegra, Mirabel—and clothed them in gossamer, spiderweb, water lily. Allegra wore her hair long and dark, and the spiders huddled there, frightened of the sunlight. But when she dove into the lake, the spiders bubbled up and swam for the lilies. They climbed, though the reeds were slippery, and found new homes deep inside the water blossoms. Dellaphina was the color of fire, her skin and her hair molten gold, for she was the light we had seen from shore, and how she danced! It was Mirabel's first time to the island; she watched everyone and everything with wide eyes the color of fir trees.

"You're both absurd," Laura said, and turned lazy circles in the water before us. "It's only ghosts. Japanese ghosts from the war. Come to haunt Father and keep him awake all night."

Father *had* stayed awake late into the night; I listened to him pace on the back porch and smelled the tang of his pipe smoke. I shivered at Laura's words, even though it was only pretend. She wanted him to tell her about the war, about killing, but he refused.

Laura asked, but I only hedged. *What was it like, Father?* was all I managed. He would scoop me up and laugh, because how could he tell any one of us what it was like? Someday, he would try, he said he owed that to us, but today was too soon; Laura's make-believe ghosts were too close.

Laura floundered in the water, making a great show of sinking. She thrashed and flung water on us.

"I'm caught, oh! The ghosts are carrying me away!"

Winnie came to her knees, wide-eyed like Mirabel, and shrieked until my sister rose, a laughing Venus from the waters.

Winnie didn't find anything remotely funny about Laura's game and stalked up the hill. She stalked slowly, though, allowing me to keep pace with her. As it neared the house, the brown sugar–dirt path forked and Winnie took the right branch, walking instead toward the gardens where hardworking bees hummed as they flitted from flower to flower. Winnie walked the row between the blackberry bushes, every now and then ripping a curling tendril of vine loose.

"I'm glad he's dead. Glad."

Winnie flung her handful of vines at me and fled faster than I could have followed if I cared to. I watched her go and even from a distance heard her cry.

ဌ   ဌ   ဌ

Every night, Father paced the back porch. I kneeled in bed and peered through the filmy curtains that covered the window. When I felt especially brave, I parted the curtains and looked beyond my father, to the lake and its island with the flickering gold light. Don't go out there, Father had said. *Ghosts*, I thought, and dived back under the covers.

The night after, I looked out and saw, instead of Father, the tail of my sister's pale nightgown whipping down the stairs and into darkness. I watched her run barefoot down the sloping lawn and vanish.

I sat on the edge of my bed and waited, watching, but Laura didn't come back. The hands on the clock moved through half an hour, and still she did not come. At an hour, the sky outside was beginning to brighten. I changed my nightgown for blouse and skirt, shoes and cane, and quietly made my way out of the house.

The lawn was slippery with dew. I stuck to the path that led to the dock, wondering if Laura had found Winnie's island of young men, or mine of dancing women. Had the ghosts carried her away?

"That's silly," I told myself.

Not even the sound of my voice was a comfort, though, and

I walked a little faster. I pictured Laura floating in the lake, hair spreading around her, water lily vines curled around her neck. Pictured her face gone blue, her eyes as black as the hem of her gown, scorched from the island fire. I stumbled.

The ground seemed to tip out from under me. I landed in the dew-damp grass breathing hard, all the while looking for Laura. I was about to scream her name when I saw her, stretched some distance away in the grass.

Laura's hair and nightgown were wet, as though she had been swimming. The gown clung to her like a second skin, her hair madly tousled. Laura stretched, spreading fingers and toes into the first light of day, and saw me. Laughed at me.

"Where have you been?" I asked, sputtering as though I were the one wet after a dunking in the lake.

Laura said nothing. She rolled to her feet and made for the house, leaving a soaking footprint on each of those thirteen steps up. There was no towel waiting for her.

I looked at the lake, a ring of shadow even as the sky brightened; it would be some time before the sunlight touched it. I watched, holding my breath as I waited.

When the fish broke the surface, I gripped my cane and pushed myself to stand. I headed for the dock. The fish were numerous now, gathering to snatch the bugs that hovered in the half-light before dawn. They glided like magical creatures, and I kneeled on the dock to watch them.

One slithered its way to the dock. I reached down to stroke its back, but when it turned from belly to back, it was not fish scales I stroked. It was warm skin.

I pulled my hand back, staring at the young man in the water. He smiled at me, his russet curly hair dripping water into his eyes. He blinked the water away, dove beneath the surface, and came back up, breaking the water at the edge of the dock. I fell backward, afraid he would climb out and—And? I couldn't complete the thought; I had no idea *what* he might do.

"Where did you come from?" I asked in a whisper.

He laughed at me and pointed across the lake. "I saw your sister," he said, "and came to say hello."

There were other fish in the water, I could see them clearly now. Maybe they weren't fish at all. I held my cane across my chest. If he made to come closer, I could strike him. But he didn't come closer; he paddled in the water a short distance off the dock, then turned and dove and was gone.

As quickly as that, he was gone, and I didn't see him surface again. I watched and waited, and my father came to get me, and still the young man didn't come up for air. I think I was breathing hard enough for both of us.

Later in the bathroom as I tidied myself, there lingered a glimmer of fish scales on my fingertips. I washed these off as quickly as I could and hurried to join my family for breakfast.

ᔕ ᔕ ᔕ

"She couldn't have been more than five," Aunt Esme said. She wiped her ringed fingers across her apron-covered belly, leaving broad strokes of flour on the polka-dotted fabric.

"Seven if she was a day; a mother knows," Mother said.

My mother and Esme worked side by side rolling pie dough, debating when I had learned to walk again. I wanted to tell them that I was still learning, that I hadn't mastered it at seven *or* fourteen, but I kept quiet. I pressed the star-shaped cookie cutter into the dough they had rolled for me. Granny sat at my side, weaving lattice over cherry pies. Father was resting, and Laura and Winnie had left without me that morning.

"Eugene had it right though, walking her every day the way he did," Granny said.

My head came up at that. "Uncle Eugene taught me how to walk?"

Mother and Esme looked back at me together, as if they were joined at the shoulder and had to turn as one. They could have been sisters, not sisters-in-law, with their curling auburn hair and green eyes.

"He would have doctored you himself if he knew what he was doing," Esme said with a wide smile. She had a nice mouth, colored into a bow with red lipstick. "Like as not, he'd have wound you into a taffy puller to get that leg of yours pulled straight and true."

I pressed the star cutter into the dough but didn't pull it free. "I don't remember much about him." Admitting this did not shock my aunt or mother the way I thought it would. I withdrew Uncle Eugene's photograph from my pocket, and Esme sighed when she saw it.

"Lord, wasn't he as handsome as autumn apples." Esme wiped her hands clean and took the photograph. "This was taken at the Seattle house, by the pond." Her eyes flicked up to me. "I'm so sorry, sweet one."

"Talking about it doesn't bother me," I said.

"She has what you might call a fascination about it," Mother said, and smiled at me the way you might at someone who needed calming before they came unhinged.

"It's just that you'd think I would remember," I said.

"What's to remember?" Esme said. She handed the photograph back to me, before peeling the dough away from the stars I had cut and working it into another ball. "It was a warm day and you wanted to swim."

It was my unfortunate luck to go swimming in contaminated water. "I mean my uncle. He taught me to walk again. He—" I looked up at my aunt, finally putting the pieces together. "He pulled me out that day, didn't he?"

"That he did. Like I said, he would have doctored you up if he'd a known how."

I slipped the photograph into my pocket as Laura and Winnie came into the room. Their cheeks were glowing, the tips of their hair clinging wetly to their shirts. I stared at the pair of them as they danced around Mother and Esme, twirling and laughing.

"Come swim," Laura said, and wriggled her damp head in Mother's face.

"Yes, do!" Winnie snuggled up to Esme, who pushed her away and pretended revulsion.

"Since when do you swim, my daughter? Since when?" Esme laughed when Winnie took her by the hands and twirled her around.

Couldn't abide all those fish mouths.

Don't go out there.

Winnie leaned across the counter and grasped my hands, the dough stars squashed under the press of her arms. Her fingers curled into my hands, pinching. "Will you come?" she asked.

"I—"

"Oh!" Winnie's mouth widened in an O that told me she hadn't forgotten I couldn't swim, just that she didn't care if she reminded me.

Winnie gave me what probably passed as a sweet smile to everyone else, but to me it stung like a slap. I saw the void within her dark eyes and heard the echo of her words amid the blackberry vines. *I'm glad he's dead. Glad.* How could anyone think it, let alone his own daughter?

 followed by my father's voice—was he singing? I pressed my fore-

᭡ ᭡ ᭡

I waited each night for Laura to leave the house. She always went in her nightgown and grew smart enough to leave out a towel for herself. Tonight, she left even before our parents had turned out their light.

She looked small against the lawn in her bright white gown. It fluttered behind her like wings, her hair loose around her shoulders. I drew an image in my mind of her rushing off to meet a secret lover, and remembered the boy in the lake.

I watched Laura now, kneeling at the end of the dock, wriggling her hand in the water. She stood, stripped her nightgown off, and dove into the water.

In the room next to mine, my mother laughed. It was followed by my father's voice—was he singing? I pressed my forehead to the cool window and stared down at the puddle of Laura's nightgown. What was she doing? Had she lost her mind? In the distance, I saw the light on the island and shivered.

Night made the walk to the lake too dangerous for me to contemplate, but I did contemplate it. I thought long and hard, but fell asleep before I could decide. I woke with a start, to a clock that read eight A.M.

I stumbled out of my room and ran into Laura in the hall. She was humming, tying her hair with a ribbon at the nape of her neck.

"Laura—"

"Morning, sleepyhead," she said and glided past me, into her room. She closed the door behind her, and that was that.

There wasn't a moment in the day to ask what she had done. I watched as she and Winnie exchanged secretive glances, and wondered if Winnie had taken to swimming in the lake with her. Had they gone to the island?

Laura repeated the pattern over the next two nights, and I never saw any sign of Winnie. It was the following morning that Winnie came to my room, just before sunrise, in tears.

"Is she here?" Winnie looked around the room. Winnie looked in the closet and under the bed before flopping back on it with a sob.

"She?"

"'She' Laura, your sister!"

"What's happened?" I asked, and slowly lowered myself to the foot of the bed.

Winnie wiped the sleeve of her nightgown over her wet cheeks. "It was supposed to be a game, but you didn't play."

I frowned at Winnie but said nothing.

"The light on the island, the stories we told, Laura going off to swim." Winnie seemed to want to laugh, but it came out as another sob. "Why couldn't you play?"

Father's words hadn't been a game though; he was serious when he told us not to go out there. Did he know the island's secret, or was he simply being a father?

"Was I supposed to follow her?"

Winnie nodded.

I shook my head and offered my cousin a handkerchief. She took it without looking at me. "I can't walk down there at night, not safely."

"Not even for your own sister?"

The accusation, that it was my fault Laura was now missing, did not go unheard.

"I thought you two were together, that you meant to make me jealous, or that she was meeting someone—"

Winnie looked at me now, and I didn't like her expression, dark and lined and old, like someone had taken a coffee-stained cloth and draped it over her face. "Someone? What someone? What do you know?"

A knock at the door saved me from answering, from telling her about the boy in the lake.

"Lizzie, you all right?" Father asked.

I grabbed the blanket and threw it over Winnie's head before crossing to the door. I opened it and smiled at my father.

"Winnie had a bad dream," I said.

Father looked beyond me, to the lump on my bed. I followed his gaze to see Winnie's pale face emerging from the blanket.

"You all right?" Father asked her.

Winnie nodded. "Lizzie is a great comfort," she said, and smiled through a new haze of tears.

"Indeed," Father said. He kissed me on the forehead before drawing the door shut and leaving us.

"What someone?" Winnie asked again, standing so close to me that I jumped.

I turned to look at my cousin, feeling courage curl around my shoulders. "Why are you glad your father is dead?"

Winnie held my gaze and at first said nothing. When she would have turned away from me, I grabbed her arm. My arms and hands were strong, and I held her effortlessly. She squirmed and still I held on; Winnie resigned herself to captivity.

"Everything would be fine if you hadn't gone into the pond," she said, a growl shading her voice black.

I released Winnie's arm. Courage left me small as ever, and I wanted only to leave this room. But now it was Winnie who took hold of me.

"The water made you sick, and he blamed himself." She shook me hard. "Fretted over you every which way he could. Paid for doctors. Drove hours just to walk with you." Winnie leaned in so close that our foreheads almost touched. "He loved you the way he should have loved me."

"Winnie, no."

"I didn't want a sister, and neither did Laura. Wanted to toss you in the lake myself, let the fish eat you."

Laura once told me that gypsies left me on the porch one winter's evening, in a Burma-Shave box. I was a nuisance to the tribe and they could no longer stand me and my crooked body, so they deposited me at the first house that looked sturdy enough to withstand my screaming.

Father thought he had won a great contest and had been rewarded with his favorite shaving cream. When he discovered otherwise, it was too late, for that's how gypsy magic works. Take the child in, and she's yours forever.

It wasn't polio that withered my leg, Laura would say, it was the gypsy in me. Our parents overlooked it, but they loved her best, for she was their true daughter. The first time I heard such things, I cried; I cried until I was weak and empty and Father had to carry me to bed. That same feeling drew around me now, of being empty and never understanding why.

"I tried to get sick," Winnie whispered, "and couldn't, so I wished you dead, wished you dead so many times and now— And now *he's* gone—"

Winnie couldn't talk around the tears. I wanted to hug her and at the same time shove her away. Winnie turned away from me and crossed to the window, to push the curtain back and look at the lake. In daylight, everything seemed normal; the island was just a small lump of tree-covered land.

"She's out there," Winnie said. "On the island with those young men. They've snatched her away."

My heart leapt into my throat. "How—"

"What do you see when you look out there, at that tree, Lizzie?" she asked me. I came to stand by her side, seeking comfort in the lines of the old tree.

"The Madonna tree," I said.

"That's what everyone says. What do you really see?"

I looked at the tree and saw broad shoulders, two arms encircling two children. I saw my father, whole and strong, holding me and Laura, holding us beyond all danger. I shook my head, refusing to tell Winnie this.

"Only the old tree, that's all."

"I see a vulture," Winnie said. "And if we go there, it will pluck our bones clean."

ฦ   ฦ   ฦ

We disliked each other, Winnie and me, but we linked arms and pretended to be the best of friends in front of our parents and Granny. Laura had left without us that morning, we said, walking around the lake. We meant to head out the other way and catch her coming around. Granny smiled at us and offered us pocket pies wrapped in wax paper. We each took one, and left the house as fast as we could.

We walked two houses over, then cut through the yard, down to the lake. It didn't escape me that Winnie and Laura could still be playing their game. Still, I played along now, because no matter how hateful Winnie could be, her fear this morning at Laura's absence was genuine.

"We'll row out," Winnie said, and kneeled beside a small green boat lashed to the dock. "We'll—"

Whatever Winnie meant to say was lost in a scream. A glistening silver hand wrapped around her wrist. I covered her mouth to silence her and looked down into the eyes of the young man I had spoken with days before.

"Only Lizzie comes," he said.

Winnie jerked away from both of us, leaving me to sprawl on the dock. She couldn't get her feet under her though and settled for crawling some distance away.

"W-what is it?" she asked.

The morning sun draped the young man's shoulders not in gold but silver. He was silver everywhere I looked, save for the mop of russet curls on his head. Silver from scales.

"Laura needs you, Lizzie," he said and lifted a hand to me. "She's on the island."

"I can't swim," I said. "But I would try. I would."

The young man shook his head. "There's more than one way to cross water. You can row. And bring her pie," he added before slipping under the water.

I looked at Winnie and held a hand out for her pie. "You heard him."

"What—you're going? Lizzie!"

"I can't leave Laura there." Not when I knew now that this was no game of pretend.

"He'll pluck your bones clean," Winnie said, and threw her pocket pie at me before huddling on the dock. The pie fell short of my grasp, but I picked it up, looking at Winnie so small and scared. I felt a moment's pity when I climbed into the boat, feeling equally small. I set the pocket pies on the seat opposite me. "Untie me, Winnie."

She untied the boat and pushed it away while I fitted the heavy oars into their locks. I watched Winnie grow smaller and smaller while behind me I felt the Madonna tree growing larger. Its shadow spread over the surface of the lake and seemed to pull me toward the island.

When I saw the russet head in the water, I jumped in surprise, fearing I would hit it with an oar. But he moved like a fish, effortlessly under and around the boat and oars. He broke the surface of the water twice to smile at me, to beckon me onward when I felt my arms tire.

"You're almost there," he said, and a moment later the boat touched the muddy island shore.

I climbed out on shaking legs, shaking even more when the young man handed me the pocket pies and my cane. He had legs, legs like any normal man, but his feet and hands were webbed, and every inch of him was covered in shining scales.

"She's just up here, Lizzie," he said, and stepped through the trees.

I looked back at the far shore, the houses nearly swallowed by trees and greenery. How small they seemed, and I couldn't see Winnie at all but somehow felt myself being watched.

I turned and followed the young man into the trees. He guided me to the center of the island, to the base of the Madonna tree where a fire burned and my sister rested, wearing only her nightgown. Her feet and legs were flecked with dried mud.

"Laura!"

She lifted her head, eyes widening at the sight of me.

"Lizzie! Oh Lizzie, how wonderful, how wonderful! Come, you must come."

Laura drew me into her arms, and I saw then that she was clothed in a silver gown, one that sparkled like the young man's scales. When I looked for him, I found him across a grand ballroom, dressed in midnight blue from head to toe. He nodded at me, then twirled away with a woman in his arms. It was Dellaphina, liquid and gold, running into his silver and blue as they danced to a high-blowing flute. Dellaphina kicked up her feet and the world was awash in golden warmth.

"Have you ever seen anything like it?" Laura asked me. "Look!"

Allegra had come to the party, her dark hair writhing with spiders. Her gown was ebony, her lips scarlet, and no one touched her as she crossed their paths. She walked to the water and sank into it. A string of ghosts trailed behind her, gray and thin like clouds, some wrapped in foggy cloaks. Among them, I recognized Uncle Eugene, handsome as autumn apples. He raised his hand to me, and I to him. Tears blurred my vision.

"Thank you, thank you—" I said, knowing then what he meant to me, and that I could never put it into proper words. He meant what Laura meant to me, and Mother and Father and Granny. And even Winnie. Even her. We were each pieces of the other, incomplete without the other.

Eugene passed with Allegra and the other ghosts into the water, and I felt the hollow ring of my heart. I knew what Father felt, to lose his brother; knew what it would be to lose Laura.

"Oh, Lizzie, look out!"

Laura laughed as a man swept me into his arms. My feet came away from the ground and the world blurred, a confused painting of half-real dancers. I tried to free myself but could not, so I relaxed in the man's arms and felt my father's embrace. I breathed deeply and smelled the tang of his pipe and felt the world slip out from under me. Everything else could wait.

But it was Laura's face that stood out clearly as we danced; Laura's face that was sharp and real when everything else was indistinct. When I focused on my sister, I found myself able to leave the man's arms, to cross to her side and keep the whirling dance to my back.

"Lizzie? Dance with me?"

"You need to eat. Granny sent these," I said and opened the packet of pocket pies. "Here."

We ate the pies, and Granny's crust flaked over us like snow. We ate every bit, Laura's blackberry and mine cherry, and licked our fingers clean. By the time we had finished, the dancers had vanished, like a wonderful dream.

I covered Laura's fire over with dirt and made certain every bit of it was out before we left. Laura didn't laugh at the idea of me rowing here on my own; she didn't say much of anything as we left the island.

The sun was lower in the sky—had an entire day almost passed? I imagined Mirabel's wide fir-eyes watching us as we went and pulled the oars with all my strength to leave this place behind.

֍ ֍ ֍

At the neighbor's dock, Winnie hauled both of us out of the boat. Her eyes were red and swollen from crying, her clothing soaking wet, a coil of water lily vines caught in the collar of her shirt. Winnie hugged even me, blubbering apologies and something about ghosts. Had she seen her own while she waited?

The three of us were a mess when we came into the house, wet clothing, muddy feet. Granny said nothing, just handed us towels and told us to get cleaned up. My father caught me by the arm and held me back when Winnie and Laura went giggling into the bathroom.

"I told you not to go out there," he said, but his voice wasn't angry.

"I had to go."

Father understood this in a way no one else in the house could have. I knew then that he was still my father; no matter what the war had done to him, he was still a vital piece of me. He smoothed my damp hair behind my ears and kissed my nose.

In my bedroom, I stripped out of my clothes and pulled a dressing gown on. Where the curtain hung askew, I could see a sliver of the lake. Ripples too large to be from a fish moved through the water, and I held my breath.

A young man in his silver scales jumped in the air, twisted in the sunlight. He spread his hands into the air, reaching for something I could not see—

—the edge of the dock warm and velveteen under my own questing fingers—

When I looked again, he was gone. Quick and bright. I hoped Mirabel had seen.

E. CATHERINE TOBLER lives and writes in Colorado—
strange how that works out. Among other places, her fiction
has appeared in SCI FICTION, *Fantasy Magazine*, *Realms of
Fantasy*, *Talebones*, and *Lady Churchill's Rosebud Wristlet*. For
more, visit www.ecatherine.com.

Author's Note

Island Lake is a real place. My grandparents live there, and I
spent countless summers fishing and swimming its waters. My
cousins and I used to float in inner tubes to the island in the
lake, and as we went, strange things would slither past our legs
under the dark water.

Sometimes they were water lilies; other times, who knows?
Was it more than just fish nibbling at our toes? This lake watered my writer's brain from an early age. This story is one
result.

THE PUMA'S DAUGHTER

Tanith Lee

I: THE BRIDE

Since he was eight years old, Matthew Seaton understood he was betrothed to a girl up in the hills. As a child it hadn't bothered him. After all, among the Farming Families, these early hand-fastings were quite usual. His own elder brother, Chanter, had wed at eighteen the young woman selected for him when Chanter and she were only four and five.

Even at twelve, Matt didn't worry so much. He had never seen his proposed wife, nor she him—which was quite normal too. She had a strange name, he knew that, and was one year younger than he.

Then, when he was thirteen, Matt did become a little more interested. Wanted to know a little more. Think of her, maybe, just now and then. "She has long gold hair," his mother told him, "hangs down to her knees when she unbraids it." Which sounded good. "She's strong," his father said. "She can ride and fish and cook, and use a gun as handily as you can, it seems." Matt doubted this, but he accepted it. Up there, certainly, in the savage forested hills that lay at the feet of the great blue mountains, skills with firearms were needed. "Can she read?" he had asked, however. *He* could, and he liked his books. "I've been told," said Veniah Seaton, "she can do almost anything, and finely."

It wasn't until the evening of his fourteenth birthday that Matt began to hear other things about his bride.

Other things that had nothing to do with skills and virtues, and were not fine at all.

✿   ✿   ✿

Matt was seventeen when he rode up to Sure Hold, now his brother's house, wanting to talk to Chanter.

They sat with the coffeepot before a blazing winter hearth. No snow had come yet, but in a week or so it would. Snow always closed off the outer world for five or six months of each year, and Chanter's farm and land were part of that outer world now, so far as Veniah's farm was concerned. This was the last visit, then, that Matt could make before spring. And his wedding.

For a while they talked about ordinary things—the crops and livestock, and a bit of gossip—such as the dance last leaf-fall, when the two girls from the Hanniby Family had run off with two of the young men from the Styles. Disgrace and disowning followed, it went without saying.

"I guess I'd fare the same way, wouldn't I, Chanter, if I just took to my heels and ran."

"I guess you would," Matt's brother replied, easy, only his eyes suddenly alert and guarded. "But why'd you run anyhow? Have you seen someone you like? Take up with one of the farmgirls, boy. She'll get it out your system. And you'll be wed in spring."

"To Thena Proctor."

"To Thena Proctor."

"I've never met her, Chant."

"No you haven't, boy. But others have on your behalf. She's a good-looking lady. Our pa wouldn't ever pick us any girl not fit. Take my wife. Pretty as a picture and strong as a bear."

Matt looked off into the fire with his blue eyes full of trouble.

Chanter waited.

Matt said, "Did you ever hear—a tale of the Proctor girl?"

"Yes." Chanter grinned. "Gold hair, waist narrow as a rose stem, and can wrestle a deer to the ground."

"How does she do that then, Chant?"

"How the heck do I know, Matt?"

Matt's eyes came back from the hearth and fixed like two blue gun-mouths on Chanter's own.

"Does she perhaps leap on its back, sink in her claws, fangs in its neck—drag it to the earth *that* way?"

Chanter winced. And Matt saw he wasn't alone in hearing stories.

Matt added, slow and deadly, "Does her long hair get shorter, yet cover her all over? Do her *paws* leave pad-marks on snow? Are some of her white front teeth pointed and long as my thumb?"

Chanter finished his coffee.

"Where you hear this stuff?"

"Everywhere."

"You must see it, sometimes men get jealous—our pa is rich and so we'll be too—some men want to fright you. Malice."

"Chant, you know I rather think these fellers were set—not to scare—but to *warn* me."

"Warn you with horror tales."

"*Are* they tales? They said—"

Chanter rose, angry and determined.

So Matt got up too. By now they were almost the same height.

They stood glaring at each other.

Chanter said, "They told you old man Proctor is a shape-switcher. He sheds his human skin of a full moon midnight and runs out the house a mountain lion."

"Something like that. And she's the same."

"Do you think our pa"—shouted Chanter—"would hand-fast you to a—"

"Yes," said Matt, cool and hard and steady, though his heart crashed inside him like a fall of rocks. "*Yes*, if the settlement was good enough. Enough land, money. The Proctors are a powerful Family. Yet no one else made a play for Thena."

"Because they knew we Seatons would ask for her."

Matt said, "This summer, late, about three weeks back, I had to ride up that way, through the forests. Let me tell you, brother, what I saw *then*."

§   §   §

That evening Matt hadn't been thinking at all of the Proctors. Some cattle had strayed, so he and his father's hands rode into the woods above the valley. The landscape here was like three patterns on a blanket: the greener trees, birch, maple, oak, amberwood, with already a light dusting of fall red and gold beginning to show; next up the forests on their higher levels, spruce and larch and pine, dark enough a green to seem black in the leveling sunlight; last of all the mountains that were sky-color, etched in here and there by now with a line of white.

In less than two hours it would be sunfall. Once the cattle had been found, on the rough wild pasture against the woodland, they minded to make camp for the night and ride back to the Seaton farm the next day.

Matt had known most of these hands since boyhood. Some were his own age. They joked and played around while the coffee boiled on the fire. Then Ephran remembered a little river that ran farther up, where the first pines started. He and Matt and a couple of others decided on some night fishing there. It would be cooler, full moon too, when the flap-fish rose to stare at the sky and were easy caught.

After supper, going to the river, it was Ephran who spoke to Matt. "I guess you know. Joz Proctor's place is all up that way."

Matt said, "I suppose I did." It was perhaps strange he hadn't recalled. But then, he'd never been exactly certain where the Proctor farm and lands began. Hadn't ever tried to learn. Never been tempted to come up and see. It seemed to him right then, as they walked on into the darkness of the forest, he hadn't cared to, nor even wanted to remember now. He added, lightly, "Ever been there, Ephran?"

"Not I. It's all right, Matt. We're at least ten miles below the place."

"Think old man Joz would reckon I was out to spy on him otherwise, to see what I was getting? Run me off?"

"No. Not that."

They walked in silence for a while after this. The big moon was rising by then, leftward, burning holes between the trees.

Ephran, who was eighteen now, had never been one of the ones Matt had heard muttering about Joz and his golden daughter. The first time, when he had been fourteen, Matt had felt he *overheard* the mutters, anyhow. Later though he'd wondered if they meant him to, less from spite or stupidity than from that idea of forewarning—just as he was to say to Chanter.

What had the men said? ". . . bad luck for the boy. He don't know no better. But Veniah Seaton should've." "By the Lord, so he should." And the lower, more somber voice of the old man in the corner of the barn: "Not a wife he'll get, but a wild beast. A *beast* for a bride. God help him."

There'd been other incidents through the years after that. In front of Matt even, once or twice—given like a piece of wit: "Proctor, that old puma-man—" "Joz *Puma's* Farm . . ." Matt took it all for lies. Then for games. Then—

Then.

The river appeared.

It was slender and coiling, moonlit now to sparkling white.

The other men went on, and Ephran paused, as if to check his line.

"Listen up, Matt," said Ephran, "you don't want to worry too much. About her."

"Why's that?" said Matt, again light and easy.

"Because there are ways. Do your duty by her. There'll be no hardship there. Do that, and let her keep her secrets. Then when the time's right, you can be off. Not leave her, I don't mean that, Seatons and Proctors have a union, you'll have to stay wedded. But big place, the Proctor lands. Plenty to do. Just let her be. Don't—try an' rule her, or get on her bad side—jus' do as you want and let her do as *her* wants. That's the bestest way."

Matt said, "So you think it's true?"

Ephran scowled. "I don't think no thing at all."

"She's a shape-twist."

"I never said—"

"And her daddy before her."

Ephran glared in his face. "Don't you put words in my mouth. You may be the boss's second-born but I'm freer 'an you. *I* can go off."

Matt had the urge to punch Ephran in the mouth. So instead he nodded. "Fair enough. Let's go fish."

They fished. And the moon and the fish rose high. They laid the slim silver bodies by for breakfast, and not another word was spoken of the Seaton hand-fast or the Proctor house not ten miles away above, beside the forest.

It was when they had enough catch and were making ready to go back down to the camp.

Matt glanced up, and there across the narrow river, less distance from him than the other men, it stood, pearl in moonlight, and looked at him.

He hadn't seen one alive. In fact only the drawn one in the book of pictures, when he was schooled.

They haunted the forests and the lower slopes of the mountains. But they were shy of men, only slipping from the shadows of dawn or dusk, once in a while, to kill them. The last occasion one of their kind had killed one of Matt's had been in his childhood, about the time, he thought, he had seen the book-picture. Puma.

None of the other men seemed to have noticed. They were busy stringing the fish.

For the strange moment then, he and it were alone in utter silence, total stillness, unbroken privacy, eye to eye.

Its eyes were smoky and greenish, like old glass, and they glowed. Its coat was smooth and nacreous, glowing too.

Matt thought it would spring at him, straight over the

water for his throat or heart. Yet this didn't quite matter. He wasn't afraid.

He could smell the musky, grassy-meaty odor of it.

It opened its red mouth—red even by moonlight—and for a second seemed to laugh—then it sprang about, and the long thick whip of its tail *cracked* the panes of the night apart like glass as it sped away.

All the men whirled round at that and were staring, shouting. Old Cooper raised his gun. It was Ephran bellowed the gun down.

Like a streak of softest dimmest lightning, the racing shape of the great cat slewed off among the pines, veering, vanishing. Behind it, it left a sort of afterimage, a kind of *shine* smeared on the dark, but that too swiftly faded.

None of them spoke much to Matt as they trudged down to the pasture. In the camp, each man quickly settled to rigid sleep. Matt lay on his back, staring up at the stars until the moon went all the way over and slid home into the earth like a sheathed knife.

§   §   §

"So I wondered to myself," said Matt to his brother Chanter in Sure Hold now, "if that was Thena Proctor, I mean, or her daddy, come down to take a look at me."

Chanter strode to the fire and threw on another log.

"You pay too much mind to the chat of the men. Are you sure you even saw that big cat?"

"Oh, I did. All of us did. Ephran was white as a bone. He stopped Cooper shooting it. Could it even have died though, I wonder?"

Then he left off because he saw Chanter's face, and it had

altered. He had never seen Chanter like this before. Not in a good humor, or in a rage, nor with that serious and uneasy expression he had whenever he had to pick up a book, or the daft, happy smile he gained if he glanced at his wife. No, this was a new Chanter—or maybe a very young one, how Chanter had been perhaps when *he* was only a child.

"Matt, I don't know. How can I know? I know our pa meant well by us—both. But I think—I think he never thought enough on this. Probably it's all crazy talk and damn foolery. Those upland Families—they go back a great way, hundreds of years, deep into the roots of the Old Countries. . . . What you saw— what Joz Proctor is—and she, the girl—I've only ever gotten sight of a little sketch someone made of her. Good-looking as summer. But Pa met her. He liked her mightily. Uncommonly fine, he said."

"The puma," said Matt on a slow cold sigh, "was beautiful. Silk and whipcord. Pearl and—blood."

"God, Matty. Thena Proctor's a human girl. She has to be. She *must* be. Human."

Matt smiled. He said, softly, "*Puman.*"

2: THE MARRIAGE

A spring wedding.

The valleys and hills were still wet with the broken snows, rivers and creeks thick and tumbling with swelled white water. The scent of the pines breathed so fresh, you felt you had never smelled it before.

In the usual way among the Families, neither bride nor groom had been allowed to look at each other. That was custom. The old, humorous saying had it this was to prevent either, or both, making off if they didn't care for what they saw.

None had the gall to try that in the prayer house. Well, they said, ha-ha, only a couple of times, and those long, long ago.

And Matt? He hadn't taken to his heels. He had left off asking questions. He simply *waited*.

No one around him among the Seaton clan acted as if anything abnormal went on. Even Chant didn't, when he and his Anne came to call. He didn't even give Matt a single searching glance.

Matt had anyway grasped by then that he was quite alone.

He'd dreamed of it, the mountain cat, two or three times through the winter. Nothing very awful. Just—glimpsing it among trees by night, or up on some high mountain ledge, its eyes—*male*—*female*—gleaming.

They drove, trap horses burnished and a-clink with bells, to the prayer house, done up in their smartest, Matt too, bathed and shaved and brushed, the white silk shirt too close on his neck.

What did he feel? Hollow, sort of. Solid and strong enough on the outside, able to nod and curve his mouth, exchange a few words, be polite, not stammering, not stumbling, not in a sweat. His mouth wasn't dry. He noticed his mother, in her new velvet dress, haughty and glad. And Veniah, like a person from a painting of *A Father*: *The Proud Patriarch*. . . .

They are stone-cut crazy. So he thought as they drove between the leafing trees and into the prayer house yard. *They don't know what they've done*. And along with the hollow feeling, he had too a kind of scorn for them all, which helped, a little.

Inside the building there were early flowers in vases, and all the pewter polished, and the windows letting in the pale clear light. Everyone else, the representatives of the Families, were well dressed as turkeys for a Grace-giving Dinner.

He stood by the altar facing forward, and the minister nodded to him. Then the piano-organ sounded in the upper storey, and all the hairs on Matt's head and neck rose in bristles. For the music meant that here she was, his bride, coming toward him. He wouldn't turn and look to see—a mountain cat in human form and wedding gown, on the arm of her father, the other human mountain cat.

She wore a blue silk dress.

That he *did* see from the corner of his eye, once she stood beside him.

She had only the kind of scent he would have expected, if things were straightforward, cleanness and youngness, expensive perfume from a bottle.

When they had had their hands joined, hers was small and slender, with clean short nails, and two or three little scars.

"And now, say after me—"

He had to look directly down at her then. Not to do so as he swore the marriage vows would have been the action of an insulting dolt—or a coward. So he did. He looked.

Thena Proctor, now in the very seconds of being made over as Thena Seaton, was only about three inches shorter than he.

She was tanned brown, as most of the Farm Family daughters were, unless kept from learning on the land—brown as Matt. Her eyes were brown too, the color of cobnuts.

She was attractive enough. She had a *thinking* face, with a wide, high forehead, arched brows, straight nose, a full but well-shaped mouth with white teeth in it. Not that she showed them in a smile.

She met his eyes steadily with her own.

How did *she* then reckon all this? Oh, marry him for the

Seaton-Proctor alliance, the benefit of extra land and power for her clan. And then, when bored, kill him one night out in the fields or forest, with a single swift blow of her puma paw—pretend after, with help from her pa, some other thing had done for him.

Matt had shocked himself.

He felt the blood drain from his face.

That was when her cool hand, so much smaller than his own, gave his the most fleeting squeeze. She shut her right eye at him. So quick—had he imagined—she *winked*?

Taken aback, yet she'd steadied him. He thought after all she was real. Or was it only her animal cunning?

Her hair was arranged in a complicated fashion, all its gilded length and thickness braided and coiled, part pinned up and part let fall down—like corn braids made for Harvest Home.

Matt liked her hair, her eyes, the way she had winked at him. He liked her name, the full version of which the minister had said—Athena. Matt knew from his books *Athena* was the wise warrior goddess of the Ancient Greeks. It might have been fine, really fine, if everything else had been different.

꙳ ꙳ ꙳

They ate the Wedding Breakfast in the prayer house Goodwill room, among more bunches of flowers.

Here Matt finally met Joz Proctor, an unextraordinary, rangy, dark-haired man, who shook Matt's hand, and clapped him on the back, and said he had heard only worthy and elegant things of Matthew Seaton, and welcome to the Upland Folk.

There was wine. Matt was now like a pair of men. One of

whom wasn't unhappy, kept glancing at his new young wife. One of whom, however, stood back in hollow shadows, frowning, tense as a trigger.

Joz had given them a house, as the head of each Family generally did with the new son-in-law. Chanter's house was like that too, gifted by his Anne's father. So after the Breakfast, under a shower of little colored coins of rice paper, Thena and Matt climbed into a beribboned Proctor trap, and Matt snapped the whip high over the heads of the beribboned gray horses, and off they flew up the hill, in a chink of bells and spangle of sunlight. Just he and she. They two.

ঌ   ঌ   ঌ

"I guess you'd like to change out of that."

This was the first real thing she said to him since they'd been alone—really since they'd met by the altar.

"Uh—yeah. It rubs on my neck."

"And such smooth silk too," she said, almost . . . playful.

But anyhow, they both went up the splendid wooden staircase and changed in separate rooms into more everyday clothing.

When he came down, one of the house servants was seeing to the fire, but Thena, *Athena*, was lighting the lamps. The servant seemed not to mind her at all. But then, even wild animals, where they had gotten accustomed to people, might behave gently.

They ate a late supper in candlelight.

"Do you like your house, Matthew?" she asked him, courteously. This was the very first she had spoken his name.

"Yes."

"My father spent a lot of thought on it."

A lot of money too, obviously. "Yes, it's a generous and magnificent house."

"I'd like," she said, "to alter a few small things."

"I leave that to you, of course."

"Then I will."

The servant girl came around the table and poured him more coffee, as Maggie would have at home. But *this* was home, now.

"Tomorrow I'll ride out, have a word with the men, take a look at the land," he said in a businesslike way.

"No one expects it, Matthew, not on your first day—" she broke off.

Indeed, nobody would, first morning after the bridal night.

He said, "Oh, well, I'd like to anyhow. Get to know the place."

He had already seen something of the grand extent of it as he drove down in the westering light. Cleared from the surrounding woods and forest, miles of fields awaiting the new-sown grain, tracts of trees kept for timber, cows and sheep and goats. Stables and pigpens, orchards with the blossom flickering pink. The house was called High Hills.

There was an interval after the brief discussion. A log cracked on the hearth. But the servants had gone and let them be. Over the mantel, the big old clock with the golden sun-face gave the hour before midnight.

"Well," she said, rising with a spare seamlessness, "I'll go up." Then she made one flamboyant gesture. She pulled some central comb or pin from her braided hair and it rushed down around her, down to the backs of her knees, as promised. As it fell, it frayed out of the braids like water from an unfrozen spring and seemed to give off sparks like the fire.

She turned then to look at him over her shoulder.

"No need for you to come up to me yet, Matthew Seaton." She spoke level as a balance. "Nor any need to come upstairs at all. If you'd rather not."

"Oh but I—" he said, having already lurched to his feet as a gentleman should.

"*Oh but.* Oh but you don't want me, that's plain enough. I have no trouble with *you*. You're a strong, handsome man, with very honest eyes. But if you have trouble with me, then we can keep apart."

And so saying she left him there, his mouth hung open.

It was nearly midnight, his coffee cold on the table and the candles mostly burned out, when he pushed back his chair once more and went after her up the stair.

At her door he knocked. He thought perhaps she was asleep by now. Did he hope so? But she answered, soft and calm, and he undid the door and went in.

The big bedroom, the very bed, were of the best. White feather pillows, crisp white linen sheets, a quilt stitched by twenty women into the patterns of running deer and starry nights.

Thena sat propped on pillows. Her hair poured all around her like golden treacle. She was reading a book. She glanced at him. "Shall I move over and make room, or stay put?"

Matt shut the door behind him.

"You're a splendor," he said, coloring a little at his own words. "All any man'd want. It isn't that."

She looked at him, not blinking. In the sidelong lamplight her eyes now shone differently. He had seen a precious stone like it once—a topaz. Like that.

"Then?" she quietly asked.

What could he say?

Something in him, that wasn't him—or was more him than *he* was—took a firm sudden grip on his mind, his blood, even perhaps his heart. He said, "I'd like it goodly if you would move over a little, Thena Seaton."

While he took off his boots, she lowered the lamp. And in the window he saw the stars of the quilt had gotten away, and were returned safely to the midnight sky.

3: THE WIFE

Summer came. It came into the new house too, unrolled over the stone floors in transparent yellow carpets, sliding along the oak banister of the stair, turning windows to diamonds.

Outside the fields ripened through green to blond. In the orchard, apples blazed red. The peach vine growing on the ancient hackwood tree was hung with round lanterns of fruit.

He got along well with the hands, some of whom were Joz Proctor's, some the roving kind that arrived to work each summer for cash but were known and reliable for all that. Once they were sure Matt knew his business with crops and beasts, they gave him their respect with their casual helpful friendliness. None of them had anything to say about Joz Proctor but what you'd expect, seeing they dealt here with Joz's son-in-law.

None of them seemed at all uneasy either. Even when their tasks kept them near the house. And none of them had a strange look for Thena—save now and then, on seeing her, one of the newer younger boys colored up or smiled appreciatively to himself.

Every night when Matt went home to the house, the big, cool rooms, well swept and polished, would light with lamps as the day went out. Coming in he might hear Thena too, playing the old pianotto in the parlor. She played quite brilliantly, though she never sang. Sometimes she persuaded Matt to do that. He had a good tenor voice, she said, true to the note. Otherwise, when the meal was done, they'd sit reading each side the fire, which even in summer was generally needed once the sun went down. She might read something out to him, some story from a myth, or piece of a play by some old dramatist or poet. He might do the same. But they seldom went up late to bed. They told each other things besides about their childhood—how he had hitched his first dog to a cart, and ridden over the fields, pretending he was a charioteer from Roman times; how she had seen a falling star once that was bright blue, and no one believed her, but Matt said he did.

She wasn't one for chores, darning or sewing, left all that to the house girls. But frequently she drove them laughing out of the kitchen, and cooked up a feast for him. Some days they rode out together along the land, debating the state of this or that.

Did he love her by then, so fast? He couldn't say. But he was glad to come back to her, glad to be with her, always. Thought of her often in the day, especially when he was far off on the outskirts of the mountains, and wouldn't see her or lie at her side that night.

And she. Did *she* love *him*?

A woman did, surely, if she acted to you as Thena did to Matt. The other girls he had known who had definitely loved him, at least for a while, had acted in similar ways, though none so intelligently and wonderfully as she. She was like a young princess, regal in her generous giving, strict only with herself, and even in that never cold.

How had he ever been wary, been afraid of her? Why hadn't he known that the stupid tales were only that, just what Chant had warned him of, jealousy and empty-headed gossip? Aside from all else, five full moons had by then gone by. She had been in his arms on each of those nights and never stirred till morning.

For Matt's wife was no more a were-beast, a shape-twister, than the sun was dead when it set.

§   §   §

It was getting on for leaf-fall, and the farm busy and soon to be more so with harvest.

That night they went upstairs directly after supper, around nine by the sun-clock, for Matt needed to be away with the dawn.

He was brushing her hair. His mother had let him do this too, when he was much younger. It had fascinated him then, did so now, the liveness of a woman's hair, its scents and electric quiverings, as if it were another separate animal. . . .

"When will you be home again?" Thena asked, her eyes shut as she leaned back into the brush. Any woman might ask this of her young husband.

"Oh, not for a night, I'd say. More's the pity."

"I see," she said. She sounded just a touch—what? Unhappy? He was glad to hear.

"Maybe," he said, "I *can* get back tomorrow, very late—would that do better?"

"No, Matt," she said. "Don't hurry home."

Something in him checked. He stopped the brushing.

As if joking, he said, "Why, don't you want me home if I can be? Would I disturb you so much arriving in the little hours? You don't often mind when I wake you."

She put out one of her slim calloused hands, and covered his wrist. "Come home if you want, Matt. It's only, if you do, I may be from the house."

The pall cleared from his brain. Of course. There was a baby about to be born, several miles off at the next big farm. Joz's other kin, one of the Fletcher family. Probably they had asked Thena, now a married woman, to help out when the time came.

"Well I'll miss you. I hope Fletcher's wife is swift in delivery, for her sake—and mine."

"Oh, Matt, no, I'm not going there. That child's not due till Honey-mass."

Again taken aback, he left off brushing completely. He stepped away, and with a mild *Thank you*, she gathered all her hair in over her right shoulder like a waterfall. She was going to braid it and he wanted to stop her. He loved her hair loose in their bed. But he said nothing of that now. He said, "Then why won't you be at home at our house, Thena?"

Her hands continued braiding. He couldn't see her face.

Matt moved around her and seated himself across from her in the large carved chair in the corner. He could still tell nothing from her face. Nor did she reply.

He said again, very flat, "Do you want me to think you have some fancy lover you like better'n me? If not, say where you're going."

Then she answered promptly. "Into the forest."

The bedroom lamps were trimmed and rosy. None of them

went out. But it was as if the whole room—the house—the land outside—plunged down into a deeper, *darker* darkness.

All these months he had disbelieved and nearly forgotten his earlier fears. Yet instantly they returned, leaping on him, sinking in their fangs, their claws, lashing their tails to break the panes of night and of his peace.

"The forest? *Why?* No, Thena. Look at me. And tell me the truth."

She let go of the braid.

She raised her head and met his eyes with her topaz ones, and abruptly he knew that no woman's eyes, even in sidelong lampshine, ever went that color.

As if she simply told him the price of wheat, she said to him, "Because I have a need now, sometimes, to be that other thing I am. The thing not human, and which once you saw, when I came down from the woods to look at you as you fished, by the river in the moon."

Matt shook from head to foot. He could barely see her, she seemed wrapped in a mist, only her eyes burning out at him. "No—" he said.

"Yes," she said. "It's how it is with me. It isn't at full moon I have to change, nor any other time, not in that way. But sometimes—as another woman might want very much to wear a red dress, or to eat a certain food, or travel to a certain house or town—like *that*. I have a choice. But I want to and *choose* now to do it."

He saw in his mind's eye what she had chosen then—as another chose to visit or wear red: the mountain cat with its pelt of dusk. The puma. *The shape-twist.*

"No, Thena—no, no."

She left him immediately. She walked out of the bedroom,

and went to the other little bedroom, and shut the door. And Matt went on sitting in the carved chair. He sat there until four in the morning, when anyway he must get up for the dawn ride.

ᏍᎢ   ᏍᎢ   ᏍᎢ

Afterward he never recalled much about what he did that day. It was to do with the stock, fences, something of that sort. But though he dealt with it, it was never him. And by sunfall he and the men were up along Tangle Ridge, the black forests curling below, and the house he shared with Thena far away.

He always thought of her. But today he had thought of nothing else.

Matt kept asking himself if he had heard her rightly. Had she truly said what he recollected? Or was he losing his wits? But even though he couldn't fully involve himself in his work, he knew he had seen to it. And what he had heard the other men say to him had been *logical* and *coherent*. While everything he'd looked at was what you would reckon on. The sun hadn't risen in the north, and now it didn't sink in the east. So he hadn't gone mad, nor had the world. What she had said, therefore, she had said. He'd not imagined it.

He did wonder—why? for it scarcely mattered—how she had known he was fishing that past night at the river. But it seemed to him, uneasily, the puma side of her had sharper senses—perhaps she had picked up the *scent* of him, found him in that animal way. *Tracked* him.

Or was she only *lying*?

Was it *all* some damned lie, meant to throw him, scare him—yet why'd she do that? She loved him—maybe she didn't.

Maybe she hated his guts and it was all a plan to be shot of him, or else *send* him crazy and get rid *that* way.

By sundown his head ached.

He wanted only to go to sleep, off beyond the fire, solid rock under him, and the stars staring back in his eyes.

But instead, having let the horse rest herself a while, and having shared a meal without appetite, Matt swung again into the saddle. The men laughed at him, just a bit, not unkindly. He and his wife had been wed less than six months. No wonder he'd want to ride home through the night.

The horse picked her way off the ridge, and an hour later, delicate and firm footed, in among the pines.

The trees had the tang of fall already on them, and the streams were shallow as they trickled downhill.

Every glint of moonlight, every deeper shadow, took on the form for him of topaz-green-glass eyes, a slink of four-legged body, round ears, pointed teeth—

But it never was.

The moon was only a little thing, thin and new and curved. Like the shed claw-case of a cat.

Three more hours he rode down through the forest, into stands of larch and oak and amberwood. In the end he must have fallen asleep, sitting there on the sure-footed mare. But the horse knew the way, the way home.

ş ş ş

Matt reached the house before sunrise. By the time he went up to the bedroom, he was thinking in a sort of dream. He thought she would be there, asleep, her gold hair on the pillows. But she wasn't there. And in the house no one was about, and outside the man who had come to stable the horse, old Seph, was the same as he always was. Not a sign anyplace that anything was wrong. Except the empty bed and, when Matt tried the door, the other smaller room was also empty. He slept in there anyway, in the smaller room.

When he woke again it was full day and everything going on at its usual pace. And when he went down, Thena was in the parlor, helping one of the girls to clean some silver, both of them laughing over something. And Thena greeted him apparently without a care, and came over to kiss his cheek. And murmured, "Don't upset the girl. Make pretend all's well." So he did. And having had his breakfast, he went out to the fields.

They didn't meet, after that, he and Thena, till supper.

ß ß ß

Silence had come back with him. It made a third at the table. When the servants left them, there they were the three of them: he, Thena, the silence.

In the end he spoke.

"What shall I do?"

He had thought of all sorts of things he might say—demands, threats, making fun of it even. Or saying she had made a fool of him because he'd believed her.

But all he said was that. *What shall I do?*

She answered him straight back. "Come out with me to-night."

"—come out—"

"Come out and see for yourself. Oh," she added, "I don't think you'll faint away, will you, Matthew Seaton? Or *run* away. I think you'll take a book-learned scientific interest in it. Won't you?"

"To see you change—"

"To see me change into my other self."

"My God," he said. He gazed at the plate, where most of his food lay untouched. "Is it true?"

"You know it is. Or why this fuss?"

"Thena," he said.

He put his head into his hands.

At last she came and rested her own hand, cool and steady, on his burning neck. How human it felt, this slim hand with its scars, human and *known*, and kind.

"In God's world," she said, "so many wonders. Who are we to argue with such a wise magician as God? Midnight," she whispered, as if inviting him to an unlawful tryst. "By the old door."

Then, she was gone.

The old door led from the cellar. You got down there by way of the kitchen, but only Thena and he had a key to the cellarage. Going to meet her there he partly feared, his distress so overall he barely felt it, that already she would be—*in that other shape*. But she wasn't. She was just Thena, her hair roped round her head, and dressed as she did to go riding.

Together they slipped out into the soft cold of an early fall night.

Stars roared like silver gunshot in the black. No moon was up, or else it had come and gone; Matt couldn't recall what the moon did tonight, only that it wasn't full, was in its first quarter, and that the moon had no effect on her. To *alter* was her *choice*. Puman . . .

They didn't take the horses. They strode from the house and farmland, up through the tall tasselled fields, reached the woods and went into them.

Again, silence accompanied them all this while.

Then, all at once, Thena turned and caught his face lightly in both hands and kissed his mouth.

"This is mountain country, Matt, it isn't the Valley of the Shadow."

And *then*—she was darting away among the trees, and he too must run to keep her in sight.

The trees flashed by. Stars flashed between. The mountains lifted beyond, very near-seeming, very high, a wall built around everything, keeping everything in. Was it possible to climb right up those mountains? Get over them to the other side? Tonight it seemed to him nothing *lay* on the other side. For here was the last border of the world, what the ancients had called *Ultima Thule*.

She stopped still in a glade, where already the rocky steps showed that were the first treads of the mountain staircase. A creek ran through, and Thena pulled off her clothes, everything she wore, and loosed her hair out of its combs as she had that very first night. Clothed now quite modestly in the striped dapple of the starlit pines, she lay down on her knees and elbows and lapped from the stream, as an animal did.

He couldn't see her clearly. Couldn't see—Only how the shadows shifted, spilled. Fell differently. She was a young woman drinking from the water, then a creature neither woman nor beast—and next, in only half a minute—or half a year, for that was how slow it seemed to him—she was the puma in its velvet pelt, raising its muzzle, mouth dripping crystal from the creek, its eyes marked like flowers, and tail slowly lashing.

This—my wife.

They stared at each another. To his—almost angry—astonishment Matt felt no particular fear. He was terrified and yet beyond terror. Or rather all things were so terrible and fearful and Thena and the puma only one slight splinter dazzling from the chaos.

And dazzled he was. For too—so beautiful.

The puma—was beautiful.

It slinked upright and shook away the last beads of water.

When it spun about, it moved like quicksilver, mercury in the jar of darkness—It. *She.*

He couldn't follow her now. He would never catch her, as she had become. How curious. There was suddenly, to all of it, a sense only of the *normal.*

Matt sat down by the creek, where her clothes sprawled in a heap as if dead. Idiotically he had the urge to pick them up, spread them, perhaps fold them in a tidy way. He didn't.

He tried to decide now what to do, but in fact this seemed redundant. There was no urgency. Was he tired? He couldn't have said. He selected pebbles, and dropped them idly in the water.

When she came back, which was perhaps only two hours later, she brought a small slain deer with her, gripped in her jaws. He was not shocked or repelled by this. He had expected it, maybe. It had been neatly and swiftly killed by a single bite to the back of the neck. Matt had seen even the best shots among the hands, even Chant, who was a fine hunter, sometimes misjudge, causing an animal suffering and panic before it could be finished. When she, the puma, sat across the carcass from him, watching him, he thought he was sure that what Thena said to him, if wordlessly, was, *See, this is better.*

And it was. All of it—was.

They slept by the stream, he and the cat, a few feet between them—but when he stirred in sleep once, they were back to back, and her warmth was good. She did him no harm. Though he couldn't bring himself to touch her with his hands, this was less nervousness than a sort of respect. She smelled of grass and balsam from the pines, of cold upper air, of stars. And of killing and blood.

He hadn't meant to sleep. Somehow he hadn't been able to make himself understand.

But in the sunrise when he wakened, the trees painted pink along their eastern stems, Thena was there as a woman. She had dressed and set a fire, portioned the deer, and was cooking it slowly. The glorious savor of freshest roasting meat rose up on a blue smoke.

"Well," she said.

"Did I dream it?" he said.

"Maybe you did too."

"No, I didn't dream. Oh, Thena—what's that *like*? To be— *that*?"

"It's wonderful," she answered simply. "What else."

"But you knew me, even then?"

"I know you all. It isn't I cease to be myself. Or that I forget. Only I'm another kind of *me*. The true one, do you think?"

After they ate the meat and drank from the stream, they lay back on the pine needles. If until then he hadn't quite loved her, now he did. That was the strangest part of it, he thought ever after. That he *loved* her fully then, once he had seen her puma-soul. And he believed, that day, that nothing now could destroy their union. He had confronted the terror, and it was *no* terror, only a great, rare miracle, the blessing of God. And there was magic in the world, as the myths and stories in books had always told him.

4: THE BEAST

Years on, when he was older, Matthew Seaton sometimes asked himself if this was, precisely, what was at the root of his reaction—magic. Sorcery—a spell. She had put some sort of hex on him, bewitched and made him her dupe.

It hadn't felt like that. Rather, it had felt like the most reasonable *natural* thing. And the love—that too.

Surely something wicked might inspire all types of wrong emotion, such as greed or cruelty or rage. But it wouldn't bring on feelings of pure happiness. Or such a sense of rightness, harmony. Hope.

This then was the worst of it, in one way.

Yet only in one.

🔊   🔊   🔊

They did talk afterward, after the night in the forest. She let him ask his questions, answered them without hesitation. The substance of it was that her shape-switching had begun in infancy. It was the same, she implied, for her father, and when young he had often taken cat form—but it seemed with age he turned to it less and less. Nor had she ever seen it happen. None had. It was for him a private thing. He only told *her* when he became aware that she also had the gift. And *gift* was how he termed it, comparing it as she grew older to her talent for the pianotto. He said he had heard his great-grandmother had powers of a similar sort. He never revealed who told *him* about that.

As to whether Thena had been afraid when first she found what she could do, she replied no—only, perhaps oddly as she was then a child, she had known intuitively to keep it hidden from others. Yet something had prompted her to tell Joz. But it had *frightened* her not at all. It had seemed always merely what *should* happen, as presumably it had when she had learned to walk and talk, and presently to read. She said that some of the commonplace human changes that occurred in her body as she became a woman had alarmed her far more.

Again, much later, Matt—looking back at it—was startled by his calm questions and her frank answers. He could remember, by then stunned and oppressed, that at that time nothing about her "gift" anymore disquieted him. Indeed, he left her to indulge in her *other* life, felt no misgiving, let alone horror. And this of course *was* horrible. Horrible beyond thought or words.

Stranger too—or not strange, not at all given the rest—was how he began almost to lose interest in her uncanny pursuit, leaving her to solitary enjoyment, just kissing her farewell on such nights, letting her go without a qualm. As if she only went on a visit to some trusted neighbor.

It had seemed to him then that everyone in the house called High Hills, and on their land, knew what Thena did. They must see her come and go but were reassured they need fear nothing from her. Perhaps even the very cattle and sheep that grazed the slopes saw her pass in her shadow-shape, the blood of deer on her breath, and never even flicked an ear. Thena would not prey on her own. Thena, even when puma, stayed mistress and guardian.

Besides, anyhow, by the time the first snows began to arrive, she had told Matt *they* had something far more important on their hands. She was pregnant. He and she were to have a child.

§ § §

Thena withdrew into herself in the last months of her pregnancy. Some women did this. Matt had seen it with his own mother, when the younger children came. Rather daunted by the idea of fatherhood, he already treated her with a certain awed caution. Still he was happy, and as the good wishes of the hands poured over him, pleased with himself.

Once the snow eased away, the Family visits began. The Seaton clan was followed by Proctors and Fletchers. He saw people young and old he'd met once at the wedding and barely once since. Joz was just as he recalled, well humored and approving of both the baby, and the running of the farm. But he too was remote somehow, as he had seemed before. It came to Matt, though he scarcely considered it then, that this ultimate remoteness belonged in Thena too. However close and connected he and she might become, some part of her stayed always far off, behind her eyes, beyond the mind's horizon. As with her father, the puma part of her? The sorcerous and elemental part . . .

As the fields greened with new summer, Thena told Matt she believed the baby might come a little early.

Soon heavy with the child, she hadn't, from her fourth month, gone off anymore at night. They did not discuss it. It seemed to him only sensible that she didn't indulge the shape-switch at this time. Though she had done it, he realized at the beginning of her pregnancy, perhaps not yet aware she carried. What effect would such an action have on the growing being inside her? He never asked her that and never himself fretted. He trusted Thena. Again, in the future, he would remember that. And curse himself as blind.

Now and then, on certain nights, he did find her at a window, gazing out toward the forests and mountains. He noticed, when she gazed—he liked to see it—one of her hands always rested protectively on her swelling stomach.

Thena was right. The child was nearly two weeks premature.

He was away the day her labor started. Returning he found the house moving to a kind of ritualistic uproar. The doctor's trap stood in the yard, women ran up and down the staircase. No one, however, forgot Matt's comforts. Hot coffee and fresh water stood waiting. The bath had been drawn. His evening meal, he was assured, was in preparation.

When urgently he asked after his wife, they tried to keep him from her. The doctor was there, and two of the Proctor-Fletcher women. Finally he let them see his anger—or his nerves—and they allowed him to go up too.

Thena was in the bed, blue rings round her eyes, but smiling gravely. "Brace up, Matthew," she told him. "Within the hour I'll have it done."

Then they shooed him out again, the women. And twenty minutes after he heard Thena give a loud savage cry, the only violent noise she had made. He dropped the china coffee cup and bounded up the stair, where the doctor caught him. "All's nicely, Matt. Listen, do you hear?" And Matt heard a baby crying.

"My wife—" he shouted.

But when they let him go in again Thena lay there still,

still gravely smiling, now with the child in her arms.

The baby was a girl. He didn't mind that, nor the fact the fluff of hair on her head was dark, not golden. And he praised the baby, because that was expected, and too, if he didn't, some of them might think he sulked at not receiving a son. But really he hardly saw it—her, this girl, if he were honest. She was just an object, like a dear little newborn lamb, useful, attractive— unimportant. All he cared about was that Thena had come through the birth, and held out her hand to him.

Fatherly feeling might have found him later. He didn't seek it. More than all else, as the month went on, he felt a sort of confusion. For now another was with them. He and Thena— and the child. Three of them. Like the silence that had been with them that other time, he and she, and it.

꙳ ꙳ ꙳

He had a dream one night, and for a while on other nights. Always the same. There was no definite image, only vague shiftings of shade and moonlight in what might be forest. And an unknown voice, not male or female. Which said quietly to him in his sleep, "Thena." And then, "The puma's daughter." And this upset him in the dream, as if he didn't know, had never heard even a rumor of shape-twisting, let alone *seen* her change, lain back to back with her in that form, eaten of her kill, loved her better for all of it.

꙳ ꙳ ꙳

There was a piece of music Thena had sometimes played. Matt couldn't ever remember the composer; he'd never liked it much. Beginning softly and seeming rather dull to him, so his thoughts wandered, then abruptly it changed tempo,

becoming a ragged gallop full of fury and foreboding, ending
with two or three clashing chords that could make you jump.

The sun-clock showed the days and nights as they went
by. The farm's work-journal showed the passage of weeks and
months. The seasons altered in their ever changing, ever unal-
terable fashion. As did the moon.

People came and went as well, in their own correct stages
of visit, hire, service.

It wasn't so long, anyhow. Far less than a year. Far more
than a century.

In this space they grew apart, the husband and his wife.
Like two strong trees, one leaning like a dancer to the breeze,
the other bending at a tilt in the earth, backward, sinking.

It was Matt who sank and looked backward. He tried to
recapture what they had been before the child came. Or what
he believed they'd been. But the child was always there somewhere, needing something. Present—if not in the room, then
in the house—and a woman would appear to fetch Thena, who
left her cooking or the pianotto, or put down her book, and
went away.

But then Thena too began to go away on her own account.
There was a nurse at such times, for the child. The notion was
that this allowed Matt and Thena a night together. But on
those nights she didn't remain with Matt. It was the forest she
went to, like a lover.

For she never said to him now, *Come with me*. And he never
offered her company. She wouldn't want it, would she? She
had company enough, her own.

How thin, he thought, *her profound patience must be wearing with her child*. She was its slave. *He* must let her go.

The baby was starting to toddle and was due to be God-blessed soon at the prayer house, and there was to be a big party. Spring was on the land again also, calling up sap, and extra work, and memory.

And a night fell when Matt was exhausted, sleeping as hard as if he were roping cows or tying the sheaves. Yet he woke. Something wakened him.

He lay on his back in their bed and wondered what it was— and then saw the moon burning in the window, full and white as a bonfire of snow.

The room was palest blue with light, and in a moment more he saw Thena was gone from the bed. Putting out his hand, he felt that her side of the mattress was cold.

Nor was this a night for the nurse to watch the baby. It must be lying in the cot in the corner, and would wake and begin it—her—loud lamb's bleating for Thena—and Thena wasn't there. So Matt sat up and looked at the cot, and it was empty. Empty as the bed, and as anything meant to hold something else safe, when a theft has happened.

If never before had the child meant anything to him, now suddenly she did.

Her name, at the God-blessing, was to be declared as Amy.

Matt called it aloud, *Amy! Amy!* and sprang from the covers. He rushed to the small room, where the nurse slept when the cot was moved there—but no one was there now, not the nurse, never Thena and the child. He'd known this would be so.

Matt flung on his clothes, his boots. He dashed down through the house. Nobody was about. Not even out in the stable. He slung the saddle on his horse and galloped away, straight through the young-sown fields, cleaving them.

He knew where she'd gone, Thena, his wife.

His heart was pounding in his brain, which was full too

of one terrible picture. He thought of the old religious phrase: *And the scales drop't from mine eyes*.

Blind—blind fool. She was a *beast*, daughter of a *beast*. A mountain cat—and she had taken his child with her up into the wilderness of pines and rocks under the glare of the bitter, burning moon.

Oh, the picture. It lit his mind with terror as the wicked moon the world. A puma running with its red mouth just ajar on a thing held clamped within its jaws, a small bundle, with a fluff of darkish hair, faintly crying on a lamb's lost bleat.

It was as he entered the first mass of the trees, looking up, he saw. Bright-lighted on a shelf of stone above, trotting through from one tree line to another. The silver puma with the little bundle, exactly as he saw it in his head, gripped in by the sparkle of white teeth.

He pulled the horse's head round so sharply she swerved and almost unseated him. Frozen, he clung there, staring up at his baby in the fangs of death.

Peculiarly none of this had made a sound, or attracted the attention of the cat. The child didn't cry. Could it be—*she* had already killed it?

Then the pines reabsorbed them, those two joined figures, and the hex broke from him and he floundered from the horse and left her, and ran, *ran* up the chunky side of the mountainous forest, with his hunting rifle in his hand.

In any myth, or tale like that, he must have located them. In reality it wasn't likely. He knew it, and took no notice. Matt was *living* in a legend. And this was finally proven, when at last he ran to the brink of the cold blue moonlight. And there they were, on the ice-blue grass, Thena and her baby. And they—

They were playing. But not as a human mother and her

human infant ever play. For Thena was a mountain lion, and Amy was her cub. No room was ever shined up by a lamp so bright to show Matt, clear as day, the sleek puma mother, rolling and boxing with the energetic cub, it carelessly nipping her, and she gentle and claw-sheathed, while both their dusken pelts gleamed from moon-powder, and their crimson mouths were open, the mother to mimic growls, the infant to spit back and warble as best she could. Openmouthed, they seemed to be both of them, laughing. But when the play ended and the puma lay down to lick the cub for a bath, her hoarse purr was louder in the night than any other sound.

Matt stood by the tree that hid him. He thought after, they should surely have known he was there, only their total involvement with each other and themselves shut out his presence. Hidden as if invisible, he might have ceased to exist.

So he watched them for a while. And when the moon passed over, and the edge of the forest was no longer a flame of light, but a shattered muddle of stripes and angles, he was yet able to watch one further thing. And this was how both creatures changed, quick and easy, back into their human form. Then there she was, Thena. And her baby. And Thena picked up the child, and kissed her, and humanly laughed and held her high, laughing, proud and laughing with joy, and the little child laughed back, waving at the night her little hands which, minutes before, had been the paws of a cat.

She had never been his. Neither of them. Not Thena. Not Thena's daughter. No, they came of another race. The shape-twisting kind. *Him* she had used. And could Thena harm her baby? Never. Thena loved her. *Knew* her. They were to each other all and everything, and needed no one else on earth.

He'd wondered in the before-time, if it was possible to ride all the way up to some mountain pass, and so cross the mountains and get over to the other places, where other people were. Human people. Ordinary.

That night Matt Seaton, with only his horse and his gun, and the clothes he stood in, climbed up the side of the world, and combed the ridges until he did find some way through. He left all behind him. His kinfolk, the Seaton-Proctor alliance and the Families, his property, himself. His marriage and his fatherhood he didn't leave, they'd been stolen already. Stolen by his jealousy. By his cheated humanness, and his lonely human heart.

TANITH LEE has written nearly 100 books and over 270 short stories, besides radio plays and TV scripts. Her genre-crossing includes fantasy, SF, horror, and young adult, historical, detective, and contemporary fiction. Plus combinations of them all. Her latest publications include the Lionwolf Trilogy: *Cast a Bright Shadow*, *Here in Cold Hell*, and *No Flame But Mine*, and the three *Piratica* novels for young adults. She has also recently had several short stories and novellas in *Asimov's SF Magazine*, *Weird Tales*, and *Realms of Fantasy* as well as the anthologies *The Ghost Quartet* and *Wizards*.

She lives on the Sussex Weald with her husband, writer/artist John Kaiine, and two omnipresent cats. More information can be found at www.tanithlee.com.

Author's Note

The Beastly Bride is a very evocative title. From it I got the instant idea of a reverse of the usual "Beauty and the Beast" scenario—this time the reluctant and alarmed young *man* going uneasily to wed an unknown and supernaturally beastly young woman.

(Of course, sometimes one forgets, in any strictly arranged marriage sight unseen, there may well be severe qualms on both sides.)

Then I needed to decide what *kind* of beast. I chose the puma (or mountain lion) because though I've always loved its beauty, its *cry*, heard by me in a movie when I was about eleven, seemed terrifying. (Strangely, that cry is the one puma-esque attribute not mentioned in this tale.) With the puma settled on, its natural habitat was also immediately there, less a backdrop than a third main character: a parallel North American Rockies, probably around 1840.

MAP OF SEVENTEEN

Christopher Barzak

Everyone has secrets. Even me. We carry them with us like contraband, always swaddled in some sort of camouflage we've concocted to hide the parts of ourselves the rest of the world is better off not knowing. I'd write what I'm thinking in a diary if I could believe others would stay out of those pages, but in a house like this there's no such thing as privacy. If you're going to keep secrets, you have to learn to write them down inside your own heart. And then be sure not to give that away to anyone either. At least not to just anyone at all.

Which is what bothers me about *him*, the guy my brother is apparently going to marry. Talk about secrets. Off Tommy goes to New York City for college, begging my parents to help him with money for four straight years, then after graduating at the top of his class—in studio art, of all things (not even a degree that will get him a job to help pay off the loans our parents took out for his education)—he comes home to tell us he's gay, and before we can say anything, good or bad, runs off again and won't return our calls. And when he does start talking to Mom and Dad again, it's just short phone conversations and e-mails, asking for help, for more money.

Five years of off-and-on silence and here he is, bringing home some guy named Tristan who plays the piano better than my mother and has never seen a cow except on TV. We're supposed to treat this casually and not bring up the fact that he ran away without letting us say anything at all four years ago, and to try not to embarrass him. That's Tommy Terlecki, my big brother, the gay surrealist Americana artist who got semifamous not for the magical creatures and visions he paints but for his horrifically exaggerated family portraits of us dressed up in ridiculous roles: *American Gothic*, Dad holding a pitchfork, Mom presenting her knitting needles and a ball of yarn to the viewer, as if she's coaxing you to give them a try, me with my arms folded under my breasts, my face angry within the frame of my bonnet, scowling at Tommy, who's sitting on the ground beside my legs in the portrait, pulling off the Amish-like clothes. What I don't like about these paintings is that he's lied about us in them. The Tommy in the portrait is constrained by his family's way of life, but it's Tommy who's put us in those clothes to begin with. They're how he sees us, not the way we are, but he gets to dramatize a conflict with us in the paintings anyway, even though it's a conflict he himself has imagined.

Still, I could be practical and say the *American Gothic* series made Tommy's name, which is more than I can say for the new stuff he's working on: *The Sons of Melusine*. They're like his paintings of magical creatures, which the critic who picked his work out of his first group show found too precious in comparison to the "promise of the self-aware, absurdist family portraits this precocious young man from the wilderness of Ohio has also created." Thank you, Google, for keeping me informed on my brother's activities. *The Sons of Melusine* are all bare-chested men with curvy muscles who have serpentine tails and faces like Tristan's, all of them extremely attractive and extremely in pain: out of water mostly, gasping for air in the back alleys of cities, parched and bleeding on beaches, strung on fishermen's line, the hook caught in the flesh of a cheek. A new Christ, Tommy described them when he showed them to us, and Mom and Dad said, "Hmm, I see."

He wants to hang an *American Gothic* in the living room, he told us, after we'd been sitting around talking for a while, all of us together for the first time in years, his boyfriend Tristan smiling politely as we tried to catch up with Tommy's doings while trying to be polite and ask Tristan about himself as well. "My life is terribly boring, I'm afraid," Tristan said when I asked what he does in the city. "My family's well-off, you see, so what I do is mostly whatever seems like fun at any particular moment."

Well-off. Terribly boring. Whatever seems like fun at any particular moment. I couldn't believe my brother was dating this guy, let alone planning to marry him. This is Tommy, I reminded myself, and right then was when he said, "If it's okay with you, Mom and Dad, I'd like to hang one of the *American Gothic* paintings in here. Seeing how Tristan and I will be staying with you for a while, it'd be nice to add some touches of our own."

Tommy smiled. Tristan smiled and gave Mom a little shrug of his shoulders. I glowered at them from across the room, arms folded across my chest on purpose. Tommy noticed and, with a concerned face, asked me if something was wrong. "Just letting life imitate art," I told him, but he only kept on looking puzzled. *Faker*, I thought. He knows exactly what I mean.

§   §   §

Halfway through that first evening, I realized this was how it was going to be as long as Tommy and Tristan were with us, while they waited for their own house to be built next to Mom and Dad's: Tommy conducting us all like the head of an orchestra, waving his magic wand. He had Mom and Tristan sit on the piano bench together and tap out some "Heart and Soul." He sang along behind them for a moment, before looking over his shoulder and waving Dad over to join in. When he tried to pull me in with that charming squinty-eyed devil grin that always gets anyone—our parents, teachers, the local police officers who used to catch him speeding down back roads—to do his bidding, I shook my head, said nothing, and left the room. "Meg?" he said behind me. Then the piano stopped, and I could hear them whispering, wondering what had set me off this time.

I'm not known for being easy to live with. Between Tommy's flair for making people live life like a painting when he's around, and my stubborn, immovable will, I'm sure our parents must have thought at some time or other that their real children had been swapped in the night with changelings. It would explain the way Tommy could make anyone like him, even out in the country, where people don't always think well of gay people. It would explain the creatures he paints that make people look nervous after viewing them, the half-animal beings that roam the streets of cities and back roads of villages in his first paintings. It would explain how I can look at any math problem or scientific equation my teachers put before me and figure them out without breaking a sweat. And my aforementioned will. My will, this thing that's so strong I sometimes feel like it's another person inside me.

Our mother is a mousy figure here in this little town in the Middle of Nowhere, Ohio. The central town square is not even really a square, but an intersection of two highways where Town Hall, a general store, beauty salon, and Presbyterian church all face each other like lost old women casting glances over the asphalt, hoping one of the others knows where they are and where they're going, for surely why would anyone stop here? My mother works in the library, which used to be a one-room schoolhouse a hundred years ago, where they still use a stamp card to keep track of the books checked out. My father is one of the township trustees, and he also runs our farm. We raise beef cattle, Herefords mostly, though a few Hereford and Angus mixes are in our herd, so you sometimes get black cows with polka-dotted white faces. I never liked the mixed calves, I'm not sure why, but Tommy always said they were his favorites. Mutts are always smarter than streamlined gene pools, he said. Me? I always thought they looked like heartbroken mimes with dark, dewy eyes.

From upstairs in my room I could hear the piano start again, this time a classical song. It had to be Tristan. Mom only knows songs like "Heart and Soul" and just about anything in a hymn book. My parents attend, I don't. Tommy and I gave up church ages ago. I still consider myself a Christian, just not the churchgoing kind. We're lucky to have parents who asked us why we didn't want to go, instead of forcing us like tyrants. When I told them I didn't feel I was learning what I needed to live in the world there, instead of getting mad, they just nodded and Mom said, "If that's the case, perhaps it's best that you walk your own way for a while, Meg."

They're so *good*. That's the problem with my parents. They're so good, it's like they're children or something, innocent and naïve. Definitely not stupid, but way too easy on other people. They never fuss with Tommy. They let him treat them like they're these horrible people who ruined his life and they never say a word. They hug him and calm him down instead, treat him like a child. I don't get it. Tommy's the oldest. Isn't he the one who's supposed to be mature and put together well?

I listened to Tristan's notes drift up through the ceiling from the living room below, and lay on my bed staring at a tiny speck on the ceiling, a stain or odd flaw in the plaster that has served as my focal point for anger for many years. Since I can remember, whenever I got angry, I'd come up here and lie in this bed and stare at that speck, pouring all of my frustrations into it, as if it were a black hole that could suck up all the bad. I've given that speck so much of my worst self over the years, I'm surprised it hasn't grown darker and wider, big enough to cast a whole person into its depths. When I looked at it now, I found I didn't have as much anger to give it as I'd thought. But no, that wasn't it either. I realized all of my anger was floating around the room instead, buoyed up by the notes of the piano, by Tristan's playing. I thought I could even see those notes shimmer into being for a brief moment, electrified by my frustration. When I blinked, though, the air looked normal again, and Tristan had brought his melody to a close.

There was silence for a minute, some muffled voices, then Mom started up "Amazing Grace." I felt immediately better and breathed a sigh of relief. Then someone knocked on my door and it swung open a few inches, enough for Tommy to peek inside. "Hey, Sis. Can I come in?"

"It's a free country."

"Well," said Tommy, "sort of."

We laughed. We could laugh about things we agreed on.

"Sooo," said Tommy, "what's a guy gotta do around here to get a hug from his little sister?"

"Aren't you a little old for hugs?"

"Ouch. I must have done something really bad this time."

"Not bad. Something. I don't know what."

"Want to talk about it?"

"Maybe."

Tommy sat down on the corner of my bed and craned his neck to scan the room. "What happened to all the unicorns and horses?"

"They died," I said. "Peacefully, in their sleep, in the middle of the night. Thank God."

He laughed, which made me smirk without wanting to. This was the other thing Tommy had always been able to do: make it hard for people to stay mad at him. "So you're graduating in another month?" he said.

I nodded, turned my pillow over so I could brace it under my arm to hold me up more comfortably.

"Are you scared?"

"About what?" I said. "Is there something I should be scared of?"

"You know. The future. The rest of your life. You won't be a little girl anymore."

"I haven't been a little girl for a while, Tommy."

"You know what I mean," he said, standing up, tucking his

hands into his pockets like he does whenever he's being Big Brother. "You're going to have to begin making big choices," he said. "What you want out of life. You know it's not a diploma you receive when you cross the graduation stage. It's really a ceremony where your training wheels are taken off. The cap everyone wants to throw in the air is a symbol of what you've been so far in life: a student. That's right, everyone wants to cast it off so quickly, eager to get out into the world. Then they realize they've got only a couple of choices for what to do next. The armed service, college, or working at a gas station. It's too bad we don't have a better way to recognize what the meaning of graduation really is. Right now, I think it leaves you kids a little clueless."

"Tommy," I said. "Yes, you're eleven years older than me. You know more than I do. But really, you need to learn when to shut the hell up and stop sounding pompous."

We laughed again. I'm lucky that, no matter what makes me mad about my brother, we can laugh at ourselves together.

"So what are you upset about then?" he asked after we settled down.

"Them," I said, trying to get serious again. "Mom and Dad. Tommy, have you thought about what this is going to do to them?"

"What do you mean?"

"I mean, what the town's going to say? Tommy, do you know in their church newsletter they have a prayer list and our family is on it?"

"What for?" he asked, beginning to sound alarmed.

"Because you're gay!" I said. It didn't come out how I wanted, though. By the way his face, always alert and showing some kind of emotion, receded and locked its door behind it, I could tell I'd hurt his feelings. "It's not like that," I said. "They didn't ask to be put on the prayer list. Fern Baker put them on it."

"Fern Baker?" Tommy said. "What business has that woman got still being alive?"

"I'm serious, Tommy. I just want to know if you understand the position you've put them in."

He nodded. "I do," he said. "I talked with them about Tristan and me coming out here to live three months ago. They said what they'll always say to me or you when we want or need to come home."

"What's that?"

"Come home, darling. You and your Tristan have a home here too." When I looked down at my comforter and studied its threads for a while, Tommy added, "They'll say the come home part to you, of course. Not anything about bringing your Tristan with you. Oh, and if it's Dad, he might call you sweetie the way Mom calls me darling."

"Tommy," I said, "if there was a market for men who can make their sisters laugh, I'd say you're in the wrong field."

"Maybe we can make that a market."

"You need lots of people for that," I said.

"Mass culture. Hmm. Been there, done that. It's why I'm back. *You* should give it a try, though. It's an interesting experience. It might actually suit you, Meg. Have you thought about where you want to go to college?"

"It's already decided. Kent State in the fall."

"Kent, huh? That's a decent school. You wouldn't rather go to New York or Boston?"

"Tommy, even if you hadn't broken the bank around here

already, I don't have patience for legions of people running up and down the streets of Manhattan or Cambridge like ants in a hive."

"And a major?"

"Psychology."

"Ah, I see, you must think there's something wrong with you and want to figure out how to fix it."

"No," I said. "I just want to be able to break people's brains open to understand why they act like such fools."

"That's pretty harsh," said Tommy.

"Well," I said, "I'm a pretty harsh girl."

§   §   §

After Tommy left, I fell asleep without even changing out of my clothes. In the morning when I woke, I was tangled up in a light blanket someone—Mom, probably—threw over me before going to bed the night before. I sat up and looked out the window. It was already late morning. I could tell by the way the light winked off the pond in the woods, which you can see a tiny sliver of, like a crescent moon, when the sun hits at just the right angle toward noon. Tommy and I used to spend our summers on the dock our father built out there. Reading books, swatting away flies, the soles of our dusty feet in the air behind us. He was so much older than me but never treated me like a little kid. The day he left for New York City, I hugged him on the front porch before Dad drove him to the airport, but burst out crying and ran around back of the house, beyond the fields, into the woods, until I reached the dock. I thought Tommy would follow, but he was the last person I wanted to see right then, so I thought out with my mind in the direction of the house, pushing him away. I turned him around in his tracks and made him tell our parents he couldn't find me. When he didn't come, I knew that I had used something inside me to stop him. Tommy wouldn't have ever let me run away crying like that without chasing after me if I'd let him make that choice on his own. I lay on the dock for an hour, looking at my reflection in the water, saying, "What are you? God damn it, you know the answer. Tell me. What *are* you?"

If Mom had come back and seen me like that, heard me speak in such a way, I think she probably would have had a breakdown. Mom can handle a gay son mostly. What I'm sure she couldn't handle would be if one of her kids talked to themselves like that at age seven. Worse would be if she knew why I asked myself that question. It was the first time my will had made something happen. And it had made Tommy go away without another word between us.

Sometimes I think the rest of my life is going to be a little more difficult every day.

When I was dressed and had a bowl of granola and bananas in me, I grabbed the novel I was reading off the kitchen counter and opened the back door to head back to the pond. Thinking of the summer days Tommy and I spent back there together made me think I should probably honor my childhood one last summer by keeping up the tradition before I had to go away. I was halfway out the door, twisting around to close it, when Tristan came into the kitchen and said, "Good morning, Meg. Where are you off to?"

"The pond," I said.

"Oh, the pond!" Tristan said, as if it were a tourist site he'd been wanting to visit. "Would you mind if I tagged along?"

"It's a free country," I said, thinking I should probably have been nicer, but I turned to carry on my way anyway.

"Well, sort of," Tristan said, which stopped me in my tracks.

I turned around and looked at him. He did that same little shrug he did the night before when Tommy asked Mom and Dad if he could hang the *American Gothic* portrait in the living room, then smiled, as if something couldn't be helped. "Are you just going to stand there, or are you coming?" I said.

Quickly Tristan followed me out, and then we were off through the back field and into the woods until we came to the clearing where the pond reflected the sky, like an open blue eye staring up at God.

I made myself comfortable on the deck, spread out my towel and opened my book. I was halfway done. Someone's heart had already been broken and no amount of mix CDs left in her mailbox and school locker was ever going to set things right. Why did I read these things? *I should take the bike to the library and check out something classic instead*, I thought. Probably there was something I should be reading right now that everyone else in college would have read. I worried about things like that. Neither of our parents went to college. I remember Tommy used to worry the summer before he went to New York that he'd get there and never be able to fit in. "Growing up out here is going to be a black mark," he'd said. "I'm not going to know how to act around anyone there because of this place."

I find it ironic that it's this place—us—that helped Tommy start his career.

"This place is amazing," said Tristan. He stretched out on his stomach beside me, dangling the upper half of his torso over the edge so he could pull his fingers through the water just inches below us. "I can't believe you have all of this to yourself. You're so lucky."

"I guess," I said, pursing my lips. I still didn't know Tristan well enough to feel I could trust his motivations or be more than civil to him. Pretty. Harsh. Girl. I know.

"Wow," said Tristan, pulling his lower half back up onto the deck with me. He looked across the water, blinking. "You really don't like me."

"That's not true," I said immediately, but even I knew that was mostly a lie. So I tried to revise. "I mean, it's not that I don't like you. I just don't know you so well, that's all."

"Don't trust me, eh?"

"Really," I said, "why should I?"

"Your brother's trust in me doesn't give you a reason?"

"Tommy's never been known around here for his good judgment," I said.

Tristan whistled. "Wow," he said again, this time elongating it. "You're tough as nails, aren't you?"

I shrugged. Tristan nodded. I thought this was a sign we'd come to an understanding, so I went back to reading. Not two minutes passed, though, before he interrupted again.

"What are you hiding, Meg?"

"What are you talking about?" I said, looking up from my book.

"Well, obviously, if you don't trust people to this extreme, you must have something to hide. That's what distrustful people often have. Something to hide. Either that or they've been hurt an awful lot by people they loved."

"You do know you guys can't get married in Ohio, right? The people decided in the election a couple of years ago."

"Ohhhh," said Tristan. "The people. The people the people the people. Oh, my dear, it's always the people! Always leaping to defend their own rights but always ready to deny someone else theirs. Wake up, baby. That's history. Did that stop other people from living how they wanted? Well, I suppose some-times. Screw the people anyhow. Your brother and I will be married, whether or not the people make some silly law that prohibits it. The people, my dear, only matter if you let them."

"So you'll be married like I'm a Christian, even though I don't go to church."

"Really, Meg, you do realize that even if you consider your-self a Christian, those other people don't, right?"

"What do you mean?"

Tristan turned over on his side so he could face me, and propped his head on his hand. His eyes are green. Tommy's are blue. If they could have children, they'd be so beautiful, like sea creatures or fairies. My eyes are blue too, but they're like Dad's, dull and flat like a blind old woman's eyes, rath-er than the shallow ocean with dancing lights on it blue that Mom and Tommy have. "I mean," said Tristan, "those people only believe you're a real Christian if you attend church. It's the body of Christ rule and all that. You *have* read the Bible, haven't you?"

"Parts," I said, squinting a little. "But anyway," I said, "it doesn't matter what they think of me. I know what's true in my heart."

"Well, precisely," said Tristan.

I stopped squinting and held his stare. He didn't flinch, just kept staring back. "Okay," I said. "You've made your point."

Tristan stood and lifted his shirt above his head, kicked off his sandals, and dove into the pond. The blue rippled and rippled, the rings flowing out to the edges, then silence and stillness returned, but Tristan didn't. I waited a few moments, then stood halfway up on one knee. "Tristan?" I said, and wait-ed a few moments more. "Tristan," I said, louder this time. But he still didn't come to the surface. "Tristan, stop it!" I shouted, and immediately his head burst out of the water at the center of the pond.

"Oh, this is lovely," he said, shaking his wet brown hair out of his eyes. "It's like having Central Park in your backyard!"

I picked my book up and left, furious with him for frightening me. What did he think? It was funny? I didn't stay to find out. I didn't turn around or say anything in response to Tristan either, when he began calling for me to come back.

🌀   🌀   🌀

Tommy was in the kitchen making lunch for everyone when I burst through the back door and slammed it shut behind me, like a small tornado had blown through. "What's wrong now?" he said, looking up from the tomato soup and grilled cheese sandwiches he was making. "Boy trouble?"

He laughed, but this time I didn't laugh with him. Tommy knew I wasn't much of a dater, that I didn't have a huge interest in going somewhere with a guy from school and watching a movie or eating fast food while they practiced on me to become better at making girls think they've found a guy who's incredible. I don't get that stuff, really. I mean, I like guys. I had a boyfriend once. I mean a real one, not the kind some girls call boyfriends but really aren't anything but the guy they dated that month. That's not a boyfriend. That's a candidate. Some people can't tell the difference. Anyway, I'm sure my parents have probably thought I'm the same way as Tommy, since I don't bring boys home, but I don't bring boys home because it all seems like something to save for later. Right now, I like just thinking about me, *my* future. I'm not so good at thinking in the first person plural yet.

I glared at Tommy before saying, "Your boyfriend sucks. He just tricked me into thinking he'd drowned."

Tommy grinned. "He's a bad boy, I know," he said. "But Meg, he didn't mean anything by it. You take life too seriously. You should really relax a little. Tristan is playful. That's part of his charm. He was trying to make you his friend, that's all."

"By freaking me out? Wonderful friendship maneuver. It amazes me how smart you and your city friends are. Did Tristan go to NYU too?"

"No," Tommy said flatly. And on that one word, with that one shift of tone in his voice, I could tell I'd pushed him into the sort of self I wear most of the time: the armor, the defensive position. I'd crossed one of his lines and felt small and little and mean. "Tristan's family is wealthy," said Tommy. "He's a bit of a black sheep, though. They're not on good terms. He could have gone to college anywhere he wanted, but I think he's avoided doing that because it would make them proud of him for being more like them instead of himself. They're different people, even though they're from the same family. Like how you and I are different from Mom and Dad about church. Anyway, they threatened to cut him off if he didn't come home to let them groom him to be more like them."

"Heterosexual, married to a well-off woman from one of their circle, and ruthless in a boardroom?" I offered.

"Well, no," said Tommy. "Actually they're quite okay with Tristan being gay. He's different from them in another way."

"What way?" I asked.

Tommy rolled his eyes a little, weighing whether he should tell me any more. "I shouldn't talk about it," he said, sighing, exasperated.

"Tommy, tell me!" I said. "How bad could it be?"

"Not bad so much as strange. Maybe even unbelievable for you, Meg." I frowned, but he went on. "The ironic thing is, the thing they can't stand about Tristan is something they gave him. A curse, you would have called it years ago. Today I think the word we use is *gene*. In any case, it runs in Tristan's family, skipping generations mostly, but every once in a while one of the boys are born . . . well, different."

"Different but not in the gay way?" I said, confused.

"No, not in the gay way," said Tommy, smiling, shaking his head. "Different in the way that he has two lives, sort of. The one here on land with you and me, and another one in, well, in the water."

"He's a rebellious swimmer?"

Tommy laughed, bursting the air. "I guess you could say that," he said. "But no. Listen, if you want to know, I'll tell you, but you have to promise not to tell Mom and Dad. They think we're here because Tristan's family disowned him for being gay. I told them his parents were Pentecostal, so it all works out in their minds."

"Okay," I said. "I promise."

"What would you say," Tommy began, his eyes shifting up, as if he were searching for the right words in the air above him, "what would you say, Meg, if I told you the real reason is because Tristan's not completely human. I mean, not in the sense that we understand it."

I narrowed my eyes, pursed my lips, and said, "Tommy, are you on drugs?"

"I wish!" he said. "God, those'll be harder to find around here." He laughed. "No, really, I'm telling the truth. Tristan is something . . . something else. A water person? You know, with a tail and all?" Tommy flapped his hand in the air when he said this. I smirked, waiting for the punch line. But when one didn't come, it hit me.

"This has something to do with *The Sons of Melusine*, doesn't it?"

Tommy nodded. "Yes, those paintings are inspired by Tristan."

"But, Tommy," I said, "why are you going back to this type of painting? Sure it's an interesting gimmick, saying your boyfriend's a merman. But the critics didn't like your fantasy paintings. They liked the *American Gothic* stuff. Why would they change their minds now?"

"Two things," Tommy said, frustrated with me. "One: a good critic doesn't dismiss entire genres. They look at technique and the composition of elements and the relationship the painting establishes with this world. Two: it's not a gimmick. It's the truth, Meg. Listen to me. I'm not laughing anymore. Tristan made his parents an offer. He said he'd move somewhere unimportant and out of the way, and they could make up whatever stories they wanted about him for their friends, to explain his absence, if they gave him part of his inheritance now. They accepted. It's why we're here."

I didn't know what to say, so I just stood there. Tommy ladled soup into bowls for the four of us. Dad would be coming in from the barn soon, Tristan back from the pond. Mom was still at the library and wouldn't be home till evening. This was a regular summer day. It made me feel safe, that regularity. I didn't want it to ever go away.

I saw Tristan then, trotting through the field out back, drying his hair with his pink shirt as he came. When I turned back to Tommy, he was looking out the window over the sink, watching Tristan too, his eyes watering. "You really love him, don't you?" I said.

Tommy nodded, wiping his tears away with the backs of his hands. "I do," he said. "He's so special, like something I used to see a long time ago. Something I forgot how to see for a while."

"Have you finished *The Sons of Melusine* series then?" I asked, trying to change the subject. I didn't feel sure of how to talk to Tommy right then.

"I haven't," said Tommy. "There's one more I want to do. I was waiting for the right setting. Now we have it."

"What do you mean?"

"I want to paint Tristan by the pond."

"Why the pond?"

"Because," said Tommy, returning to gaze out the window, "it's going to be a place where he can be himself totally now. He's never had that before."

"When will you paint him?"

"Soon," said Tommy. "But I'm going to have to ask you and Mom and Dad a favor."

"What?"

"Not to come down to the pond while we're working."

"Why?"

"He doesn't want anyone to know about him. I haven't told Mom and Dad. Just you. So you have to promise me two things. Don't come down to the pond, and don't tell Tristan I told you about him."

Tristan opened the back door then. He had his shirt back on and his hair was almost dry. Pearls of water still clung to his legs. I couldn't imagine those being a tail, his feet a flipper.

Surely Tommy had gone insane. "Am I late for lunch?" Tristan asked, smiling at me.

Tommy turned and beamed him a smile back. "Right on time, love," he said, and I knew our conversation had come to an end.

ᔕ   ᔕ   ᔕ

I went down the lane to the barn where Dad was working, taking his lunch with me, when he didn't show up to eat with us. God, I wished I could tell him how weird Tommy was being, but I'd promised not to say anything, and even if my brother was going crazy, I wouldn't go back on my word. I found Dad coming out of the barn with a pitchfork of cow manure, which he threw onto the spreader parked outside the barn. He'd take that to the back field and spread it later probably, and then I'd have to watch where I stepped for a week whenever I cut through the field to go to the pond. When I gave him his soup and sandwich, he thanked me and asked what the boys were doing. I told him they were sitting in the living room under the *American Gothic* portrait fiercely making out. He almost spit out his sandwich, he laughed so hard. I like making my dad laugh, because he doesn't do it nearly enough. Mom's too nice, which sometimes is what kills a sense of humor in people, and Tommy was always testing Dad too much to ever get to a joking relationship with him. Me, though, I can always figure out something to shock him into a laugh.

"You're bad, Meg," he said, after settling down. Then, "Were they really?"

I shook my head. "Nope. You were right the first time, Dad. That was a joke." I didn't want to tell him his son had gone mad, though.

"Well I thought so, but still," he said, taking a bite of his sandwich. "All sorts of new things to get used to these days."

I nodded. "Are you okay with that?" I asked.

"Can't not be," he said. "Not an option."

"Who says?"

"I need no authority figure on that," said Dad. "You have a child, and no matter what, you love them. That's just how it is."

"That's not how it is for everyone, Dad."

"Well thank the dear Lord I'm not everyone," he said. "Why would you want to live like that, with all those conditions on love?"

I didn't know what to say. He'd shocked me into silence the way I could always shock him into laughter. We had that effect on each other, like yin and yang. My dad's a good guy, likes the simpler life, seems pretty normal. He wears Allis Chalmers tractor hats and flannel shirts and jeans. He likes oatmeal and meat loaf and macaroni and cheese. Then he opens his mouth and turns into the Buddha. I swear to God, he'll do it when you're least expecting it. I don't know sometimes whether he's like me and Tommy, hiding something different about himself, but just has all these years of experience to make himself blend in. Like maybe he's an angel beneath that sun-browned, beginning-to-wrinkle human skin. "Do you really feel that way?" I asked. "It's one thing to say that, but is it that easy to truly feel that way?"

"Well it's not what you'd call easy, Meg. But it's what's right. Most of the time doing what's right is more difficult than doing what's wrong."

He handed me his bowl and plate after he'd finished, and asked if I'd take a look at Buttercup. Apparently she'd been looking pretty down. So I set the dishes on the seat of the tractor and went into the barn to visit my old girl, my cow Buttercup, who I've had since I was a little girl. She was my present on my fourth birthday. I'd found her with her mother in a patch of buttercups and spent the summer with her, sleeping with her in the fields, playing with her, training her as if she were a dog. By the time she was a year old, she'd even let me ride her like a horse. We were the talk of the town, and Dad even had me ride her into the ring at the county fair's Best of Show. Normally she would have been butchered by now—no cow lasted as long as Buttercup had on Dad's farm—but I had saved her each time it ever came into Dad's head to let her go. He never had to say anything. I could see his thoughts as clear as if they were stones beneath a clear stream of water. I could take them and break them or change them if I needed, the way I'd changed Tommy's mind the day he left for New York, making him turn back and leave me alone by the pond. It was a stupid thing, really, whatever it was, this thing I could do with my will. Here I could change people's minds, but I used it to make people I loved go away with hard feelings and to prolong the life of a cow.

Dad was right. She wasn't looking good, the old girl. She was thirteen and had had a calf every summer for a good ten years. I looked at her now and saw how selfish I'd been to make him keep her. She was down on the ground in her stall, legs folded under her, like a queen stretched out on a litter, her eyes half-closed, her lashes long and pretty as a woman's. "Old girl," I said. "How you doing?" She looked up at me, chewing her cud, and smiled. Yes, cows can smile. I can't stand it that people can't see this. Cats can smile, dogs can smile, cows can too. It just takes time and you have to really pay attention to notice. You can't look for a human smile; it's not the same. You have to be able to see an animal for itself before it'll let you see its smile. Buttercup's smile was warm, but fleeting. She looked exhausted from the effort of greeting me.

I patted her down and brushed her a bit and gave her some ground molasses to lick out of my hand. I liked the feel of the rough stubble on her tongue as it swept across my palm. Sometimes I thought if not psychology, maybe veterinary medicine would be the thing for me. I'd have to get used to death, though. I'd have to be okay with helping an animal die. Looking at Buttercup, I knew I didn't have that in me. If only I could use my will on myself as well as it worked on others.

When I left the barn, Dad was up on the seat of the tractor, holding his dishes, which he handed me again. "Off to spread this load," he said, starting the tractor after he spoke. He didn't have to say any more about Buttercup. He knew I'd seen what he meant. I'd have to let her go someday, I knew. I'd have to work on that, though. I just wasn't ready.

ᛰ   ᛰ   ᛰ

The next day I went back to the pond, only to find Tristan and Tommy already there. Tommy had a radio playing classical music on the dock beside him while he sketched something in his notebook. Tristan swam toward him, then pulled his torso up and out by holding onto the dock so he could lean in and kiss Tommy before letting go and sinking back down. I tried to see if there were scales at his waistline, but he was too quick. "Hey!" Tommy shouted. "You dripped all over my sketch, you wretched whale! What do you think this is? SeaWorld?"

I laughed, but Tommy and Tristan both looked over at me, eyes wide, mouths open, shocked to see me there. "Meg!"

Tristan said from the pond, waving his hand. "How long have you been there? We didn't hear you."

"Only a minute," I said, stepping onto the dock, moving Tommy's radio over before spreading out my towel to lie next to him. "You should really know not to mess with him when he's working," I added. "Tommy is a perfectionist, you know."

"Which is why I do it." Tristan laughed. "Someone needs to keep him honest. Nothing can be perfect, right, Tommy?"

"Close to perfect, though," Tommy said.

"What are you working on?" I asked, and immediately he flipped the page over and started sketching something new.

"Doesn't matter," he said, his pencil pulling gray and black lines into existence on the page. "Tristan ruined it."

"I *had* to kiss you," Tristan said, swimming closer to us.

"You always have to kiss me," Tommy said.

"Well, yes," said Tristan. "Can you blame me?"

I rolled my eyes and opened my book.

"Meg," Tommy said a few minutes later, after Tristan had swum away, disappearing into the depths of the pond and appearing on the other side, smiling brilliantly. "Remember how I said I'd need you and Mom and Dad to do me that favor?"

"Yeah."

"I'm going to start work tomorrow, so no more coming up on us without warning like that, okay?"

I put my book down and looked at him. He was serious. No joke was going to follow this gravely intoned request. "Okay," I said, feeling a little stung. I didn't like it when Tommy took that tone with me and meant it.

I finished my book within the hour and got up to leave. Tommy looked up as I bent to pick up my towel, and I could see his mouth opening to say something, a reminder, or worse:

a plea for me to believe what he'd said about Tristan the day before. So I locked eyes with him and took hold of that thought before it became speech. It wriggled fiercely, trying to escape the grasp of my will, flipping back and forth like a fish pulled out of its stream. But I won. I squeezed it between my will's fingers, and Tommy turned back to sketching without another word.

⚸　⚸　⚸

The things that are wrong with me are many. I try not to let them be the things people see in me, though. I try to make them invisible, or to make them seem natural, or else I stuff them up in that dark spot on my ceiling and will them into nonexistence. This doesn't usually work for very long. They come back, they always come back, whatever they are, if they're something really a part of me and not just a passing mood. No amount of willing can change those things. Like my inability to let go of Buttercup, my anger with the people of this town, my frustration with my parents' kindness to a world that doesn't deserve them, my annoyance with my brother's light-stepped movement through life. I hate that everything we love has to die, I despise narrow thinking, I resent the unfairness of the world and the unfairness that I can't feel at home in it like it seems others can. All I have is my will, this sharp piece of material inside me, stronger than metal, that everything I encounter breaks itself upon.

Mom once told me it was my gift, not to discount it. I'd had a fit of anger with the school board and the town that day. They'd fired one of my teachers for not teaching creationism alongside evolution and somehow thought this was completely legal. And no one seemed outraged but me. I wrote a letter to the newspaper declaring the whole affair an obstruction to teachers' freedoms, but it seemed that everyone—kids at school and their parents—just accepted it until a year later the courts told us it was unacceptable.

I cried and tore apart my room one day that year. I hated being in school after they did that to Mr. Turney. When Mom heard me tearing my posters off the walls, smashing my unicorns and horses, she burst into my room and threw her arms around me and held me until my will quieted again. Later, when we were sitting on my bed, me leaning against her while she combed her fingers through my hair, she said, "Meg, don't be afraid of what you can do. That letter you wrote, it was wonderful. Don't feel bad because no one else said anything. You made a strong statement. People were talking about it at church last week. They think people can't hear, or perhaps they mean for them to hear. Anyway, I'm proud of you for speaking out against what your heart tells you isn't right. That's your gift, sweetie. If you hadn't noticed, not everyone is blessed with such a strong, beautiful will."

It made me feel a little better, hearing that, but I couldn't also tell her how I'd used it for wrong things too: to make Tommy leave for New York without knowing I was okay, to make Dad keep Buttercup beyond the time he should have, to keep people far away so I wouldn't have to like or love them. I'd used my will to keep the world at bay, and that was my secret: that I didn't really care for this life I'd been given, that I couldn't stop myself from being angry at the whole fact of it, life, that the more things I loved, the worse it would be because I'd lose all those things in the end. So Buttercup sits in the barn, her legs barely strong enough for her to stand on, because of me not being able to let go. So Tommy turned back and left because I couldn't bear to say good-bye. So I didn't have any close friends because I didn't want to have to lose any more than I already had to lose in my family.

My will was my gift, she said. So why did it feel like such a curse to me?

When Mom came home later that evening, I sat in the kitchen and had a cup of tea with her. She always wanted tea straightaway after she came home. She said it calmed her, helped her ease out of her day at the library and back into life at home. "How are Tommy and Tristan adjusting?" she asked me after a few sips, and I shrugged.

"They seem to be doing fine, but Tommy's being weird and a little mean."

"How so?" Mom wanted to know.

"Just telling me to leave them alone while he works, and he told me some weird things about Tristan and his family too. I don't know. It all seems so impossible."

"Don't underestimate people's ability to do harm to each other," Mom interrupted. "Even those that say they love you."

I knew she was making this reference based on the story Tommy had told her and Dad about Tristan's family disowning him because he was gay, so I shook my head. "I understand that, Mom," I said. "There's something else too." I didn't know how to tell her what Tommy had told me, though. I'd promised to keep it between him and me. So I settled for saying, "Tristan doesn't seem the type who would want to live out here away from all the things he could enjoy in the city."

"Perhaps that's all grown old for him," Mom said. "People change. Look at you, off to school in a month or so. Between the time you leave and the first time you come home again, you'll have become someone different, and I won't have had a chance to watch you change." She started tearing up. "All your changes all these years, the Lord's let me share them all with you, and now I'm going to have to let you go and change into someone without me around to make sure you're safe."

"Oh, Mom," I said. "Don't cry."

"No, no," she said. "I want to cry." She wiped her cheeks with the backs of her hands, smiling. "I just want to say, Meg, don't be so hard on other people. Or yourself. It's hard enough as it is, being in this world. Don't judge so harshly. Don't stop yourself from seeing other people's humanity because they don't fit into your scheme of the world."

I blinked a lot, then picked up my mug of tea and sipped it. I didn't know how to respond. Mom usually never says anything critical of us, and though she said it nicely, I knew she was worried for me. For her to say something like that, I knew I needed to put down my shield and sword and take a look around instead of fighting. But wasn't fighting the thing I was good at?

"I'm sorry, Mom," I said.

"Don't be sorry, dear. Be happy. Find the thing that makes you happy and enjoy it, like your brother is doing."

"You mean his painting?" I said.

"No," said Mom. "I mean Tristan."

ဪ ဪ ဪ

One day toward the end of my senior year, our English teacher, Miss Portwood, had told us that many of our lives were about to become much wider. That we'd soon have to begin mapping a world for ourselves outside of the first seventeen years of our lives. It struck me, hearing her say that, comparing the years of our lives to a map of the world. If I had a map of seventeen, of the years I'd lived so far, it would be small and plain, outlining the contours of my town with a few landmarks on it like Marrow's Ravine and town square, the schools, the pond, our fields, and the barn and the home we live in. It would be on crisp, fresh paper, because I haven't traveled very far, and I've stuck to the routes I know best. There would be nothing but waves and waves of ocean surrounding my map of my hometown. In the ocean I'd draw those sea beasts you find on old maps of the world, and above them I'd write the words "There Be Dragons."

What else is out there, beyond this edge of the world I live on? Who else is out there? Are there real reasons to be as afraid of the world as I've been?

I was thinking all this when I woke up the next morning and stared at the black spot on my ceiling. That could be a map of seventeen too. Nothing but white around it, and nothing to show for hiding myself away. Mom was right. Though I was jealous of Tommy's ability to live life so freely, he was following a path all his own, a difficult one, and needed as many people who loved him to help him do it. I could help him and Tristan both, probably just by being more friendly and supportive than suspicious and untrusting. I could start by putting aside Tommy's weirdness about Tristan being a cursed son of Melusine and do like Mom and Dad: just humor him. He's an artist after all.

So I got up and got dressed and left the house without even having breakfast. I didn't want to let another day go by and not make things okay with Tommy for going away all those years ago. Through the back field I went, into the woods, picking up speed as I went, as the urgency to see him took over me. By the time I reached the edge of the pond's clearing, I had a thousand things I wanted to say. When I stepped out of the woods and into the clearing, though, I froze in place, my mouth open but no words coming out because of what I saw there.

Tommy was on the dock with his easel and palette, sitting in a chair, painting Tristan. And Tristan— I don't know how to describe him, how to make his being something possible, but these words came into my mind: *tail, scales, beast,* and *beauty.* At first I couldn't tell which he was, but I knew immediately that Tommy hadn't gone insane. Or else we both had.

Tristan lay on the dock in front of Tommy, his upper body strong and muscular and naked, his lower half long and sinuous as a snake. His tail swept back and forth, occasionally dipping into the water for a moment before returning to the position Tommy wanted. I almost screamed but somehow willed myself not to. I hadn't left home yet, but a creature from the uncharted world had traveled onto my map where I'd lived the past seventeen years. How could this be?

I thought of that group show we'd all flown to New York to see, the one where Tommy had hung the first in the series of *American Gothic* alongside those odd, magical creatures he had painted back when he was just graduated. The critic who'd picked him out of that group show said that Tommy had technique and talent, was by turns fascinating and annoying, but that he'd wait to see if Tommy would develop a more mature vision. I think when I read that back then, I had agreed.

I'd forgotten the favor I'd promised: not to come back while they were working. Tommy hadn't really lied when he told me moving here was for Tristan's benefit, to get away from his family and the people who wanted him to be something other than what he is. I wondered how long he'd been trying to hide this part of himself before he met Tommy, who was able to love him because of who and what he is. What a gift and curse that is, to be both of them, to be what Tristan is and for Tommy to see him so clearly. My problems were starting to shrivel the longer I looked at them. And the longer I looked, the more I realized the dangers they faced, how easily their lives and love could be shattered by the people in the world who would fire them from life the way the school board fired Mr. Turney for actually teaching us what we can know about the world.

I turned and quietly went back through the woods, but as I left the trail and came into the back field, I began running. I ran from the field and past the house, out into the dusty back road we live on, and stood there, looking up and down the road at the horizon, where the borders of this town waited for me to cross them at the end of summer. Whether there were dragons waiting for me after I journeyed off the map of my first seventeen years didn't matter. I'd love them when it called for loving them, and I'd fight the ones that needed fighting. That was my gift, like Mom had told me, what I could do with my will. Maybe instead of psychology I'd study law, learn how to defend it, how to make it better, so that someday Tommy and Tristan could have what everyone else has.

It's a free country after all. Well, sort of. And one day, if I had anything to say about it, that would no longer be a joke between Tommy and me.

CHRISTOPHER BARZAK'S stories have appeared in *The Year's Best Fantasy and Horror, Salon Fantastique, Trampoline, Asimov's Science Fiction, Nerve,* and other magazines and anthologies. His first novel, *One for Sorrow,* won the 2008 Crawford Award for Best First Fantasy and was nominated for the 2008 Great Lakes Book Awards. His second novel, *The Love We Share Without Knowing,* was published in 2008. Chris grew up in rural Ohio, has lived in a beach town in Southern California, and in the capital of Michigan, and returned in 2006 from a two-year stint in Japan, where he taught English in the Japanese school system outside of Tokyo. He now teaches writing at Youngstown State University in Youngstown, Ohio.

His blog is at christopherbarzak.wordpress.com.

Author's Note

A lot of people think small towns in rural America are either charming and quaint, like in a Norman Rockwell painting, or backward and scary, like in a Shirley Jackson story. Both depictions can be true, of course, but despite the smallness of rural America you'll find a wider range of people living there than this.

I grew up on a small farm in Ohio, grew out of it and into the wider world beyond it, and found not only that much of what I expected of the world was different from what I'd been told but also that people who grow up on small farms like me are different from what people who grew up in cities and suburbs tend to expect. So when I wrote "Map of Seventeen" I wanted to write about a rural midwestern family struggling with a conflict between the expectations of their norms and those of the cosmopolitan world outside their boundaries. And I wanted to write about how people we perceive to be beasts or monsters in the world because of their difference from us are really beautiful if we can look at them in the right way.

THE SELKIE SPEAKS

Delia Sherman

My mother said:
> Don't swim too far from home.

My mother said:
> Don't tell men what you are.

My mother said:
> Men are not like seals. They hunt for pleasure and
> for gain.

Restless, impatient
Of my narrow bay, my narrow life,
My own ungainly desires,
I swam far and far from home,
Along the whale roads
Threading the jeweled reefs
To the islands where turtles breed.
And I watched.

I saw:
> Nets like giants' hands scoop fish from the sea

I saw:

Opalescent filth clog the waves.

I saw:

Men hunt seals for pleasure and for gain.

Enflamed, enraged,
I chose a beach littered with men
And surged from the waves,
Shedding my seal skin as I came.
I seized a knife, I ripped their nets,
I roared aloud my grief at what I'd seen,
The proof of all my mother's warning words.

The men ran from the beach.
All but one.

He said:

You are far from home.

He said:

You are magnificent.

He said:

I fish to eat. Like you.

Our house is built on a rock above the sea.
My pelt warms the foot of our bed.
He teaches our children to build and sail.
I teach them how to swim and fish.
Together we teach them the ways of wave and wind,
To fight when they must and love when they can.
At night, they sleep warm under their own pelts.

We tell them:
> Swim to the limits of your strength.

We tell them:
> Rejoice in who you are.

We tell them:
> Men and seals are hunters both. But not for pleasure
> and never for gain.

DELIA SHERMAN'S stories have appeared in the anthologies *The Green Man, The Faery Reel, The Coyote Road, Poe,* and *Naked City.* Her adult novels are *Through a Brazen Mirror* and *The Porcelain Dove* (winner of the Mythopoeic Award), and, with Ellen Kushner, *The Fall of the Kings.*

She has coedited anthologies with Ellen Kushner and Terri Windling, as well as *Interfictions: An Anthology of Interstitial Writing,* (with Theodora Goss), and *Interfictions 2,* (with Christopher Barzak).

Changeling was her first novel for younger readers. Its sequel, *The Magic Mirror of the Mermaid Queen,* was published in 2009.

Delia is a past member of the James Tiptree Jr. Awards Council, an active member of the Endicott Studio of Mythic Arts, and a founding member of the Interstitial Arts Executive Board. She lives in New York City, loves to travel, and writes wherever she happens to find herself. Her Web site is www.deliasherman.com.

ꙅꙅ

Author's Note

All the folklore about seal maidens tends to focus on the forced marriages, the romantic betrayals, the unhappy relationships ending with the seal wife finding the skin her (at best) clueless husband has hidden under the thatch and swimming away, with or without her selkie children. I began by thinking about one of those traditional seal mothers, embittered and traumatized by her sojourn in the world of men. But I ended up writing about her daughter's journey. My thanks to Claudia Carlson and Ellen Kushner, who both gave me very helpful advice in working out the pattern of my seal maiden's story.

BEAR'S BRIDE

Johanna Sinisalo
Translated by Liisa Rantalaiho

Kataya lies among the lichen, enjoying herself. In front of her runs the path the ants have furrowed in the moss, and she finds the seemingly pointless yet purposeful dashing to and fro very funny. She is playing; she puts little obstacles on the ants' path: pine needles, cone scales, new spruce shoots, her own hairs. The ants just keep on creeping over, past, or under the obstacles; or, in the best case, they accept her gift and bring it inside their nest, even if they don't actually know what to do with it.

Kataya concentrates, telling the ants in which direction she wants them to take a pine seed. She knows she cannot order the ants to take the booty far from the nest, or into a puddle, for instance. That's not for *tsirnika*. But she may guide the ants. Kataya starts on the ant struggling next to her. She partly closes her eyes and tries to reach the ant's mind. It's a small mind, divided into tight compartments, tasting sour, very simple, and strong in its simplicity.

The ant is quite stubborn and goes its own way, and Kataya doesn't approve. She lifts up her hand, but doing that, remembers the teachings. She imagines a huge hand rising up from behind the spruce tops, rising and then descending to crush her. Kataya shivers and looks again at the ants. It may be that her *tsirnika* isn't very strong yet, only what any girl possesses from birth and what will be completed and thoroughly learned only by *tsirnikoela*, but she is capable of something. At least she knows enough not to break the rules *of tsirnika*.

Tsirnikoela.

Kataya shivers again; she doesn't want to think of *tsirnikoela*. It is something each woman of the tribe will experience, one way or another, either while it's happening to her personally or while participating in the ritual, and although the event is fascinating and right and proper, it's also scary. Kataya remembers at least two girls who never returned from *tsirnikoela.*

Kataya would rather be concentrating on the ants. The one she's been observing hesitates, as if reconsidering its direction. Lightly, she senses the ant's mind, how it brushes on the edges of her own; the little mind of must-go-forward, the mind of part-of-tribe, and the large mind of doing-what-is-necessary.

Kataya concentrates very hard. She weaves a large pattern in her head, a pattern even the ant can understand, and there's a place in the pattern for what she wants the ant to do. It seems to work. For a moment, she feels the colors of sunset spreading over herself, and, hesitatingly, the ant on the path drops its burden.

"Kataya!"

Kataya recognizes the voice. Yes, she has been expecting

this, and yet she had chosen to come to her favorite place to play, right up to the last moment.

Tsirnikoela.

𝔰   𝔰   𝔰

Kataya had been very young when she'd heard the story of *tsirnika* for the first time. Since then, it has become her favorite tale; although it's not just a tale. It had really happened, many, many, many generations ago. When they were little, even the boys of her tribe listened to the *tsirnika* story with shining eyes; but as the boys grew up, they found the story harder and harder to understand, while the girls began to talk about *tsirnika* only among themselves.

Kataya can still hear the voice of Akka Ismia, the eldest of the tribe women, beginning the tale of *tsirnika*:

> *"Ancient times our tribe remembers,*
> *weak of leg were all the people,*
> *spying after speedy reindeer,*
> *ever chasing elk in forests,*
> *always left behind were people.*
> *Ancient times the tribe remembers,*
> *weak of spirit, weak of power;*
> *at their heels the wolves were hunting,*
> *yet behind were lynxes leaping,*
> *ever worse in fight the people.*
> *Weak and weaker yet the people:*
> *famished were they, fearful children,*
> *silly sisters lacking counsel,*
> *close to death the dainty daughters.*

𝔰   𝔰   𝔰

"First was Akka, mindful maiden,
far she did in woodland wander,
strolling through the fen and forest.
Thunder rumbled in the woodland
lightning lit the fen and forest.
Spirit from the skies descended,
from up high appeared Gift Giver.

"Where's the place of Bruin's birthing?
Where the home of Honey-eater?
House of Moon and home of Daystar,
high up on the Dipper's shoulders;
down from there to earth was lowered
silver shining by the beltings,
golden glimmers on the cradle."

"What did the Bruin bring us?" Akka Ismia would ask the children at this point.

"Tsirnika," even the smallest ones knew to answer.

Although Kataya has herself retold the story numerous times by now, the way Akka Ismia tells it is the most proper and traditional.

It was the first Akka who had seen the golden cradle of the Bruin descending from the heavens and the Heavenly Honeypaws walking toward her. He'd been fur covered, like the Brown One of the forest, but he'd walked on two legs and could talk and had a human mouth. Touching her, the heavenly Bruin had given the first Akka the *tsirnika*, as well as the ability to teach its use. And then he had returned to the golden cradle with its silver belt, and the cradle had ascended like a bird back to the heavens—rising toward the Big Dipper, the group of stars that the tribe now calls the Bruin Stars.

Now this Akka discovered that she was able to control animals: to chase off the wolf and call the deer, to charm the trout from the brook and ask the snake to yield way. But then one day she slept with a man, and *tsirnika* disappeared. The gift had been given to an untouched one, and the Bruin had not known that the woman might change. But over time the Akka bore many daughters, and each of her daughters was born with the gift of *tsirnika*, just like a singer's daughters may have the gift of singing. And the Akka taught them to use their gift, and so the tribe grew and prospered.

When Kataya had first received the blood sign of the moon that marked her transition from child to woman, Akka Ismia had spoken with her seriously. "Kataya, you'll have to decide soon whether you wish to keep your *tsirnika*. Each daughter of the tribe has the Bruin's gift, but only the ritual of *tsirnikoela* will make it as strong as it was with the first Akka's daughters. Unless you wish to have children straightaway?"

"No, not yet," Kataya had answered.

"That's good, for it's much better to have some *tsirnika* years before children—the children will be stronger and the mothers healthier."

Now, as her *tsirnikoela* approaches, Kataya curses the day she decided to keep the Bruin's gift and acquire a real, strong *tsirnika*. She remembers the horror stories about *tsirnikoela* that the old men spread by evening fires, stories the women meet with snorts of contempt, yet still they fill Kataya with fear.

But it must be done.

Kataya walks toward the commanding voice of Akka Ismia, toward the familiar gathering place of the village, which looks foreign to her now, almost menacing. As she enters the crowd, Akka Ismia is still speaking.

"For as clay spreads out in water, so is the ability of *tsirnika* spread out in the tribe, spread out and thinned. As the blood of the Brown-furred One would spread in water, so has the gift of the heavenly Bruin spread out and thinned. And that is why we ourselves have to strengthen it."

The other women of the tribe stand back as Kataya approaches Akka Ismia, looking her straight in the face. There are no men in sight. The women carry a big leather container and a small basket made of birch bark.

> *"What's the secret of the sky vault?*
> *High to heavens curves the sky vault,*
> *with the stars its dome is dotted:*
> *that's the womb of Bruin's present.*
> *Where's the sister of the sky vault?*
> *By the alder, near the thicket,*
> *by the bark of pine tree branches*
> *hiding under juniper bushes*
> *on the boughs of summer birches. . . ."*

As Akka Ismia recites the traditional story, two women, Aella and Mitar, come forward, carrying the big leather container between them. They put it down, grip Kataya's clothes, and undress her, leaving only her birch bark shoes. Kataya is startled when they open the container. Inside is a red-brown, black-spotted swarm of ladybugs, or bloodsisterbugs, churning about in the container. It must have taken the whole of the summer so far to collect so many.

"Only when it's a proper kind of year, only then can we

gather enough sisterbugs for *tsirnikoela*," Akka Ismia explains. Kataya realizes two things at once: that the shield of the blood-sisters, domed and spotted, resembles the vault of heaven; and that it's true there weren't as many ladybugs every summer, but this summer there had been enough to cover their favorite places in red. The ladybugs are red-brown like blood, which gives them their second name.

Kataya stands naked, shivering, as Aella and Mitar lift wooden cudgels and give the mass of ladybugs a crushing blow. There's crackling and rustling, and a sharp smell reaches Kataya's nostrils. She remembers playing with bloodsisterbugs as a child, and how they left small orange-red drops on her skin if she poked them carelessly. Now the leather container is filling with a red and black paste of ladybug shells and wings, but also with that sharp excretion.

It takes a long while to crush all the bloodsisterbugs—but for Kataya, the moment when Aella and Mitar straighten their backs seems to come all too soon. Akka Ismia steps close to her and, taking a handful of the sticky crushed stuff from the container, spreads the paste on Kataya's neck and breasts and behind each ear. She then signs to Aella and Mitar to do the same, and soon all the other women have joined in, except Arrah, who holds the birch bark basket. They cover Kataya with the crushed reddish spread, rhythmically rubbing it everywhere, especially on places where her skin is thinnest and the veins show dimly through.

> "Fly bloodsister, fly to forest,
> fly with wings of heaven's image,
> fly to roots of biggest boulders,
> fly to crag and fly to crevice,

fly and find the first Birth-Giver,
fly and find the highest Mother
who gives life to all the creatures,
who gives food to all who hunger."

As the women recite the ritual words, Kataya is covered completely with bloodsisters. She is feeling giddy, her skin tingles, and suddenly all sounds are enormously loud.

"Fly off east and fly off westward,
fly to far up northern corners,
fly to south of noon-sun's shining.
Raise the Bruin up from his burrow,
heave the Honeypaws from hideout.
Shroud the sight and veil the seeing,
fog the eyes of Forest Apple,
mist the mind of Hairy-Muzzle."

Arrah steps forward and presents the birch bark basket. Inside is the cap of a mushroom, bright red and spotted with white. Another image of the vault of heaven.

"Get the boy," Kataya hears Akka Ismia say, as though from a great distance.

Aella runs off and returns with Kesh, a young man a little older than Kataya. He cannot hide his curiosity as he stares at Kataya, who's covered with crushed bloodsisters up to her hair and face. Arrah hands the basket to Kesh, who swallows nervously as he takes the mushroom cap out of the basket, breaks off a bit, and puts it in his mouth. He chews a moment, makes a face, then spits the mass out on a piece of birch bark that Arrah holds out to him.

Arrah gives the chewed-up mass to Kataya, who is feeling increasingly tingly and strange. She keeps noticing everything around her with a wonderful clarity and yet, at the same time, she also feels as if nothing matters. The mass is still warm, soft, and a bit slimy as she takes it into her mouth and swallows. At the same moment, she sees Kesh bend double and start to throw up violently.

"There's always some poison in *shomja*," Akka Ismia explains to Kataya, who doesn't care. "The bad effect of the poison goes away when it's been chewed."

Akka Ismia retrieves Kataya's clothing from the ground and helps her to put it on, then she scoops up a handful of the crushed bloodsisters and rubs it into Kataya's dress. Far in the background, Kesh is kneeling in the lichen, gray faced, covered with sweat, and spitting yellow bile.

As Kataya stands surrounded by the women, a feeling like a wave flushes through her head.

"Go, my child," Akka Ismia says, passing the birch bark basket from Arrah to Kataya. "Go and find your Bruin."

§   §   §

Kataya takes root and joins into a tussock. Kataya drinks the forest and the air and the night. How long? Kataya doesn't know. Kataya is sitting and Kataya is lying down; her skin itches and burns with the skysister excretion and her soul itches and burns with the skymushroom poison. Except it's not poison. *Shomja* no longer makes her throw up; she has eaten all the *shomja* there was in the basket and has searched for new ones. The red sky vault of *shomja* might shine by any thicket, near any alder. Inside her head, Kataya is humming.

Come and meet your humble maiden.
Come to jolly woodland wedding.
Have a happy feast in forest.
So I wait for Brown-furred Beastie
as a bride waits for the bridegroom.
Woodland Beauty, good Stout Fellow,
drink the drops of forest honey
off the armpits of your maiden.
Take to thee to learn the forest.

The bear arrives so quietly she doesn't even notice.

The bear sees her, smells at her, but Kataya's smell is the smell of earth and insects.

The bear looks at her with Akka Ismia's eyes, and since Kataya is but a spot of earth and tussock, the bear has nothing against her. Over the next three evenings the bear comes to eat crowberries in the neighborhood, and on the third night, Kataya follows the bear.

Kataya is learning.

When the bear walks in the bog, eating cloudberries—it knows how to pick only the ripe ones with its lips, as if with fingers—Kataya walks a couple of steps behind, head humming with *shomja*, and picks berries. She is the bear's shadow. When the bear opens a rotting stump with its fierce paws, rips it open and eats the grubs, Kataya follows and finds a few more grubs, swallowing them quickly. Bit by bit, Kataya is learning to read the bear's mind. And at the same time, thousands of other minds are impressing themselves on her: the mind of a red-breasted bird in the trees above and the mind of a fox speeding far away and the mind of a hare scared off by the bear and the mind of a badger digging in its hummock.

When the bear dines on delicious mushrooms in the spruce copse, Kataya picks both those and *shomja* and eats. When the bear finds a young deer with a broken leg, Kataya is the one who helps the bear; she calms the deer and lets the bear do the killing. And after the bear has eaten, Kataya goes and gnaws on what's left. Kataya is the bear's shadow, Kataya is the bear's bride. Kataya eats cranberries, and Kataya walks behind, the corners of her mouth red. Kataya is there. Kataya is the breathing, Kataya is the shredding of fur. Kataya is part of the bear's life.

Kataya's bear is a female, a friend of Akka Ismia. By and by, that too is coming clear to her. Kataya is there, watching everything, experiencing everything, even when the she-bear finds a suitor. Kataya feels the mind of the male bear too but she's careful not to intrude herself. That is only the beginning.

Nights and days melt together. And then one night there comes the first freeze. That night Kataya sleeps side by side with the bear, and the bear allows her to do so. As Kataya humbly lies down with the bear, the bruin lifts its muzzle and sniffs at Kataya's face, deeply, like a kiss.

Kataya will never forget the smell of the bruin's breath. Nor the still-quivering suspicion toward her that she senses in the bear's mind. Nor the feeling of relief when the bruin accepts her, recognizing the touch of *tsirnika*.

Very soon after this the bear starts digging a winter lair beneath the roots of a big spruce, throwing earth several paces off while Kataya helps by scattering the dirt, for that's what the bear wants. She gathers spruce needles, dwarf-birch twigs, pungent marsh tea, bunches of heather, grass, and moss. The last of the frostbitten *shomja* too. When the lair is finished and the bear crawls in, Kataya follows behind on all fours, head humming. There's hardly any space for her, however much she pushes, and she senses a fierce hostility; but Kataya has learned. She strokes the bruin's mind and sweet talks it and soothes it with her own mind. The moons-old bloodsisterpaste on Kataya's skin is peeling off. She swallows the last pieces of *shomja*, presses herself to the bear's side, and closes her eyes. Outside it is snowing. The snow makes the silence grow, deepens the bear's sleep and Kataya's sleep.

The silence grows, and Kataya grows along with it. The bear's mind fills the cramped winter lair, and Kataya's mind sucks at the bear's, catching parts of it, assimilating it, while the seed of *tsirnika* germinates inside her.

Kataya sucks on the bear's mind. She sucks it like a cub sucks on its mother's teat, and tiny particles in Kataya's body change direction and form and function. Burrowed in the lair, Kataya should have perished of thirst and the poisons of her own body, but the same forces that govern the bear's mind and body now also govern Kataya's mind; and the wastes of her body turn into her body's powers, and the powers of her body turn into its sleep. And all the while, the bruin's mind is feeding the *tsirnika*.

Kataya sleeps, the bear's muzzle on her shoulder.

ॐ ॐ ॐ

One midwinter day, Kataya wakes up.

For a moment she's filled with a choking fear. A grimy, frosty ceiling of roots is half a finger above her nose and eyes, and the air is thick with the smells of marsh tea, dirt, excretion, and beast. She finds herself lying tight against the side of a female bear, as if grown into its pelt. She is weak, dizzy, about to throw up. The bear has been pregnant since the middle of summer, and now Kataya's *tsirnika* has grown strong enough to reach the minds of the bear's two cubs. She senses that they are ready to be born, and she knows that she must leave. Later, she will recognize the minds of these cubs too. Though now they are small and blind, unborn, nonetheless they are known to her. Yes, she will meet them yet.

Kataya moves with the uttermost care. Little by little, she creeps toward the lair's snow-covered opening, her fingers scratching on ice caused by the warm fumes of their breath. She knows that breaking the snow-sealed door is likely to disturb the bear, so she covers it up behind her, using *tsirnika* to sing the bruin back to sleep.

That done, she straightens and looks up at the sky. Akka Ismia will be expecting her.

§   §   §

Kataya walks toward the tribe's abode with hunger-heavy, dragging steps. She is filthy, thin, a mere skeleton, smelling of bloodsister paste and *shomja* and bear, and she can no longer say whether these are bad smells or good smells; they're just part of her, a part of her forever.

Her feet, in their ragged birch bark shoes, do not feel the cold of the snow-covered path. Her mind is empty, her mind is full. Kataya stops by her favorite place, where snow now covers the trails made by the ants. When she remembers playing here only a few moons back, she no longer knows that Kataya.

The anthill by the path is a sizeable one, and Kataya is beginning to understand that it's the *tsirnika* of the tribe's women that has kept the bears away from places like this. One of the bruins would have made its winter lair out of this very anthill had they not been told to stay farther from the village. Kataya knows that now, for half of her being is still thinking like a bear.

As she stands above the hill, her *tsirnika* swells up inside with such a fierce surge that Kataya feels dizzy and sick. The winter day hums and rustles around her, the gray sky hangs low upon the tops of the spruce. And out of the snowy cover of the anthill, small dark spots begin to erupt. The ants do not know why they are on the move when it's quite the wrong season to leave the hill, but they pour out of the ground, seized by a power too great to withstand.

Kataya smiles a tired smile. She knows she's guilty of pride, and of abusing *tsirnika*, so she quickly sends the ants back into their hill, to sleep their little death. She kneels, and with her own hands, she covers up the hole the ants have made in the snow, so the frost will not wreak destruction inside the anthill.

Kataya straightens up and sighs. Her steps a little brisker now as she heads for home.

✿   ✿   ✿

Akka Ismia comes to meet her. Akka Ismia knows she has left the bear. Of course. It's as simple as that.

All the women of the tribe have gathered in the open. They watch her arrive expectantly. And Kataya knows that, after all she's been through, nothing ought to feel difficult. But this is. This is difficult. The song of *tsirnikoela* is important; it's the song that cleanses; it's the song that tells how one has taken possession of *tsirnika*; it's the song that sparks the souls of the younger girls; and above all it is the song that confirms that a woman has really done what must be done.

Singing the song of *tsirnikoela* is one of the greatest acts of a woman's life.

But she remembers when Aella came out of the forest, how Aella's eyes were filled with horror and madness. Aella had fallen on her knees in the middle of the women's circle and screamed so long that everyone's ears ached. The women had waited silently until Aella finally quieted; she had lifted up her dirty, teary face, and her eyes again had a true expression. Then Akka Ismia lifted her to her feet, telling the others, "That was her song."

Now it is Kataya who stands before Akka Ismia, surrounded by the women's circle. Kataya tries to stand up straight and proud, although her head is spinning. With a look somehow both friendly and stern, Akka Ismia intones the ritual question:

"Kataya, fair forest maiden,
do you bear the Beast within you,
in your womb the Woodland Spirit?"

The old woman's voice is soft but demanding.

Kataya knows the answer. Yes, she is full of bear, as if a bear were growing inside her, as if a bear's heart were beating in her breast; even now she senses the mind of the sleeping bear like second thoughts, like a stranger inside herself, but so familiar, oh so familiar.

Kataya feels for the right words:

"Oh, should my Known One come and meet me . . ."

She feels encouraged, hearing the new strength in her own voice. Memories of the summer fill her mind. *Horrible* and *beautiful* are equal words for the summer she has spent, rooted in tussocks, grown into moss, not letting the bear go for a moment. She knows the bear like only a bear's bride can know it.

> *"Should my Known One come and meet me,*
> *should my Seen One see me coming,*
> *hand in hand would I be taking,*
> *were a snake between the fingers . . ."*

Kataya shakes, remembering the day that the bear had swept its ferocious paw at the heather, and how a snake had hurtled from the underbrush—black, shining, poisonous. The bear broke the creature in two, and then ate the snake halves, growling and snorting.

> *"Mouth to mouth would I be kissing,*
> *though the tongue of wolf's blood tasting . . ."*

The bear had found an elk carcass, and a wolf, pale pelted, had come to the same catch. When the wolf drew close and spotted Kataya, she hadn't even had enough time to get scared before the bear showed its teeth with a hollow rumble and the wolf sidled off into the spruce copse. The bear, it seemed, was now protecting her, the silent, stubborn shadow that had become part of its life.

> *"In my arms the Known One holding*
> *were a bear upon the neck bones . . ."*

A hum of laughter goes through the group of women: this

is very daring. Surely no one has ever dreamed of disturbing a bear as it mates! Kataya's allusion to this is, of course, a proud exaggeration; and saying the bruin's holy name aloud is something that may only be done in situations like this. But Kataya remembers the terror and excitement when the big male was covering her bear, just a few steps away from where she sat. She'd felt the hot, rumbling thoughts of the female bear, and the bittersweet lust that filled its every cell while the male kept puffing and growling on its neck, biting the neck-skin hard, without giving hurt.

> *"Self next to my Seen One setting*
> *be there blood upon the side!"*

Kataya finishes the song, chest heaving, heart beating wildly. The women of the tribe look at one another. They have heard something new today, something quite different from any other *tsirnikoela*, ever. It is, perhaps, the best *tsirnikoela* song that has ever been made.

Especially the final lines, which refer to the power of the bloodsister paste and the mushroom to stop the moon-cycle blood during *tsirnikoela* so that the bear is not enraged by the smell of blood. Here Kataya proclaims that she knows her bear well enough to approach it while she bleeds. Oh, that is a proud and beautiful song! Akka Ismia steps forward and grips Kataya's shoulders.

"Men!" she shouts.

The men of the tribe approach cautiously, looking askance at the emaciated, filthy, but triumphant young woman who has come back from the forest. Kataya sees Kesh among them, and to her eyes he seems a little boy, though when she'd left for *tsirnikoela*, Kesh had looked like a young man to her.

"Akka Kataya," says Akka Ismia, and the men understand. They all go down on one knee in the snow and bow their heads.

It's only then that Kataya lets herself weep.

🎵　🎵　🎵

Stepping firmly, Kataya walks toward the dwelling she now knows has been reserved for her. Tears have rinsed the last traces of bloodsister paste off of her cheeks. Pots of water have been warmed up for her, and young boys stand ready to wash her up in the *shouna* dug into the riverbank. Behind her, she hears the women celebrating. They are singing her song.

> *"Should my Known One come and meet me*
> *should my Seen One see me coming,*
> *hand in hand would I be taking,*
> *were a snake between the fingers,*
> *mouth to mouth would I be kissing*
> *though the tongue of wolf's blood tasting,*
> *In my arms the Known One holding*
> *were a bear upon the neck bones,*
> *Self next to my Seen One setting*
> *be there blood upon the side!"*

And it's then Kataya dares to laugh.

By the time **JOHANNA SINISALO** left her fifteen-years-long career in advertising and decided to be a full-time writer in 1997, she had already won the Finnish national award Atorox six times for the year's best science fiction and fantasy short story. (Today, she's got seven of them.) In 2000, she published her first novel *Not Before Sundown* (published in 2004 in the United States as *Troll, a Love Story*). It won both the foremost Finnish literature award, Finlandia, and a James Tiptree Jr. Award in the United States in 2004. Since then, she has published three more novels and a collection of short stories, and edited anthologies such as *The Dedalus Book of Finnish Fantasy*.

Sinisalo's story "Baby Doll," first published in English in 2007, was a final nominee for the Theodore Sturgeon Memorial Award and the Nebula Award. Sinisalo is especially proud of the fact that her short story "Red Star" has been included on the international DVD multimedia disc "Visions of Mars," which was sent to the planet Mars with the Phoenix lander and reached the planet's surface in 2008.

Sinisalo has written movie, television, and comics scripts, articles, columns, and essays. Mythology, feminism, and ecological issues are the themes central to her prose writing.

ᴐᏨ

Author's Note

Old Finnish folklore tells about a rite in which a slain bear is symbolically wedded with a virgin maiden. In ancient Finland, and as a general rule among all primitive peoples, the bear was a highly respected and awe-inspiring animal, a spirit of the woods who merited all kinds of homage to appease him when he was slain. Even the bear's name should never be said aloud; instead, people used various roundabout expressions.

Our national epic *Kalevala* tells that the bear hails from space and landed on Earth in a golden cradle. Such a detail cannot but fascinate the mind of a science fiction writer. In 1985 I wrote a story about the roots of the virginity myth and constructed a fictive ancient Finnish tribe where the maidens who kept their virginity were able to communicate with animals. In "Bear's Bride" I returned to that tribe and set out to combine the idea with the bear myth.

The association of the fly agaric with the sky-vault and the shamanistic dimensions of their resemblance (including of course the narcotic qualities of the mushroom) are part of Finnish folklore, as is regarding the ladybug as helper and guide. Incantations asking for the ladybug's help are kept alive to this day as nursery rhymes. It was gratifying to combine all these elements when I considered what kind of a practical basis such myths might have.

It should be mentioned that Kataya's song at the end of the story is a genuine, well-known, and very old piece of Finnish folklore, a song sung to one's beloved. Not a single word was changed in the original text, and it felt bewildering to notice how well the poem fitted, even when addressed to a bear.

This is the first English translation and publication of "Bear's Bride," which originally appeared as "Metsän tuttu" in the Finnish magazine *Aikakone*.

THE ABOMINABLE
CHILD'S TALE

Carol Emshwiller

Did Mother say to always go down?

But maybe she said always go up.

Did she say follow streams, and then rivers? First paths and then a road? And then a road all covered with hard stuff? Did she say there'd be a town if you go far enough?

Or did she say, whatever you do, don't follow roads? Stay away from towns?

She always did say, "You're not lost." She always said, "You're my forest girl. You know which way is up." She didn't mean I know up from down, she meant I always know where I am or that I can find out where I am if I'm not sure.

But Mother didn't come back. Even though she's a forest girl, too. She had her best little bow, her slingshot, and her knife.

I waited and waited. I made marmot soup all by myself. It turned out really good, so I was especially sorry she wasn't here. I barred the door, but I listened for her. I studied my subtraction and then I read a history lesson. I didn't sleep very well. I'm used to having her, nice and warm, beside me.

Did she say, "If I don't come back after three days, leave?" Or did she only say that when I was little and not that much of a forest girl like I am now? Way back then I would have needed somebody to help me.

She *did* say that I never listen and that I never pay attention, and I guess this proves it.

But what if she comes back and I'm not here? What if she's tired? I could help. I could pump up the shower.

Except what if she doesn't come back?

I was always asking if we couldn't go where there were people, and she was always saying, "It's safer here." And I'd say, "What about the mountain lions?" And she'd say, "Even so, it's much safer up here—for us."

She said not to let anybody see us, but she didn't say why.

She did say people are always shooting things before they even know what they are.

What if I'm some sort of a creature that *should* be shot? Eaten, too?

Or is *she*? We don't look much alike. Maybe *she's* the odd one.

I asked her about all that once, but she wouldn't talk about it.

Now and then, in summer, when there are people camping all the way up here, we go yet higher and hide out until they're gone. Mother always said, "Let's *us* go on a camping trip, too," but she couldn't fool me with that. I knew she wanted to keep us secret, but I played along. I never said I didn't want to go. If we were in trouble some way I wanted us to stay out of it.

I know a lot more than she thinks I do.

ঙ ঙ ঙ

I wander all over, trying to see what happened to her. I see where she crossed the stream and started down to the muddy pond, but then I lose track. I check the pond, but she never got there. There's a fish on the line. I bring it home for supper.

The thing is, do I want to spend my life here alone? Waiting? Does Mother even want me to? I can come back after I see what's beyond the paths. Mother said two-storey houses and even three-storey. Also I'd really, really like to see a paved road—once in my life anyway.

I wait the three days, looking for her all that time, then I leave. I take Mother's treasure. She had this little leather book. Even when we just went up to hide, she took that with her and kept it dry.

There are lots of books here—actually twelve—but I don't take any except the one Mother always wrote in and locked shut.

I stop at the look-over and think to go back, just in case she came home exactly when I left, but I did leave a note. Actually two notes, one on the door and one inside. The one inside I shaped like a heart. It was on the paper we made out of stems. I don't need to tell her where I'm headed. She'll see that. I'm leaving a lot of clues all along the way.

ॐ ॐ ॐ

It turns out exactly like Mother said it would: a river and then a bigger river and a path and then a road, and after that the wonderful, wonderful paved road. Pretty soon I see, in the distance, a town. Even from here I can tell some of the houses are tall.

I wait till dark. I'm not sure what's wrong with me, but it's a town with plenty of bushes around. I don't think it'll be hard to hide. I never had a good look at those people that come in the summer. Mother tried to get me away as fast as she could. I've only seen them from a distance. Besides, they were all covered up with clothes, sunglasses, and hats.

We have those.

I want to see what they're like so I can see what might be wrong with me. Though maybe Mother did something really, really bad a long time ago and had to hide out in the mountains. They couldn't put me in prison for something she did, could they?

୧   ୧   ୧

I wait till dark and then I creep into town. Everything is closed up. Hardly any lights on. (I know all about electricity, though I've never seen it till now.) I wait till everything except the streetlights are out. I wait for them to go out, too, but they don't.

I wander backyards. I try to see into windows, but I waited too long for those streetlights to go out. Every house is dark, except for now and then an upstairs window.

In one yard I hide behind laundry where somebody's mother forgot to bring it in before dark. Mother sometimes did that, too, but I didn't. She had a lot on her mind. She was always worried.

I just about give up—everybody seems to be in bed—but then I see somebody sneaking out a window, trying to be quiet. It's that very yard where the laundry is still out.

I hide behind the sheets, but so does whoever crawled out the window. We bump right into each other. We both gasp. I can see on that one's face that it's going to yell but I'm about to, too, and then we both cover our mouths with our hands, as if we both don't want to attract attention. Then we stare.

If this one is how I'm supposed to be then I'm all wrong. This one looks like Mother, not like me. I have way too much hair. All over. Are they all like this? But I've suspected something was wrong with me for a long time, else why did Mother act as she did, always keeping us away from everybody?

I can't tell if it's a boy or a girl. I'm not used to how they look here or how they dress. Then I see it's got to be a girl. She's wearing this lacy kind of top. I never had anything like that but Mother did. This girl seems to be just my size. At least my size is right.

She's like Mother, no hair anywhere except a lot on her head. Mother always said it was a disadvantage, not having hair all over. And it was. She was always cold. But I'd rather be like everybody else.

So we're standing there with our hands over our mouths, staring at each other.

Then she says, "Can you talk?"

And I say, "Of course. Why not?"

What an odd question. What does she think I am? Except I *am* all wrong. I was afraid of that. But we're exactly the same height, and both of us are skinny. I'm wearing shorts and a T-shirt. She wearing shorts, too, and this fancy blouse. And I see now she has the beginnings of breasts just like I do. Hairiness looks to be our only difference. I don't have that much on my face—thank goodness. I guess.

"Am I all wrong?"

It's the question I've been wanting to ask just about all my life but didn't know it till right now.

I can tell from the way she says "Well . . ." that I am and that she wants to be nice about it.

She says, "Come."

Way back at the end of her yard, there's a funny little house that we have to lean over to go in. It has two tiny rooms that you couldn't lie down straight out in unless you put your feet through the door into the other room. It has a little table and chairs, too small for any regular-size person. Are there people I never knew about?

The girl lights a candle, and we squinch into the little chairs next to the little table.

Even in this light I can see her eyes are blue just like mine. We're an awful lot the same.

"Dad was going to take this house down, but I said, not yet."

She has a dad!

"So what about you? What are you, anyway?"

I can't answer. I feel like crying. I have to say, "I don't know."

"We could look you up online. There's a lot of choices: Yeti, Abominable Snowman, Sasquatch, Bigfoot. . . ."

She knows more about me than I do.

"I suppose abominable."

"I don't think so. You're too nice-looking. Are you crying?"

I thought I was holding it back but that makes me feel worse than ever. I really do start to cry. Mother would be saying, "Where's my forest girl?"

"That's all right, go ahead and cry. I'll make you tea, and there's cookies, too. I don't have a stove in here, Dad wouldn't let me, this is just sun tea, but it's good. I know I'm too old to have a playhouse like this, but I want it, anyway. It comes in handy, like right now."

The tea is nothing like anything I've had before, even though we have lots of teas up there. And the cookies are like nothing I ever had either. I say, "I never had these."

"Oatmeal with raisins. Mom thinks they're good for you. She's a great believer in oatmeal."

I guess her mother is right. I feel better after the tea and a couple of cookies.

But I'm thinking maybe she has a bad mother. I've heard of that. After all, she sneaked out the window.

"Were you escaping? I thought maybe your mother was mean and you were running away."

"Oh no, my folks are fine. I sneak out lots of times when there's a moon like this. I'm fourteen. I'm old enough to be on my own."

"I'm fourteen, too, and I *am* on my own, but I don't want to be."

"I don't know what Mother would do about you, though. Call the police . . . or the doctor. Or maybe the zoo."

"Am I all wrong?"

"You're probably some sort of mutation."

How can she be so sure of herself all the time? But she does seem to know a lot.

"I don't want to be put in the zoo."

"That wouldn't be so bad. I wouldn't mind at all if it were me. I'd come visit you. But I don't even know your name. Mine is Molly. I picked it out myself two years ago when I started junior high."

"You named yourself?"

"Lots of people do. You could, too. But do you have one?"

"Of course I do. I'm not . . ."

But maybe I am—sort of an animal. "Mother calls me Binny. It's short for Sabine."

"Sabine!"

She looks impressed.

"Don't change it!"

ɕ   ɕ   ɕ

We both get tired at the same time. Molly goes back in through her window and brings me a pillow and a blanket. Tells me to keep quiet and she'll bring me breakfast after her parents go to work. She says, "Not to worry. Nobody . . . *Nobody* would dare go in my playhouse unless invited."

It feels good to stretch out all the way through the two rooms after hunching over all that time. And I've never had such a soft pillow before.

ɕ   ɕ   ɕ

I wake at dawn, as I usually do. Things are pretty much quiet all over the whole town. I hunch myself around the little house. I didn't get a good look at it last night in the candlelight. There's a mirror. I see me. Actually Molly and I look kind of alike. Our eyes are blue. Our hair is tawny.

Hair!

On a shelf I find a doll . . . a very worn-out doll (not hairy), and a worn-out (hairy) dog doll beside it.

ɕ   ɕ   ɕ

The town starts waking up. Doors slam. Cars drive by, but out along the front of the houses, way across the lawn from me. I saw those last night. Some even came right close to me while I was waiting for it to get dark. Trucks, too. I saw everything Mother talked about and drew pictures of. I even went up to a car and looked in. I saw the steering wheel and the pedals. I can't wait till I get to ride in one. Maybe Molly can get me a ride. A truck would be even more fun than a car, the bigger the better. I'll ask her.

I wait and wait for Molly to bring breakfast. Finally she does. Stuff I never had before. Toast and sausages. Actually, enough for both of us. She wants to eat with me. First thing she says is, "I hate eggs."

I've had eggs lots of times and I like them but I don't say it.

"I have to go to school. Whatever you do, don't leave here in the daytime. I'll take you out tonight. We have to figure out what to do about you."

I say okay, but I'm not sure I'm going to stay shut up here all day.

"When do you get back?"

She looks at her watch. (I know what that is, too.) She doesn't notice I don't have one.

She says, "Three thirty, thereabouts."

§   §   §

Pretty soon everything gets very quiet. All the cars and all the children are gone. I'm tired of hunching over. I'm not going to stay in here, but I'm a little scared about just walking right out. Then I think about Molly's back window. I cross the lawn (by now the laundry's brought in) and climb in Molly's window.

Here's a nice place! Pale yellow walls, an all-white, really, really soft bed (I try it), a not-so-worn-out stuffed dog on the pillows (even fuzzier than the one in the little house), and a wonderful lot of books. Must be twenty or so on a nice little shelf. I recognize schoolwork things. There's a notebook exactly like Mother has for me.

Time goes faster than I thought it would. I spend a lot of it looking at the books, but then I get hungry. I find the kitchen. The refrigerator! In there it's like winter. I eat a lot of things that I don't know what they are. I've heard of cheese. Besides, I can read the labels: cold cuts, cheddar, cottage cheese. . . . I taste everything. There's radishes. I'm glad Mother saw to it that I knew about these things. I think she was homesick for all this, so she talked about it. Actually she talked about a lot more than I wanted to hear—then, anyway. Talk about not listening! It's a wonder I even remember radishes.

I wander around the whole house. Turns out they have lots of books. And all over the place. I start reading several of them, one after the other, bits and pieces of all sorts of things. Magazines, too. I've been missing a lot. Mother knew it. She tried to make it up to me. When I see all this I realize how hard she worked at it. I start feeling tearful. I wonder where she is and if she's all right.

Their clocks already say after two. I think I'd better go back into that little house.

I bring some books and magazines, but I don't read them. I start thinking about dads. I know enough to know I must have had one. I haven't thought much about it. I thought the way Mother and I lived was the usual way. Like bear cubs and fawns, always a mother and a child or two. And here's a dad living right with them. Out of the little windows, I saw whole families leaving all together. The dads were living right there with everybody.

There's a lot Mother told me, but a lot she didn't. I'd ask her, Where is my dad? Who was he? And, especially, how hairy?

I must have fallen asleep by mistake because Molly wakes me.

"Come quick," she says, "before my parents come home. We'll look you up on the Web. If Mother comes in . . . she always knocks first . . . you just scoot under the bed."

"Scoot?"

So then I get my first lesson in computer stuff. We look all over the place, but not a one looks at all like me. They're all chunky and have terrible faces.

Molly says, "You're much nicer looking than any of these. I like your hair color. There's a lot of gold in it."

I'm glad she said that, but it worries me that one of these might be my dad. How could Mother have even gotten close to somebody like that? I hope at least he was a nice person . . . *if* I can think of him as a person.

I ask Molly, "You have a dad. What's that like?"

"Oh, he's okay. He thinks I'm a kid, though. I'll be forty-five before he'll think I'm grown up. Don't you have your dad? Well, you don't or you'd already know what he looks like."

I'm thinking, looks aren't everything. Molly's father might not be so handsome either. But that's too much to hope for. And, anyway, why would I hope for that? That isn't nice.

Then I remember about cars and trucks. I ask Molly if she can take me for a ride in a truck.

"Truck! Of course not. We don't have a truck. But I could take you in our car—after everybody's gone to bed. I don't have a license, but I do know how to drive. Dad already taught me. You're not supposed to drive until you're sixteen. I don't know why they make you wait so long."

I go to the little house before her mother comes back. Molly loads me up with cookies and milk (I never had milk before), just in case she has a hard time bringing me a supper.

"Don't light the candle until all our lights are out here in the house."

♫   ♫   ♫

Finally she comes to get me.

She brings me a big floppy hat, one of her father's white shirts, pants, socks, and sandals. The sandals are terribly uncomfortable.

She says, "I guess you really are a Bigfoot."

I must look hurt because right away she says, "Sorry, that was supposed to be a joke. Not a very kind one. Look." She puts her foot next to mine. "We're almost the same size." Then, "You don't have to wear the sandals. I don't suppose anybody will see your feet anyway."

She tells me to button up the shirt and raise the collar to cover my neck as much as I can.

If I need all these clothes and to button up just to go for a ride in a car, I guess I really am entirely wrong.

♫   ♫   ♫

Even just getting in the car is exciting.

Then it jerks forward.

"Sorry. I haven't driven very much. But this will be good practice. Better put on your seat belt."

We drive, and it's wonderful. We go out in the country so we can go fast. She says in town we can only go twenty-five. We open the windows and get the breeze.

She says, "I'll go even faster if you stop saying 'Thank you' all the time."

I stop and she does.

She turns on the radio, which is another new thing—not that I haven't heard all about it. She pushes buttons to get the right music. She says, "Dad has it on news all the time." I wouldn't have minded hearing news.

We start around a curve and all of a sudden we're in the ditch. Then bouncing up and down, and then upside down.

We're not hurt, but the front doors won't open. Molly finally gets a back door open, and we crawl out.

She doesn't look like Molly anymore. She looks scared and like she doesn't know what to do.

She says, "I don't even have my cell phone."

It's still the middle of the night. There's not a light in sight. She starts to cry. I feel like I'm the strongest one now. I say, "Come on. Let's start back to town."

"I wish I hadn't gone so fast. We wouldn't be so far away if I hadn't done seventy. Daddy's going to kill me."

"Your dad will kill you?"

"No, silly, of course not. Don't you know anything?"

Getting angry at me makes her feel better. She starts walking down the road in the dark and trips and falls flat. And then she's crying again.

My eyes must be better than hers. I can see a little bit. There's the sliver of a moon. I say, "We'll be all right. Hang on to me."

Pretty soon it starts getting light and we see a farmhouse and head for that.

"I'll go in and telephone Dad. You have to hide. Don't let anybody see you."

The more she says things like that, the more I worry about myself.

"What will Daddy do? And we don't even have a car now. And what will we do with *you*?"

"I don't want to be put in the zoo."

"Look, there's a barn. Go hide there while I go in."

In the barn there's stalls, mostly empty, but there are two horses at the back. There's a ladder up to a loft full of hay. That's where I'll go, but I've never seen horses—except in picture books. I check on them first. I worry they might kick or bite, but they come right up to me to see who I am, friendly as can be. It makes me feel better, stroking something big and warm. Then I go up and lie down in the hay.

It takes so long for Molly to come back I think maybe she's just left me here. I'm too shaken up to sleep. I go down again and talk to the horses. I get right in with them. I call one Spotty and the other Brownie.

Finally Molly comes.

"I couldn't get away from the people here. They're too nice. They were going to drive me home, since they had to go to town anyway, but I said I needed to call Daddy. They went off to town. I know their kid. He's a couple of grades ahead of me in school. He's still here. He takes the school bus. Daddy's renting a car. He'll be here as soon as he can, but it'll take a while. I didn't tell him about you. What'll we do about you?"

I don't say anything. What do I know?

But suddenly here's the boy. First he says, "What are you doing out here?" And then he sees me and gasps.

I'm still dressed, head to toe . . . to almost toe, but even so I'm too much for him.

"What *are* you?"

I say, "Bigfoot."

Right away he looks at my feet. Then he laughs. And we all laugh.

He says, "I don't believe in you."

I say, "Nobody does."

And we laugh all the more.

He decides not to go to school—after all, Molly isn't going either—and invites us in for breakfast.

He keeps staring at me as he cooks us pancakes. And he keeps spilling things.

He says, "You're a nice color," and, "I didn't think a Bigfoot would be so attractive," and, "You have nice eyes," until I'm a little worried. Though he could be trying to make me feel good about myself. I suppose I should appreciate it.

He says, "I don't think you should go back with Molly. I think you should stay here where you have a nice barn to hide in."

Molly looks relieved.

I'd really rather be back in her little playhouse, but I don't know how we can get me there.

Then he says, "We could go horseback riding," and I think, maybe it wouldn't be so bad here. I'm learning so many new things. Including rolling over in a car. Horses would be nice.

Molly's father comes by in a rented car. He barely stops, honks, opens the door, and yells. I guess he's really angry. She looks at us, scared, then rushes out. There's no way I could have gone with her even if I'd wanted to.

§   §   §

The boy's name is Buck. He changed his name, too. I didn't know everybody could do that. He used to be Judson. He says, "Judd isn't so bad but I like Buck better."

He goes to put on his riding clothes. He has the whole out-fit, cowboy hat and boots and all. I've seen pictures. I think he's trying to impress me. And maybe himself. He does look as if he likes himself a lot in these clothes.

He brings a bag of stuff for a picnic, and we go out and saddle up. First he has to brush the horses so there's no dust and stuff under the saddle. He shows me how, and I help.

I feel funny, getting up on something I just talked to and petted, but he doesn't seem to mind.

Buck heads us up into the hills and pretty soon we're in the trees. He makes us canter even though he can see I'm bounc-ing and hurting. Trotting isn't much better. He doesn't say a word about what to do. It looks as if he likes to see me not knowing how to do it. He's got this funny little smile all the time. He's laughing at me.

We get to a nice shady spot and get off and tie up. He spreads out a blanket, he says, for our picnic.

He takes off half his fancy cowboy outfit. And then he takes off even more. Is this what people do?

But I start to know what this is all about. I remember things Mother warned me could happen. I wasn't listening, but some of it must have gotten through.

He's a lot taller than I am and stronger, too. He tears Mol-ly's father's shirt practically in two. I have to really fight and I'm losing.

Finally I grab a stone and knock him away.

He says, "What difference does it make? You're just an ani-mal. Why should you care?"

"I'm not an animal, or if I am, I'm only half. My mother was your kind."

He comes after me again but I run . . . uphill. I'm thinking of getting back to our cabin and maybe finding out what happened to Mother.

I'm way faster than he is. I guess from all my hiking around the mountains. Pretty soon he gives up. From way above I see him put on his costume, mount up, and ride away, leading the other horse.

I sit down and catch my breath. I feel like crying, but I'm angry, too. Molly didn't think I was an animal. Or am I? I wish I was back with her.

I'm glad that, up in the mountains, it's always just mothers and children off by themselves. I was thinking I wanted to meet my father someday, but now I'm not sure. And he'd be more of an animal than I am. Though if Mother liked him he couldn't be that bad. Or maybe she didn't like him. Maybe she couldn't fight him off.

And then I think how Mother's little book is in the pocket of my shorts back in the little house. I have to get back there.

I walked there once before, I guess I can walk there again. I'm going to stay in the foothills and walk mostly at night. I'm pretty well covered up with Molly's dad's shirt, even though it's torn and has lost some buttons, and the slacks are okay. I don't have the hat anymore.

I wonder what Molly is expecting to do about me. She might try to come and get me. For sure not driving a car. I wonder what she'll do when she finds out I'm gone. I wonder if she knows about how Buck is. Except maybe he's only that way with somebody who's an animal.

I'm too impatient to wait for dark. I start heading back toward the town, but I keep well away from any roads or houses. I suppose it's pretty far, considering how fast Molly was driving. I don't even know the name of the town, but it has a special smell. I'd recognize it right away.

Later, when I come to a river and a nice pile of brush next to it, and berries, I decide to rest there until dark.

Except I can't rest. I'm too angry and upset. I need to talk to Molly. I keep on across the rocky foothills.

§   §   §

I should have stayed and rested.

At first I think they're wolves, but then I see it's a pack of all sorts of dogs. I climb a juniper. They're making a terrible racket.

Practically right away, here comes a man with a rifle. He shoots toward the dogs, and they run off. Then he comes to see what they've treed. He stares. Walks all around the tree to look at me from every angle. The shirt and slacks don't hide that much. My Bigfoot-big-bare-fuzzy-feet are just above his head.

He isn't dressed like Buck, though he is wearing a cowboy hat. He has a bushy mustache that's mostly gray. He's a lot older than Buck. I don't know if that's good or bad. He might, all the quicker, take off his clothes and grab me. Is he going to climb the tree and pull me down and then try to do what Buck tried?

"Can you talk?"

Why does everybody ask me that? Do I look so animal? I guess I do.

"Of course I can."

And I climb a little higher.

"Don't be scared. I won't hurt you. I won't. I promise. Are you hungry?"

Yeah, lure the animal down with a little bite of food.

He sits under the tree and takes off his hat. He's got a *very* high forehead. I've seen pictures of that. That's being bald. Maybe when I'm older I could get bald all over.

He takes out an apple and a sandwich and begins to eat. He's in no hurry. As he eats, he keeps looking up at me and shaking his head, as if, like Buck, he doesn't believe in me.

"I've heard tell of your kind, but I've never seen one. Where did you come from, anyway?"

I don't know what to say.

"Do you have a name?"

What does he think I am? Well, I know what he thinks.

"Of course I do."

"Mine's Hiram. People call me Hi."

"Mine's Sabine."

"I never knew a Sabine. Is that from your people?"

"My people?"

"Your kind of . . . Whatever you . . ."

I never thought about being "a kind." Was he going to say, your kind of animal?

For a minute we just look out at the view of the fields far below us with the sprinkling of black cows, both of us as if embarrassed. Then he says, "You might as well come down. You'll have to one of these days. It might as well be now as later. When I leave those dogs might come back. You can have half my sandwich and this apple."

He's right, I might as well come down, so I do.

I take the sandwich and sit a couple of yards away. I hope I'm not eating like an animal or sitting like an animal. I sit as he's sitting. I'm hungry, but I slow down. I try to keep the torn shirt shut as best I can.

He leaves his clothes on all that time, and afterward we just sit quietly. I'm thinking maybe I should ask about men taking their clothes off, but then I think I'd better not. Even if he is a man, maybe he can help me get back to the town.

He keeps looking me up and down. He just can't stop. Then he says, "Sorry, I shouldn't stare. I'd like to take a picture of you. Of course nobody will believe it. They'll think I made it up on the computer."

"Can you drive a car? I'm trying to get back to the town. I'll let you take my picture if you help me get back. It would have to be at night. And I only need to go to the edge. And if you could lend me a hat, I'd try to get it back to you."

☙ ☙ ☙

He takes me down to his house. I won't go in. I don't care if he thinks I'm a scared animal, I just won't, and I *am* a scared animal. He gets his camera and takes a lot of pictures, all different views. I'm worried about it because Molly said I should hide, and this sure isn't hiding, but this is the only way I know of to get back to her. If he's going to bother helping me, I have to do something for him.

Then we wait till the middle of the night. I apologize for keeping him up.

He never once takes his clothes off. Maybe all men don't do that. I'll have to ask Molly. She said everything is on the computer. If she doesn't know, we can look it up.

He makes me supper. A kind of stew with everything in it. He says it's called slumgullion. He says it's kind of a guy thing. He serves it outside on his picnic table so I won't need to go in. I'm beginning to think I shouldn't be so scared. I wonder if my father is as nice.

He sits down to eat across from me.

"You've had a bad experience, haven't you. Or are you just scared of all of us?"

"I like Molly. That's where I want to get back to. But I had a bad experience with Buck. He took his clothes off and grabbed me."

Then I tell him all about Molly and the car rolling over and about Buck. I tell him, "You don't seem like him."

"I'm not. And when any man takes his clothes off, you take care. I have a daughter about your age. I live by myself, except my daughter comes here for the summer. If I show those pictures I took of you around, you're in trouble. Everybody will be after you. They'll chase you wherever you try to hide. You ought to go back up into the hills and let yourself be a legend like the rest of your people are. I'll hang on to these pictures until you get well away."

"But I don't know my people. I've never met my father. My mother's one of your kind. Molly wanted to shave me all over with her dad's electric razor. Do you think that would work?"

"Not a good idea. You'd prickle. Nobody could get near you. Here, feel my cheeks. I haven't shaved since yesterday."

I reach across the table and feel them.

"You sure you don't want me to take you up into the mountains far as I can drive and drop you off? I'll give you a knapsack and water bottle and food for a couple of days. That would be best for you."

"I'd like to see Molly first. Besides, I left Mother's book there."

He gets me a shirt of his that isn't torn. It's dark green. Better for hiding in than this white one.

We spend time looking up at the stars. He knows the names

of everything up there. I tell him my mother did, too. Then we have coffee, though he doesn't let me have much. He says if I'm not used to it it'll make me jittery. And then we go—in his rickety old truck. He gives me a stained old cowboy hat. He says it may not look so good but it's beaver so it's waterproof.

He drops me off at the edge of town like I want him to. I think I can smell my way back to Molly's house, but not if I'm in the truck.

When he lets me off he says, "You know I'll not use those photos. Better you folks stay a myth. And you better hurry back in the hills. That's where you belong."

I'm glad I met him after Buck. I was ready to never get near a man again.

🔊 🔊 🔊

It doesn't take me long to find Molly's place. I kept pretty good track of where I was. I always know where I am when there are trees and rocks, but I knew I'd have trouble finding my way with all these streets and houses.

I go right back to the playhouse and settle in to get some sleep for what there is left of the night. The pillow and blanket aren't there anymore, but I take the old dog doll for a pillow. Hi's shirt will keep me warm.

But first I find my shorts just where I hid them, and Mother's book is still in the pocket.

I want to let Molly know I'm here, but I don't want to wake her up in the middle of the night. But then I oversleep. Everybody in the house has gone off just like before. I wonder if Molly tried to find me at Buck's and if Buck tried . . . that with her? But I suppose not. I'm the one who doesn't count. But I don't see what difference it makes. Animal or not, I shouldn't have to get forced into doing something I don't want to. Hi didn't think so, either.

So then I have to wait around for Molly to come back. I sneak in and get myself some food. I snoop around again. I wish I knew how to use the computer. I don't dare try without Molly. She said you could learn about everything there.

I grab some books and go back. I start reading and don't even notice when Molly comes home. When I realize she must be back, I go look in her window. There she is, on the bed with a magazine. I tap on the window. She gives a shriek when she sees me. It's good nobody else is home. She opens the window and hugs me. She climbs out, and we go back to the playhouse.

She says, "I was so worried, and I didn't know how to come and get you back, and Daddy won't let me go *anywhere* now that I ruined our car. I'm going to have to stay home for months and I have to do chores to help pay for the new car." She starts to cry.

I don't know what to do. Mother would have held me, but that's different. At least I think it is. Finally I reach out and pat her shoulder. That seems to be all right. She does stop.

I ask, "Is it all my fault? You were driving for me."

"Of course not. I know it's my fault. I don't even have a license. Daddy says I have to take the consequences."

"Can I help?"

"I don't know. Maybe keep me company, now that I have to stay home every single night there is."

"I'll do it. Besides, I want to learn more things on the computer. About men." Then I tell her what Buck tried to do.

She gets really mad and tells me not every boy would be

that way, and she is never going to speak to him again, and she's going to tell all her friends to watch out for him.

"Yes, but I'm an animal."

"You're a girl. Anybody with any sense can see that."

"Thank you."

"I like your looks."

I feel like crying, too, but one of us in tears at a time is enough.

"Actually, in your own way, you're quite decent-looking."

In my way.

"Maybe there's some kind of medicine you can take that would make all your hair fall out. I'll bet there is. These days there's something for everything. I'll go online and look it up."

I don't trust Molly anymore. She doesn't know as much as she thinks she does. I don't want to take some pill that will make my hair fall out.

I don't tell her, but, even though I owe it to her, I'm not sure I want to stay here much longer. Maybe just look up some more things on the computer. Get her to print some pictures of my possible fathers. I don't belong down here. Hi said so, too. And I miss the mountains. Mother said I was made for them. I was always warm enough up there, even my feet. Mother's feet were always cold. What if she's back there by now? Though I know I shouldn't get my hopes up.

§ § §

Next day Molly pretends to go to school and then comes home. She's going to go back to school for her dad to pick her up. I guess her dad can't keep tabs on her all the time.

(Here I am wishing I could go to school and she can and doesn't do it.)

So we print out all the pictures of Sasquatch, and Yeti, and Bigfoot. None of them look very nice. I like having their pictures, though. I fold them up and button them in the pocket of the shirt Hi gave me.

The next day Molly does go to school. She says she can't afford to miss too much. She's not doing very well in French (French! I wonder if I could ever get to take that) and math. She says her dad is already angry enough without her failing two subjects. So I have the whole place to myself again.

I go to the house and bring back food and books, but then I think I should be reading that little book of Mother's. Maybe I can find out why she went with such an odd . . . creature. I almost thought "person," but I'm not sure if either my father or I can be called a person.

I pry open the lock on Mother's little leather book and there, right on the first page in big letters, she'd written:

A TALE OF TRUE LOVE ! ! !

And underneath that:

Except at first I didn't know it.

I shouldn't have been climbing alone in such a dangerous place, but I like being on the cliffs by myself. I was having an exciting time on a dangerous little trail. I remember falling . . .

. . . and then, there I was, looking up into big brown eyes. The creature—Mother calls him a creature, too—was mopping my forehead with a cool cloth. He was grunting little sad grunts. As if he was sorry for me. The way he looked—completely hairy—I never expected him to be able to speak, but when he

saw my eyes were open, he said, "I thought maybe you were dead."

I tried to get up, but I hurt all over.

"Lie still," the creature said. And then he brought me water in a folding cup, held my head so I could drink.

I had broken my leg and my arm but I didn't know that then.

He whistled a kind of complicated birdsong and right after that another one just like him came. They've got a whistling language. Lots of it exactly like real birdsongs. I love that. I never mastered it though. They use our language, too.

The other one wore a fisherman's vest full of pockets. He had soft vinelike ropes. They tied my arm and leg to pieces of wood to keep them from moving. They put me in a kind of hammock, and took me to their hidden village. Movable village. They hardly spend two nights in a row in the same place.

Then there's a break and the start of a new page.

Dear Sabine,

So this is for me. I'm *supposed* to read it.

As you see, that's what I wrote shortly after the accident, and then such a lot happened that I stopped writing. Actually for years. It was partly because I had to take care of you. But now it's because of you that I'm writing again. I want you to know about us, Growen and me. It was Growen's brother, Greener, who helped Growen rescue me. All the others were against it. They thought helping me was dangerous. I must *have lain unconscious for most of the day before they finally decided to help. If not for Growen, they never would have. I think Growen fell in love right then, but it took me a little longer.*

You know, Binny, they're beautiful. Not like any of the pictures people make of them. You must NOT think they're like those. And you should know how beautiful you are, too.

Am I really?

At first I couldn't tell them apart. I mean Growen and Greener, or any of them for that matter. Well, I could tell the men from the women. Then I saw that Growen looked at me in a different way. Hopeful. I almost wrote yearning, but it wasn't that because he always looked sure of himself. As if what he wanted would come true, it was just a matter of when. As if he knew I'd soon see how worthy he was.

Binny, I hope you're a grown-up as you read this and have fallen in love, too, so you understand.

Should I stop reading and keep this until I'm older? Besides, I haven't even met anybody to be in love with. Or maybe I can read it twice, now, and then again later.

Of course I didn't fall in love right away. Everybody and everything was too odd, but when you're hurting and are treated with kindness, it makes all the difference. Growen was so concerned and helpful and kept looking at me with such admiration.

Except for Growen and Greener, none of the others liked me. They built our cabin and sent me and Gro-

wen down from their cliffs and caves and nests.

I don't know what they'd do about you now. You're so much more them than me. I hope they find you, though as long as I'm around they don't want either of us. I'm a danger. Everything is a danger to them and I suppose they're right. They can't have been kept secret all this time without taking great care.

I hope nothing I do reveals them. Can you imagine, all of them shut up in the zoo? Or tourists swarming all over taking their picture? Or yours? Be careful!!!!! Don't ever, ever, ever go down where it's so hard to hide!!!!!!!!!!!!!!!!!

Oh, my God. What have I done!

I didn't realize how important it is for me to be a secret. Me just being down here is a danger to all of them . . . I should say, all of *us*. And now Hi and Buck and Molly know about me. Hi said he wouldn't show the pictures, but I'll bet Buck will tell about me. He can't prove it, though. At least I hope not.

And all of a sudden I want to find my kind so much I can't stand to sit here one minute more. I have to get back. But I already roamed all over the place and none of them came to me and I never saw a single sign of them.

Though there are several more pages in the book, Mother only wrote a phrase here and there, as if she was going to go back and fill them in. One just has: *Today Growen died.* Maybe she felt too sad to go on except with these little notes.

῾᾽ ῾᾽ ῾᾽

I put on my shorts and T-shirt, and on top of that Hi's green shirt, and then his wonderful waterproof hat. I don't take anything of Molly's, not even cookies. Except I wonder if she'd mind if I took her social studies book. I like the idea of all these different kinds and colors of people, even though nobody in it has hair all over. Besides, I don't think Molly cares anything about social studies.

It doesn't fit in Hi's big pockets, though Mother's book does. I'll have to carry it separately. I'll pick up one of those plastic bags that keep blowing around everywhere.

I feel bad that I'm not going to say good-bye. Molly got in a lot of trouble because of me. I ought to stay and help, but I'm not going to.

I'm going to find my people if it takes falling off a cliff and lying there with a broken leg.

But what if I don't belong with them either? What if I don't belong anywhere?

᭞   ᭞   ᭞

I follow the signs I left for Mother so she could follow me. I find my way back to our cabin, no problem. There's quite a bit of snow. It's getting too cold for most of the regular people to be in the mountains. I only have to avoid a few.

I get excited when I get close. Maybe Mother is waiting for me.

The cabin door is open. She must be there.

But then I get worried. Maybe somebody broke in. Maybe somebody like Buck, not like Hi.

I back away and hide.

And then a beautiful creature comes out, looks up and sniffs. He probably can smell even better than I can. I'll bet he knows I'm hiding here.

He's a tawny golden color—all over. He has a wide forehead, a lionlike look. No wonder Mother fell in love. His face
is bare, like mine. I can't believe how beautiful he is, and I'm
pretty much just exactly like him.

He's wearing a fisherman's vest with all the pockets bulging. And he has a belt with all sorts of things hanging from it.

"Sabine? Binny?"

He knows me. Do I dare show myself?

His voice is deep and kind of whispery—breathy.

"I'm your uncle, Greener. Come on out."

I don't.

"Your mother . . . I'm sorry. She . . . We found her not far
from Rock Creek. Come on out. Let me tell you face-to-face."

So it's true. What I suspected. But I can't come out.

He sits down and turns away so his back is toward my hiding place. A broad, strong, golden back.

"I've come to take you home. You'll like it. Your Aunt Sabby
is there. You're named for her, you know."

I can't come out.

"We have a pet fox. We've got jays that eat out of your hand."

I can't.

"I'm sorry I didn't get here soon enough—before you went
down. I hope you didn't have a bad time there."

I don't come.

"Come on out. I'll teach you how to hide. I'll teach you
how to sneak away without making a sound. I'll teach you our
whistle language. Come on. I'll take you home."

I'm glad I have Hi's big black hat. I pull it low over my eyes
and I come.

CAROL EMSHWILLER grew up in Michigan and in France and currently divides her time between New York and California. She is the winner of two Nebula Awards, for her stories "Creature" and "I Live with You." She has also won the Lifetime Achievement award from the World Fantasy Convention.

She's been the recipient of a National Endowment for the Arts grant and two New York State grants. Her short fiction has been published in many literary and science fiction magazines. Her most recent books are the novels *Mr. Boots* and *The Secret City* and the collection *I Live with You.* Her Web site is www.sfwa.org/members/emshwiller

ᴌᴐᴄᴌ

Author Note

I've always liked the idea of a child growing up in the forest . . . half-wild or all-wild. I had the first few paragraphs of this story written before Ellen asked me if I'd write something for *The Beastly Bride.* Usually I can't write "on demand," but this was already started, and I thought it might fit.

I didn't know then that my girl would be fuzzy and have a Sasquatch/Bigfoot father. Those elements entered the story because Ellen and Terri's description of their anthology seemed to ask for them. I had thought of a wild child, but one just like us. It was because of Ellen that Sabine turned out as she did, and I'm so glad that happened! I love my beautiful fuzzy people. I think the story is much more interesting than it would have been if Ellen hadn't asked for "Beastly."

THE *HIKIKOMORI*

Hiromi Goto

"**M**asako-chan." Her mother's slightly muffled voice was inflected with a smile. "A young lady from Community Health is here to see you."

Despite the wall and closed door, her mother's voice nonetheless quavered with layers of feelings. Masako could identify each of them with a coroner's disengagement: guilt, shame, pride, resentment, a clasping love, pity, self-pity. Hate.

Masako did not respond.

"Please," her mother begged, her voice beginning to rise. "She's here to help you. To help us! I can't bear it anymore! Just open the door!" She was beginning to shatter. The sharp edges in her voice. Masako imagined shards of glass inside her throat. Rising up to fill her mouth.

Go away! I can't go back! They hate me. I can't bear it. They hurt me. They'll see me. I can't bear their eyes. They whisper. Don't find me. You're not coming in! There's something wrong with me. There's something wrong with me. Leave me. Alone.

"Masako-san!"

The voice, crisp, clear, unfamiliar, cut through Masako's darting, sweaty fears.

"My name is Moriya. I am your liaison from the Community Health Center, Family and Youth Department. I will be arriving every morning at nine A.M. to visit you, Monday through Saturday. You will grow accustomed to me over time. And you will open your door. You will be able to join society once more. You are not alone."

Masako stared at the blue screen of her laptop. Who was this stranger? Who did she think she was? To think that she, a stranger, could march into their house and tell her what would happen. With her life. As if she knew her already.

Would she force the door? Would she? Break into her sanctuary?

"I look forward to meeting you." The woman's voice rang clearly. "I'll be here tomorrow," she promised.

Voices murmured in the hallway. Masako could almost *feel* her mother bowing her gratitude to the stranger. Appalling. The voices receded with the creaks of the wooden staircase as they descended to the first floor.

She could hear the front door open, then close. The Moriya woman had left their home and entered daylight.

Masako knew if she stepped out into sunlight, now, it would eat her up. She only made rare forays outside in the stillest part of darkness. When distant sirens wailed the tragedies of others. When her shame-filled parents were folded into exhausted sleep. When night people were in the middle of their shifts and day people lay unconscious to the life of shadow. Then people like her crawled out of their sanctuaries.

If only for a brief moment of starlight. To breathe moonlight and drink in the sweet night air.

Masako shuddered with longing and fear. It was growing more and more difficult to leave her room. And now, this Mori-ya creature here to harass and torment her during the days. It was unbearable.

If only she could leave. Cast everything from her, like an exoskeleton, and emerge new and naked into a new life. She would do it gladly.

But fifteen-year-old girls trapped in a Chiba suburb did not do such things, especially someone like her.

Outcast from school, fat in a land of skinny, and named after the Imperial Prince's neurotic bride, Masako was trapped in this hell until she died.

"Princess Lump," they had sneered. "Princess Landfill." They had filled her plastic slippers with shit. They had snapped photos of her sitting on the toilet with their cell phones and had posted them on student Web sites. They had mashed her face into skinny Ryo's acne-filled cheek screaming, "Love! Love! Love!" And the teachers just turned aside their gaze. As if in witnessing this abuse they would somehow be sullied themselves. The teachers had no authority. The cliques of students, sneering and aloof, ruled the school.

One morning she had changed into her school uniform, but she could not leave her room. She had crawled back into bed and retreated into silence. All of her mother's entreaties, threats, bribes, manufactured kindness, and a final failed attempt at spanking had done nothing to change her mind.

Masako had become a *hikikomori*.

ṡ   ṡ   ṡ

The three-quarter moon streamed a pale light through the gauzy curtains. Masako shook her head, blinking her eyes in confusion.

She had been standing at the open refrigerator, cramming leftover croquettes and salty cucumbers into her mouth, gulping sweet liquid yogurt. She could not remember entering the living room. She wiped her mouth with the back of one hand. Bread crumbs fell to the floor.

The hard edges of the neighborhood were softer in the night. There were shadows, plenty of dark pockets where one could hide, and the narrow street, aglow with orange lights, looked as if it had been washed in a golden rinse. Like old-fashioned tinted photos. It beckoned.

 க   க   க

The cool night air sank into her face, her skin, and she raised trembling hands to push back her monstrous hair. Her fingers caught in the unwashed hanks of her knotted strands. But she felt like she was aglow.

Her slippers slid and slopped on the pavement, her bare feet simultaneously sweaty and cold. The sound echoed against the city of concrete. Masako glanced down. She had left the house wearing her inside Hello Kitty slippers, her filthy school uniform, without a jacket.

She must look appalling, she thought. But the air was as sweet as sugar water. Masako slip-slopped down the dark sidewalk, eyes half-closed, mouth half-open. She wanted to swallow the night and carry it inside her.

Masako wasn't mad. She knew that she *looked* mad, and that if anyone saw her in public this way they would call the police or chase her away. So she turned away from the headlights of some four A.M. shift employee on their way to work and ducked down a side street.

In the near distance a dog barked, a hopeful ring in the sound.

Teeth clacking, fingers aching, she walked more quickly, moving with purpose toward a glowing Lawson's sign. She cast furtive glances all around as she stood by the door. She peered into the hyperbrightness of the interior, her eyes tearing even more at the shocking artificial lighting. The late-night convenience store was empty. The clerk sat propped behind a book, his head bobbing with sleep. Probably a university student, she thought.

The door chimed its two tones, and the store clerk jerked upright. "Wel—" choking off when he caught sight of her hair, her filthy and crusty school uniform. Her indoor Hello Kitty slippers on bare feet.

The clerk cleared his throat, loudly, as if to assert something. Masako's ears burned. She stared at the display of manga, tabloids, and soft-core porn magazines. They were all wrapped in plastic so that no one could browse. Her lower lip wobbled, her vision blurring.

The door chimed once more.

The store clerk made his noise again: disapproving and also a warning.

Someone shuffled. The slap, pad, slap, pad of uncaring feet. Masako, eyes cast downward, watched as a pair of filthy sneakers came into view. The wearer had to drag his shoes, which were devoid of laces, in order to keep them on. The hems of the navy blue school uniform pants were ragged and caked with mud and pine needles. The cloth tattered and worn.

That smell.

He did not reek with the tang of urine and unwashed flesh. Of the musty sweet animal oil of filthy human hair.

He smelled of trees.

A bony hand clamped around her wrist.

Masako froze.

The too-thin hand, almost tenderly, turned her wrist over so that her palm faced upward.

He gently placed a small something in her hand. Then folded her fingers to close over it.

Masako shook and shook. Someone had touched her.

She could feel something small, slightly oblong, inside her fist.

He had touched her.

Unable to help herself she glanced upward. Just as the thin dirty young student strode on, his gaping sneakers dragging loudly. She only caught one glimpse of a pockmarked profile before he was past her.

His face.

Were there wrinkles? Gray stubble mixed in with black? The student looked like he was over thirty years old. Was he an old pervert, pretending to be a high school student?

Masako grimaced.

The tiny object enfolded in her fingers burned. What vile thing had he put into her hand? Quaking, she slowly revealed the dubious gift.

On her dirty palm lay what could only be a seed. Pale yellow. Slightly conical. She had seen it somewhere before, she was sure of it. But she couldn't say what it was. Gross. It almost looked like a little tooth. What did the *hentai* want?

She raised her head to glare angrily at the middle-aged man.

But he wasn't there.

Masako's arms pimpled with a skittering cool breeze and the hairs on her neck tingled.

A motion. Low. Upon the floor. Masako's eyes shifted in time to see the long naked tail of a rat disappear behind an ice cream freezer.

She shook her head. It didn't make any sense. What did it mean? How could a man disappear? He had to have been at least 185 centimeters tall! There wasn't an exit in the back of the store. The only way out of the Lawson's was the way they had come in.

Could it be . . . ?

The tiny dubious gift clenched inside her hand, Masako lowered to her haunches and peered cautiously behind the freezer. It was dark and dusty. Was there a small hole in the wall?

"Kora! Kora!" A rude foot jabbed her right buttock. "You're not going to puke inside. Get out! Get outta here, you freaky kid!"

Masako, startled, began to topple, and she extended her hands to catch her fall. The little seed fell to the dirty floor.

She desperately scrabbled after the tiny gift.

"Hey!" the store clerk exclaimed. "What did you steal! Give it back, I'm calling the police!"

Masako popped the seed into her mouth.

She squeezed her molars together, grit from the floor grinding disgustingly against her tooth enamel, then a rich oily flavor began to fill her mouth, nutty and slightly sweet.

Pine nut.

The store clerk angrily grabbed the back of her neck.

But she never felt his touch.

The ground zoomed toward her as everything swelled, up, away, the tins of food, the shelves of sanitary napkins and contact lens solution rearing away from her, receding into a blurry backdrop. The floor accelerated, growing suddenly enormous, the details of the seams between tiles in high resolution, filled with crumbs, rock particles, oily smears, and strands of long black yarn.

She had lost her slippers. Because she was on all fours, upon the ground.

"Oh!" Masako gasped.

But the sound that escaped her mouth was a high-pitched squeal.

Her hands.

They were not her own.

The nails were thin, narrow claws. A fine pale fur covered them. In wonder, she turned one over. It was as close to a hand as it could be. But it was still a paw.

"Uhhhhh! Rat!" a voice bellowed, the sound of thunder. An enormous shoe swung toward her with the slow-fast speed of a pendulum.

Instincts took over. And she flipped with a twist, shooting into the safety of darkness behind the refrigeration unit.

Masako could smell something clean and fresh. It was coming from the small hole in the wall. She shot through as a foot dropped downward, just missing her tail by a hair's width.

Hair's width, she thought in one part of her mind. The strands of black on the floor weren't lengths of yarn; they were human hair. . . .

She had become so very small.

She slowed her headlong plunge and came to a stop. She sniffed and sniffed in the darkness, her whiskers bobbing.

A most marvelous breeze stroked each and every whisker; she could scarcely bear the pleasure. Like when she was a small child and her mother scratched her back for her with long slow strokes . . . except that the delicious sensation ran along the length of each and every one of her strands of hair.

And the smells. She could smell *everything*! Each scent was as precise and individual as snowflakes. Wet mud, loamy and rich. She could virtually taste the acid in the soil, as sour as grapefruit. The spiciness of pine and cedar, sweet and sharp. The nuanced flavor of rain. A banquet of complex and compelling scents—

And a rat.

He was middle-aged, with his own signature scent.

He did not reek with testosterone and aggression. . . . He was tired. But not exhausted. He'd eaten a Mossburger with rice in the past two hours. No potato fries. He had two sisters and one older brother. His father was dead. She could smell-taste all his details from the tiny droplets of urine markings he'd left behind. In the minute vapors that hung in the air.

Come outside.

If it was a voice, it was without words. And if anything had been uttered, she had not heard it with her ears, but with every sense of her body.

She had been turned into a rat.

Delayed reaction set in, and she began to shiver. She crouched low, pulling her legs beneath her body, curling her tail around her. A rounded hump of fear.

Her tail . . . She clutched it with her front paws. It felt cool in the furrowed heat of her ratty palms. It was a small comfort.

Come with me, the voice called once more. *Don't be frightened.*

Masako ground her teeth. The loud noise filled her sensitive ears. She clutched her tail firmly and shook her head.

It's nice here, the voice continued. *That's why I thought you'd like to join me. But it's not for humans. That's why you had to change, first. Into your true form.*

Masako froze. In the silence her heart tripped faster than it had ever beat before. Her true form?

You better hurry, the voice continued. *I have things to do.*

Masako turned her muzzle toward the enticing scent of fresh green forest. It was dizzying in its complexity and richness. A pale golden light shone through.

I'm going . . . The voice was receding.

Wait! Masako actually squeaked.

Startled at the foreignness of her own voice, she bolted outside.

She plunged blindly. All or nothing. It could be a trap, but it was too late. She was out in the open, terror vibrating in each and every hair on her body, running as if she were being chased by demons.

She crashed into coarse, thick fur, and they both squealed, tumbling end over end in a flurry of leaf litter and small snapping branches.

Claws clamped down upon her, and Masako realized that she was going to die now. She was probably actually dead, in fact. She had died and been reincarnated as a rat, moving down the enlightenment path, because she had brought shame and suffering to her parents, and now, after so briefly being a rat, she was going to be killed probably to be reincarnated even lower down the chain, as a slug or mollusk.

She heard a strange sound. On the highest threshold of her

auditory frequency. A barely discernible chirping chortling rat laughter.

The tickling contagious sound filled her senses, and she began chirping her pleasure.

Don't be stupid, the male rat said affectionately. *Your true form is rat. Your true form will always be rat. I recognized you for who you were as soon as I saw you in the store.*

Come. And the male rat turned and ran into the underbrush. *It is not entirely safe here, as we might wish it to be, but it is more beautiful than we could ever speak of.*

But I can barely see, Masako complained, still clinging to her memories of human sight.

See with all of your senses, her friend said. *See with your entire body and spirit.*

ᔕ   ᔕ   ᔕ

They dashed through patches of dark and light, staying close to shadow and narrow spaces. The night was thick with currents of air, water vapor dense with flavors. It was so overwhelming, and Masako soon grew tired as they scurried on, between brief moments of rest, deeper, deeper into the forest.

They scuttled for what felt like hours.

Wait. Masako could scarcely stand.

Here. Her friend passed her a pine nut, and she greedily snatched it with her mobile paws. Fingers, she thought. They were more like fingers than animal paws. But the rich oils and sugars of the pine nut overwhelmed her, and she began nibbling furiously.

Masako sighed with contentment. She could not remember the last time she felt so—so complete. And to think that she could feel this way by being a rat instead of human.

Where are we going? Masako asked.

I'm taking you to the Lady, so she can explain. The male rat's back was turned toward her. His posture rather stiff.

What lady? Masako looked around, the surrounding blur of forest night. Explain what? For some reason she had imagined she had come to a place far from human. And it had been such a relief. Dismay began to grow inside her, as if the seeds she'd eaten were beginning to sprout.

The Lady of the Pine was the one who first came to me. The male rat's whiskers bobbed in the sweet breeze. *To tell me about my true form. She set me free. Come,* he said rather urgently. *Rat time moves far more quickly than human.* They raced on, from shadow to shadow, following the most sheltered trail, until they finally came to a stop.

Look. Her friend actually pointed.

Masako looked up, up. She saw the dark blurry shadow of an enormous tree. The monstrous limbs grew broad and wide, bark thick and deeply ridged. Masako's whiskers quivered. Something was missing. . . . The tree should have smelled sweet and biting with sap and needles, but the odor was faint. She blinked nearsightedly.

The branches were practically bare.

Only the lowest branches retained their needles. The upper branches of the tree were already dead. A violent storm would likely snap the tree in half. Something gray ringed the torso of the enormous, dying tree. Masako could not make out what it was.

Lady, her friend called out. *Lady of the Pine. I have found another.*

Masako began to shiver. Another what?

A pale figure seemed to slip out from the trunk of the tree. Her long hair was pale and bright, the color of moonlight. Her face was young and worn with age. Her dress made of the thinnest silk, woven lovingly by the multitude of spiders she housed in her ample branches. Masako breathed with wonder. The Lady was so very lovely. She felt coarse and common before her. She wrapped her tail tightly around her body and quivered with self-consciousness.

The Lady slowly swept her gaze about until she caught sight of the small creatures in the deep moss. She crouched down with a groan, as if carrying an unbearable weight.

Masako anxiously glanced up at her glorious beauty.

The Lady's skin was pale and smooth, but dark worn shadows cupped her eyes, and her eyelids were wrinkled with age and experience. She looked like she could be sixteen or a hundred years old.

Friend Rat. She smiled. Her breath was sweet, but her eyes were dark with pain. *Guardian. Protector. I am most honored by your kind visit.*

Me? Masako squeaked disbelievingly.

Yes, you. The Lady lowered her hand, and Masako crawled upon her palm. She bowed her head, humbled by the Lady's demeanor. The pale Lady raised her hand, and Masako resisted the urge to dig her claws into her skin.

The Rats have always been my most trusted guards: loyal, wise, brave. But for a thousand years I have been bound by a curse, dying so slowly, every day. My Guardians were scattered and lost. Lost from me, and lost in themselves. My Guards were flung to the outer realms, far beyond the Forest of Dreams. As the centuries passed, I learned to pull my spirit from my body. The Lady stroked her free hand lovingly against the coarse bark of the great pine. She took that hand and then rested the palm upon her chest. *In this form, I traveled to distant realms to search for my trusted Guards who have lost all memory of their origin.*

A golden tear of sap slowly formed in the corner of her pale eye. *I had thought that if they ate a seed from my tree they would remember and return to me. Return they did, but only to ravage my branches for more seeds, ripping off my needles in their need to consume them. They ate and ate until they died. And yet I am not yet free. Of the hundreds of Rats I have found and brought back to me, none remain except this one.* She gestured gracefully toward the middle-aged male rat.

He had been raising a pine nut to his incisors, but he dropped it with a sudden flurry, transparently trying to hide the evidence beneath his hind paw.

The Lady of the Pine smiled sadly. *And my most loyal one; even he is rather flawed.*

Masako blinked her small black eyes. She sniffed and sniffed, her whiskers sweeping. How many pine nuts were left? How could there be any left if the tree was so barren?

Masako-san, the Lady said gently.

Masako stopped sniffing the air and rose up on her hind legs.

Can you free me from my thousand-year-old curse?

Masako nervously scrubbed her whiskers with both paws. *I'll try*, she squeaked. *I can try.*

The Lady of the Pine closed her eyes. Her eyelids were ridged like tree bark. Suddenly she looked so very ancient, Masako could not help but bow with reverence.

The Lady of the Pine began to lower Masako, but she stopped at her midriff. *See*, the Lady whispered. *I am bound, here, and it is killing my spirit, stopping the flow of my life sap.*

Masako gasped. There. A cord. It was tightly bound around her middle. But it was much too narrow and it cut into her dress, her flesh, down to the bone. Golden sap oozed from the circumference of pain. She was slowly being cut in half.

A great spasm shook the Lady, and Masako clung desperately to her fingers with her claws.

The Lady regained control and gracefully dabbed the sleeve of her dress to the corner of her lips. A golden stain marked the silver cloth. I fear my time is near, she said calmly.

What must I do? Masako held the Lady's thumb with both tiny paws. She could try. She could try to get through to the rope with her teeth.

The Lady sadly shook her head. *If it was such a task, little Guardian . . .* she whispered. She raised her free hand toward the great barren tree and pointed upward. High above them, perhaps twenty feet or more, Masako could make out something lighter colored than the bark encircling the massive trunk.

There, the Lady said gently. *That is the binding that is upon me. That is the binding that must be broken.*

Masako closed her eyes. Her tiny heart tripped like a wind-up toy. She didn't have to help her. The pine tree and her spirit were nothing to her. She could just turn around and follow the loud scent trail back to the store and crawl back out to her own world. She had no obligation to come to the Lady's aid. Masako sighed. Opened her eyes.

She leapt.

The thick hide of the tree was ridged and provided easy paw-holds for a scampering rat. But the vertical climb was intense, and Masako was soon panting and wheezing with exhaustion. She was not made for endurance, only for brief spurts of speed. She was extremely grateful not to be able to see details farther than a few feet away. She had a horrible fear of heights.

Masako climbed and climbed. Her paws were growing raw with pain. She could scarcely breathe. She had no idea how much farther she had left to go, and she was growing so weary. But she continued her upward clamber long after she had burned through her initial altruism. Now she was frightened that the only thing keeping her from falling was her upward momentum.

A humming vibration broke through her flutter of heart, the blood ringing inside her ears. Something glowed, pale, white, like a winter grub.

The rope! She had reached the rope that choked the great tree!

Masako set a quivering paw upon the binding, but as soon as her tiny nails pricked the surface, the great rope moved, turning half an inch clockwise away from the point of contact.

From deep inside its roots the tree groaned.

Far, far below a woman's voice gasped.

Oh! Masako gnawed her teeth together, her fur standing on end, her whiskers horizontal with horror.

The rope was alive. And it tightened when it was touched.

How? How on earth was she to take it off if she couldn't touch it?

Incisors clattering, Masako began to crawl horizontally around the tree trunk, directly beneath the squeezing white rope. It was much more difficult going around than it had been climbing upward. Stretched out to the tips of her hind paws, she reached for a distant protrusion of bark. Just as her tiny claws made contact, the brittle piece flaked beneath her weight. Gravity yanked at her round middle, and she screamed as she began to plummet. Her tail, with a life of its own, swung desperately toward the tree and embedded its length inside the ruts of bark just as her opposite paw found purchase. She dug her tiny claws into the bark and sobbed with relief.

When she finally opened her eyes, the great white rope was right before her.

The rope. It was much thicker, here, than it had been where she had started.

It was not the same width all the way around.

What did that mean?

Masako climbed more carefully, planting her tail in the grooves of the tree before moving forward. One inch at a time, she slowly made her way around the trunk, her ears and tail growing red from the blood and exertion. She would climb around the ring of rope. To see if there was a flaw, a weakness that she might discover. To somehow break the binding.

She had rounded over three-quarters of the massive trunk. The rope had gradually widened, until, at one point, it was easily three times her width, but after that it had begun to slowly taper once more.

She had never once seen a spot where it was weakened or frayed. She dared not touch it again, to check, in case it choked the Lady further. She wouldn't even let her sensitive whiskers whisper over the surface.

The rope that had been narrowing so subtly suddenly bulged. Thick, rounded. The fur along her spine tingled with abject disgust. She would have retched if rats were capable of retching. But she only convulsed with revulsion, red tears of stress forming in the corners of her eyes.

Even as her very essence screamed at her to flee, she continued onward. Looking for the weakest point of the binding rope.

The bulging roundness continued until it came to a point where what might be the tail end of the rope seemed to be embedded *inside* the bulbous portion. There was nothing on the rope that suggested weakness. The only change was one thick black vertical line, a marking of some kind, and the place where the two ends appeared to be attached.

Movement. The vertical black line was slowly growing thinner, finer, even as it drew closer toward Masako, who clung fiercely to the bark with all her claws.

It was an eye.

The black vertical stripe was its pupil.

Of a snake.

The largest snake in the world. Squeezed tightly around the Lady Pine, its tail clamped inside its jaws.

Masako screamed.

The snake tightened its noose; a wet cracking sound rang from below.

No! Masako screamed. She flung herself at the snake and began biting in a crazed frenzy. But the snake's scales were not mortal. Masako's teeth skittered and clattered against its skin, as if she were biting metal. And still she did not desist. She bit and screamed, bit and screamed, until her small ineffectual teeth splintered into fragments. Her muzzle red with blood, she spat out her teeth, despair filling her tiny fluttering heart.

She could not help the Lady.

They would both die.

Why should two die? When it could be one?

Masako shivered with exhaustion. Her mouth, her paws, a mess of broken teeth, ripped claws.

She moved. Crawled toward the rounded point of the snake's snout and discerned its narrow nostrils. She scrambled up the slippery form to crouch enticingly close. Her shivering rodent life, her tripping vibrant heart. The scent of her rich blood, the pulsing warmth of her individual life. She twitched her tail so that his eyes had something seductive to trace as her scent began to seep into his time-dulled reptilian brain.

Come, take this life, Masako invited. Flicking her paws. Scraping her claws against the coarse bark.

The snake's scales shrieked metallic as he loosed his hold from his tail and whipped his head around.

He clamped down with the hunger of a thousand years.

Bright red light roared behind Masako's eyes.

She thought she heard a gasp far far below.

She could not feel the snake's fangs as they began to plummet. They twisted through the cold night, like acrobats, like falling angels.

The air was screaming.

It came so fast she didn't gasp.

She was surrounded in darkness.

Falling, falling.

ჩ   ჩ   ჩ

Rain fell upon her face, icy cold, shocking. She opened her eyes, and her entire body seized with pain. She felt as though she had been crawling over a mountain of broken glass.

Copper taste in her mouth.

She could see. Forest. Wet and cold with morning. Her

breath misting in front of her face. Blood on yellow fallen leaves. She ran her tongue over her teeth.

Several were missing. And her head ached. Like she had been punched and kicked. An aching fire in her fingers. She raised her hands and stared with confusion.

Not at the raw, bloody palms and lost fingernails.

But her hands.

They were like a stranger's.

Creased and worn, filthy, bloody, and so human. No longer a rat. She shook her head. And frowned at the heaviness of her head, the weight and the surreal length of her matted locks.

Her wretched hair, covered in pine needles, twigs, and brambles, was long enough to reach the back of her calves. . . .

Her thoughts churned so slowly. There must be a reason, she thought vaguely. The Lady . . . Had she failed her after all?

Masako raised her head.

She was in a forest. Early evening, a red cast to the glimmer of skies between the thick branches of trees, birds twittering and chirruping unseen, and somewhere a woodpecker's staccato. The distant roar of traffic, commuters wending their way home. The dark silhouette of a torii against the backdrop of trees.

It was the gate at the Shinto shrine. The one she had gone to during a school trip in elementary school when they were studying leaves. She had friends, then. It had been such a pleasant excursion. . . .

Something caught the corner of her eye.

A ragged piece of rope.

Lying on the moss at the base of a large worn pine tree with a curiously pinched middle.

Masako's breath caught in her throat.

She stumbled toward the tree and gently traced her fingers over the indented bark, the place of its deformity. Small threads were caught within the tree's fiber, as if it had tried to grow around the binding. It oozed with golden sap, but the rope had been somehow torn off. The tree was wounded, possibly mortally, but it was finally free.

It was one of the knotted ropes that Shinto priests tied around special trees. But this pine—it had somehow been forgotten a long, long time ago. Off the main pathways, away from the shrine, it had continued growing with no one to loosen the binding as she grew, no one to tend to her needs.

As Masako turned away, she let the rope fall to the moss bed. Plastic Hello Kitty slippers. There. She would have laughed if she had any strength remaining. She toed them on and began walking toward lights that were beginning to wink into existence as evening turned toward night.

卐 卐 卐

She finally reached her neighborhood as the sun was beginning to rise. She had no recollection of the path she took. Only the numbed sense of relief when she saw the familiar streets.

Only—

Only . . . they were familiar . . . but there was a certain *off*-ness. Like how she would feel if someone had gone into her bedroom while she was away, and then she had returned to find that everything had been rearranged.

The houses were almost the same. The trees were almost the same.

I am half-dreaming, Masako thought. I am half-asleep.

She clattered through the metal gate of her house and opened the door with her key.

The house smelled familiar. Yet musty. A little dirty. How unlike her mother, Masako thought numbly as she toed off her house slippers.

Her legs wobbled so much she had to crawl up the stairs on her hands and knees. Her raw palms, which had dried out during the long walk home, broke open beneath the weight of her body. She left red bloody handprints on the pale wood floor, her dirty long hair trailing behind her. She crawled down the hallway and rose up, once, to her knees, to open her door. She crawled into her room, her den, her safe hollow. And locked the door.

ᔆ   ᔆ   ᔆ

Knocking.

Insistent.

Masako pulled her blanket over her pounding and aching head. Something prickled unpleasantly beneath her back. She reached down and retrieved a dried twig. She slid her hand out the side of her comforters and dropped the debris onto the floor.

"Masako-chan," her mother's voice called. It was toneless. Nothing inflected. It wasn't a collage of emotions. But flat. As if she didn't feel any longer.

Masako raised her head.

Her mother's voice.

The same.

But different.

"Masako-chan," her mother repeated. "Moriya-san from Community Health is here to see you."

Moriya, Masako mouthed, painfully with her swollen mouth.

"Masako-san," a female voice rang out, like a wind chime on a clear summer morning. "Please come out. I would like to see you to thank you."

A choking sound.

Her mother wasn't crying.

She was laughing.

"Thank her!" she exclaimed. "Thank her for what? You are madder than she is. Coming here for fifteen years, every Monday through Saturday. And she has never once opened the door. Never once acknowledged you. And you want to thank her!" She laughed and laughed, and it was the ugliest thing Masako had ever heard.

Fifteen years?

What was her mother talking about?

Masako stared down at her ravaged hands.

The skin was slightly wrinkled. Diamond-patterned, with a crisscross of lines. The skin was not fine and smooth with the elasticity of youth.

Hand trembling, she grabbed her hank of long hair. There were white strands in among the black.

Fifteen *years* . . .

She tottered to her vanity, which was covered in a dusty blanket. She ripped it off, the clatter of items knocked off the stand as the clouds of dust were caught in diagonal lines of golden light.

Fifteen years . . .

Three stripes of light fell across her face.

A tormented overweight girl did not look back at her.

The person looking back was a woman. Grime and years

etched into her skin. A mass of knotted and filthy hair surrounded her face. Her mouth an open pucker of newly lost
teeth.

The floor tilted to one side and she staggered, grabbing
hold of the stand with one grubby hand.

What had happened to her? What had been done to her?

Masako's lower lip wobbled.

How could she have lost so much?

So quickly?

Fury roared inside her ears. It burned her throat and filled
her maw.

She lurched to her bedroom door and wrenched it open.

Her mother, back curved with age, hair white and bedrag-
gled, raised a trembling hand to her wrinkled mouth. Her eyes
were wide with shock.

Masako stared back. Disbelievingly.

Everyone . . . not just her . . .

"Masako-chan?" her mother croaked. "Masako-chan . . .
you've opened your door. After fifteen years. After fifteen
years," her voice quavered in a low wail. Of relief, of sorrow.

A strong odor. Sharp. Sweet.

A second person, slightly behind her aged mother, stepped
forward.

The woman, dressed in a navy blue skirt suit, looked like
any middle-aged government employee. She even had a name
tag clipped to her chest. MORIYA. Her eyes. They were filled with
myriad emotions. But strongest of all was respect.

The neat nondescript woman gracefully knelt to the dusty
hallway floor without a hint of distaste or self-consciousness.
She placed something at Masako's feet, then bowed low.

"Thank you, Masako-san," she said, her voice throbbing.

"You have saved my life. I am in your debt. I, and all of my kin, will always be here for you should you ever need assistance. We will never forget." The woman rose. She did not wipe the dust off her knees. Moriya-san's eyes blazed, and Masako lowered her gaze with fear and confusion.

"You succeeded when everyone else failed," Moriya-san said softly. "You are truly remarkable."

Masako blinked, rubbed her eyes with the back of her hand.

The thing on the floor.

It was a length of tattered rope, gray with lichen and years.

The air in the hallway was filled with the biting sweet scent of pine.

Moriya-san held out her hand.

Masako, after several seconds, raised her arm waist high, palm facing upward.

Yes. She wanted to return to the forest. Let her leave human life with its pain and disappointments. She had never felt so alive as she did in that night forest. She wanted a pine seed with every cell of her body. Let it take her back to that place. She did not care that time passed more quickly for rats if she could live so vibrantly.

Moriya-san wrapped her fingers gently around her hand.

There was no seed.

"Come," Moriya-san said softly. "You may return to the forest when you come to your life's end, but you still have much to do in this world, my Guardian and Hero."

Masako slowly raised her head.

A roaring filled her head, a thundrous waterfall.

To leave her sanctuary without the cover of night—

To leave her sanctuary in the company of others—

She would self-destruct, she would fall to dust. She would be a mortal, exposed, naked among strangers. . . .

Moriya-san's eyes shone with a golden light. "Come," she said firmly.

Masako closed her eyes.

She stepped over the threshold.

Her mother gasped.

The floorboards of the hallway were cool beneath Masako's aching feet. She could feel her heart pounding in her palm. Moriya-san squeezed her hand with gentle strength.

Outside a small bird trilled, liquid, melodic. A distant train's clatter punctuated the tofu seller's scratchy nasal recording as he peddled his wares in their neighborhood. The sound of the plaintive horn on his small truck receded as he turned onto another street.

Moriya-san slowly led Masako toward the stairs that descended into light.

Masako did not burst apart into atoms.

She lived.

HIROMI GOTO was born in Japan and immigrated to Canada as a young child. Her novel *The Kappa Child* was the 2001 winner of the James Tiptree Jr. Award and was on the final ballot for the Sunburst Award and the Spectrum Award. In the same year she also published a children's fantasy novel, *The Water of Possibility*. Her first novel for adults, *Chorus of Mushrooms*, was the recipient of the regional Commonwealth Writer's Prize for Best First Book, and was a co-winner of the Canada-Japan Book Award. Her first collection of short stories, *Hopeful Monsters*, was published in 2004. Her latest novel, an epic genre-bending fantasy called *Half World*, was published by Penguin Canada in 2009 and will be published by Viking in the United States.

Her Web site is www.hiromigoto.com

⟡⟡

Author's Note

Currently I live and dream in British Columbia. Every day, I read, rather compulsively, several online newspapers, one of them the English version of a Japanese journal. I like to have a window open, even if it's not a "neutral" framing, into the happenings of the country and people of my cultural heritage. And I can't help but see how despair manifests in different ways in different cultures/countries. Long-term acute social withdrawal wreaks devastation upon the sufferers and their families. It has taken a particular form in Japan, but the triggers to the withdrawal are experienced the world over. Excessive social pressure, rigid parental expectations, school bullying; sometimes, hiding away is the most rational thing to do. But the retreat can turn into a prison sentence . . . and the *hikikomori* can lose the capacity to reenter the world. But I believe. I believe in the power of transformation, both literal and symbolic. Before we can change we must be able to imagine it. And if there is no spirit left inside you to begin this journey of the imagination, turn to the earth. The forest. The stream. Touch the bark of a living tree. See the flit of a chickadee. The perfection of the dragonfly's flight. The loyalty of rats. Leave the concrete and the walls. Enter the living. Breathe.

(And a really good counselor is also capable of bringing light to a darkened path—so I have found.)

THE COMEUPPANCE OF CREEGUS MAXIN

Gregory Frost

A curious event happened this morning when I read the latest news from my brother, and it caused me to cast my mind back some twenty years to the spring of 1908. That was the spring when Mary had to sell off her father's farm, and most of the folks in the _____ Valley had rode up for the auction of the farm tools and possessions and whatnot, and I suspect many of them were bidding high 'cause they felt kindly toward Mary.

The fall before, her daddy'd up and left her all by herself out there. Mary's mama had died bringing her into the world, and there weren't any brothers or sisters. Maybe that was just as well, because Creegus Maxin wasn't much good as a farmer and was worse as a man.

A bunch of us boys was sitting there that day, talking about nothing in particular. We'd been dragged out to the farm by our parents, but we weren't bidding and had no opinions anybody wanted to hear, so we'd been turned loose.

Even though the nights were near freezing lately, that day

it was Hades hot, and we sat on some hay bales against the barn side. That hay had been baled by none other than Mary herself, and we took turns sneaking glances at her across the yard, not wanting to reveal how impressed we all were. I don't believe there was a boy in fifty miles that wasn't sweet on Mary. She was a year older than me, and a tomboy who could match all of us in any roughhousing we had in mind.

About the time the auction started in on the household furnishings—I remember them bidding on a piecrust table— Doc MacPhellimey wandered over to us. Doc was a tall, you might say spindly, man, much admired if not outright loved for his gentle ways and his healing gifts. Doc had "the sight," as they say. He could look at someone who was sick and just know what was to be done, even when there was nothing could be done at all. Among the men, our fathers, he was also particularly popular for his loquaciousness over a pint or two of beer. Doc could take the simplest recounting of events and make it magical when he talked of it.

That afternoon he sat down with us on the hay and said, "So, you fellers, what's the topic of the hour?"

Davy Crockett (I swear that was his name) answered, "Oh, Doc, you know. We's feeling kind of bad about Mary, and wonderin' 'bout what's gonna happen to her."

"And," I added, because I wasn't going to leave it with that joker Davy, "thinking that maybe she's better off without that Creegus Maxin in her life."

Doc took out his clay pipe and a small oilcloth pouch of tobacco, and he started packing the pipe while he spoke. "Well, now, she's like kin to you all. You've grown up with her, and you know things about her and Creegus that your parents probably pretend you don't, just like they pretend they don't know 'em, neither."

That right there was one of the things about Doc MacPhellimey and us—he could get inside the truth of something in a way you trusted, when you knew the rest of the grown-ups would hem and haw and change the subject.

"Also, you're right," he said, looking at me. "She's had the devil of a winter, but she's *much* better off without him."

Johnny McClendon put in, "My da says he run off with a floozy. Run off to Chicago."

"What's a floozy?" asked Luke Willette, who was eight that year.

Doc didn't answer Luke's question, but he leaned in close, real conspiratorial like, and said, "I'll tell you boys a secret. I *know* what happened to Creegus Maxin." The way he said it, his eyes aglitter, made the hair prickle on my arms. He leaned back then for a moment and, producing a match, struck it against a barn door hinge. With Doc, this was an indication that he was going to launch into a story, and I saw a couple of men on the outskirts of the auction crowd nudge each other and turn in our direction while he was getting the pipe lit. A moment later he crushed the head of the match between his nicotine-brown fingers, then leaned forward again.

"Were any of you boys in town last October when Mary brought Creegus in to see me? She was driving the buckboard, looked to be alone, and I noticed as she pulled up outside my office that she was sitting kind of hunched and uncomfortable herself. I was all alone at the time, and I got up from my desk to see what it was about.

"Creegus, he'd been lying flat in the back of the wagon. He

pushed himself up as I came out, and kind of skooched to the end of the buckboard. Before he got down he slid out a long-handled shovel that had been at his side. I looked to Mary as I passed her, but she just sat staring into her hands, as if the reins had burned the skin off 'em and she didn't know what to do next.

"Her old man, now, he was hobbling around the wagon, all his weight on that shovel head, and his knee bent, his foot up behind him. I asked him, 'What is it happened to you, Creegus?' When he came near, I could smell the whiskey coming out of his skin in the heat and see that his eyes were swimming with it—something I never want to see on you boys, ever.

"Creegus, he launched into his story so hard that I could tell he'd been worrying it the whole way in from his farm. 'That damn dray did it,' he said. 'I thought he'd gone lame on me, but he'd just throwed a shoe off'n that hind leg of his, and I had took him in the barn and had ahold of him by the pastern, bent and trapped betwixt my knees and I guess I'd put one or two nails into him and was reaching for the next. They was on the sawn-off stump right beside me, and that damned horse pulls hisself right outten my grip and drops that hoof straight down to my foot. And that iron shoe come loose on the way down, so it hit me first and then his hoof 'bout drove it into the ground right through me. Doc, it was like my toes was being sliced off, and my whole head had like a sun explodin' in it.' And then he cursed and he spat. 'When I could see clear again,' he said, 'I grabbed my birch switch and I flogged that damn dray within an inch. My foot was like fire itself but I wasn't gonna let him off on account of that, nossir!' And I shook my head and told him, 'Yes, certain I am you taught that horse his lesson.'"

Luke had his face all screwed up. "But that horse didn't do nothing," he said. "Was the man dropped his foot."

Doc nodded and said, "You're right about that, young Luke." Four or five of the men had come up by then. One of them set a Mason jar on the hay beside Doc and then moved off to listen with the others.

Doc paused to take a sip, and he smiled. "I helped Creegus inside. Mary hung back on the wagon. Now that boot was on him so tight that I wanted to cut it off, but he wouldn't have it. Said he couldn't afford boots and I wasn't about to ruin that one. He said he'd wear the boot till he healed if he had to. But you know, I couldn't have that or I'd be cutting his leg off by Christmas. I soaked a cloth in ether and held it to his face and put him out cold. Then I worked that boot off like he'd asked, even though it surely didn't improve things for him. The foot was filthy, but even after I washed it clean, it looked like an eggplant with toes. That horseshoe had come down on what's called the cuneiform, and I expect it had fractured right straight across his foot. If you break one bone in your foot, boys, you're like to break a dozen. I bandaged it up tight so everything would line up all right, and left him sleeping on the table. He was going to have to be off that foot the whole of the winter, and that meant Mary would have to make do all by herself as well as tending to him. So I needed to talk to her.

"She was still sitting up behind the horse. I made her get down and come inside with me. She wouldn't meet my eye, and about every step she took she winced. She didn't want to go first through my gate, but I insisted, and when I got a look at her from the back I could see why. There were blotches on that gingham dress. I knew well enough it was blood. I took her into the back room, away from her old man. Turned up a lamp and said, 'All right now, Mary, you need to take down your dress and let me have a look at that back of yours. You don't have to say one word to me, because I'm going to know when I see it. So you can tell your daddy that you said nothing to Doctor MacPhellimey.'

"She had tears on her face, but she nodded and did as I told her. The camisole she had on was worse than the dress. Fairly striped with blood, it was. I saw clear enough that the plow horse wasn't the only thing Creegus had beaten that morning. Mary, that brave girl, had gotten between the poor horse and her crazy father and Creegus had kept right on going. Terrible welts. The camisole was stuck to her, so I had to peel it off. She near fainted from that, and then she hugged herself to me and cried her heart out. Creegus'd whipped her all the way to her legs. I cannot imagine how she'd driven the buckboard into town. And you just imagine, you boys—she'd had to change clothes first, to hide what he'd done before she brought him in to me. Well, I dressed her wounds and let her rest awhile, but when I tell you she's a strong young woman, I mean she's stronger than most of the men hereabouts to take what she did."

He didn't have to convince any of us how tough she was, and I think in some way he was speaking more to the men.

"When her father woke up, I loaded him none too gently in the back of his wagon, helped her up onto the seat, and off they went. I gave it a full day, and then I went out there.

"I'd told him to stay off the foot, and he took to that as you would expect. Had himself propped up in the front room in the rocker with his foot up on a keg, like some grand old king. The place reeked on account of him using his chamber pot that she had to empty whenever he gave a holler. The foot was still ugly and dark, but the swelling had gone down. Since he couldn't follow us anyhow, I had Mary take me out to the barn so I could look at her back once more. It was bruised all over, but the wounds had responded to the salve and were healing. I'm certain she has scars from it to this day. I applied more salve to her, and then I looked in on the horse. Poor old thing had done nothing to deserve the beating he'd taken—across his flanks, throat, even his muzzle. Insects crawled all over him, feeding off his open sores. They rose up like a cloud when I stepped into the stall. He was lucky he hadn't lost an eye. I spent some time on cleaning his wounds, too, and I feared for him.

"I walked Mary back inside, where Creegus demanded to know what I was doing. 'Fixing your damage,' I told him, and he snarled back at me, 'Who told you to fix anything?' Now, you know, for an ailing patient to ask you that, they just aren't right in the head.

"People do rarely appreciate hearing about their own short-comings, but I couldn't hold my tongue. 'You know,' I said, 'for a man who can't afford a pair of boots, you've maybe killed your plow horse. You going to strap that plow to yourself come spring?' He laughed and said he'd strap it onto Mary if that horse died, and just maybe he'd nail some shoes onto her feet if he felt the urge. I told him then he had no business beating animals and children for his mistakes.

"He tried to shoot straight out of that rocker, but all he managed to do was knock over the keg. It rolled aside and his heel hit the floor so hard you could hear his teeth creak with the pain. 'She's my *property*, same as that dray. I got the right to treat her howsoever I like, and nothin' wrong about it. I go to church same as you, Doc, same as any. I'm as God-fearing as the whole damned town put together.'

"'Yes, you are,' I replied, 'on account of you have a lot more *cause* to fear Him than any of your neighbors do.' We both knew what I knew then, and there was no reason pretending otherwise. He told me to leave and not return. He'd have his foot rot and kill him before he'd let me in his house again. I tell you, the thing I wonder most about Mary's mother is that she survived with that bastard long enough to deliver a child."

He paused then. His pipe had gone out. He'd been so intent, telling us boys this story, that now he took stock, as if surprised by the audience he'd acquired: maybe a dozen adults, and all of them solemn and a little shy, embarrassed by the things they knew about Maxin, things they'd let be. And all of them, I suspect, knew there were no secrets from Doc MacPhellimey.

He knocked his pipe and lit it again, then continued.

"I had Mary come by my house whenever she went to town, or my office if I wasn't at home. She healed up fast, but the dray died and there was nothing to be done. She couldn't drag him out of the stall, either, so she covered him up there and left him. Her daddy's foot ought to have healed, but that fool just couldn't stay off it. He'd get liquored, tell her what she cooked was no good, and throw the plate at the fireplace, and then try to grab her, so blind in his fury that he forgot he couldn't stand. I told her to tell him we'd have to cut that foot off if he didn't take better care. I should have known better, because when he learned that I'd spoken to her, he just got up on that foot again and tried to thrash her. There are some people, boys, who are just too stupid. Don't ever be one of them."

Doc smoked awhile in silence then. Finally, I had to ask. "Well, what happened?"

Doc pointed that pipe at me. "Well, Thomas, come November first, Creegus Maxin himself rolled up to my house on his buckboard. All alone he was. Had a shotgun next to him on the seat. He got down out of that wagon and he was truly what you'd call hopping mad. He'd cut himself a kind of crutch out of some branch, or maybe Mary had done it for him, and he limped about on that with his shotgun tucked up under his arm. I could see his toes, which were pinkish from the cold but otherwise down to normal size. He was healing in spite of himself. He glared at me with those bloodshot eyes, jerked that shotgun around, and told me I wasn't caring for him properly. And he accused his daughter of trying to poison him."

McClendon's pa was the sheriff, and all steely-eyed he said, "You think she did, Doc? You think that young woman poisoned her father?"

Doc blinked, as if the idea astonished him. "Why, Rory," he said, "that's ridiculous. Not that I'd blame her if she'd put an ax through his skull, but fact is, I *know* what happened to him, as I was after telling these boys here. That's where this story's heading."

The sheriff said, "Wait now. You've known all this time and you never said a thing? We've ridden the countryside this winter looking for him. He left debts he's run away from. Why do you think she's selling off most of the house?"

"I never said a thing because it has no bearing. The man is gone, the farm belongs to his daughter, and there's no one going to dispute it. The debts were there no matter what, and she's paying them off, after which she'll own the farm free and clear if she wants it."

McClendon huffed but said, "All right, what *did* happen to him?"

Doc said, "Well, I'm coming to it." He picked up the Mason jar and had another sweet long pull on that clear liquor before setting it down. "I intended to tell these boys, but now you're here, I guess you'll hear it, too, and be remanding me over soon enough."

The men exchanged startled glances, and we boys did likewise. Was our decent, kind Doc MacPhellimey confessing to a murder?

"I said to Creegus, 'I want to show you something down in the stable.' He demanded to know what it was. 'Well,' I told him, 'you killed off *your* horse, and I've got a special one to take his place.' He wanted me to bring the horse up to the house, but I refused, and he grumbled and cursed all the way down there. We reached the shadows of the stable and I asked him, 'Do you know what day this is?' Sure he did, it was November the first. 'That's so,' I agreed. 'And did you know, also, that my people come from Ireland?' Well, sure, he thought he knew that and what difference did it make anyway? I said, 'The thing of it is, in Ireland, there's a fella called a *poukha*. He's a fine feller all in all. And every year on November the first he receives the gift of prognostication. That is, he can look into the future and see how things will go, and if you catch the *poukha* in the mood, he'll share what he knows with you.'

"Creegus blinks at me, finally says, 'So what?'

"'So,' I says, 'do you want to hear it for yourself then?'

"'What, that you're one of them *poukha* fellas?' I nod, and he sneers and says, 'Sure, you tell me my future.' Then he trains that gun on me, like if I don't give it up to his satisfaction he'll shoot me right there.

"And so I did. I told him, 'The most important thing is your line, and that's good news, on account of your daughter's going to do well for herself. She's going to marry a fine young fella name of Thomas.'"

He stared straight at me when he said it, and Davy and Charlie and the others hooted and shoved at me till one of the men told them to settle down.

Doc said, "Creegus sneered at me, 'Well, isn't that fine? Why would I care a whit what happens to that girl? I want to know about *me*, Mr. Fortune-teller.'

"'You?' said I. 'Ah, the truth of that is, you have no future at all.'"

Doc leaned back on the hay and smoked with an odd smile on his face. To no one in particular he added, "And wasn't I right, too?"

McClendon spluttered, "But what happened to him, dammit? You keep putting that off."

"I showed him that special horse I'd told him about. You'll know this, McClendon, even if the others don't."

"I know what a *poukha* is, all right. It's a nightmare horse that you never want to ride, so help ya God."

"Just so. Well, right there in front of Creegus I changed so fast he couldn't even find the trigger on that shotgun. I flipped the damnable fool up on my back and rode away with him, all the way out to Shandhill Butte. There I stamped the ground three times and the hillside split wide apart and I rode him right inside. He screamed the whole way till the earth closed up on him. And if anyone's to ask, that's where he is right now."

Doc hoisted the jar and toasted the openmouthed crowd. I think I could have counted to ten before they all burst out laughing. McClendon slapped both thighs and doubled over.

He waved his hand and said, "Doc, you old coot. First you're avowing I have to lock you up for murder, and then you're after telling me that you're a *poukha*!"

"Jiminy Christmas," Alan Petris guffawed. "Ever'body knows Creegus skedaddled to Chicago, where he's got some cousins or something stashed away."

"With a floozy!" cried Luke, and that set everybody off again. They slapped Doc on the back and clinked jars with him, and the conversation slowly turned into a round of stories about Mary's father and where he'd gone, and even some reminiscences of things they'd seen him do. Doc, the mad storyteller, had got their goat, and now somehow it was all right to speak of things otherwise withheld.

One by one, we all went off to the auction or to the trestle table that had been set up and now brimmed with food. Slowly after that, folks headed home, most with a few items in their wagons; parents called their boys to come along. About half the people were gone by sunset.

Later, after dark, I was out strolling on my own, just killing time. Somebody'd stoked up a bonfire because the night had gotten cold. My family were one of the last to leave, as my mother was part of a committee at the church that were taking it upon themselves to help Mary settle things after the auction.

As I passed the barn someone said, "Thomas," and I must have jumped halfway to the moon. There was Doc, still sitting on that hay bale like only a minute had gone by.

"Why, Doc," I said, "you gave me a fright."

"Oh, now, I couldn't frighten you, lad." He struck a match, and the flame caught and glimmered in his eyes as he lit his pipe. The fire seemed to be watching me. "Tell me something, Thomas. Shandhill Butte, that'd be on your property, wouldn't it?"

My family owned the land, right enough, and I agreed with him.

"That's good, because, you know, when I split that hillside open, I saw the richest vein of gold in there. Rich as the gold rush itself. I'm thinking you might be sure to keep that parcel of land in the family, as your young lady will be needing to live in style, and you'll wish to provide for her."

I looked at him, at his eyes that I knew to be gentle gleaming like hellfire in the glow of that clay pipe. "How can you know that about Mary? About me?"

"How?" he answered, and drew the pipe from between his lips. "How does anybody know about anybody?" That was all he would say on the matter.

§　§　§

I probably hadn't thought about Doc MacPhellimey since his funeral. He was right about Mary. She'd had her eye on me for awhile, and with my mother taking her under her wing, we were thrown together, and something caught between us. In a year's time we were engaged. The other boys telling everyone about Doc's prediction probably helped things along considerably, too. When my father died in '14, I took over the farm. Next year we sold off a piece of it, but I hung on to that seemingly worthless Shandhill Butte, and paid an assayer to take a look at it. Sure enough, just like Doc had sworn, there was gold in it. More gold than you'd know what to do with. With the money that brought us, I bought this ranch in Oregon, and Mary, the children, and I moved up here. My brother and his wife took over the farm. I guess it was two years after that he

wrote to tell me Doc had passed. The entire town turned out
for his wake. I'd have liked to have been there, too. They filled
the whole of the day and night, my brother wrote, with stories about Doc, including how he claimed to have taken away
Mary's father in fair payment for his cruelty. Sometime in the
night, a couple of the revelers came stumbling inside to announce they'd seen a black horse with flaming eyes run past
the house. Nobody believed them, and a few of the more sober
participants pointed out that you couldn't *see* a black horse at
night in the first place.

While I'd never quite forgot nor resolved that story of Doc's,
much less his forecast of my future, what brought him to mind
today was another letter from my brother. He wrote:

*Today, Tommy, the mining crew found the oddest thing
in the hillside at Shandhill. It was a body. It was too
deep in the ground to have been a proper burial. There
was bits of cloth, like from rotted denims, so it wasn't
any native burial either. The strangest thing, Tommy,
was that the fella'd been buried along with a length of
wood tucked under the bones of his arm like a crutch.
Nobody has the slightest idea how that body got wedged
in that hill so deep they didn't come upon him for all
these years, and nobody has any idea who it might have
been, save for your old friend Davy Crockett. He's now
the foreman of the crew, by the way. Davy swears on a
stack of Bibles that we've found us Creegus Maxin for
sure and that Doc MacPhellimey must have been, he
says, "a pooka." He says you'll know what that means,
even if hardly anybody else does, including me. I expect*

you won't want to mention any of this to Mary on ac-
count of him saying it's Creegus we found, but I thought
you might want to know.

My brother was right about that. Nobody's likely to believe
Davy, what with his reputation for pulling folks' legs, but I
know. I've known ever since that night at Mary's farm when I
took one last look back at Doc across the yard and saw instead
that black horse just disappearing beyond the barn, silent as
moonlight.

GREGORY FROST is a writer of fantasy, science fiction, and supernatural thrillers. His latest work is the critically acclaimed Shadowbridge fantasy duology, *Shadowbridge* and *Lord Tophet*.

His previous novel was the historical thriller *Fitcher's Brides*, a reimagining of the fairy tale "Bluebeard." Recent short fiction includes contributions to *Realms of Fantasy* magazine, to Ellen Datlow's *Poe: 19 New Tales Inspired by Edgar Allan Poe*, an anthology commemorating the bicentennial of Poe's birth, and to the anthology *Urban Werewolves*, edited by Darrell Schweitzer. He is one of the Fiction Writing Workshop Directors at Swarthmore College in Swarthmore, Pennsylvania. His Web site is www.gregoryfrost.com and his blog is at frostokovich.livejournal.com.

i⅄ C⅄

Author's Note

The first thing I should tell you is that I've no idea just where this story came from. My experience of *poukhas* involves Jimmy Stewart, taverns, and invisible rabbits. But I have a number of books on Celtic lore, and one of them mentioned in its description of the *poukha* (spelled one of at least ten different ways), that on November first it is gifted with the ability to see the future. That, and that it isn't generally a giant rabbit, it's a "nightmare" horse, black and terrifying, with fiery eyes, and it has a habit of taking hapless individuals for some *serious* rides. Somewhere out of that mix of research and a few days of contemplation—which for me is unusually quick—I came up with a rough outline of the story you've read. I thought I'd invented the name of the villain, but it turns out there are Cree-guses in the world, too. Beyond that, I had enormous fun with the voices of it—the first a sort of Mark Twain or Garrison Keillor narrator's voice, the second a bit more Irish on the part of the good doctor. His name, by the way, was lifted from a Flann O'Brien novel. It was the name of a *poukha* in *his* book, too. So you might say I had a bit more experience of the dark pranksters than I realized. Sneaky buggers.

GANESHA

Jeffrey Ford

On a floating platform adrift in the placid Sea of Eternity, Ganesha sat on his golden throne beneath a canopy of eight cobras. The eyes in his elephant head gazed out past the moon; his big ears rippled in the breeze. Each of his four human hands was occupied, so his trunk curled up to scratch his cheek; the itch was a manifestation of evil in the million and second reality. In one hand he held the pointed shard of his broken tusk, using it to write on parchment held by a second hand. In his third hand was a lotus flower, and his fourth hand was turned palm out to show a red tattoo of a cross with bent arms, meaning, *be well*. He wore baggy silk pants the color of the sun, but no shirt to cover his chest and bulging gut. His necklace was a live snake, as was his belt. At his feet sat Kroncha, the rat, nibbling a stolen *modaka* sweet.

In the west, something fell out of the sky, sparking against the night. Ganesha watched its descent, and when it collided with the sea, a great sizzle and a burst of light becoming dark again, he marked the spot by pointing his trunk. He stood and stretched. "A journey," he said to Kroncha. The rat followed, and they went to the edge of the floating platform where a boat had appeared, an open craft lined with comfortable pillows. In a blink, they were aboard. Ganesha rested his weighty head back, one hand holding a parasol to block the moonlight, and crossed his legs. They remembered only after they had pushed off to bring the *modaka* sweets, and so the sweets appeared. The wind picked up and gently powered the boat to sea.

After a brief eternity, they reached the spot where the object had fallen.

"There it is," said Kroncha, who was sitting atop the parasol. As Ganesha rose, the rat scurried down his back.

The boat maneuvered next to the floating debris. Ganesha leaned over and picked something out of the water. "Look at this," he said, and held up a prayer. It wriggled in his hands for a moment before he popped it in his mouth and ate it.

"Where to this time?" said Kroncha, leaning his elbow against the bowl of sweets, shaking his head.

"My favorite, New Jersey," said Ganesha, and his laughter, the sound of OM, gave birth to realities.

They took the turnpike south from the Holland tunnel, Ganesha perfectly balanced on Kroncha's small back. The rat did seventy-five and complained bitterly of tailgating. At the traffic tie-up, they leaped in graceful arcs from the roof of one car to the next, landing in perfect silence and rhythm. Back on the road, Ganesha eventually gave instructions to take the number 6 exit south. Kroncha complied with relief.

In the next instant, it was the following afternoon, and Kroncha carried Ganesha across a vast, sunburned field toward a thicket of trees next to a lake. In among the trees, there were picnic tables, and sitting at one of them, the only person in the entire park, was a dark-haired teenage girl, smoking a cigarette. She wore cutoff jeans and a red T-shirt, sneakers without socks. When she saw the elephant-headed god approaching, she laughed out loud and said, "I thought you might show up this time. I burned five cones of incense."

"A tasty morsel," said Ganesha as he dismounted from the rat with a little hop. His stomach and chest jiggled. The girl stood and walked toward him. When she came within reach, he lifted his trunk and wrapped it around her shoulders. She closed her eyes and patted it softly twice. "Florence," he whispered in an ancient voice.

"I changed my name," she said, turning and heading back toward the table.

Ganesha laughed. "Changed your name?" he said and followed her. "To what, Mithraditliaminak?"

She took a seat on one side of the bench, and he shimmied as much of his rear end as he could onto the opposite side, lifting hers a couple of inches off the ground. The wooden planks beneath them quietly complained as the two leaned back against the edge of the table.

"Call me Chloe," she said.

"Very well," said Ganesha.

"Florence is a crappy name," she said, "like an old woman with a girdle and a hairnet."

"You have wisdom," said Ganesha, and allowed the bowl of sweets to appear on the table between them.

"Chloe's much more . . . I don't know . . . I love these things," she said, lifting one of the golden rice balls. "How many calories are they, though?"

"Each one's a universe," he said, lifting a *modaka* with the end of his trunk and bringing it to his mouth.

"I'll just have a half," she said.

"She'll just have a half," said Kroncha, who sat at their feet.

"If you bite it, you'll be compelled to finish it," said Ganesha.

Her lips were parting and the sweet was just under her nose. Its aroma went to her eyes, and she saw a beautiful garden alive with butterflies and turquoise birds, but even there she heard his warning.

"No," she said and put the sweet back into the bowl.

"Ah-ha!" he said and picked up the abandoned *modaka*. He stood up suddenly, her end of the bench falling three inches, and he waddled a few feet away from the picnic table. Standing in a small clearing amid the thicket, his elephant head trumpeted, his human legs danced, and his four arms spun. As his clarion note echoed out through the trees and across the field and lake in all directions, he gave a little kick and threw the *modaka* into the sky.

Her gaze followed its trajectory, first golden against the blue day and then, of a sudden, a ball of fire streaking away through the night. The eyeblink replacement of sun with moon nearly made her lose her balance. Still, she managed to watch until the sweet became a star among the million other stars. When Ganesha, glowing slightly in the dark, turned to face her, she clapped for him. He bowed.

Once they were situated back on the bench, the girl lit a cigarette. Ganesha gently waved her smoke away with his ears and curled his trunk over his left shoulder. Kroncha climbed on the bench between them, curled up, and went to sleep.

She leaned forward, her elbows on her knees, and turned her head to look at him. "It's night now?" she asked.

He nodded, pointing to the moon and stars with three of his hands.

"What happened to the day?" she asked.

"You'll get it back later," he said.

"Got my report card today," she said, and took a drag.

"A triumph, no doubt," he said.

"When my father saw it, he checked my pulse. My mother was in tears. I can't help it, though; their frustration is comical to me. A report card. What does it really mean?"

"An excellent question," said Ganesha.

"Should I care?"

"Do you feel as if you should?"

"No," she said, and flicked the glowing butt away onto the dirt.

"You've outwitted that conundrum, then," he said.

She leaned over slightly and began petting the sleeping Kroncha.

"When I saw you in the time of the red leaves, you told me you were in love," said Ganesha.

She smiled. "An elephant never forgets," she said. "I hate that part."

"The young gentleman with the tattoo of Porky Pig on his calf?"

She nodded and smiled. "You know Porky Pig?" she said.

Ganesha waved with all four hands. "Th-th-that's all, folks."

"Simon," she said. "He was okay for a while. We used to bike out to the forest, and he helped me build a little shrine to you out of cinder blocks from the abandoned sand factory. I brought out your picture, and we'd go there at night, drink beer and light incense. He was really cute, but under the cute there was too much stupid. He was always either grabbing my tits or punching me in the shoulder. He laughed like a clown. After I dumped him, I rode out to the forest to the shrine one day and found that he'd wrecked it, torn your picture to scraps, and kicked over the thing we'd built, which, now that I think about it, looked a lot like a barbecue pit. Then he told everyone I was weird."

"Aren't you?" asked Ganesha.

"I guess I am," she said. "Poe's my favorite writer, and I like to be alone a lot. I like the sound of the wind in the trees out by the abandoned factory. I like it when my parents are asleep at night and aren't worrying about me. I can feel their worry in my back. I have a lot of daydreams—being in a war, being married, making animated movies about a porcupine named Florence, running away, getting really good at poetry, having sex, getting really smart and telling people what to do, getting a car and driving all over."

"Sounds like you'll need to get busy," said Ganesha.

"Tell me about it," she said. "My specialty is napping."

"A noble pursuit," he said.

"The other day," she said, "when I took a walk in the afternoon, I went all the way out to the factory. I sat on that big rock next to it and watched the leaves blowing in the wind. In a certain configuration of sky and leaves, I saw this really detailed image of a mermaid. It was like she was there flying through the air."

He closed his eyes and tried to picture it.

"A rabbit hopped out from behind a tree then, and I looked away for a second. When I looked back to the leaves, she was gone. No matter how I squinted or moved my head, I couldn't find her there anymore."

"Nevermore," whispered Kroncha from sleep.

"I thought it might have been a sign from you."

"No," said Ganesha, "that was yours."

"I've wanted to write a poem about it," she said. "I can feel it inside me, there's energy there to do it, but when I sit down and concentrate—no words. All that happens is I start thinking about other stuff. I'm afraid I'll look away from her one day, and she'll be gone, as well, from my memory."

"Well," he said, sitting forward, "am I the destroyer of obstacles or am I not?" As he spoke, the color drained from him and he became gleaming white. Out of thin air appeared four more arms to make eight, and in his various hands he held: a noose, a goad, a green parrot, a sprig of the *kalpavriksha* tree, a prayer vessel, a sword, and a pomegranate. His eighth hand, empty, he turned palm up, as if offering something invisible to her.

"You are definitely the Lakshmi Ganapathi," she said, laughing.

The seven items suddenly disappeared from his hands, but he remained the color of the moon. "Show me the things you think about instead of the mermaid," he said.

"How?"

"Just think about them," he said. "Close your eyes."

She did, but after quite a while, she said, "I can't even picture . . . Oh, wait. Here's something." Her eyes squinted more tightly closed. She felt the image in her thoughts gather itself into a bubble and exit her head. It tickled the lobe of her left ear like a secret kiss as it bobbed away on the breeze. She opened her eyes to see it. There it floated, five feet from them, a clear bubble with a scene inside.

"Who's that?" asked Ganesha.

"My mother," she said.

"She's preparing something."

"Meat loaf."

"Do you like it?" he asked.

"Gross," she said.

"Not exactly a *modaka*," he said. "Let's see more."

She closed her eyes and thought, and eventually the bubbles came in clusters, exiting from both ears. Each held a tiny scene from her life. They bobbed in midair and sailed on the breeze, glowing pale blue. Some had risen to the tallest branches of the trees and some lit snaking paths through the thicket toward the lake or field.

"There goes Simon," she said as the last few bubbles exited her right ear.

"Call them back," said Ganesha.

"How?"

"Whistle," he said.

She did, and no sooner had she made a sound than all of the glowing bubbles halted in their leisurely flights and slowly reversed course. She whistled again, and they came faster and faster, flying from all directions, each emitting a musical note that made their return a song that filled the surrounding thicket. Their speed became dizzying, and then, at once, they all collided, exploding in a wave of blue that swamped the picnic table. The blue blindness quickly evaporated to reveal a man-shaped creature composed of the bubbles. Now, instead of scenes, each globe held an eye at its center. The thing danced wildly before Chloe and Ganesha, sticking out its long, undulating tongue of eyes.

She reared back against the table. "What is it?"

"A demon. We must destroy it," said Ganesha, and leaped off the bench. The ground vibrated with his landing, and this startled the demon, which turned and fled, its form wavering, turning momentarily to pure static, like the picture on the old television in her parents' den.

"Kroncha, to the hunt," said Ganesha, his color changing again, blue and red swirling through moon-white and mixing.

The rat rubbed its eyes, stood up, and jumped down to the ground. As Ganesha squatted upon Kroncha's back, the rat asked, "A demon?"

Ganesha now brandished the point of his broken tusk as a weapon. "Correct," he said. Kroncha inched forward, building speed.

Chloe was stunned by what she'd seen. She wanted to follow but was unable to move.

"I suspected as much from the moment she refused the *modaka*," said the rat.

Ganesha nodded, and they were off.

It wasn't until god and vehicle were just a faint smudge of brightness weaving away through the trees that Chloe overcame the static in her head and woke from amazement. The thought that called her back was that the demon could easily return and she would have to battle it alone. She tasted adrenaline as she bolted from the bench. Across the clearing and into the trees she sprinted, afraid to call out for what might be watching.

At one point, early on, she thought she would catch them, but Kroncha moved deceptively fast, and suddenly the path had disappeared. The ground was uneven and riddled with protruding roots. She hurried as best she could, still driven by fear. "Where's my day?" she whispered. The night was getting cold. She passed through a forest she'd not known existed, waiting for the demon to pounce at any moment and thankful for the moonlight.

The trees eventually gave way to a sandy mountain path littered with boulders. She knew there were no mountains within a hundred miles of where she lived. *I'm in a dream within a dream*, she thought, and climbed up onto a flat rock to rest. Her legs hurt, and she realized she was exhausted. She lay back and looked for her star, but it was lost among the others.

If I fall asleep here and then wake, I'll wake from this dream and be back at the picnic table in late afternoon, she thought. She closed her eyes and listened to the breeze.

She knew she'd slept, but it seemed only for the briefest moment, and when she opened her eyes she groaned to see more night. There was soft sand beneath her, not rock, and it came to her that she was in a new place. Remembering the threat of the demon, she stood quickly and turned in a circle, her hands in fists. The moonlight showed, a few yards away, a mountain wall with a cave opening. Within the cave, she perceived a flickering light.

It's in there, she thought, and at that instant, Ganesha's broken tusk appeared in her left hand. "We must destroy it," she remembered him saying and realized that she'd never retrieve her day unless she confronted the demon. An image came to her mind of her mother making meat loaf and it weighed her down, slowed her, as she moved toward the opening in the mountain. She fought against it, as if against a strong silent wind. And then a cascade of other memories beset her—Simon, her father, her condescending English teacher, a group of kids snickering as she passed, her image in the bedroom mirror. . . . Still she struggled, managing to inch along, drawing closer to the light within. At the entrance, she hesitated, unable to move forward, and then holding the tusk in front of her, point out, she swung her arm, slicing a huge gash in the malevolent resistance. There was a bang, the myriad bubble eyes that composed her demon exploding, and its power over her bled away quickly into the night.

The cave's interior was like a rock cathedral, the ceiling vaulting into the shadows above. Instead of the demon there was a shining blue woman holding a lotus flower, floating six feet off the ground. She wore a jade green gown and a helmet made of gold. The blue vision smiled down upon Chloe, and the girl felt a beautiful warmth run through her, putting her at ease and filling her with energy.

"I am the *shakti*," said the blue woman.

"The power?" asked Chloe.

The woman nodded. She motioned for the girl to sit at the table between them where lay a blank sheet of paper. Chloe sat on the stone bench and turned the tusk around in her hand, from a weapon to a pen. The *shakti* gave her light, and she wrote, the tusk moving like an implement made of water over the page, birthing words almost before she thought them.

A WEEK OF FACES IN THE TREES

I saw her there
with flowing hair
green against the blue

A woman in a tree
a woman of the sea
and then I thought of you

Her tail of leaves
swam through the breeze
she nodded into light

Her eyes were figs
her fingers twigs
outstretched as if in flight

Then I thought of you and me
alone together by the sea,
beneath the sun some time ago

We found blue glass there
amid the clumps of mermaid hair
and I quoted Edgar Allan Poe

"Everything we see and seem
is but a dream within a dream."
You smiled and shook your head

When summers into winters passed
through every different color glass
I learned the lie in what I'd said

The woman in the tree is gone
Out beyond the blue beyond
I turn away and slowly walk

Wondering tomorrow what I'll see
who the blowing leaves will be
what I'll have to say to me when we talk

Back in the late afternoon, at the picnic table in the thicket
by the lake, Florence folded the piece of paper that held her
poem and slipped it into her back pocket. Then she capped her

pen and climbed up on top of the table to sit with legs crossed, staring out at the sun's last reflection on the lake. She had a smoke and watched the world turn to twilight, the stars slowly appear. Among them, she was surprised to be able to identify her own, and she reached up into the sky for it. It burned in her hand at first with a cold fire, but as she drew it toward her mouth, it became the sweet *modaka*.

"A universe," said Kroncha, sitting at the foot of Ganesha's throne on the floating platform in the Sea of Eternity. "She'll have no room for meat loaf tonight."

Ganesha nodded and his stomach jiggled when he laughed, the echo of his mirth pervading a million realities, crumbling a million obstacles to dust.

JEFFREY FORD is the author of the novels *The Physiogno-my*, *Memoranda*, *The Beyond*, *The Portrait of Mrs. Charbuque*, *The Girl in the Glass*, and *The Shadow Year*. His short fiction has been published in three collections: *The Fantasy Writer's Assistant*, *The Empire of Ice Cream*, and *The Drowned Life*. His fiction has won the World Fantasy Award, the Nebula Award, the Edgar Allan Poe Award, and the Gran Prix de l'Imaginaire. He lives in New Jersey with his wife and two sons and teaches literature and writing at Brookdale Community College.

ᓂᎧᏟ

Author's Note

I can't recall when I became aware of Ganesha, the elephant-headed god of the Hindu religion, but it was quite a few years ago. I do recall that his image was immediately pleasing to me. I felt a cosmic mirth behind it—the idea of an elephant head on a man's body, his shameless girth, the fact he rode on a rat, his many arms. After my first meeting with him, I occasionally, over the following years, did haphazard research about his story. What I didn't suspect from the beginning was how very powerful this god was. He's one of the most important figures in the Hindu pantheon. The stories told about him feature earthly desires and mythic implications. He's the Destroyer of Obstacles.

I'd wanted to write about Ganesha for a long time. I could readily see him behind my eyes, involved in a drama. There was one huge obstacle, though. I really didn't know that much about him. The Hindu religion is extraordinarily old and complex, and the more you study Ganesha the more your perception of him changes to reveal some new aspect you'd been previously unaware of.

A few semesters ago, I was teaching a creative writing class, and one of the students was an older gentleman, a retired physician, Dr. Patel. He was a good guy, very smart but very laid-back and with a sense of humor. One day after class, I asked him about Ganesha. Having been born in India and brought up in the Hindu religion, he had what seemed to me a very deep understanding of the subject. He had all kinds of interesting insights and stories about the god.

I told the doctor my plans to write about Ganesha, and I also told him about my trepidation, worrying I didn't know enough. He thought for a moment or two and said to me, "If you write with an open heart, Ganesha will accept it." I thought about that for a year and a half, and then I wrote the story.

If you're interested, there's a lot of information online about Ganesha. As a reference for this story, I used the book, *Ganesha: The Auspicious . . . The Beginning* by Nanditha Krishna and Shakunthala Jagannathan. It's a general source with stories and information and has a lot of great pictures.

THE ELEPHANT'S BRIDE

Jane Yolen

The Elephant's Bride
was not as wide
as her husband, or as deep.

The only trunk she had
was filled with clothes.

Her nose was small,
the septum deviated,
she snored in her sleep,
but not loud enough to wake
her big husband.

The Elephant's Bride
had never slept alone.
Sisters do not own
a single bed,
but sleep

cocooned, spooned
together,
head to heart, heart to head.
She was still a girl
when she was wed.
Now her gargantuan lover
was dead.

He who had been so huge,
was made small by illness.
His ears drooped,
his tail shed hairs,
his eyes seemed scaled,
gray skin paled.
Slump went his great back
And he dropped
right in his track.

She touched one long, cold, tusk,
whispered as he became a husk,
"Go, love, and I will follow."
Better that than a dead elephant's wife.
Widows in her world
had less than a half-life.

It took a derrick and ten men
to lift the corpse
onto the bier.
She set the fire,
then climbed on
the bed of flame,

folded her arms,
closed her eyes,
waited to claim
sweet heaven's surprise.

But with a horrible crack
and a worse crash,
her hopes of heaven
were quickly dashed.
She arose, small,
gray
and covered with ash.

A miracle
or an allegory?
There is no moral here,
no jokes either.
You have a heart of stone
or else you are a believer.
I am neither,
just a teller of gossip,
a memorist, a liar.
Some of us bring water,
some bring alcohol
to fuel the funeral pyre.

JANE YOLEN just counted up her books published—and under contract to be published—and the astonishing number is 320. Of course if you counted her single poems, the count would be much higher. Her first love has always been poetry.

Her Web site is www.janeyolen.com.

Author's Note

I have long been fascinated by the horrifying tradition in India of suttee, in which a widow climbs onto her dead husband's funeral pyre to die with him. I am a recent widow myself. So when I was invited to contribute to this anthology, I was at last able to write about the custom (and my own widowhood) one step removed.

THE CHILDREN OF CADMUS

Ellen Kushner

THE DAUGHTER SPEAKS:

The daughters of Cadmus have a duty to their father's house, and so do all of the sons, as well. And thus it is that we can never be truly happy, my brother and I.

For he loves the night, the strange time when all men are asleep. He loves the swoop and glitter of the stars that the gods have set in the heavens, loves to watch the heroes and the monsters cartwheel their way across the sky until rosy-fingered Aurora strokes them away before Apollo's chariot. Only then will he fall into bed, my big brother, sprawled out on his couch half the day until the sun has passed the zenith of the heavens, when he comes lumbering out of his chamber, blinking and rubbing his eyes, looking for something to eat. I can usually find him something.

It's a wonder my brother and I ever meet at all. For I love the cold gray dawn, when the grass is still wet with dew. I love to be up before everyone except the household slaves, and the keepers of the hounds, readying for the hunt, which I love best of all. The chase through the woods in the waking dawn, the dappled trees and morning shadows, pursuing the sweet, swift animals that we love even as we seek to break them and bring them to their knees to furnish our tables and our bellies and our feasts. I love to run with my spear and my hounds in my short chiton, legs free and arms free. . . .

But those days are finished for me. I am Creusa, the daughter of Autonoë, the daughter of Cadmus, king of Thebes. I am of an age to be married, now.

You will have heard of our grandfather, Cadmus: he who sowed the serpent's teeth, and brought forth a race of warriors to build our fair city of Thebes. He did not do all this alone. The god Phoebus Apollo told Cadmus where to find his fate, and Pallas Athena herself stood by him as he scattered the dragon's teeth across the fields of Boeotia. The gods love our grandfather Cadmus.

And we, in return, must love and honor them.

And so I do. I make my sacrifices to Zeus the Thunderer, to Hera of the Hearth, and to red Mars, fierce in War, who is father to my grandmother Harmonia, whose mother is sea-born Aphrodite.

But it is Artemis, virgin goddess of the hunt, I love. And that is my despair.

THE SON SPEAKS:

My sister Creusa is quite mad. I said as much to my tutor, Chiron the Centaur, and he chided me, as he so often does. He is always whisking his tail at me—it stings but does not really hurt. And I would take ten times that sting to remain his pupil. For while Cadmus and my parents think the great centaur is teaching me hunting, we left that behind long ago. Chiron is a noble archer, true, and I'm not a bad shot thanks to him. But Chiron is a master of the art of healing and knows the movements of the stars.

The stars tell stories. Some of the stars are our own people, taken from the pains of this life up into the heavens. The stars make patterns, too, and surely it all means something. Here on earth, there is pain and blood and strife. But the stars move in an orderly way, pacing out a huge dance across time that no man has seen the end of.

If I watch long enough, I think I might learn.

As it is, I am often forced out of my bed into a cold and drippy day and expected to run about, shouting, following smelly dogs howling to wake the dead. They are perfectly nice dogs, ordinarily, but they become monsters when we hunt. And so I run after poor wild beasts that never did me any harm, to open great wounds in their sides with my spear or my arrows—if the dogs' teeth don't get to them first—to rip open their sleek and beautiful hides and ruin them forever, letting out their life's blood in the process while the poor animals writhe and froth trying to escape.

When I leave this earth, I would not mind becoming a star, or even a full constellation. People will look up at me and tell my story. And I will become part of the great pattern, the great dance.

Chiron says that I should not mock my sister's dreams. He says that our dreams are our truth, even if we cannot achieve them. He says that I should help my sister, if I can, to bear whatever fate the gods choose for her. I'll try.

ॐ   ॐ   ॐ

THE DAUGHTER SPEAKS:

I cannot bear it. I cannot bear to think, because I am a girl, almost a woman now, that my fate will be to become the wife of any man. I wish to follow the goddess. I wish to run with her in the hunt by day, and lie with her and her nymphs by night.

Instead, a man's hands on me? A man's mouth on my lips, a man's body on mine?

The only rough hair and rough skin I want anywhere near me is that of my kill. Rather than yield to a man's touch, I would *become* a lion, a boar, a hare, or a deer, myself.

Such transformations are not unheard of. The stories abound of men and women turned to animals, to trees or flowers or even stars, in order to escape a more terrible fate. The gods can be cruel, but they have always helped our house.

Whom shall I pray to, then?

To Phoebus Apollo, who desired and chased the fair nymph Daphne, she who ran from him—as I would run, even from a god—screaming for help? Just as his hands reached her, Daphne turned into a laurel tree. Her toes became roots, her skin bark, her hair leaves, leaving the god unsatisfied. . . . I don't want to be a tree. I want to run, and run free.

To the great Zeus, lover of the beautiful mortal Io? The god was powerless when his angry wife, Hera, turned pretty Io into a cow, afflicted by flies and unable to speak her torment.

No help from the gods, then, and what goddess would hear my prayers? Hera, goddess of wives and hearths, wants me for her own. Wise Athena would mock me. And Aphrodite . . . her kind of rapturous love is not for me. Only Artemis the Hunter can save me.

All my life I have prayed to her. But if she has heard me, she does not care.

Is it because of my impiety? Do I love the goddess Artemis too much? There is a marble statue in her temple, with high round breasts and long white thighs. Once, when I was alone there, I reached out and touched them, running my fingers along all that whiteness, cool as stone but smooth as perfect flesh. Nobody saw me, I'm sure. I dream of touching them again. But I'm afraid of how even the thought makes me feel, all hungry with a hunger there is no food for, and aching like pain, only strangely sweet. All I have to do is think about touching her, to feel that way again. I don't think there's even a name for how I feel. It fills me utterly, and I am almost powerless before it. So I dare to call it love. Maybe this is why Zeus could not leave pretty Io alone, though it meant her doom. Or why Apollo ran after the screaming Daphne.

Maybe the goddess does not want such love from me. But it is hers, all the same.

THE SON SPEAKS:

My sister grows pale. It is terrible to see. She weeps and spins, and burns herbs at the altar of Artemis. Now Creusa wants to build her own special altar to the goddess. Yesterday she begged me to bring her horns from a mighty stag, the finest in the forest.

I'll do a lot for poor Creusa. So I suppose I'll take a good sharp saw, and hack away at the next deer we kill. It's not really the season for the great-horned stags. The older ones are cunning in the hunt, and the young ones not yet grown. But for my sister, I will make a stag appear, if I can. If it will make her happy.

THE DAUGHTER SPEAKS:

The suitors are coming. Four from the north, three from the south, and two from the east. They will expect hospitality befitting the House of Cadmus. I must be here to welcome them when they come.

Or I must flee.

What will I do, oh, what will I do? Choose the least horrible of them, and submit?

Or could I leave the safety of our city and of my mother's house, to live outcast and alone in some wasteland without people? Live all by myself in a cave by a spring, devoting my life and my virginity to her who hunts by day and shines by night? My hair would grow tangled, my clothing the skins of the beasts I caught. I would drink only water, eat the flesh of my prey. The only fire I'd ever see would be my own, the only voice the voices of my dogs, and of my kills. Can I do it?

THE SON SPEAKS:

I found Creusa with a knife in her hand, lifting her blade to her own neck.

"Stop!" My hand is so much bigger than hers, now. It was not hard to circle hand and knife in my grasp. "Sister, I beg you! No matter how hard this life is, it is better than wandering with the starless shades."

"You big star-gazing ox," she said, but she wasn't angry. "I was just cutting my hair."

She wore a short chiton, and her cloak was on the chest next to her, even though the weather is very hot.

I saw it then. "You're going?"

"Yes," she whispered. "It is my fate."

"A nameless, homeless wanderer? Oh, Creusa, no!"

"What else can I do? Grandfather will not let me dedicate myself to Artemis and live chaste. While I am under his roof, I must obey his will." She patted my hand, releasing her knife into it. "And so I'm leaving. I will seek the goddess all my life, and maybe she will take pity on me and let me find her."

"And if she doesn't? Creusa, what then?"

Her eyes filled with tears. "I don't know. I don't know what else to do."

I took both her hands. They were so cold. I looked hard into her eyes, which shone with unshed stars. "Don't go. Not yet. Once you have gone, you can never come back. There's still time."

"Time for what?"

"I'll think of something," I promised her. "I'll watch the skies. There is a pattern, there is a dance. . . ."

She shook her head. She doesn't believe the night skies hold any answers. But she put her knife down, pinned up her hair again, and folded up her cloak.

THE DAUGHTER SPEAKS:

What a fool I've been! The answer to my escape has been before me all along.

As I sat spinning under the great tree in the courtyard, in he walked, grandfather's old friend, gray and gnarled as the staff he stretches before him to find his way.

The seer Tiresias.

I flung myself at his feet, kneeling in supplication, clutching the hem of his robe. I would not rise, but made the old seer bend down to hear my whispered plea: "Prophet, blinded by the gods for what you saw—I beg you, tell me the secret of your transformation!"

"Rise," he said, "and sit with me. Does the daughter of the House of Cadmus wish to become a prophet? Or blind, or old? Those last two may be easily achieved, given enough years and patience."

"I don't have years!"

"Nor patience, either, it would seem."

I picked up my spindle and put it down. But then I placed it in his hands. "Remember this?" I said. "Remember when you wore a woman's body as your own?"

I had always doubted the tale. Tiresias is so dry, so unlovely, so gnarled and hairy and *male*. But when he took the spindle from me, he naturally maintained the tension and the twist with a sureness no man's hands could ever know.

"It's true," I marveled. "You were a woman seven years, before you came again to your manhood."

"But it is not my manhood you seek, little princess."

"Yes, it is!" The prophet eased away from me in his seat uncomfortably, and I laughed. "Not that. Never that."

Tiresias shrugged, and laughed himself. "What, then?"

"I wish to leave my father's house."

"And so you shall, when you are wed."

"I do not wish to marry. I wish to follow the goddess."

"Have you asked your family's permission?"

"They only laugh at me. They say a girl never knows her own mind." The old man nodded. "But when I say I *do* know, they tell me a princess must wed, to carry on her noble line."

"You think they are wrong?"

I hung my head, ashamed of what I must ask. "Is it possible, Seer, for someone to be born into the wrong body?" I waited, tense, to see if he would pull away. But he turned the spindle in his hands. He did not spin.

"Go on."

I leaned closer, whispered in the grizzled hair that fell over his ears. "I don't want what women want. I don't want a husband, or children, or a house. I want—what I want is what men want!" There. I had said it. My heart hammered, and my cheeks were hot. But I felt strangely glad, and lighter, now. The words came tumbling out of me: "I want to run free, to hunt, to kill, to glory in my fleetness and my strength! If I can't have them as a woman, then let me have them as a man!" Hardly knowing what I was doing, I grasped his old shoulders between my hands. "Tell me your secret! Tell me what you did, how you changed your shape, and how I may do it, too!"

Tiresias did not move. But his blind eyes turned up to mine. "And if I do? What is it you hunt, Child of Cadmus? What is your true desire?"

"Artemis," I whispered, her very name a prayer I breathed into his face. "I would seek Artemis of the Hunt."

I don't know where he found the strength to push me away. It was as if another touched me, threw me backward to the ground. Tiresias towered above me, his staff raised, a howl like an animal's coming from his throat: "*Woe!* Woe to the House of Cadmus! Blood and terror, terror and blood and the great deer running!"

"Stop!" I crawled to the edge of his robe, pulling on it to draw his attention, but it was as if I were not even there.

"O terrible transformation!" He flung up his arm again, as

though to hide the vision from his sightless eyes. "The hunter hunted and the terror loosed! Alas for a house made barren! Alas for a seed made cold!"

The prophecy was terrible enough. But what if people heard the shouting, and came running to listen?

"I didn't mean it," I babbled. "I beg you, stop, I didn't mean it—"

Slowly, the prophet lowered his staff until he was leaning his full weight on it. His knees were shaking. "Oh, little princess, what I saw!" Slowly, he lowered himself to his knees before me. "I beg you, for your grandfather's sake and mine, do not pursue the goddess. Such a terrible transformation. Death and madness. Terrible, terrible . . ."

The old man was weeping at my feet. I had to kneel before him myself, and clasp his ankles and promise I would never seek to become other than that I am.

But what is that?

THE SON SPEAKS:

My sister rose in the middle of the night to tell me of the bloody prophecy. She found me up on the roof, where I'd gone to watch the progress of Saturn as it met for the first time in my life with Alpha Serpentis.

Her face was the color of the moon, silver, all the blood washed away by starlight. She did not weep, but I held her by her stiff shoulders to comfort her anyway, in the cold night air.

"I dare not go," she said. "I dare not run." She looked out over the sleeping fields to the woods beyond. "And yet, I almost wish I could. To seek the goddess, to look on her once before I die. . . ."

"Creusa!"

"It's the way I feel. I can't explain."

"No need," I said. "I just don't want you to die, that's all."

She smiled, and touched my cheek. "You big star-gazing ox."

That's when I realized how I could help her. I was a fool not to have thought of it before. Chiron was right: the gods decide our fate, but it is ours to look squarely on it, to take up what we have been given, and to use it the best way that we can.

If fate decreed me for a hunter, why then, I would hunt. But my quarry would be for my sister's sake. The goddess loves one who hunts with spirit and true purpose.

Creusa yawned. She really isn't much good at night. "I'd better get to bed," she said sadly. "The suitors are coming, and I have household matters to attend to."

"I'd better get to bed, myself." I forced a yawn, too. "The hunt starts bright and early, and I've got a lot of meat to catch for all your suitors."

She said, "I hope they like rabbit; it's all you're likely to get this time of year."

"Whatever it is, I'll dedicate my catch to you, and to your future happiness."

That's what I told her. But my true quarry, *that* I'll keep a secret, until I can return to my sad sister with news to turn her pale cheeks bright with joy.

THE DAUGHTER SPEAKS:

Actaeon is gone. He's been gone for five days and four nights. The skies have been clear. Maybe he has finally wandered off, star-struck, star-gazing, at last.

His companions say they lost him on the second day of the hunt. They'd been running hard, and their nets and spears were full of the blood of the wild animals they'd caught. It was midday, sunny and hot, and even in the tangle of bushes and scrub, the shadows were short. Hunting was over for the day. They cast themselves down in whatever shade they could find, and drank from streams and cleaned their nets. They'd begin again early the next morning.

They say my brother wandered away, following the music of a rocky stream that led deep into the shady wood. They saw him disappear into a grove of pines and cypress, and that was all.

Hours passed, and he did not return. They thought he'd fallen asleep in the shade somewhere, and let him be. Then a wonderful thing happened so late in the day: a huge stag came running out of the pines, scattering bright drops of water from its brows. The dogs were excited; it was as if they'd been waiting all day for this particular stag, as if they'd already had its scent. Weariness forgotten, all gave it chase.

The stag ran blindly, crashing through the brush in terror. But the fierce dogs were always on its trail, never resting or letting go. When the great stag finally turned to face the dogs, instead of attacking them with its horns, it stretched out its neck and bellowed, as if its voice were calling them to stop! The dogs fell back, confused, but the men surrounded it, urging them on.

"Where's Actaeon?" they cried. "He really should see this. Actaeon! Actaeon!" The forest rang with my brother's name.

The deer turned its head then, and cried again, a noise almost like a human voice. Its eyes rolled wildly from one to the other of them, looking for escape, but the circle was too tight.

As the hounds closed round it, the deer fell to its knees, for all the world as though begging them to spare it. But the dogs brought it down at last, tearing at its flanks until it could cry no more. There really was nothing to save, by the time the dogs were done; the men were distracted, calling for my brother, who never came, not even to see the kill.

But then, I know he never really liked hunting. He was just pretending, so as not to shame our house.

They have tried setting the dogs to follow his scent. But the dogs will only go so far into the grove of pine and cypress before they become confused and frightened and lose the trail. They keep returning to the place they slew the deer. Silly creatures.

Chiron has searched the stars. My brother is not there among them.

THE DAUGHTER SPEAKS AGAIN:

Artemis has come to me at last.

She came in all her beauty, bathed in moonlight so clear it looked like water—or was it water so bright it was like the moon? I saw her body clearly through it, curved and strong like a bow.

"Follow me now," she said, "if you will."

I rose from my couch and followed her on the moon's path, which led from my chamber window to the meadow beyond my grandfather's house. Where her feet trod, night flowers bloomed, and small animals, the mice and voles and even rabbits—for she carried no bow but the moon's curve on her brow—looked up to adore her.

At the edge of the wood, the goddess paused.

"Here, I am the only light. Will you follow?"

I nodded.

The woods were dark, but she was the moon, and I moved fearless by the light of her body between the trees. I heard the sound of rushing water, then. A fountain, gushing naturally from the rock, formed a sweet pool where ferns grew among the stones.

Artemis stood at the edge of the pool. The water reflected her brightness now so strongly that I could hardly see. One foot was in the water, the other on a rock. She turned her back to me, and smiled over her shoulder as she undid one sandal, and then the other. The curve of her back, drawn like a bow, the hair pulled up from the nape of her neck. . .

"Look your fill, virgin daughter of the House of Cadmus. To such as you, nothing is forbidden."

I felt the hungry ache I had known for so long grow in me a hundred hundredfold. The more I gazed on her, the more it grew, until my legs shook so I could hardly stand. The silver water stood between us.

The goddess held out her hand. "Will you cross the water and come to me?"

I would have crossed fire for her. I set one foot on the edge of the pool.

"But remember," she said, "there is a price to be paid by mortals who look upon the goddess in her nakedness. Will you remember that?"

I nodded. She dipped one white hand in the water. Moon-struck drops flew through the air into my face.

My whole body shivered. I felt my skin shudder on my bones, as if trying to shake them off. I felt strange, and light, and my balance left me. I pitched forward but caught myself on the edge of a stone.

And then I saw my own face in the pool.

I screamed, and heard a deer's cry tear the night air. Saw the black mouth and black tongue of a doe parting to give that cry again.

The goddess leapt on my back. Her thighs straddled my flanks like fire, and her weight on my spine was a terrible glory. I fled through the night woods, more terrified than I have ever been, and more completely consumed by a happiness I hope I never feel again.

It might have been hours, or it might have been years. I remember nothing of where I've been. Until she guided me back to the pool, urging me on until I submerged my panting, sweating, hairy body in its icy silver waters, and came to, gasping and trembling and choking to the surface of the water, in my own form again.

"You shiver, daughter of Cadmus."

I tried to hide my nakedness with my hands, my hair. I was so ashamed. Ashamed of what I'd been; ashamed of what I was.

The goddess took my face in her hands and kissed me. I felt the deer's power coursing through my veins, the deer's joy in its own wildness running in my own body. But my hands were my hands, my voice my voice as I moaned my pleasure. It might have been heartbeats, it might have been years. My aching turned to sweet pain, and then only to sweetness. And so, finally, I knew what it was to have my strange hunger satisfied.

The goddess cradled my head in her hands. "In the full heat of the day, when I rested with my maidens, and bathed in the cool water, your brother came to me here." Her lips spoke against my lips. "And so he saw what is forbidden men to see. And paid the price. Do you remember the price, Child of Cadmus? Do you understand what I say?"

I understood. Woe to the House of Cadmus, the terrible transformation. I tasted my own tears on both our lips.

"Do you understand, then, that his own dogs savaged him while his friends looked on and cheered?"

Woe to the House of Cadmus, the terror and the blood. I felt my own groan twist against her body.

"But before the power of human speech left him, he cried out your name. And before his hands became hooves, he held them out, begging me to pity him. And so I came to find you, and to tell you of your brother's fate."

Her arms were around me then, holding what was left of me together while I shivered into little pieces.

"You should have come to me," the goddess said. "You should never have sent a man to do your work for you."

I heard a high mewing keen like the lost birds that fly in from the sea.

"Do you still wish to be my votary? To serve me all your days?"

She had given me everything I thought I ever wanted, and taken from me what I held most dear. The gods love our house, and we must love them.

"Speak," she said. "You still have the power of human speech."

My voice was hoarse. "I do."

"And?"

"I will be your servant always."

"Will you come with me into the woods? I will make you forget all human sorrow, and your name will be a whisper on the wind."

I yearned for her. "And my brother's name?"

"The same."

"I must go home. They are waiting for him. I must speak

of my brother's fate, that all may mourn him, and know what price is paid for your terrible glory."

"Go, then, Child of Cadmus. I accept your service. And serve me still."

Her kiss on my brow burned like silver horns, the twin crests of the moon.

I felt no different when I returned to Cadmus's house. But the suitors were all sent quietly away, with gifts. I serve the goddess now, as she has promised. I sing songs in her honor, and keep the fires lit at my brother's shrine. I hunt what I can: the flies that buzz around sleeping babies' eyes on hot days; the sun that robs the color of our wool; the mice that steal the grain. I speak for the goddess, and no one contradicts me.

There seem to be two ELLEN KUSHNERs: the public radio personality who hosts the national series *PRI's Sound & Spirit*, in which she explores the music and myth, traditions and beliefs that make up the human experience around the world and through the ages; and the author who wrote the "mannerpunk" novels *Swordspoint* and *The Privilege of the Sword*, and the mythic novel *Thomas the Rhymer*, among others. Some people are shocked to discover they both inhabit the same body, taking along with them the Ellen who performs live shows, lectures, teaches writing, and loves riding trains. Ellen Kushner grew up in Cleveland, Ohio, and now lives in New York City. She has two younger brothers and is married to Delia Sherman.

All is revealed at her Web site, www.ellenkushner.com.

᠅

Author's Note

We love Greek tales of gods and heroes; but the gods can be cruel, and the greatest tales can be fraught with great injustices.

When I was six, I had just learned to read when my dad took us all to live in France for a year. We had very few books in English, and I was desperate for more. So were my parents, I guess; my father went down to the American Library and bought some old volumes they were clearing off the shelves. I glommed onto a pale blue clothbound volume with a broken spine (published in London before I was born), a retelling of Greek myths mostly taken from the Roman poet Ovid's collection, *Metamorphoses*. Checking the title page now, I see it was called *Men and Gods*, by Rex Warner—but I just thought of it as My Blue Greek Book, and I read it over and over. I loved the tragedies the best.

For *The Beastly Bride* I have turned back to one of my favorites, the terrible story of Actaeon. Several Ancient Greek writers wrote their own versions of Actaeon's story, each offering a different rationale for his cruel punishment. In some of them, it's because he was intentionally spying on the goddess Artemis to see her naked. In Ovid, he is just a poor luckless guy who wanders into the wrong place at the wrong time.

In all of them, the young prince Actaeon is an enthusiastic hunter.

None of them mentions any sister.

THE WHITE DOE: THREE POEMS

Jeannine Hall Gailey

THE WHITE DOE MOURNS HER CHILDHOOD

Kept safe in a home made of stone
with no windows
with no glass to catch the light
or sun streaming in,
I grew paler each year, as pale as the moon,
as pale as doves, and soft to my own touch.

Until I'm fifteen, and betrothed,
I must hide from the light:
from the company of trees,
of birds, of others I hear through the walls,
the horses' whinnies, the song of day,
although I creep out at night, while the bats sing and
    sweep.

No company, for fear they might open the door,

just books, and my paintings, and jewelry, and mirrors.
A quiet life, not merry, lonely and slow.
Not even sure if it was death or just sorrow or lies
that kept me imprisoned in a world of darkness,
a world of candlelight; the uncertain glow of fire
my only hint of what the sun might hold for me.

When a young man swore he loved me
just from a picture he saw (fell in love
with a picture, that foolish child)
and would not listen to my mother's entreaties
but swung my door open, wounding me with light,
I bounded into the forest, turned into a white doe.

Cursed during the day, unable to speak,
this new body darting like moonlight through
        unfamiliar woods,
this young hunter kept pursuing me,
not safe even in this form from his love;
he shot me with an arrow not far from the water
and I bleed, and I sleep, and wait for my own death.

Oh if I was only safe, back in my room,
where the darkness embraced me, and kept me alive.
This cruel brightness descended,
the fury of sunbeams on my delicate skin . . .
Forbid him, mother, from touching me now
as the sun sets, as my human form returns.
He may not mourn me, whose selfish desire doomed me
        to this.

ৎ ৎ ৎ

THE WHITE DOE'S LOVE SONG

You may not touch me;
you may not enter.
If you swing open my door
I will turn into a white doe.
I will leap through the woods faster than water
and you shall not have me.

Young man, I cannot face this sun
in human form, the sun burns me,
cursed as a child to hide in the dark,
the shadows my friend, the cooing of night birds
my only companion. But here, in this body,
I cannot speak, I cannot sing,
another kind of prison, first the windowless castle,
now this body, these four legs.

And you, so greedy to have me,
my portrait on your wall,
think long about how you will slow me down
will you shoot me, will you hunt me,
will you open the door,
will you wound me with brightness
unwelcome and hard?
Sunbeams on human skin, arrows on deer hide,
either way, you menace, with your young man's desires,
so foolish, so hasty, entranced by your own thoughts.

ৎ ৎ ৎ

You don't know the real me,
just a pale girl on a wall,
who never speaks, who doesn't dream,
who never escapes your fantasy of her.
So fall ill for love of me, come to the woods,
seek me there and hurt me, and maim me,
clutch my neck as you will:
you will not have me, a trophy for your wall.

THE WHITE DOE DECIDES

If she cannot have the sun, she will have freedom. She jumps through snatching hands and cutting tree branches, blindly. She does not believe she ever slept well. The villagers call her a ghost, accuse her of spooking the hunt. She keeps time with rabbits and egrets, eats flowers, green hostas, and white lilies. Alone, alone, all this time pursued by vain princes. Finally she lies down beside the water, the moon rises, and she becomes herself again. She grabs a bleeding ankle, wanders back to an empty bed, hair tangled and skin scratched by briars, a different princess from before. When the sun rises she will be animal again, she will leap up, wild heart beating against her thin hide. It gets easier every day, having four legs, heeding the morning glory's old song, the strange warmth of sun on her neck. This is better than a palace, she thinks, to run faster than she's ever run, to outpace her old fears, the hands that would hold her down. Her feet nothing but flashes, blue eyes still human and shadowy, peering through white pine.

JEANNINE HALL GAILEY is the author of *Becoming the Villainess*. Her work has been featured on NPR's *The Writer's Almanac*, *Verse Daily*, and in *The Year's Best Fantasy and Horror*. In 2007, she was awarded a Washington State Artist Trust GAP Grant and a Dorothy Sargent Rosenberg Poetry Prize. She is currently working on two manuscripts, one about Japanese folktales of animal transformation and another on the inner lives of sleeping princesses. Her Web site is www.webbish6.com.

ιϽCι

Author's Note

I've always been fascinated by stories of transforming women, from Greek mythology's Daphne and Ovid's Philomel to changelings and shape-shifters in folk tales, science fiction, and comic books. It seemed to me these tales connected women to unearthly powers and magical abilities, while also communicating man's uncertainty and, sometimes, squeamishness toward women's "otherness." After all, a lot of the magical transformations—like the dragon-woman Melusine's—happen around childbirth and other womanly rituals.

"The White Doe" is a French fairy tale that I always thought had a terrible ending for the poor princess—first a random prince falls in love with her picture, then he curses her by opening the door to her tower (though everyone warns him not to) and exposing her to sunlight for the first time, which leads to her transformation to deer form, then he shoots her with an arrow while she is in magical white doe form . . . and she still marries him! I thought I might let the princess voice some ambivalence toward her princely suitor and toward her "curses," first being locked in a tower away from the sun, then being in animal form. It's always fun to rewrite fairy tales with an eye toward giving those poor princesses a bit more freedom and authority.

COYOTE AND VALOROSA

Terra L. Gearhart-Serna

Many years ago among the burnt hills and dry winds of the Southwest, there lived a girl named Valorosa and, though she didn't know it yet, the trickster god of the native tribes. His name was Coyote, because he was one. Not just *any* coyote, *mijita*, my little one, but the biggest, cleverest, most beautiful coyote on the mesas. Coyote could trick anyone, even himself! Valorosa, on the other hand, had just turned fifteen, and she knew that she must be a woman because the priest at her *quinceañera* had said so. Her mother had named her "Valorosa" so that her daughter would know that she had *valor*, courage, and also *valor*, great value. Her father, who was a mostly good man with a big nose and a cruel voice, called Valorosa "Rosa," his *rosita*, a lovely little Spanish rose with round red cheeks and shining dark hair. Her mother thought that Valorosa's father had missed the point. But what can you do, when you marry a man because your papa makes you? You can give your daughter a good name and hope that *un día* she will live up to it. *Las madres siempre* *esperan así, mijita*—mamas always want such things for their daughters.

Valorosa was a proud girl, and fearless; she knew that she was meant for great things, or at least a great husband. After all, her father was the *comandante* of a great territory, and Valorosa knew that he was considered very important. Her mother told Valorosa that she would still be an important girl even if her father were a simple man with nothing more than a burro to his name, but Valorosa thought this was a bit silly. Jose Bañaco, down in the village, was a simple man with only a burro to his name, and no one thought very much of *him*.

Ahora. Ya al cuento. To the story. One day, Valorosa's father heard news of trouble brewing among the tribes in a far-off corner of the territory. Since he was charged with keeping proper order in the name of His Majesty, the king of Spain, he immediately made preparations for travel to this troublesome native village. Before he left, he asked Valorosa: *"Mi rosita lindíssima, ¿no quieres nada de tu padre? ¿No quieres un regalo de los salvajes?"* "My pretty little Rose, don't you want something from your father? Don't you want a gift from the savages?" He told her that he would bring her some beautiful jewelry, perhaps a necklace made all of bright turquoise and shining silver. But Valorosa shook her head and asked if he could pick her some sand verbena flowers instead. She loved those hardy little pink blossoms that bloom in hot, sandy, barren places. Her father was taken back. "But you already have roses, *mija!*" he cried. "Beautiful roses, the only ones to be found in the whole territory, right here in our courtyard! Why, they were planted just for you." But Valorosa asked again for the sand verbena blossoms, and finally her father promised to bring them for her.

When Valorosa's father arrived in the Indian village that had been causing trouble, he and his men were very tired. The Indians seemed meek and sorry, and asked if he would only accompany their two head men, the chief and the medicine man, out into the hills. They wanted to speak with him, and then they wouldn't cause any more mischief. The *comandante* agreed, and he followed the chief and the medicine man into the dry desert hills outside the village. Of course, these native men were not so stupid as the *comandante* thought. They had made a deal with Coyote, the trickster: they would bring the Spanish general out into the desert, and Coyote would give him a good scare, to teach him some respect.

Soon Valorosa's father and the two Indians arrived on top of a big hill out in the desert. The two Indians lit a fire from dry brush and bade the *comandante* sit while they went hunting for a rabbit for their supper. The *comandante* sat down, nearly crushing a little sand verbena plant growing near his foot. "*Qué grosera,* what a disgusting little flower," he muttered to himself when he spotted it, wrinkling his nose at its sharp, tangy smell. But he was a dutiful father, so he leaned over to pluck one of the pretty little flower stems. Suddenly, he stopped and rubbed his eyes in disbelief. Only a few feet away, near the edge of the firelight, was a beautiful vine of wild roses, draped over a thorny old mesquite bush. These were not just any roses, *mijita*! They were in glorious full bloom, and they smelled like something from *el Cielo*—from heaven. Unable to believe his luck at finding this much more suitable flower, the *comandante* reached out and picked one of the roses. Immediately, a crackling, roaring voice cried: "THOSE ARE MINE!" It was Coyote. He had been making the roses grow as a way to pass the time while he waited for the Spanish *comandante*, and he had so amused himself that he hadn't realized that the *comandante* had arrived.

The *comandante* began to quiver and shake. Like many men with military jackets and impressive mustachios, the *comandante* was really a bit of a coward at heart. *"Por favor, señor,"* he cried, trembling like a leaf in a dust storm. *"Por favor, ¡no me mate!"* "Please, sir, do not kill me!" *"Es sólo para mi hija, mi Rosa, la rosita de mi vida!"* "It's only for my daughter, my rose, the little rose of my life!" Coyote, who realized now who this silly man must be, chuckled to himself so that the *comandante* couldn't hear. "Well, *ladrón*, my petty thief," he said (in a very cross, dangerous voice), "daughter or no, I will tell you this: those roses were my pride and joy! I cannot let you steal one from me without punishment, so here is what I will do. First, I will let you return to your home to kiss your woman and get your things in order. When seven suns have set, you must return to me and be my servant for ten years. After that, I will give you back to the desert." With that, he let out a frightening, unearthly howl, and the *comandante*, that silly *bobo*, that fool, ran as fast as his legs could carry him away from the hill and the demon that lived on it. He didn't stop running until he got back to the village, where he leapt onto his horse and rode back to his mansion, just as quick as a scared jackrabbit.

Coyote laughed to see the Spanish fool flee and was sure he had done a good job and taught the man some respect. He didn't intend to make the *comandante* his servant—in fact, he didn't care if the *comandante* returned at all! Satisfied, he went back to his lair to chew on quail bones and laugh a coyote laugh.

The *comandante*, *pobrecito*, poor little man, had a lot less imagination than Coyote suspected. He never guessed that it might be a trick, and he was white and shaking and moaning when he came home. He shut himself up in his study, where he paced the floors and shivered with fear. Finally, Valorosa came and tapped on his door. "What's wrong, Papá?" she asked. *"¿Qué le sucedió?"* Her father tried to be brave for a few moments but soon he told Valorosa the whole story. "Why, Papá!" Valorosa exclaimed, "You can't go! You are the *comandante*! But *I* will go—I am your daughter, and I will tell this demon that he can take *me* in your stead! Surely *la Virgen* will protect me." Her father cried out and forbade her to go, but Valorosa wasn't paying attention. In her head, she was thinking: *Won't this be a grand adventure? I'll show that demon a thing or two!* But her father continued to protest, so Valorosa said no more about it.

That night, Valorosa snuck out her bedroom window, saddled her horse, and rode away across the desert toward the Indian village that her father had fled so quickly. She told herself that she was such a good daughter, so dutiful, so loving! But she knew that really, she was a bit bored of making tamales, and wanted an escape. *¡Aventura, mijita!* Adventure! It calls to us all.

When Valorosa arrived at the spot where her father had met the demon, she let her horse go to find some scrub to eat, and called out: *"¡Diablo!* Demon! I am here in place of my father, and *la Virgen Santíssima* will protect me!"

Coyote heard her and laughed to himself in amazement. He came out from behind the mesquite bushes and circled the girl. "So you are the *rosita*, eh?" he asked, slyly. "You are not so fragile, not so delicate as my roses here."

"Pah!" said Valorosa. "I am Valorosa, *la valiente*, the brave! I am not afraid."

At this, Coyote became a bit annoyed, and he decided that

Valorosa might do very well for a new trick. *I'll keep her here with me,* he thought. *Her family will think that she has disappeared forever, taken by the powers of the desert! I will send one of my bitches, my woman-coyotes, to walk through the girl's village with a rose in her mouth. Hah! They will all think that I have turned her into a coyote. That will teach the proud and pompous* comandante *a lesson!* And he grinned a big coyote grin.

Meanwhile, Valorosa was examining this big golden-gray beast with a curious eye. He could speak and he had managed to scare her father witless, which meant that he was no ordinary animal; however, Valorosa had a bit more imagination than her father, so she knew that this could well be a local spirit, perhaps even a god. Not every powerful thing in the world is either evil or Catholic, *mijita*. Remember that.

Coyote, who had come to a decision about his trick, told Valorosa his plans for her. He told her that she would stay with him as his servant to cook him good food and groom his dusty coat, and eventually he might release her.

Valorosa stamped her foot and stared him down. "Pah!" she said again. "I will have no part in a trick played by such a dirty little animal!" Coyote was taken aback. What did she mean? "Why, if you had any *real* power," said Valorosa contemptuously, "you would turn yourself into a man! Don't you know that humans are made in God's image, so God must be a man? No real god would be a *coyote!*"

Coyote was now more than a little angry, though secretly he was also quite impressed. "Oh, yes?" he cried boastfully, "Well, *hormiguita*, my little ant, watch this!" And with that, he turned himself into a man—a tall, muscular, sandy-haired man. Frowning because he was starting to wonder if *he* might be the tricked one, he carted Valorosa off to his lair.

Many weeks passed. Valorosa was forced to do chores for Coyote, but she didn't really mind; at least there was no embroidery! Coyote brooded to himself, wondering whether and when he should complete his trick, and mulling over the words that Valorosa had thrown at him.

Despite herself, Valorosa rather missed that trickster's grin that he had worn when they first met on the hilltop, and even though she thought him quite handsome in his human form, she didn't really like the change in him. Finally, she came to him one evening and begged him to turn himself back into a coyote.

Coyote smiled. "Oh? So you do not think being an animal is so bad after all?"

Valorosa looked at her dirty feet and said, quietly, "No, perhaps not." Coyote changed himself back on the spot, and he and Valorosa went for a wild moonlit ramble out across the mesas.

Eventually, after many such runs in the moonlight, Coyote let Valorosa go; he did not want her to leave, but he knew that some things must be simply because they must be. That is wisdom, *mijita*.

Valorosa returned to her father's mansion, where her father welcomed her with open arms and wept tears of gratitude for the mercy of God. Her mother, sensing that perhaps Valorosa herself might have had something to do with her return, simply smiled.

After a few months, a new man came to serve under the *comandante*, a man with an easy laugh and a good mind. He and Valorosa became engaged, and Valorosa was content.

Just before the priest began the wedding ceremony, Valorosa's mother gave her a little bouquet, a *ramillete*: two stems of sand verbena and a sweet wild rose. Tucked in between the rose petals were a few golden-gray hairs. Valorosa looked at her mother, who grinned her own coyote grin. And I'll tell you, *mijita*, there were many times after that when people swore that they saw a girl and a coyote running across the mesas together under the moon, howling and yelping and grinning. If Valorosa's husband heard about any of this, he didn't seem to mind; maybe he went along. Which just goes to show you, *mijita*, that you should never marry a man who does not like coyotes.

Though **TERRA L. GEARHART-SERNA** has been writing short stories since the age of ten, "Coyote and Valorosa" is her first published work. It was written for an undergraduate class at the University of Pennsylvania and wound up in this anthology thanks to the encouragement of a truly exceptional English professor. Terra is currently a student at Yale Law School, where she writes legal essays consisting of more footnotes than text.

Author's Note

I originally wrote "Coyote and Valorosa" as a midterm essay for a college class called "Feminist Fairy Tales." In order to give the story its bilingual/multicultural flavor, I paid a return visit to my childhood memories of reading both Western fairy tales and the bilingual *cuentos* of the much-loved Santa Fe storyteller Joe Hayes.

We tend to think of shape-shifting as a purely physical thing, but as a young Latina my experience of "changing shape" has been a constant shift between my mother's Hispanic family in the West and my father's Anglo family in the East, between English and Spanish, between the interwoven threads of New Mexico's Native American, Hispanic, and Anglo heritage, and most recently between the deserts of the Southwest and an East Coast university. "Coyote and Valorosa" also seesaws between various identities and traditions: English and Spanish, Hispanic and Indian, male and female, pride and humility. Valorosa achieves her metamorphosis from child to woman as she struggles with a new and different cultural and life experience; given this kind of change, what does it matter if she becomes a coyote or if Coyote becomes a man?

ONE THIN DIME

Stewart Moore

I t had to be a great house for candy. Anyone who decorated their house that much for Halloween must have great candy, and lots of it. Old-style carnival posters filled the yard, proclaiming the wonders of Doug the Dinosaur Boy, the Real Jack Pumpkinhead, the Mysterious Black Widow, and Kate the Lion-Tailed Girl. Each poster was carefully framed, its yellowing paper sealed behind glass. Each one hung from a stake driven deep into the dew-damp grass. They stood, arrayed like a band of goblins, guarding the house. That house itself—so white and plain by daylight—was draped in shadows that dripped from the branched fingers of old oak trees. A simple, single-toothed jack-o'-lantern grinned its candlelit grin from the porch, and right at the top of the steps, a real, honest-to-goodness, enormous witch's cauldron smoked and steamed. There had to be great candy in there.

The problem was that there were no lights on in the house, no lights at all, and so the little pirate stood on the sidewalk, shifting from foot to foot, trying to decide whether to go up and knock. In the glass frame of every poster, his reflection danced nervously.

The little pirate's mother had warned him not to go up to any house that didn't have its lights on—and especially not to go up to this house. This house had been empty for years and years, but just last month someone had moved in. Grown-ups never talked about the new owner except in whispers. The little pirate watched the cauldron steam. He was sure he had heard his mother whisper the word *witch*.

It didn't help that the moon was full, that the last dry leaves on the trees rattled like tiny bones in the cold wind, and that somewhere in the darkness, an owl was hooting. These things didn't help at all.

Finally, the little pirate decided not to try it. As he turned to go to the next, friendly, well-lit house, a shadow moved among the deeper shadows of the porch, and a smooth, clear voice spoke: "And what are you tonight, my dear little monster?"

The trick-or-treater froze. It was a woman's voice, a young woman's voice: younger than his mother, older than his babysitter. The voice spoke quietly, but still he could hear it clearly over the soft bubbling of the cauldron. "Well?"

The trick-or-treater began his shuffling dance again. He looked down at his costume, as if to be sure: at his oversize white shirt, his black pants, his buckled shoes; at the shiny plastic hook that hid his left hand. He felt the eye patch and the bandanna he wore on his head. Finally, uncertainly, he croaked an answer. "I'm a pirate?"

The woman in the shadows laughed. It was a friendly laugh, not the sort of gurgling chuckle you might expect to hear from a darkened porch on Halloween night.

"That I can see," the voice said. "But which one? Are you

that Blackbeard, Edward Teach, who died with twenty-six bullets in his body and his beard full of other men's blood? Or perhaps you're Jean Lafitte, the voodoo master of New Orleans, who used his own dead sailors to guard his treasures? Or even—no, you couldn't be—so bloody a man as Captain William Davey, a man so evil he named his ship *The Devil*? They say that before he was caught and dangled, he made his crew swallow his gold and jump overboard, so that they could bring his treasure back to him in Hell, ten thousand doubloons clinking in their bellies. Are you such a man as that?"

The trick-or-treater's ideas concerning pirates came mostly from *Scooby-Doo*. The names the shadowy woman had rolled out to him spoke of blood, and he didn't like them. He tried, quickly, to think of a name for himself, a good piratical name, but now all the names he could think of sounded like they belonged to very, very bad men. At a loss, he looked down at his feet and mumbled, "I'm a pirate."

"And a fine one you are, too. But you weren't going to pass me by, were you?"

"Your light's a-pposed to be on." The little pirate felt that on this point the Halloween rules, as they had been explained to him by his mother, were quite clear, and he felt confident enough to assume a reproachful tone.

"I know," said the voice, unfazed even by this clear admission of rule breaking. "It burned out. Don't you want a trick-or-treat?"

The little pirate's father was fond of this exact same trick question, and so he knew the proper follow-up: "Which one?"

The voice laughed again. "A treat. For you—most certainly a treat. All you have to do . . ." The voice paused for a very long time, as if waiting for an owl to hoot eerily in the silence—which, at last, one did. "All you have to do is reach into the pot."

The cauldron still bubbled and steamed but did not choose this moment to do anything threatening, like spitting out a shower of multicolored sparks or allowing a greasy gray tentacle to slither briefly over its lip. Uncertain, but drawn on by the promise of treats, the little pirate began inching his way up the walkway. "What's your name?" he asked. With a name, he would at least be on firmer ground.

"Oh, no," the voice purred. "You're not supposed to tell names on Halloween. It's dangerous. You don't know what might be listening. Do you?"

The shadow that spoke from the shadows finally stirred and stepped forward into the light. A young woman appeared, with long golden hair and tawny skin, wearing a red lion-tamer's jacket and a black top hat. She also had a long, golden-furred tail that swished idly back and forth behind her.

"But Long John Silver," she said, "where's your parrot?"

The little pirate looked at the poster nearest the house: Kate the Lion-Tailed Girl looked exactly like the coolly smiling woman standing over the cauldron.

"You're in the poster," he said.

"Yes . . ." Kate winked. "Well, don't you have something to say?"

The pirate only looked down at his hook.

"Trick . . ." Kate prompted.

". . . or treat?"

"And which would you prefer?"

"Treat, please," said the pirate quickly.

"Of course!" Kate opened her arms in a wide gesture of welcome. "Go ahead. I've got very good candy. Reach in. I won't move a muscle."

The little pirate climbed the steps to the porch, much more slowly than many a real pirate had climbed the stairs to the gallows. He stopped on the last step, refusing actually to stand on the same porch as the lion-tailed girl. Her tail, he saw, was twitching much faster now. He tried to look into the cauldron, but all he could see was white smoke bubbling inside it.

"You said . . . good candy?"

"Very good, I said." Kate grinned.

The white cloud inside the cauldron spat out a tendril of mist, and the pirate shrank back. The candy he'd already collected rattled inside his plastic pumpkin: not very much so far. And the cauldron was very, very big. There was a lot of room for a lot of candy. Finally, he screwed his courage to the sticking place and, squinting his eyes tightly, reached into the pot. His hand sank beneath the surface of a cold liquid. He'd expected heat and snatched his hand back. It was covered in strawberry syrup, but it wasn't strawberry syrup. He knew what it was. He knew what it was, it was—

"Oh, how silly!" Kate laughed. "You said treat, didn't you?" Cat-quick, she reached into the cauldron herself, and her hand came out, not scarlet, but clutching a crinkling mass of candy bars. She held it out, patiently waiting for the little pirate to hold up his pumpkin. Trembling, he did. But before she dropped the treasure, she tilted her head and asked, "But are you sure you wouldn't like to see what the real trick is?"

He shook his head so violently his eye patch slid down to his cheek. Kate laughed and dropped the candy into his pumpkin. On the instant, the pirate ran off like a cannon shot for saner quarters. She called after him, "I hope you find your parrot!"

A little ways down the road, under a streetlight, an old, old man was watching, his hands buried deep in the pockets of a coat that might have fought at Verdun. As the boy ran off, the old man walked nearer, stopping at the same spot where the little pirate had stood for so long before his fateful decision to go up the walkway. The old man tipped his hat. "You set to bothering the young ones there?" he asked.

"Can I help you?" Kate asked, stepping back slightly toward her shadows.

The old man took off his hat. His wisps of white hair shivered in the wind. He held his hat like a bowl. "Trick or treat?"

"Where's your costume?" Kate took a half step back toward the light.

"Right on my face!" the old man said. "I'm a genuine Egyptian mummy, ten thousand years old and falling to pieces right before your eyes. You got any magic tannis root in that pot there?"

Kate regarded him sidelong, her arms crossed. "Reach in and see."

"Oh, no. Not after what I just saw. My heart couldn't take the strain, I'm afraid."

"That is a pity," Kate said, and tossed him a candy bar. He caught it in his hat and slipped it in his pocket.

"Much obliged, Miss Kate," he said as he put his hat back on.

"That's trouble," she said. "How do you know my name?"

"Well, there's the convenience of putting it on that poster there."

"That poster," she said, "is older than you are."

"And besides that, you're about the only thing this town

has talked about since you moved in last month. It's behavior like this—plus having a tail, I suppose—that's done it all, you know."

Kate half-smiled. "So it's Halloween night, and you know my name. That gives you quite an advantage. But who are you?"

The old man tipped his hat once more, and said, "Name's William Wildhawk."

Kate laughed, surprised, delighted. "No, it isn't!"

"Of course not. But it sounds like the sort of name a fellow ought to have when the woman he's talking to has a tail, doesn't it?"

"It does indeed," she said, and her tail arched upward with pleasure. "But what brings a man named William Wildhawk to my doorstep on such a night as this? Surely not free candy bars. With a name like that, you need dragons to slay."

The old man looked around, as if Kate might have a dragon waiting in the shadows on a leash. "No, not me," he said. "I doubt I have anything that would slay a dragon. Why, do you know where one might be found?"

"I used to," Kate said, a faraway look coming over her face. William glanced at the poster of Doug the Dinosaur Boy, a tyrannosaurus in a schoolboy's tie and short pants. Would he be the sort of thing that counted for a dragon in this mechanized day and age? he thought.

Kate shook her head. "But I think he's most likely moved on by now." Far away, something howled. It was certainly a dog. It couldn't possibly be a wolf. It couldn't possibly be a lonely timber wolf keening over its empty belly. The wind cut through the thin places in the old man's coat. He shuddered and wrapped his arms around himself.

Kate forced a smile. "You should think about getting yourself home soon, William. It's Halloween, and things will be coming out to play soon. This is a night for haunts and fairies."

William winked. "Goblins, too?"

"What!" gasped Kate, in tones of deepest mortification. "A goblin, me?"

"And where else would a tail like that come from?"

Kate huffed. Her tail flicked indignantly. "From my mother's side of the family. And you watch your mouth, or you'll be a toad come morning."

"Your mother had a tail, too?" William asked.

"She had a nicer tail than I, but she took better care of it. French shampoo, German vitamins, and plenty of exercise."

"And what about her mother?"

Kate looked down at William for a long time. Her tail was stiff and still. "My grandmother's tail was the world champion. She could serve tea with it. She even traveled around with a carnival for a while. That's where all the posters come from." She stepped down off the porch, standing on the first stair, her hands on her hips, her tail slowly arching. "You knew her, didn't you?"

William shook his head. "No. But I saw her once, just once, when her circus passed through. I must have been, oh, twelve. Around there. That was the last year before I was too old to let my friends know that I still liked circuses and too young to know that they all felt the same way. In fact, that was the last circus I ever went to, till I had kids of my own and a good excuse. And I was just on my way home that night, licking the cotton candy off my fingers, when I saw the Lion-Tailed Girl herself in front of the old freak show tent, working the crowd for their last dimes."

Kate jumped down onto the grass in the midst of her posters, landing on her feet without a sound. "Ladies and gentlemen!" she called out to an invisible crowd, and though she did not shout, still every word rang down the street and around the corner. Her voice circled around William's ears and would not be ignored. "Ladies and gentlemen! Every one of you knows the wonders that God made in the six days of Genesis. But have you seen what his hands made in those same six nights, in the dark, when no one was looking?"

She strode over to a poster filled entirely by a mass of swirling darkness, with two large eyes in the midst of it. "Have you seen our famous Black Widow, the most horrifying perversion of nature in history? She's inside, just a dime away."

Kate's fingers slipped into a jacket pocket and came back up with a thin dime flashing, rolling over her knuckles. "Have you seen the real refugee from Oz, our own Jack Pumpkinhead?" She pointed to a poster of a huge, smiling, orange, empty-eyed face. It must have been a mask, because it looked exactly like a tall, thin man with a pumpkin for a head.

"They're all inside, and it only takes a dime to see them, just the skinniest coin of all, slap it down and walk on in." Kate hopped back onto her porch and flung her front door open wide. Darkness gaped inside. "If you walk away now, you'll wake up in the night, in the dark, and wonder what it was you missed. But you can see it now. For one dime. Just one—thin—dime!"

Kate froze in a theatrical pose, both hands pointing into the darkness inside her house. William had watched it all with misty eyes. He shook his head.

"You are her spirit and image," he said. "You are that."

Kate relaxed and leaned against her porch railing. "So I'm told." She shrugged. Her tail drooped.

"You know," William said, "I always wondered what was that Black Widow's 'perversion of nature' that was so horrifying."

"You mean you didn't go in?"

"No. I spent my last dime on one of the games. Throwing baseballs at milk bottles." He reached into one of his deep pockets and pulled an ancient flattened rag doll into the light: a lion with a mangy mane and a windup key in its back. "I won this for knocking them over three times in a row. I named him Raleigh. He used to play a little song when you wound him up."

"What was the song?" Kate asked.

"I don't really remember anymore. It was . . ." He closed his eyes, and, after a moment, began to hum. He hummed a tune that was somehow melancholy and jaunty at the same time: the sort of tune you might want to hear after a long, bad night, in the blue, foggy light, just before the sun rose. Finally, he gave up. "But it wasn't really like that at all. . . . Oh, well. It's a funny thing about music, isn't it? You can still feel what it sounded like, years and years ago, even if you can't really remember how it went."

"And what happened to Raleigh?" Kate sat down on her top step, her chin in her hands, her tail curled around her side. "One day you wound him up too tight, and something deep down inside of him snapped?"

"No, no. Truth to tell, I just set him down one day and forgot all about him. I found him in a box, years later. And he just wouldn't play anymore. I turned the key, and nothing happened. I kept him around, ever since, but . . . nothing, of course. I took him to a toy shop once, to see if I could get him fixed, but the man said he'd have to cut Raleigh open, and I couldn't do that."

"May I see him?" Kate asked. William slowly walked forward, through the midst of the faded carnival posters, and gently laid the little lion in her hands.

"You know," he said, "I thought, that night, I might give him to your grandmother. But she'd already gone inside the tent. I'm sure she could have gotten one of her own, of course, but . . ." He shrugged. "I was twelve."

Kate gently turned Raleigh over and over in her hands. "Those carnival games were all rigged," she said softly. "Grandmother told me. The balls were full of sawdust, and the bottles were nailed down."

"Maybe I really wanted that lion." William chuckled. "Maybe I just believed I could do it." He reached into yet another pocket and brought an ancient yellow baseball up into the light. He tossed it from one hand to the other. "Maybe I switched the balls. This one has lug nuts in the middle."

"What don't you have in that coat?" Kate asked.

"The devil's three golden hairs and a cure for cancer. I've got just about everything else, though."

Kate smiled and held Raleigh out for William to take back. William shook his head.

"No," he said. "He's most of why I came by. He's always been your grandmother's, really, at least to my mind. So that pretty much makes him yours."

"Thank you," Kate said, and she hugged the little lion tightly.

"Not at all," said William. He touched the brim of his hat, and turned away.

"Black Widow's act," she said, and he stopped. "It was pretty simple. She could swallow a four-inch-long tarantula and bring it up again, alive."

William shuddered. "That's it?"

"Well, she could do some other things, too, but they were too much for the show. And you don't want to know, even if you think you do."

"Ah, well. I suppose that's what I get for spending my dime on milk bottles instead of on the show." He walked back down the walkway, but stopped on the curb. He half-turned back. "So your grandmother's name was Kate, too, then?"

Kate's tail twitched. "And my mother's. It's a popular name in the family."

William tipped his hat one last time. "You have a good rest of your Halloween, Miss Kate."

As quick as a big cat pouncing, Kate jumped down from the porch and ran up to William. She pressed her dime into his palm and whispered, "One more ticket to see the show." She smiled. "Save it this time."

"Thank you much," said William, closing his hand tightly around the little coin.

"Good night to you, William Wildhawk," said Kate over her shoulder as she walked back to her house, her tail swishing.

"Good-bye," said William Wildhawk. Kate ran lightly up the stairs and inside, shutting the door behind her.

For a long time, the old, old man did not walk down the road. He stood beneath the streetlight, looking at the dime flashing in his hand: purple-white, when it reflected the halogen lamp above his head; blue, when he tilted it to catch the moonlight. And then there was another light caught in the coin's face, a warm and golden light that he hadn't seen in years, the kind of light you could only get from old, old bulbs, like the ones over a carnival midway. He looked up and saw that warm light flashing inside Kate's house. She passed by a window, and she waved to him, a flourish of fingers matched by a flourish of her tail, and then the curtains fell closed, and the lights went off.

As William turned away, he thought he could hear music playing from somewhere far away: a simple music-box tune, somehow both jaunty and sad, the sort of tune you might hear at the end of a long, cold night as the sky grows blue, just before the sun rises.

He held the dime tightly, and shoved both hands deep into his pockets. "Just one thin dime"—he chuckled—"to see the show." And he walked slowly toward home, humming the little tune to himself as he stepped into the shadows.

STEWART MOORE has spent more time onstage than is really good for him, as Kate the Lion-Tailed Girl could tell you. He has worked as an actor, a lighting designer, a director, and a playwright. He has also been a legal proofreader, which is a good deal less interesting, and is a husband and father, which is considerably more interesting. His work has been published in *Palimpsest* and *The Encyclopedia of Early Judaism*.

Currently, he is pursuing a doctorate in the study of the Hebrew Bible, but no, he doesn't know the meaning of life—yet.

⏴⏵

Author's Note

When I lived in Manhattan, I worked nights and would often walk home in the early morning hours through Central Park. One of my routes would take me through the zoo when the only things moving would be the seals, swimming around and around and around in their tank . . . and, if I arrived just in time, there was the Delacorte Music Clock. At 8:00 A.M. precisely, a bronze penguin would chase a kangaroo chasing a goat chasing a hippo chasing a bear. All the while, a calliope would play—usually a treacly, tinkly round of "Frère Jacques" or "Mary Had a Little Lamb."

One morning, the little windup animals started up their round as I passed by, and they played the saddest song I'd ever heard. I have no idea what the tune was, and though I can almost hear it again now, it slips away from me. Being at that time young enough to think myself old, I imagined an old, old man, holding a windup toy that once, long ago, had played a sad, sad song, but now only sat in silence. It was the sort of tune I associated with the carnivals of my youth (even then a dying breed): cotton candy, carousels, and freak shows.

Kate leaped up onto the stage immediately. After that, it was only a matter of typing.

THE MONKEY BRIDE

Midori Snyder

Salim shaded his eyes from the blazing sunlight that burnished the desert a copper color. His horse panted as it plodded through the shifting sand. It was his own fault that he was here, Salim thought angrily; his fault that he was wandering across the desert in search of his rebellious spear.

That morning, the emir, his father, had called together Salim and his two older brothers. "My sons," he said, "you have grown into strong young men. You are excellent hunters and your spears never miss their aim. It is time now to marry the brides I selected for you many years ago when you were first born. Go to the home of the woman chosen for you and drive your spear into the ground before her door to let the family know the time has come."

Salim had watched as his older brothers, spears in hand, had ridden through the village. Jamal, the eldest, drove his spear in front of the door of a wealthy merchant, whose daughter had a gap between her front teeth. Next, his brother Suliman had planted his spear at the door of a prosperous caravan master, whose daughter had plump limbs. When it was his turn, Salim had galloped up and down, up and down through the village, the spear remaining firm in his grasp. The emir called to him: "Salim, what prevents you from claiming your bride? Have you no desire to be married?"

"Of course I wish to be married," he'd said. But not to the young woman his father had chosen. Salim had seen the melancholy way she gazed at the goldsmith's son and how she turned her head whenever they passed in the street. How could he marry a woman he did not love, and one who did not want him? In a burst of defiance, he wheeled his horse around and shouted: "I call upon the hunter's right to let my spear find a wife for me." And with that, he had cast his spear far out into the desert.

His father had been angry. "Foolish boy! I chose a bride for you that would have brought our families honor. But you scorn such wisdom. Ignore my counsel and my wishes if you will, but know that you must now follow this path alone."

Ashamed of himself for having offended his father, Salim had set off in search of his spear. Perhaps it might not be too late to make amends. But the longer he traveled in the desert not finding it, the more worried he became. "My spear has been my loyal companion, and yet now it leads me far from home. There is some strange force at work here," he told himself. "But as I chose my fate, I must follow where it leads."

A lone acacia tree appeared on the crest of a high dune. The horse hurried toward it, drawn by the scent of water bubbling in a spring nearby. As they approached, Salim saw his spear buried in the trunk. He slipped off his horse and went to retrieve it, disappointed that his journey had ended here.

Then he heard a slight cough, and looking up, he saw a girda monkey perched high in the branches.

"Are you supposed to be my future bride?" he said wryly to the monkey.

"That I am," answered the girda.

Salim was shocked by her unexpected reply, and then dismayed, realizing that he was now face-to-face with the consequences of his rash behavior. "Well," he said ruefully, "though you have no wealth to bring with you, at least you can talk."

"That I can," said the monkey, scrambling down the tree. "Remember, it was *you* who chose *me*."

"Yes," Salim said unhappily, wishing he could undo the spear's flight. He mounted his horse and, offering the girda his hand, pulled her up behind him. She laid her furred cheek against his shoulder and slipped a long arm around his waist. Salim's heart sank as the girda's musky odor filled his nostrils.

ᔍ ᔍ ᔍ

Salim was silent on the long journey home. Once there, he showed the girda to her room. Without a word, she lay down on an old *angareb* bed and promptly fell asleep. Then Salim went to give his father the disheartening news.

"Father, you were right to condemn my foolish behavior," Salim confessed, "for I cast my spear into the desert and it found the home of a female girda. She spoke to me."

"What did you do?"

"I brought her home, and now I must do the honorable thing and wed her."

The emir shook his head. "You have brought this on

yourself, my son, and it is you who must settle the matter."

In the weeks that followed his marriage, Salim traveled far distances to hunt each day, hoping to flee his own despair. Ever since the girda had arrived, the plain house of his bachelorhood had seemed particularly comfortless. A human bride would have brought a fine dowry to his home: rugs and cushions, lamps of scented oil, sandalwood tables, and copper dishes. She would have brought servants to cook and clean, and been a companion to share his bed. Instead, there was only a girda waiting patiently for his return each day. The monkey would come and sit beside him as he ate a plain meal off of clay dishes. Frustrated anger would rise in him at the prickly stench of girda fur, and then dissolve with the sound of her sighs. She was as miserable as he was, he realized. What life was this for a girda, after all? And it had been his fault, for it was his spear that had claimed her in the desert.

One night, after returning empty-handed from a long day of hunting, Salim met the emir in the village square. He greeted his father and asked what had brought him out on the streets at such a late hour.

"I have been dining with your older brothers," the emir replied. "For the last two nights I have visited their homes to discover how married life suits them."

"And how did you find them?" Salim asked, sorrow like an arrow in his chest.

"Very fine, indeed. Their wives are beautiful, and their houses are filled with every luxury. I have dined exceptionally well," the emir said, patting his stomach. "And how are things with you, my youngest son?"

"Not as well as with my brothers," Salim replied, shame darkening his cheeks. "I am sorry, Father, that I cannot ask you to dine with me." Then he turned his horse's head and quickly galloped home.

There were no lights to welcome him. Salim unsaddled and stabled his horse, then stumbled to his *angareb*, where he tossed and turned in misery until the girda came to him.

"What troubles your sleep?" the monkey asked. "Perhaps it is something we can solve together?"

Salim sat up and stared into the girda's concerned eyes. "It's kind of you to ask, but there is nothing you can do for me. My life would have been better had I married the woman of my father's choosing, just as yours would have been better had you found a male monkey for your mate, instead of me. I have ruined both our futures."

"You are a man," the girda said, "and you can't know what lies in a girda's heart. And you don't know me well enough to know what I might do for you if asked. So tell me, what is troubling you?"

Salim told her about meeting his father that night; he told her about his brothers and their wives, how they had lavishly entertained the emir. And he told her that he was filled with shame because he could not do the same.

"Is that all?" the girda asked. "We can solve this problem tonight. Take me to the desert and I will lead you to a town where all the women are rich and beautiful. There you will find many willing to marry the emir's handsome youngest son. Choose one, and she will accompany you home, bringing her wealth, her servants, and her family's blessings on such a union. In the morning, you can ask your father to dine with you, and all will be well again."

Salim's heart quickened. But he hesitated, seeing disappointment in the girda's eyes.

"You are very kind to help me," he said. "But if I choose another, what will happen to you?"

"I will die," she answered.

Salim's joy was dashed by her words. "Then I won't do it. I brought you here and I won't trade your life for my happiness. No, little girda, you are still my bride. I won't be the cause of your death."

"I tell you, Salim, there can be nothing easier than this," the girda insisted, a paw resting on his thigh. "Take me back to the desert, and you will find that beautiful wife of your dreams."

Salim closed his eyes, imagining her: a long sweep of raven hair, slender limbs, and a heart-shaped face. Then he opened his eyes, and the vision vanished as he stared into the furred face of a girda. "What will happen to you?" he asked again.

"I will die," she replied gently.

"I won't reward your kindness with your death!" said Salim, shaking his head. "No, little girda, you will remain here with me. Somehow we shall manage."

"As you wish." The little girda shrugged. "But, Salim, have you not asked yourself how it is possible that I can talk? And if I am capable of such a thing, is it not also possible that I am capable of other remarkable things?"

"Why, yes," Salim answered, surprised.

"Good," said the girda, her gentle eyes holding Salim's astonished gaze. "Then trust me. Bid your father to dine with you tomorrow. Believe that, like your brothers' wives, I, too, can entertain the emir in the manner you would wish."

"All right, I will ask him," Salim agreed, his heart lightening. And for the first time, he wondered what manner of creature his spear had claimed in the desert.

§   §   §

That night, roused by curiosity at last, Salim went to his bride's bedroom. A stray shaft of moonlight from a crack in the roof illuminated the girda as she lay sleeping. Salim moved closer and saw that her furred pelt had split open at the back. Long black hair, entwined with golden chains, spilled through the split in the monkey skin. He touched it gently, surprised by its softness. The girda sighed and turned in her sleep, and Salim, filled with puzzlement and wonder, retreated from the room.

Early the next evening, Salim knocked upon the gate of his father's house. He was welcomed by the servants and brought before the emir, who was sitting in his garden with his second wife, Salim's mother. Bowing before his parents, he said: "Father, I have come to ask you to dine with me this night. At this very moment, my bride is preparing a feast."

The emir frowned. "My son, how can you ask such a thing? You have no proper marriage, for you disregarded my guidance and chose no woman to be your wife. How can I dine in a house such as yours?"

"I promise that you will not be disappointed or dishonored," Salim replied with more confidence than he felt, pressing the invitation until, at last, the emir reluctantly agreed.

As they walked through the village together, Salim's stomach churned at the thought of the dark, cheerless rooms he'd left behind. What did a girda know, after all, about entertaining an emir? Yet when they reached the house, the light from a hundred oil lamps bloomed brilliantly through the windows. At the doorway stood serving boys holding bowls of scented water with which to wash away the dust. Inside, the floors were covered with rugs of richly dyed wools and pillows of embroidered silk. Carved sandalwood tables held golden plates laden with mouthwatering food.

"From where comes this wealth, my son?" the emir asked, amazed.

"From my bride, Father," Salim replied.

The emir walked around the room, touching everything, as though to assure himself that it was real. Then he sat amid the silken cushions and ate, but sparingly, of the lavish feast. He was not entirely pleased, Salim realized, by his son's new-found prosperity. *My father believes me a liar*, he thought, *for what girda could have such a dowry? I barely know what to make of it myself. I must find a way to learn what else is hidden beneath the monkey's skin before I explain this mystery to him.*

The following morning, Salim awoke to a house that was once more dark and dreary. He might have wondered if he had dreamed the splendor of the night before, but the residue of spiced oil on his lips and the contentment of his full stomach declared that it had all been real. He resolved to talk to the girda, but before he could find her, a messenger arrived at the door.

The messenger bowed deeply. "I bring greetings from the emir," he said, "who wishes to repay you for your hospitality, and requests that you and your wife join with your brothers and their wives to attend a feast of gratitude."

Salim was struck dumb. He could not bring a monkey to dine with his brothers and their wives; it was more shame than he could possibly bear. He buried his head between his hands as the girda entered the room.

"What troubles you?" the girda asked. "Was your father not well pleased last night?"

"He was," Salim answered, his voice muffled by his palms. "So well indeed, that he now requests the presence of his three sons and their wives at his home to dine. I don't know what to do."

"You must go, of course," the girda replied.

"I can't. My little girda, you are my wife. I shall not break that vow. But I cannot take a monkey to dine in the house of an emir."

"Take me back to the desert and I will show you where to find a beautiful new wife."

"But what will happen to you?"

"As I told you before, I will die," she said.

"And as I have told you before, I won't let that happen!"

"You must choose: honor your father's wishes and bring me as your wife to his house tonight, or take me back to the desert and find a more suitable woman to take my place."

"I will not."

"Then I *shall* go to your father's feast."

"As you wish," Salim said, with a flush of temper. "But you will go alone, for I won't come with you!" He left the room angrily, saddled his horse, and rode away.

ஞ   ஞ   ஞ

Throughout the day, Salim galloped across the desert, trying to outrun his emotions. The horse grew weary, its flanks dark with sweat. Finally, at a small oasis, he stopped to give his horse a rest. Dismounting, his anger dissipating, Salim began to think more clearly. He knew he could not betray the girda; having brought her into his home, he could not now discard her simply to save himself from shame. Despite his dismay at such a bride, the girda had shown him nothing but kindness. And what had he given to her in return? He had not even thanked her for last night's feast. Or asked how it had been possible. Obsessed with the oddity of his marriage, he'd failed to note it was also remarkable. He recalled the sight of the girda sleeping, and of moonlight shining on long black hair spilling out of the split in the girda skin. It was then that Salim decided to stop running and search, instead, for answers.

Night was falling as Salim stabled his horse at a neighbor's house and then returned quietly to his own. He crept to the roof and found the small crack in the ceiling above the girda's bedroom. With his eye to the crack, he watched as she prepared for the emir's feast.

Standing, the girda waved her paw, and a mirror appeared on the rough mud wall. She studied her reflection with interest. Then her thick-furred pelt split down the back, and a woman emerged from the ugly skin. Salim bit his hand to keep from crying out. She was young and beautiful, with shapely limbs, high rounded breasts, and almond eyes in a heart-shaped face. He watched as she donned a fine linen shift, golden bangles, jeweled necklaces and combs—each item pulled from the monkey skin. Then she wrapped herself in a large silk shawl and left for his father's feast.

The moment she was gone, Salim hastened to her room. He picked up the discarded monkey skin, turning it inside out and realizing that it was as empty as the dried husk of a locust. Whatever magic existed was not in the skin but in the woman herself. She had gone to the emir as herself, Salim thought, and no longer needed it. Impulsively, he threw the hideous skin into the fire, where it sizzled with strange blue smoke until there was nothing left but ashes. Then, he sat and waited for his wife to return home.

🍃   🍃   🍃

Fatma, the daughter of the king of Alledjenu, smiled as she walked to the emir's house, for she had loved Salim from the moment she'd first seen him riding across the desert. She'd followed him in the guise of a hawk as he hunted close to her father's land, and he'd never known that a king's daughter was tracking him from above. She'd watched him many times since then, delighting in the ebony of his skin, his bold black eyes, and even white teeth. And on the day that he'd cast his spear into the desert, she'd coaxed the spear to come to her, leading the emir's son to a small oasis in her father's domain.

But his handsome face was no guarantee that he could love Fatma as she desired, faithfully and with a generous heart. She needed to be sure of him. And so she had devised her test, changing her fine hawk feathers for the dusky skin of a girda monkey. And oh, how he had suffered for his compassion toward her! A lesser man would have seized the chance to free himself from this wretched fate and gain a wealthy, beautiful wife. But not Salim. She had offered him the easiest of all possible escapes from his misery, but he had found the price too high. Despite his deep unhappiness, he had been nothing but honorable toward his monkey bride.

Fatma raised her head, catching the acrid odor of singed fur that followed her on the wind. She had been right, of course. Salim's kindness and generosity had allowed her to abandon the monkey skin. But in so doing, the monkey girl had died to allow the woman to become his true wife. Neither of them needed the skin anymore.

Fatma arrived at the emir's house, and two servants ushered her into the private chambers where he entertained his family. As she stood in the doorway, her shawl hiding her face, Fatma could hear the whispered complaints of the other wives, distraught at finding themselves expected to dine in the company of a monkey.

The emir called to her, "My sons' wives are not veiled in this room. You, too, must remove your veil and show your face. We will not insult you."

"And why should the chosen wife of your youngest son be insulted?" asked Fatma as she pulled off her shawl, her beauty emerging like the rising sun from the folds of the dark fabric. Salim's brothers and their wives stared at her, speechless. The emir devoured her with his eyes, his displeasure in his youngest son's marriage swept away by the sight of this regal young woman covered in gold and jewels.

Fatma lowered her gaze in modesty. She unwrapped a large diamond from a length of silk and presented it to her father-in-law. "Please accept this gift from my father, the king of Alledjenu—who, knowing of my love for your son, has granted me the privilege of marriage. I know that the mysterious manner of my presence here has grieved you, my lord. I came disguised in a monkey skin to determine if your son was as good and honorable as he is handsome. The girda skin repulsed him, yet he refused to harm the girda and seek another bride. Salim has passed my test. Now, if you'll excuse me, my lord, I shall return to our home in my own true shape, as a woman and as his loving wife." Fatma bowed her head before her startled in-laws, wrapped the shawl around her shoulders, and departed.

ဖ   ဖ   ဖ

Versed in magic as she was, Fatma could sense Salim long before she could see the house. She could feel the strength of his emotions, hear his heart drumming in anticipation of her return, and she willed the dark and dreary house to be filled with warmth and light. Her thoughts flew before her, lavishly redressing each room, preparing the house for her arrival. She gave special care to the seraglio, where this night she and Salim would finally sleep together as a married couple.

Arriving home at last, she threaded her way through the now elegant rooms until she came to the seraglio, where her young husband awaited her. A blue-tinged fire blazed within the hearth. No sign of the girda skin remained. Salim grinned, shyly at first, then broadly, his gaze never leaving her face. With a joyful laugh, for she knew herself to be loved, she flew into his open arms.

MIDORI SNYDER is a writer, folklorist, and the co-director of the award-winning Endicott Studio for the Mythic Arts. She has published eight books for adults, young adults, and children, winning the Mythopoeic Award for her Italian-ate novel *The Innamorati*. Her short stories, essays, and poems have appeared in many journals, anthologies, and "best of the year" collections. Her forthcoming books include a fairy novel with Jane Yolen, and a sequel to *The Innamorati*. She currently resides with her husband, Stephen Haessler, in Arizona.

ᔕᥱ

Author's Note

Who doesn't have a list of attributes that one looks for in a boy-friend or girlfriend, a husband or wife? We may be attracted to someone because they are beautiful or handsome—but that is rarely enough to attract us for long. So we all "test" these po-tential partners based on our own private list of preferences. It is one of the reasons why I have always enjoyed the tale of the Monkey Girl from the Kordofan of the Sudan. From a great distance, a magical bride sees a young man she likes and de-vises a clever plan to test him, really test him up close. Does the handsome man have integrity? Honor? Compassion? These are the qualities that matter most to her, and happily for the couple, the young man proves to be worthy. For me, top among the usual attractive qualities was a good sense of humor, and thirty years of marriage later, I can say I am still laughing.

PISHAACH

Shweta Narayan

On the day Shruti's grandfather was to be cremated, her grandmother went into the garden of their apartment complex to pick roses for a garland. She never came back. Shruti's father and uncle went on to the crematorium with the body and the priest, while Shruti's mother sat cross-legged on the floor in her heavy silk sari and wailed on Auntie's shoulder, and the police searched for Ankita Bai.

Shruti climbed up to a sunlit windowsill, crumpling her stiff new pink dress. She leaned against the mosquito screen to peer down at the garden, its layered tops of coconut palms, mango trees, banana palms, and frangipani bushes spreading their greens over bright smears of rose and bougainvillea. Mama blew her nose noisily and sniffled, then wiped her face on the embroidered end of her sari. Auntie rolled her eyes.

The doorbell buzzed. Shruti's brother and cousin raced off to answer it, and came back almost bouncing with excitement. With them was a policeman, cap in hand.

"You should ask my sister questions," said Gautam importantly. "Ankita Nani always talked to her."

The policeman came over to the window and bent over Shruti, his hands on his knees. He was balding and shiny with sweat, and his khaki uniform bulged at the stomach. "Do you know where your Nani went, little girl?" he asked.

Shruti nodded and pointed out the window.

He looked out, sighed, patted her head, and went to talk to Mama.

Shaking Mama off, Auntie went into the kitchen. She pulled *jalebis*, bright orange and gleaming with sugar syrup, out of the fridge, and set a plate of them by the policeman. She gave one to each boy and a half to Shruti. Shruti looked down at the sticky sweet, then held it out to Gautam, but her cousin Vikram grabbed it out of her hand and ran into their room. Gautam chased after him.

Shruti sat on the window ledge in a stream of dusty golden light, watching her mother and aunt. She did not cry, and she did not speak. They never heard her speak again.

ॐ   ॐ   ॐ

Nani told me things.

She told me the forest is all around us, as close as breath, as close as my shadow to the ground. She told me there are entrances. Even here in Mumbai. I cannot get there yet, though. The city sticks to me like skin.

Skin comes off. I tried that. But it hurts, and there is blood, and Mama puts antiseptic cream on it and scolds.

Nani told me that it doesn't hurt when snake skin comes off. Only humans need blood to change. She said there will be blood when I become a woman, and change breeds change, so I'll be able to shed this skin. She told me how.

She didn't tell me where she has gone, but I know. She went back to the forest. Mama does not know, and I cannot tell her because it's a secret.

Nani told me lots of secrets. They fill my mouth and bubble on my tongue, like cola or like music. I will never ever speak them, though, even if Papa shouts and Auntie slaps me, because Nani said I mustn't.

ॐ   ॐ   ॐ

Shruti returned to school to find that she was something of a celebrity. Even the older children clustered around her, asking what had happened to her grandmother. It had been in the newspapers.

She did not answer.

They put it down to grief at first, but she didn't cry, and soon one of the popular girls decided that she was a stuck-up little bitch. She became first the playground target, then the playground ghost: nowhere to be found.

They tracked her down, finally, by her music. Found her sitting on a wall twice her height, cross-legged, playing a flute. The wall was crawling with lizards and little snakes, and a one-legged crow perched silently on Shruti's bony knee.

They started calling her *Pishaach*.

ॐ   ॐ   ॐ

They always chase me. They know I will not scream. *Pishaach*, they call me, and they glare, as if my silence were a threat. *Pishaach, Pishaach,* and they pull my hair and squeeze the juice from orange skins into my eyes.

Vikram joins them when my brother isn't there.

I can run faster, though, and I am not scared of the roof. They are. Stupid little boys.

I like the roof, though it smells like smog and piss and the *marihana* that the big boys smoke. Vikram doesn't come up here; the bigger boys would beat him if he did. I go from shadow into bright afternoon, sneeze, and make my way over the hot roof to the low wall that runs around its edge, stepping over broken glass and needles. Carefully. Gautam says they could give me AIDS.

I leave that behind, leave the rancid mattress and used condoms behind. They're all illusion anyway; Mama says everything is. Over the central partition lies my own palace, where the roof is too weak to hold the bigger children. I walk over my courtyard to my balcony: a magic princess, kept from her land and her true nature by the wicked *rakshasas*, her only solace the music of her dead grandfather's flute.

Vikram told me what the mattress and condoms were for. Gautam told him not to tell me dirty things, but I don't care.

My balcony is a brighter yellow than the rest of the wall. Sitting cross-legged, looking out over my crawling, roaring city, I pull out Nana's flute and play to the world.

ॐ   ॐ   ॐ

The flute was Gautam's, really. Nana had left it to him. The only sounds he could coax from it were hideous squeaks and wheezes, so it collected dust on the dresser until the morning Gautam woke to his Nana's music and a shape at the window, flat black against the pale gray of early dawn. Gautam sat up on his mattress and watched silently with wide eyes and dry throat until the figure moved and became recognizably his sister.

Vikram slept through it all. He didn't notice for several days that Shruti had the flute. Then he said, "You should have given it to me."

"You don't even play," said Gautam. "And he wasn't your *nana*."

"I'm the eldest."

Shruti left the flute at the feet of their idol of Krishna, though, and not even Vikram would take it from that place. Over the years, this became the flute's home.

꧁   ꧁   ꧁

The crows are my brothers, enchanted to take winged form until the sun goes down. The geckos are my cousins; numerous, scurrying, and easily scared. The snakes who find me even up here are, of course, Naga; my Nani's kin, drawn as the snake people always are to music. The sparrows are just sparrows.

Music draws my secret kin to me and lets me see with my eyes closed, see the truth. It soars, the mood poised between hope and heartbreak, weaving the story of a captive princess.

Almost full moon, and I am nearly a woman. Mama had to take me shopping for bras this week.

I must touch moonlight for three nights running—full moon and the night on either side—and pray for him to break my enchantment. It must happen while I am on this threshold. The moon will bring my period within the month, and with the blood I will cast aside this skin. Nani said it would be so. She said it would hurt, too, but I don't mind.

If I do not touch the moon I will be doomed to stay human.

꧁   ꧁   ꧁

Shruti drew snakes in art class. They started as crayon wiggles and grew into pencil studies and sketches of sinuous beauty—cobras on walls, in doorways, silhouetted against the full moon. They earned her excellent marks, except when the assignment was portraits or flowers.

She drew snakes in maths and Hindi as well, which never earned her excellent marks.

ᘓ   ᘓ   ᘓ

Full moon.

Moonlight does not truly come into our apartment; it is trapped in a watery smear by the mosquito netting. Last night I went up to the roof to find it, and the people on the mattress almost saw me. I will try the garden tonight.

Gautam sleeps soundly, and getting past the adults is easy; Papa snores louder than any noise I can make, and Auntie and Uncle sleep in the big room at the end of the hall. But last night Vikram's eyes followed me when I returned.

A lullaby on the flute sends him into a deep sleep. It almost does the same to me. I slip out of the apartment yawning.

I am silence in the building, a shadow on the path, a barefoot snake girl in the garden. I touch the moon, let him spill silvery brightness through my fingers; and turn, and sway, and dance in a wordless prayer to the soundless music of dark and light.

Behind me, the door closes. I spin. A form on the front steps, then a growing silhouette. Vikram. I step back.

"Where do you go alone at night, *Pishaach?*" He closes in on me, long-legged. His voice is a low and vicious monotone. "You live in our house, you eat our food, we put up with you—we coddle you, you freakish mute. How dare you go sneaking

out like a thief, and—don't even think about raising that demon flute. I know what you did to me."

I back into the darkness under the trees, flinch as his arm
reaches out toward me.

"Ah, now you remember your place. Maybe you remember
also what happens to little girls who don't behave." He grins
suddenly, moonlight glinting in his eyes, his teeth. "You can't
even scream. Everyone will think you were willing."

I shift my weight.

"Where will you run?" he whispers. "You didn't bring the
key. You can't get back in without me. Stupid little slut."

There is a pounding in my ears. Vikram laughs. He smells
of cologne and smoke, clogging my breath. A van, backing up,
plays a tinny "Ode to Joy." I could run for the street. But that
has its own dangers. I take another step back, and another,
and my heel touches something that is not a plant. Something
smooth and warm; something that starts sliding past me in
response, shrinking Vikram to a merely human terror. I stop.
Auto horns blare. Shapes around me spring into definition. A
motorcycle coughs.

A king cobra raises its head in a single sketched curve of
light. I take a breath. Taste jasmine, ripening bananas, blood.
The tail caresses my heel, lingers, and moves on.

I set my foot slowly down. Vikram goes still, as I did, eyes
white and wide. A breeze chills the sweat on my skin.

The snake pauses between the two of us; draws slowly
higher, barely swaying, until it is face-to-face with Vikram;
then sinks, becomes a shadow, leaves silence behind. I feel the
motorcycle's roar, the stillness of the trees, my hammering
heart. I hear nothing.

Then Vikram takes a shaky breath and bácks up onto

the path. "Good luck getting out of there unbitten, bitch," he calls. He crosses his arms over his chest and smirks. "I'll enjoy watching."

I remember my flute.

Even when the moon is full, its dark is only a few days away. I play that dark to Vikram now, play unseen terrors, images of death slow and painful, fears of life and love gone wrong. I play the hypnotic, deadly beauty of the cobra, and the nightmare chaos of an auto accident. The music tastes of bile and blood. It rushes forth, wailing, screeching—and Vikram breaks for home.

I ease out of the garden while he fumbles for the key, then run after him. I catch the door before he closes it. Look at him.

I arch forward, smile at Vikram, and say, "Boo."

ॐ   ॐ   ॐ

Vikram did not return to their room that night. He spent it shivering on the sofa, though the night was warm, and that is where Auntie found him the next day. He woke when she went to him, put his head on her shoulder like a much smaller boy, and whispered, "That demon flute, Mama. She put a spell on me."

She coaxed his version of the story out of him, then tucked him into her own bed and went seething to make the coffee.

When Shruti's mother sleepily joined her, Auntie said, "If you cannot control your—daughter—she can sleep in your room from now on."

Mama tried to understand what was wrong. She asked Auntie, and Gautam, and Vikram when he woke. But not Shruti, of course.

ॐ   ॐ   ॐ

I wait until Gautam's breathing slows into sleep, then roll to my feet and ghost into the kitchen, my steps silent on the hard, cool floor. On the way, I switch on the bathroom light and close the door.

The altar is in an alcove set into the kitchen wall. It smells faintly of sandalwood. I reach in to take my flute back from Lord Krishna.

It is gone.

I kneel before the altar, my fingers searching the space under it, the crack between its edge and the wall. They find only incense ash.

"Looking for something?"

Pale golden light washes past me. I turn to see Vikram lit by the open fridge, my flute clenched in one hand. "You thought I would let you have it, after yesterday, or what?" he asks. His voice is too calm. "And you thought that trick with the bathroom light would fool me? I'm not the dumb one."

I uncoil, coming to my feet fast, and grab for the flute. He holds it over my head with one hand, pushes me away with the other. I hit the wall.

"Come on," he says. "Give me an excuse to break it."

I turn on my heel and run for the front door. He follows me, leans over me as I reach for the doorknob, laughs softly into my ear. His breath disturbs my hair.

I need only touch the moonlight one more time. But I doubt he will even let me get downstairs. And perhaps I will not bleed until the ritual is complete. I slump, turn back to our room, drag my mattress over next to Gautam's, and settle back in. With Vikram's eyes on me, I pray to the Moon and to Durga to give me time.

My first period starts four days later. As Nani warned me, it hurts.

ॐ   ॐ   ॐ

There once lived, among the Naga people, a girl of surpassing beauty. Her tail looped in long coils and her scales looked new-molted, shining and unmarred. She was alluring even in human form, with hooded eyes and long shining hair like the dark of the moon. The fair hue of her underbelly spread to all her human skin, and she kept the serpent's grace.

Perhaps she was a princess; perhaps she was a queen. Perhaps she was merely a lovely girl from a Naga village.

Taking human form, this girl would escape her lands and come to ours, seeking music. There is no music in the Naga lands. It is their only lack, and the reason they wear our clothes and dare our world. This girl loved music even more than most, and she risked more, and lost. For she was trapped by a snake charmer, who took her home to be his wife.

So my Nani told me, and there she would always stop.

"What happened to her, Nani?"

"She learned to make rotis and curries and beds, and she learned to eat mice and rats only when nobody could see," she would say. "She had a daughter, in time, and that daughter had two children. A boy and a girl. And that girl, that Naga's granddaughter, has in her the magic of our people."

It seemed incredible, even then. Not that she was otherworldly. No, with her dark knowing eyes in her walnut face and her hair of spun moonlight, that was obvious. What stunned me was that she might once have been young. "Were you really beautiful, Nani?"

She would laugh. "For many, many years. It is only in this form that we truly age, Asha."

Asha. Hope. She called me that always. I did not understand why; I had been named after music, and she loved music.

ॐ ॐ ॐ

Mama found the flute in the back of a cupboard, behind the pressure cooker. She lectured Shruti about caring for the family heirloom, while Vikram smirked, and kept the flute locked up for a week.

Meanwhile, Vikram hid Shruti's homework. He rubbed soap into her toothbrush. He spilled black ink on her new school uniform. He left cockroaches in her pillowcase. Shruti may as well have been Untouchable in Auntie's eyes, but Mama was angry, so she cried on Gautam's shoulder. He was annoyed at first, inclined to shrug her off, but after the cockroaches he got into a shouting match with Vikram and called him a bastard. Auntie heard him.

Shruti took to hiding in her room after school. When Vikram followed her, she started disappearing, up to the roof or into the garden with the flute. But one day the downstairs grannies stopped talking and glared when they saw her, and she realized that Auntie must have told them something. She ran away.

They never found the cobra, nor any sign of it, but Shruti was blamed for every snakebite in the area thereafter. She started playing her music in the early morning, when nobody would see her. Women hawking vegetables were her accompaniment; the neighbors kept away and told their children to do the same.

Her mother stopped talking to the neighbors; Gautam

stopped playing cricket with Vikram's friends. Her father grew solemn and silent. They would not hear ill of Shruti in public.

Three years later the city had a miracle: a boy who was able to pick up cobras without coming to harm. He was on the television, and his parents were interviewed. Shruti's neighbors argued about whether the boy was blessed by Lord Shiva or Lord Vishnu.

Shruti could pick cobras up, too, but Shruti was far too unsettling to be a miracle.

ॐ   ॐ   ॐ

Mama waits until Papa and Uncle approve of the curry before saying, "Shruti made it."

Papa glares at her. "And that makes it all right? What shall we say to the young men? She does not talk, she frightens all the neighbors, worms and lizards come to hear her play that damned flute—but she makes a fairly good curry?"

Auntie adds, "When she's helped at every step."

Vikram makes a show of spitting the curry out, nose wrinkled.

Gautam looks coolly at him and takes another bite. I look down at my own plate. The smell of ghee and cardamom is cloying. What will my home be like when Gautam leaves—to go to college, to start his own life?

"She's a good girl," Mama protests, "and she learns well."

"Then teach her to speak."

Mama looks down at her plate, biting her lip.

"She's unnatural," says Auntie. "Like your mother was."

Uncle frowns at her. "That's enough."

Papa says, "But she's right."

Gautam clears his throat. "How do you think we will do in the test match, Papa?"

I look at them—at my mother trying to make herself small, my brother trying to distract Papa—and I am glad no man will have me. I get up, leaving my food barely touched, and walk away.

"Shruti!"

Papa no longer frightens me. Nani's eyes can silence him, even when they are in my face. I look at him until he looks away, then turn and leave the apartment.

ॐ ॐ ॐ

Ankita Nani's eyes never left Nana when he was playing his flute. She watched him, unblinking and adoring—as romantic to a child as any Bollywood film. Only when he died, when she told me she was going home, did I see the shadow behind the romance.

She obeyed him, of course, just as Mama obeys Papa. Is every girl a Naga, stolen away to serve her husband?

ॐ ॐ ॐ

The wall that runs around the roof bears new graffiti. Bold and elaborate in silvered red, it says VIKR. He has left cans of spray paint under the letters; Vikram does not delay when Auntie expects him downstairs. I pick up the silver, shake it, and draw a slow outward spiral centered on the K. When it is big enough I spiral back in, filling in the gaps to make a moon, so that only the huge V and the R's looping tail still show. I spray one practiced black curve over the moon: a cobra, its tail extending along the wall.

The roof was mine first.

I pick my way over to the other side. My side. I have to keep to the edges, along the wall, because the rest will not hold my weight anymore.

Cross-legged on the yellow patch of outer wall that I used to call my balcony, I play the music of moonlit gardens and enchantments that can be broken. I face the roof instead of the city so that Vikram cannot sneak up on me, and so I see the cobra raise his head.

He rises till his eyes are level with my own. His body is dappled, liquid motion. He could kill me with one strike, but that is abstract knowledge: my heart does not race, my breath does not shorten. I envy his grace; I do not fear it. Perhaps this is what it means to be *Pishaach*.

I play for the cobra, and he dances for me while sunset stains the sky orange and purple behind him.

Vikram comes through the doorway and stops, his mouth a comical O. His eyes slide from me to the snake to his graffiti, and he slips back indoors.

I lower my flute. He will be back. I am not sure how to let the snake know, but when the music stops he lowers his hood and slithers into my shadow. I look down but cannot see him.

I lower one foot to the ground. It touches ground and nothing else. The cobra has vanished.

When Vikram returns with his thugs they see only me, sitting where I should not be and playing the sun down. They come to the center partition to stare at me, at the empty roof. I smile.

Amit laughs at Vikram. Vikram punches him. Stalks away. The rest leave soon enough.

But I do not dare go home until Gautam comes to find me.

♪ ♪ ♪

Shruti passed her classes, but only just. She did not have a tutor, as most students did, and many nights she would forget her homework in music. Her teachers were less amused by her doodles every year. At the end of Tenth Standard one teacher told her parents that she was only good for the arts, if that.

Vikram and Gautam spent that summer closeted with tutors. Vikram was preparing for engineering college, and Gautam for Twelfth Standard. Most days, nobody knew where Shruti went. A frown grew between her mother's eyebrows, and she watched Shruti silently at meals.

Uncle took Papa aside one day. "You will have to decide what to do with her, you know," he said. "She's a good girl in her way, but . . ."

"Yes," said Papa. "But."

♪ ♪ ♪

I pause in the doorway to catch my breath, almost coughing at the smoke. Vikram and his gang are on my roof. I could exile them, set the snake on them. But if I did, what would Vikram do tonight?

I dodge an auntie's venomous glare and slip downstairs to hide under the bougainvillea, where sunlight falls in patches of magenta and the air is thick and sweet with mango and flowering rose.

I take one delicious breath, then pause. The air is too cool and too clean. There is no exhaust underlying the sweetness, no smog. No sound of children from the apartment beyond. The garden has lost its boundaries; when I raise the flute there are a hundred ears listening. I take a step forward, hesitate.

A hand on my shoulder. I twist, ready to strike, and find a bare chest. Skin like polished teak, and the dark smell of earth just after rain. I look up.

He is slender, and the curve of his cheek is a boy's, but his eyes are clear and old as drops of amber. His hair falls unbound to the middle of his back, and light glints from a silver circlet as he leans down. I should be frightened, and am not, and that tells me who he is.

"Asha," he murmurs, his lips close to mine, "won't you play for me?"

I play for him there in the multicolored light, in our tiny section of an endless forest, and he dances for me. Below the waist his body is a snake's.

He touches me, later, with fingers and lips and coils, making my heart hammer and my breath quicken with something other than fear. I run my fingers over coffee-bean skin, trying to find where it turns into scales.

৯   ৯   ৯

Naga do not marry.

They may build a home together, raise children together, create their lives together; but their ceremonies are only for birth and naming and death.

They tell a story about this: long ago, when the snake people married, a fair Naga girl was to marry a handsome youth. But at the wedding, with all the village gathered, her musk attracted and maddened the groom's younger brother, who claimed her for himself. The brothers fought over her, long and hard and viciously, and each died of the other's poison. In grief and shame the girl ran away, and never was seen again. The snake people have had no marriage since that day, and no true fights in mating season.

But my Nani considered herself married. "Once the gods have been called," she said, "we cannot pretend that they were not here."

ৡ   ৡ   ৡ

His lips brush against my neck. "Asha, play for me." We are in the garden again, among the dappled green scents and shadows, as we have been more often than is wise.

I find my voice. "Why." It sounds dusty.

"You know I love your music," he whispers in my ear. My breath catches at his voice, his closeness, his hands on my stomach, his heartbeat against my back; but his words are not the words I want.

I love your voice, I want to say. *I love the way you move, the way you smell, the nonexistent point where skin becomes scale. I love the way you shimmer between forms, as I cannot and ache to and never will. I love the curves and the planes of your body, and I love your shifting face. I want to know who you are, and that is who I want to keep with me. Do you only love my music?*

There are too many words. They jostle and clog in my throat. I shake my head.

"You know I do," he says, "and you know you will."

The air squeezes from my lungs. Have I no say in what I do? How dare he think so? I take a breath and start to play Nana's song.

He grows rigid, his heartbeat quickening. His hands drop away from me. "No," he says.

I turn to him; see terror, adoration; remember the way Nani looked at Nana. I stop playing.

He watches my eyes, my hands. He looks at me like I'm Vikram.

I will not be Vikram.

"No," I agree. "Go free."

His eyes widen. He shimmers, becomes first a cobra, then merely another shadow. I play then, play him the words I could not speak before, but only the shadows hear.

ʂ ʂ ʂ

Shruti started haunting the garden, playing eerie, melancholy tunes that made the babies cry. Or so the neighbors said. Vikram said she was probably making their mothers cry, too. And souring their milk, and rotting the mangoes and bananas on the branches. Auntie wanted to know why, if that girl would not make pleasant music, she was allowed to play that flute at all.

Papa told Shruti to stay out of the garden.

Two days before the full moon, she bought a child's recorder made of bright blue plastic.

ʂ ʂ ʂ

I have been mostly alone when I've played. But not every time. He must need the music like I need to shift, to escape. Unfair that he may have what he needs; but my lack is not his fault.

I touch the moonlight, feel my leaden form struggle for a moment to become fluid, to shed its skin. Feel it give up. I settle at the base of the coconut palm and play until the forest is listening. Then I pull out the recorder, play a simple tune.

"Gift," I say in my dusty, unused voice.

I set it aside and get up. When I look down again, it is gone.

ॐ   ॐ   ॐ

Anywhere three trees grow together, the land's invisible border rubs thin, and the great forest grows so close that it sometimes spills over.

The forest has no edge, but it has many, many frayed borders. It likes opening into our world for a beckoning, teasing, deadly instant. It is fully alive, this forest, with giant trees draped with giant vines, their leaves bigger than me; with dirt-colored flowers and flower-colored birds and sleek, silent predators. Naga live in the rivers, in the wet earth, and in hollow trees; the monkey people claim the canopy. Garuda sometimes nest on the highest branches, which border on their realm.

It is home to great beauty, the forest, in form and scent and movement, but the only music found there is the music of the natural world, calls and cries and falling rain.

So my Nani told me.

"Why?" I asked.

"We do not make music."

"Why not?"

"Perhaps we have not the skill."

"I do."

"It is not something we learn, Asha. We do not live as you do here." She smiled sadly, but she said no more.

ॐ   ॐ   ॐ

I play to myself in the punishing afternoon, when I know I will be alone. To myself and to the forest beyond. I play with my eyes closed, letting the world paint itself in touch and smell. Overripe bananas, frying onions and cumin, my own sweat beaded on my forehead and dampening my clothes. The occasional breeze, warm, bringing the stench of exhaust and burning garbage. My fingers, slippery on the flute.

The taste of his musk, of earth after rainfall, brings my eyes half-open. I watch for him through my eyelashes, and let my fingers and breath sing him a lonely mood. He drifts into view, shifting uncertainly from half form to cobra and back; he starts to dance and stops again.

When I draw breath, he shifts to full man, naked, too wild for modesty. I look away, shame and lust burning my cheeks.

"Show me?"

I look back. His gaze is wary, but he holds the little blue recorder as though it were precious. I hold out a hand. He edges forward. I grasp his wrist to pull him closer. He jerks back, shifts to cobra, disappears.

I pick up the recorder. Will he come back for it, if not for me? I play a note. Sniff and blink tears away. Whisper, "Come back."

I hear lorry and rickshaw horns in the silence. Then his voice, behind me. "Will you charm me?"

I shake my head.

"How can I know?"

I turn to look at him. "Could kill me," I suggest.

He stares for a second, then slides forward till I can feel his warmth. His tail curls around my ankle. "I would not." I keep looking at him, and eventually his lips twist into something that might be a smile. "But how can you know?"

I nod.

"What should we do?"

I reach out again to take his hand, and this time he does not start. I shape it around the recorder, showing his long fingers where to be.

He laughs, silently and a bit raggedly. "That is . . . not quite the answer I was expecting."

ꕯ   ꕯ   ꕯ

The monkey people are territorial. Sooner steal a Garuda's egg than seek the monkeys' great city in the trees.

Not so the Naga. They care little about land, only one race frightens them, and that race cannot find their homes.

When my Nani told me this I did not understand.

She glanced at me, cutting onions by feel. Her eyes were bright, the knife swift and steady in her wrinkled hand. "You will," she said.

ꕯ   ꕯ   ꕯ

He is waiting for me in the garden, his tail coiled under him, his head in his hands. He looks up as I hurry over, but he does not speak until I am close. Then he puts his arms around me, leans his head on my shoulder, and says, "They took it away."

"Who?" I do not have to ask what. I hold him, stroking his hair, breathing in its dark-leaf fragrance.

"The elders. Not all of them; your Nani said not to."

My arms tighten around him. "Nani?"

"She is our storyteller. But the rest are—angry—that any of us would learn your people's magic, and shocked that any of us *could*."

"Magic?" The lizards and birds do not come when he plays.

"Making the sweet sounds with your fingers. They said it was wrong, and . . . they took it away."

The grief in his voice shakes me. Even Auntie would not take music away from me. I ask, "Why?"

"They're scared, I suppose." He speaks into my shoulder. "Of course they're scared. It is our bane. So beautiful, so powerful . . ." He pulls back, looks at me, and says, "We cannot resist that pull."

I rest a fingertip on his nose. "Bane."

He blinks.

I smile and hold the flute to his lips. He reaches out a hand, slowly, to touch it, and looks wide-eyed at me.

"Blow," I say.

He does. It makes no sound at all. He looks surprised, and indignant, and I cannot help but laugh. This makes him glower, so I kiss him before showing him how to coax a sound from the flute.

Later, as his fingers trace the beadwork on my *kurti*, around my neck, across my breasts; as my lips are learning the shape and taste of him in the dark, he says, "I am not allowed to be here."

I kiss his shoulder, his neck, his jaw. Whisper in his ear, "Nor I."

ॐ   ॐ   ॐ

Papa's call pulled Mama out of the kitchen, wiping flour off her hands, and Gautam out of his room to the big, scarred-wood dining table. Vikram was at the other end, with heavy books around him, and Vikram showed no signs of leaving. Shruti was still in the garden and did not hear.

"Well," Papa said, "maybe it's for the best. She will be less of a problem if she hears it from Gautam."

Vikram looked up.

"Hears what, Papa?" Gautam asked.

Mama polished an imagined smudge from the wood with the end of her sari.

Papa sighed. "She cannot go to college," he said, "and no normal man will marry her. And Mr. Bhosle says Amit heard her playing that music of hers *with* someone. What next?"

Gautam said, "She can stay with me."

"A live-in mousetrap," said Vikram.

Auntie, coming in with a stack of stainless steel plates, laughed. "Wait until you have a wife, Gautam." She set the plates on the table with a clatter.

"But listen," said Papa, "I know a much better solution. I have written to—you know that boy, he was on television. The one who holds cobras. He is still alive; I wrote to his parents. They agreed that he should meet Shruti."

"Oh, what a good idea," Mama said. "They will have so much in common."

"They can open a pet shop," said Vikram.

Gautam glared. "Don't you have somewhere else to be?"

"Than in my own home?"

Gautam turned his back on Vikram and said, "She's never even met the boy."

"Your mother's right. They both like snakes to the point of obsession. Neither is quite—normal . . ."

Vikram snorted.

". . . but his parents are happy that she will not scream at his cobras."

"She's only sixteen, Papa."

"Am I getting her married tomorrow?"

"Are they Brahmins?" asked Mama.

"No, but they are well-off, and we cannot be too—" He stopped, and glanced at Gautam. "That is, in this day and age, it is very old-fashioned to care about caste."

Gautam pushed himself to his feet. Hands flat on the table, he leaned over his father. "You talk like she's defective," he said.

Vikram murmured, "There's a reason for that."

"She's not stupid, Vikram. She's clever enough to stay away from you."

The microwave beeped insistently into the silence that followed.

"Vikram," said Auntie, a little too loudly, "can you clear away your books and call your Papa? It's time for dinner."

"She's just . . . innocent, Papa. Look, you don't need to worry about her. She can stay with me. Really."

"What kind of life would that be for her?" Mama demanded. "Unmarried, unwanted, and underfoot in her brother's house? No!"

"Sit down," said Papa. "I know you want your sister to be happy. We all do. But you are too young to see the wisdom of age."

"Does the wisdom of age mean settling her life behind her back?"

"If she cannot even be home at dinnertime, maybe it does!"

Gautam's eyes widened. "Shit."

"Gautam," said Mama, "What have we said about language?"

"Well, it's not like her, is it? I'd better go look."

Vikram stood up, smiling. "I'll go with you," he said. "Mama, you'll clear my books, won't you? The poor darling might be in trouble."

§ § §

Knowing that we are both disobeying our elders brings us closer. I do not leave when I normally would, nor do I pull away when he tugs at my *kurti*, when he eases it over my head. My jeans follow. The bra confuses him, until I help.

He is a shadow cast by the waning moon above me, black limned with silver. His tail strokes my leg, tossing an arc of light between its coils, and light catches in his circlet. He picks jasmine flowers, lets them drift through his fingers onto my bare skin. I taste jasmine on the roof of my mouth, and crushed leaves, and arousal. He leans down. Kisses my neck. I feel teeth against my skin.

He slides a hand teasingly down my belly, and shifts. The wind grows stronger, bringing me the rich leaf-scent of the great forest. His magic tingles just under my skin. I arch up, aching to shift, and find myself pressed against him. He is in man-form. His gasp matches my own. We stare at each other.

We both hear the snap of a broken twig.

We freeze. Another footfall and he shifts, from man to half snake to snake.

I snatch my jeans and jam my legs into them. *Not Vikram, I pray, not here, not now.*

The snake melts into shadows. I grab my *kurti*, telling myself that he had no choice. A click, and the great forest is washed away on a wave of overbright blue light, leaving me alone. I hold the *kurti* to my chest.

"What have you been doing?" It is Gautam's voice. And

Gautam's LED key chain torch, the one he is so proud of. I wince.

"I think that's pretty clear, no?" says Vikram behind him. "The question is, who's Little Miss Innocence doing it *with*?"

I clutch my *kurti* closer.

"Put that on, stupid. It's not for playing with."

I twist away and pull it quickly over my head, inside out, trying not to show him more than he has already seen. Beadwork scrapes against me.

"I never would have believed it," says Gautam softly.

Vikram shoulders past him. I shrink back. "Believe what you want," says Vikram. "The question is what the neighbors—" His foot jerks sideways under him and he falls crashing through the bougainvillea bush. He screams.

Shadows swing wildly as Gautam runs toward us. He stops short of the bush, grabs his torch, points it. The shadows still. Wrapped around Vikram's ankle, gleaming black against the blue-gray garden, are cobra's coils.

Vikram tries to sit up, bloody scratches on his face and arms. The snake strikes. Vikram falls back and is still. A little wordless sobbing noise comes from my throat.

Gautam says shakily, "He—" He draws a hissing breath. "Ambulance."

The snake shimmers, shifts to half man. Says, "No need."

Gautam stares.

"No kills in mating season."

They watch each other, the Naga swaying to silent music. I smell fear but cannot tell whose it is. Gautam pulls himself up straight. The Naga rises to match his height. Like the forest, he is washed away in the LED's harsh glare; he looks as though he has gathered shadows for protection from the light.

Gautam shakes his head. "Mating," he says blankly. "Mating? You're—and she's a child."

"She was willing."

Gautam glances at me but turns back to the Naga. "How would you know?" he demands. "You're not even human."

"I know she was willing, because I saw her unwilling. When he tried." He points at Vikram, lying silent.

"What?"

I shake my head. Blood seeps from Vikram's scratches, black as the paper-thin bougainvilleas scattered around and over him.

"I don't know what you have done to my sister, but—"

"Done to her?" He draws himself higher, and higher yet, spreading his arms out like a hood. "I protect her. I hear her." He starts a slow glide toward me, looking all the time at Gautam.

"Don't you touch her!" Gautam stumbles forward, raising a fist.

The half-man shadow shrinks, becomes a snake. Hisses.

No kills in mating season.

Between rivals.

But Gautam is my brother. I shake my head again, but I am more invisible than even a shadow, and neither one sees me.

The cobra sways. I scream, "No!"

The cobra stops. Turns in a beautiful, silent arc and comes to me, slides over me, wraps himself around my arm, across my shoulder.

Gautam's hand falls, and he stares at me. "You can *talk*?"

I stare back. There is too much to say.

"What else have you kept from me, Shruti? Why? I thought we were close."

I want to run to him, to hold him. I want to explain. "Vikram talks better," I say.

Gautam's eyes widen. "Then he did . . . ?"

I nod.

"You should have told me. Why didn't you tell me? I would have believed you."

"And Papa?"

"*Aaizhavli.*" He puts a hand to his face. "Papa."

"What?"

"Papa has a suitable boy in mind for you."

I cringe, shake my head. "No," I say.

He nods. "And I don't know what I can do for you, after this."

I keep shaking my head.

The snake slips off my shoulders, shifts to half man, and wraps his arms around my waist. I twist around, rest my face against his chest, taste his wet-earth scent. He says, "Am I a suitable boy?"

I look up and meet his gaze. Warm. Anxious. He gestures wide with one hand, offering me the dark deep forest.

The elders cannot want a charmer in their land. Will they accept me? Send me back? Kill me? I am no shifter. What will they do to him? But I start to smile. If he will risk their anger, so will I. I say, "Yes."

"You must be joking," says Gautam. "Can you take him to meet Mama and Papa? Can you live in a snake hole? Think a little."

I turn back to Gautam. My best friend in this world; but I will not let him say no for me. I stare him down.

"But, Shruti . . ." Light grows in Gautam's eyes; he blinks, and it streaks down his face. "If you, well . . . I would miss you. Horribly. But would you be happy?"

"Maybe." I push my Naga's hands gently away, stand, and go to Gautam. "Best chance."

He takes a breath. Hugs me suddenly. Tight. "Then—go. And Vikram can bloody well die here, for all I care."

I hug him back. "No," I say. "Help him." I turn and walk out of the false light.

The forest looms immediately around me, its shadows half-felt, half-seen. The ground is uncertain, the sky dark, and the trees darker yet. They taste of death as well as life, their roots drinking sharp blood and slow rot. Thick vines coil and hang from branches, brushing my skin, and some are not vines at all. I see eyes, faintly golden, unblinking, watching me.

"Wait." It is faint, barely heard. I turn back.

I have to squint to see Gautam. He is faded, like an old photograph. But he is holding out the flute to me, and it is solid to my reaching fingers. He is not.

I want to say good-bye, to tell him that I love him. But he is gone, and the garden, and everything but the flute. I raise it to my lips and play a gentle song of hope and healing. Perhaps he hears it.

Then I reach out for my lover's hand, and it is warm in mine; and we turn together and go into the forest.

§ § §

On the day Shruti's father planned to tell her about her future husband, she went into the garden to play her flute. She never came back.

SHWETA NARAYAN is a cultural crazy quilt: she was born in India and lived in Malaysia, Saudi Arabia, the Netherlands, and Scotland before moving to California. She's particularly interested in boundaries and the people who cross them, and her fictional landscape is something of a Great Forest.

She grew up reading folktales and fairy tales from all over—and whatever was on the bookshelf—but didn't discover her love of short stories until she was given *The Green Man* anthology in college. She read that in one big gulp and hasn't stopped since, so she's particularly thrilled to be included in this anthology.

Shweta's a graduate of the Clarion 2007 writers' workshop, for which she received the Octavia E. Butler Memorial Scholarship. She has stories forthcoming in *Strange Horizons*, *Shimmer*, and *GUD Magazine*, and poetry in *Goblin Fruit*. She can be found on the Web at www.shwetanarayan.org.

Author's Note

I love snakes. I love the way they move, the way they feel; if I were going to be drawn away from the world by an animal-person, you can bet it would be a Naga.

"Pishaach" isn't really like the snake stories I grew up on, though. Traditional Nagas aren't even shape-shifters. I think they ought to be—they're drawn half snake half human, and snakes are a symbol of transformation the world over—but that bit came from somewhere else entirely. I'm a mix of cultures,

you see, and so are the stories I tell. I grew up reading folktales from all over, and living all over the world, too; and *"Pishaach"* is inspired by selkie stories as much as anything Indian.

I loved those stories where the man hides a seal-maiden's skin and she stays with him in human form until she finds it. And then she changes shape and is gone. She turns back into a seal, returns to the ocean, not caring who she leaves behind.

I always wondered how the selkie's children felt about that. The ones caught between worlds. Which is, of course, where Shruti comes in.

THE SALAMANDER FIRE

Marly Youmans

"Out gathering tufts of wool on some slope below the crags? Picking bits from the laurel?"

Startled, Alexander Prince—Xan to his friends—let a handful of ramps scatter onto the metal table.

"Hey, you're all right," the farmer said, clapping a hand on his shoulder and letting loose a laugh that had all the bounce and mounting roar of barrels rolling merrily down an incline. A robust fellow of in-between age, Charlie Garland had coarse, rumpled hair and an oddly pretty mouth inherited by the daughters who helped him at the open-air market.

"Sorry." Xan laughed back at him. "Maybe I *was* wool gathering: groping for wisps of a dream, listening for echoes. When I woke this morning, I heard the most bewitching music, like glass chimes—"

"You're a real glassman, for sure." Garland tweaked the bill from his fingers and filled his palm with silver. "Your kind would've cut down a myrtle tree and made a salamander in the olden days." He held out a sack of ramps and another of lettuce and radishes, far more than Xan had picked out.

"You're giving it away," he protested, but the other only laughed and waved him on, saying that it wouldn't be spring in the Carolina mountains without a fresh mess of ramps. What do you mean by 'making a salamander'?" Xan asked the farmer. "You don't mean the kind like a little wet lizard, do you?"

Garland sold more ramps and a bag of spinach before he answered. "You're right, it's not a lizard, it's a creature of fire. In the Talmud, when King Ahaz tried to sacrifice Hezekiah to Moloch, the boy's mother saved him from the fire by daubing him with blood from a salamander. "

"I've never heard of any such thing!"

Garland shrugged. "A glassblower like you ought to know the lore of fire."

"So how do you know this stuff?" Xan asked.

"Oh, I was a strange kid. When chores were done, I'd lie in the clover and read volumes of my grandfather's encyclopedia of marvels. Still have it—if you come by after lunch, I'll have my wife bring *S to T* ."

"All right, I'll do that. Look for me." Xan tossed the bags into his pack and moved off, glancing over his shoulder when he heard the farmer's laughter and thinking that Garland hadn't told him what the salamander was, not really.

The rest of the morning was spent in driving to Black Mountain. An elderly glassblower had died, leaving him a marver and a crate of straight shears, diamond shears, tweezers, and paddles. Although accustomed to rolling hot gathers of glass on a sheet of steel, Xan would now have a marver of marble.

The other glassblower's studio was strangely cool and empty.

"Russ thought the world of you," his wife, Eva, told him.

It was a funny saying. The world was a blue-green ball too

big for any gaffer to cut and tweeze into shape. Tears pressed at his eyes and Xan blotted them away. At the burial, after the others had flung their roses onto the coffin in the grave, making a bed of petals, he knelt and let fall a trillium of glass.

"My first husband was thoughtless, but Russ was tender."

"You two had a long go of it."

"Yes, there's that."

"He and Harold taught me the mysteries."

"They were such friends, one from the coves and the other from the city. Never jealous, always glad to see each other's work." Eva caressed the marver, snow-white with bolts of darkness. "There's a phrase, *lacrimae rerum*, in Virgil. This calls 'the tears of things' to mind. See?" Her fingers brushed the side of the slab where three owners of the marver had written their names and birth dates. In other hands, two dates of death were marked.

"Amazing that it's still intact."

"Here," she said, bringing a bottle of India ink and a dip pen, "add your name to the others. Just promise it to a young gaffer some year when you're getting older. Are you twenty-five now, Xan?"

"Just twenty-four." Saying it made him feel ashamed, as though it were somehow his fault that Eva had grown old.

"When he was twenty-four and I was twenty-six, we lived on an island near Charleston. Now all that's gone to condos and hotels. The world changes until it's not ours."

She dipped the pen and added a gleaming date to the marver. Afterward, Xan bent to scratch his name in ink below his friend's wavering inscription.

"You'll be the fourth to use this marver."

"Yes."

"You need a wife who'll mark the stone when you come to dust." She gave him a quirk of a smile that discomfited him.

"I hardly have time for a wife."

"You're married to the glass," Eva said.

The absence of Russ had disarranged the space between them. They both felt it. Xan was glad to ease the marver onto his dolly and load it through the hatch of the car. He felt distressed for Eva—there was something he had failed to say or that simply could not be said. Yet she was the last scrap he had of anything approaching family. Prince was a common enough name in western North Carolina, but he hadn't tried to find kin, not even up in Little Canada. He swept a hand across the marble and slid the box of tools on top.

"Good-bye, dear Eva." In his embrace she was as brittle as a green man in winter, all snapping twigs and dry stalks.

Then he climbed in his truck, and Eva diminished as he pulled away on the familiar drive that curled around the studio before slinging itself downhill. After that there was nothing but highway and mountains and an occasional flare of flame azalea until he reached the turnoff that led toward Sylva, Cullowhee, and Dillsboro.

Xan checked his watch: almost time for the market to close. Hoping Garland hadn't already left, he headed straight for the farmer's rickety table.

Garland waved him over.

"My wife brought the book you wanted. See here—"

He turned the volume so that Xan could see the heading, SALAMANDER, FIRE (NATURAL AND LEGENDARY). The farmer tapped the gilt-edged page with his thumb.

"Right here: 'If a glassblower will stoke the furnace with myrtle wood for seven days and seven nights, the great heat will give birth to a creature called *the fire salamander*. The glassblower should not let the cunningness of the form dissuade him, but cut until it bleeds plenteously. If he smears a hand or any part of the body with blood, he may become proof against fire.'"

"You don't—"

"Believe it? My young friend, wonders are all around us and we see them not. The world is a tangle of mystery, rolled into a ball, and soaked in the tears of things—"

"What?" Xan was startled, remembering Eva's words about the marver.

He thumped the book. "I learned that from the encyclopedia. It's a kaleidoscope made from splinters of wisdom and craziness. Here Pliny says that a salamander resembles ice and puts out fire. Aristotle talks about a fire moth: 'Winged creatures, somewhat larger than our housefly, appear in the midst of the fire, walking and flying through it, but dying immediately on leaving the flame.' And here's our boy the China traveler, Marco Polo, touting cloth-of-gold woven from salamanders." He slapped the page. "This is a dream hoard for artists. If you like, borrow the book—so long as it comes back—the encyclopedia's all I have from my grandfather."

"Garland, what a character you are!" said Xan, smiling at the other man's excitement. "Whoever heard of a farmer like you?"

He grinned. "There are plenty of oddballs in the farming trade. The encyclopedia forced me to be an outdoorsman— showed me nature packed with the sublime." He tucked a leaf in place as a bookmark and shoved the volume across the table. "Just don't thrust it into one of your ovens, all right?"

"I hate to take it. . . ."

"I'm pretty fond of *S to T*, but I know the best entries

almost by heart. Right now I'm reading *C to D* to my girls."

Xan settled the book in his arms. "That bit about the creatures like flies of fire? They must have been flakes of oxidized copper or some other metal."

"Then what's the salamander?" Garland asked.

"I thought you'd be telling me!" Surely the salamander was nothing but pulsating coals seen by an overtired gaffer, his eyes swimming.

Xan begged a bag from Garland and slipped the encyclopedia inside. "Come by if you need it," he said, scribbling directions on a scrap of paper, "or just stop in for a visit. Or to fish—I've got a trout stream."

And so the volume was deposited on the marver beside the box of tools.

At home Xan unloaded his inheritance, stowing the gear in his studio. The room was as tidy as a bakery after hours. Tomorrow he might be pulling glass and twisting it like taffy, but today he sat in a rocker, flipping through the book, drinking strong coffee.

"Listen to this," he said to the cat. "Magicians expected help from salamanders when their houses burned."

She lay on the ledge before the glory hole, switching her tail.

"Be born a writer, I wouldn't need to make one of those fire salamanders." He read aloud: "'The fire of hell does not harm the scribes, since they are all fire, like the Torah—if flames cannot hurt one anointed with salamander blood, still less can they injure the scribes.' Garland must have peculiar dreams after reading this book. What do you say, Fritsy?"

The yellow cat leaped down and rolled on the stone floor. Xan had tried to keep her away from the studio but eventually decided that she was indestructible. She must have eaten a peck of glass dust, and her fur occasionally glittered in the sunlight. Fritsy had learned to stay out of the batch, the powder for making glass, but loved to fool with beads or millefiori and had won her name by a fondness for playing with colored frit. More than once he had found her curled in the empty crucible.

His place was a mix of old and new. With the help of a stonemason, he had built the studio on two acres of slope deeded to him by Harold Queen—Queen was an even more common a name than Prince among mountain names—but had left the cabin that had belonged to Harold's father much as it was. His friend the mason had bartered labor for glass at a time when collectors were beginning to ask for Xan's work. He was lucky; he knew that. He had been brought along by notable craftsmen. If not for Harold and Russ taking a shine to him, he would be waiting tables in Sylva or pounding nails all summer long to support a glass habit.

He had been struck by glass fever at a fair during a demonstration of lampworking. A seldom-watched foster child of eleven, Xan stayed until dusk and returned the next morning to help the old man set up shop. By thirteen he held an apprenticeship with Harold that demanded three hours after school and all day on Saturdays and vacation days. So deep had been his unhappiness at home and school that he often said the glass saved his life. Harold introduced his young charge to buyers, provided him with tools that he still used, and treated him like family. After his mentor died, Xan dropped out of high school. He was sixteen, strong and determined. Russ and Eva took him in, insisting that he stay with them and finish out his apprenticeship. They never once suggested that he return to school, though Eva gave him books and taught him a smattering of Latin. When asked about college, Xan would declare that Eva was his Alma Mater. But Harold and Russ had made him a gaffer, and the magic and surprise in working the glass still brought him joy. He didn't need talk of fire moths and magic myrtle fires and salamanders to make him see the craft as wondrous.

The queer thing was this: he owned a load of myrtle. Crape myrtle wasn't the one proper to the Middle East, not the kind of myrtle that Zechariah saw in a vision of branches and red horses and an angel. But it was what sprang up when a Southerner thought of "myrtle." If mixed with resinous pine and the windfall oak that he had split and stacked, perhaps that would do.

"What if I did that? What if I worked the glass for seven days and seven nights? Even if I didn't end up with a living creature in the coals, it would be a feat." Like many another wedded to a craft, he'd gotten into the habit of talking to himself. Some days his own was the only voice he heard. He got up to see that his blowpipes and punty rods and all the gear and tackle of his trade—the puffer, the tagliol, the blow hose, the threading wheel, the pastorale, and so on—were in order, ready for the first gather from the furnace. He shifted squares of beeswax so that they lay beside the jacks, and ran his hand across the shears and paddles. Satisfied, he went to the door. April humus mixed with the fragrance of an unknown flower, and a rampant scent like bruised garlic pleased him—he could have gone hunting for his own greens, but he had a liking for Garland and thought that he would like to know the man better.

Xan split wood until bedtime and afterward dreamed of nothing but a slow fall through a well of night, ending with strands of a glass dawn. In the morning he kindled the fire with splinters of fatwood and some split crape myrtle. After heaping on oak, he shut the cat in the cabin—separated from the realm of flame by a dogtrot—and went out for groceries. On return he poured cullet into the furnace and began planning the day's work while Fritsy batted and chased a ricocheting pellet of glass. Animated by the blaze, glass cracked and bounced in the crucible. He left it alone and took a nap, curled on a daybed. When he woke, the fire sat just above two thousand degrees and the glass was a sunny orange in the bowl.

"For you, Russ."

The first gather of the day was colored with blue and white frit. Xan rolled the glass on the dead man's marver and afterward brought the blowpipe to the bench. He seated himself close to one of its arms, with his jacks and diamond shears on the table and wood blocks in a bucket of water. While shaping the vessel, he wished for an apprentice to help him with the large gathers. He set the pitcher in the heated garage to wait for a lip wrap and handle. When he was ready, the body would be heated once more, this time in the glory hole; using a punty rod, he would bring a dollop of glass from the furnace and attach the handle and thread the lip.

He kept quiet much of the time. If he spoke, it was to the cat. Intermittently he whistled a minor tune.

All day long he worked, moving from furnace to bench to garage, from garage to glory hole to bench, from bench to the annealers, where the pieces would slowly cool. When the cullet was finished off, he melted the batch and left it alone to "fine out," bubbles slowly seeping up to the surface. He stripped off his damp T-shirt and dozed again. On waking he took a pipe from the water barrel and heated it.

Before nightfall the annealers held bowls, pitchers, and vases. Strands of ruby and gold trailed through glass the color of a wild persimmon after first frost. A series of tiny fluted bowls and vases were blue and green with a peacock's metallic luster; he had tossed newspaper into the glory hole to rob it of oxygen and "reduce" the color.

"Today I worked fast, Miss Fritsy. Filled orders for a big sky blue pitcher and a group of smalls. Next I'll be fussy and start with a shimmery vase with green stems and leaves. Bloodroot. Or uvularia."

He yawned as he threw on more wood, and that night his brief sleeps had no trace of dream.

ॐ ॐ ॐ

Days passed, sometimes snailing as slowly as lampwork—time stretching out like a glittering length of twisted cane. Other times it seemed to fly as swiftly as a teardrop of hot golden glass spiraling around the belly of a vase.

By the sixth day, shadows had gathered under the glass-blower's eyes, and his ears rang with a noise like a hundred delicate glass ornaments shattering at once. At two A.M. he looked from the window as a twinkling star leaped over the horns of a crescent moon. He had become fixated and paused only to nap or shower. Sometimes he forgot to eat. Long moments he spent staring into the crucible, for it gave him a strange joy to see the living glass breathe and sparkle. Meanwhile the annealers were jammed with pieces, iridescent, opalescent, and clear. Half-asleep, he looked up and saw a child close to the still-hot vases, but when he cried out, she vanished. He felt more conscious of his body than ever before— the sorely tested strength in his arms and back and legs, the weariness that lay along his neck and made it droop.

On the seventh day he wanted only to rest but forced himself to go on; he was too close to success and could not let the fire die. Everything he made that day and the following night was a shadowy blue and purple and green flecked with gold. The wares in the annealers looked like dream glass—vessels the inhabitants of another world might take for granted, but never of this. The yellow cat patted at a drop of twilight sealed to the floor and bolted away. Xan caught himself reaching for the hot glow of a bowl and slapped his cheek. He was being pulled hard toward slumber. Shapes were dwindling. He made a tiny pot on four legs, the dream kettle of a witch. He made a thumbprint vase. He made a fluted vase, a flower vase, a fat-bellied vase: slightly crude but lovely. Drifting into a doze while holding the blowpipe, he ruined a calyx and woke, shaking his head like a dog fresh from the stream. The sleep flew away in drops, but a fresh tide of drowsiness rose up to drown him.

In the last hours of morning before the end, he made a vase small enough to hide in his fist. It was as mysterious and dusky as the others. Never had he made so much glass—never had it come as such a surprise. When he looked in the annealers and on the countertops, the vases and bowls and pitchers seemed a fanciful townscape from an alien realm, sweeping from the dawn brightness of the early days toward the twilight pieces of the last.

His heart was stirred by the shapes and colors and the light spangling on surfaces. Tears blurred the toy landscape.

"It's good." The words washed against his ears like syllables heard in a shell.

Glove raised to protect his face, he peered into the rippled fire of the furnace. The orange glow laved the coals like bright water over stones.

"What—"

Backing away, he stumbled. His glance settled on shadowy vases that only increased his unease. What had he seen? He groped for a blowpipe and carried it to the furnace. Probing the depths, he grew certain: something was creeping in the bed of coals.

He shivered, the tiredness in him moving like ice in his marrow.

Taking the long-handled pastorale, he scooped up coals with the flat plate and drew it from the furnace. His face burned, though the temperature was dropping; he had quit laying on fresh wood. With shears he nudged the coals away until there was only one left.

A creature had curled around the shuddering orange as if for warmth and camouflage.

Xan groped at the mystery with a gloved hand: it shrank from him. Grasping the coal with tweezers, he shook it gently. In response, the little animal hugged itself tightly against the glowing wood. Then, all at once, it sprawled onto the plate.

He spilled the incandescent creature onto the marver. As he bent to examine what the fire had done, a surge of delight made him tremble. Slowly the orange flush began to ebb. The substance of the body proved clear at the outer edges but was tinted a pale ruddy color elsewhere, with coppery flecks on the back and front legs. It was unmistakably a salamander of living glass.

He hesitated. Would it sear him? Holding his palm over the backbone, he could feel heat rolling off the skin. The creature seemed to flinch from the shadow of his hand. The ruby eyes swiveled in its head, looking up apprehensively. He dragged over a chair and waited for more of its warmth to be leached by the cold marble. The salamander played dead, eyes narrowing to slits. After some time had passed, he tested a pad with his fingernail but judged it still unsafe to touch. The skin twitched.

Hadn't he fired the furnace for seven days and seven nights—despite the fact that part of him was sure the idea was mad—in order to anoint his hands with the blood of the salamander?

He hoped that it could not feel pain.

The shears seemed too large and threatening, so in the end he used a pair of sharp tweezers to pierce the delicate hide. Though the salamander appeared to have neither heart nor veins, rosy juice spilled across the marble.

Xan washed his hands in the hot liquid. It steamed but cooled quickly on the stone. He tore off his shirt and smeared blood on his arms and neck and chest. A surprising amount remained, so he stripped naked and anointed every inch of his body, even the soles of his feet. Soaked to the roots, his hair was stiff with the life of the salamander. He splashed blood in his eyes until the room seemed rinsed red. A Fra Angelico portrait of the crucified Christ—the eyes two pools of vermilion staring at forever—glanced through his mind.

The little being drooped, its lids almost closed.

"I've killed it." Why had he hurt the thing—was it so important to be immune to fire? He had gone twenty-four years without such a gift. What nonsense to fantasize that blood could protect! The whole business seemed a madness born from lack of sleep.

With tweezers, he slowly pinched shut the gaping hole. The head wavered, as if to look up.

Need to sleep pressed down on his shoulders. Closing watery eyes, Xan stood as still as one of his own vessels. He appeared to have been sprinkled with sadness.

"What should I do?" The words fell from his mouth, startling him.

Forgetting the risk, he cupped the salamander in both hands and found the skin had cooled. He was so spent, any idea that the blood had already worked its magic did not occur to him.

Drenched by pity and hot grief, he impulsively lifted the creature to his cheek and held it there. In his weariness, tidal feelings seemed liable to wreck him. From a distance came a sound like a thousand windblown bells.

"Glass would crack. I wonder if you will. Maybe you'll be nothing but morsels of frit in the morning."

He reeled, shivering, his body wanting nothing but to lie prone. But there were the soft pads, tacky against his flesh. Using the pastorale, he slipped the salamander onto the coals. The cooling glory hole might be right to help in healing.

It lay without moving in the oven.

"Let it live." His mouth could hardly form the words.

Sleep slammed against the naked man. He pulled on his pants, staggered forward, and collapsed onto the daybed. Like a stone shot from a sling, he plunged into the deep.

᠗   ᠗   ᠗

He woke to Fritsy's damp nose pushing against his neck, her breath whiffling—evidently he smelled interesting. A tongue rasped against his jaw. Rolling onto his side, Xan groaned.

She settled on his ribs, purring and kneading her paws.

"Out." When he flailed an arm, the cat arrowed from the bed. He cracked open an eyelid; it was daylight, though earlier than before—he must have slept for a day and a night. The glory hole had come open. Closing his eyes, he tried to dive back into sleep, but an image of the door ajar kept niggling at him.

"All right," he exclaimed, setting his feet on the cold stone and rubbing his face. When he felt his hair, clumped and stiff, he remembered.

Alarm flashed through him; a sheet of spun glass, coppery in color, hung from the ledge. He coaxed the door open the rest of the way, standing several feet back.

Cramped in the glory hole was a naked girl, who now opened her eyes and stared at him with eyes the color of pennies. She pushed herself up on one extraordinarily pale arm.

He knew; knew instantly. He didn't have to ask who or how and wasted no time in doing so. Her oval face was ruddy on the upper cheeks, where freckles like bits of copper seemed to float. The rest of the skin was fair and so translucent that he could see the blue veins in her neck. A great eagerness seized him. Would she have a tail and legs with pads or be human in appearance? Reaching for her hands, he helped her from the glory hole. She gave off an attractive odor of burned myrrh and cinnamon and proved to be without tail and completely human in limbs. A faint silvery sheen lay in hollows around her collarbone, at her temples, and on her eyelids. Her body was perfectly formed and as smooth as glass. Suffice to say that there were portions of her more beautiful than any seen since Eve walked in the garden, as innocent and bare as the dawn. Xan, a well-built specimen of the male mortal, felt coarse and unfinished next to her.

"Can you speak? Do you have a name?"

She didn't answer. The gaffer shut his eyes, opened them again. Still there: she wasn't a dream; he was wide awake. Joy cut through him straight to the heart. He had never imagined a woman so mysterious and lovely, and he could have stared at her for hours had it not occurred to him that nakedness was no longer the natural state of Eve's children. He jerked the rod from the window and slid the curtain away. She seemed not to know what he meant by this offering, so he began to wind the cloth around her, his hands trembling. Tucked into place, the fabric made a passable sarong.

Taking her hands once more, he stared into her eyes, wondering at the fine crackled lines—bright gold and pumpkin had infiltrated the iris. She didn't seem to mind his attention and soon leaned against him in a way that suggested trust. He didn't mean to kiss her, but he did and not just once. She was a quick learner, pressing against him as eagerly as he against her.

"Xan! Xan!"

The voice called, a world away. Slowly he drew back from the girl, yet not so far that—being mesmerized by its sparkle— he couldn't comb his fingers through the spun threads of her hair.

He turned to see Garland at the screen door.

"I'm sorry—"

"Don't be! Come in, please." Xan was glad, because who else in all the known universe could understand what had happened?

The girl looked from his face to Garland in surprise. Perhaps she had thought him the only such being in the world.

"This is my friend," he told her.

"I didn't mean to interrupt. Just dropped by to pick up *S to T*. You're a bit of a mess, aren't you?" Garland laughed, surveying him. The farmer held out his hand to the young woman, introducing himself, and she took it between her own and began scrutinizing the green-stained nails and the dark hair at the wrists. Clearly he admired her and had politely failed to notice that her spring attire was somewhat lacking.

"A mess? It's nothing, just the blood. This is—"

Xan hesitated, unsure how to explain, but the other man simply smiled at the girl's odd behavior and tweaked her nose, as though she were one of his own daughters. "The salamander."

"What?" Garland tilted his head.

"I made it. The salamander. Well, I didn't make—it appeared. Not like this but like a newt. And I punctured its side and blood spurted out, the way the book said. See, look at the marble—"

Garland's lips had parted, as if to drink in the news.

"I felt terrible knowing it would die. The creature was marvelous—not as beautiful as the girl but a wonderful glass creature—and I was so happy and even a little afraid to see the thing—a miracle of glass—my heart went out to it—I couldn't bear for it to be lost—"

His voice died away. Was he babbling? Perhaps there was no fit way to tell the shape-shifting strangeness of what had happened.

Putting her arms around his waist, the girl leaned her cheek against his bare chest. Xan wrapped his arms around her, and in that instant knew that he loved her because she was everything otherworldly that he had tried to claim in his art, the visionary beauty that he saw in glimpses of glass or some-times in the fire heaving with life.

"And so I pinched the wound together and thrust the body into the glory hole and hoped—prayed it would live. While I slept, the salamander changed."

Garland stared at the girl in a handwoven curtain and the young gaffer.

"You must be careful, Xan. She has no soul—"

"What do you mean?"

"Don't be angry with me—the angels have no souls. And don't need them. Fairies as well. Demons most of all."

Xan pulled her close. "She's no—she's not any of those things. She's a woman; I'm sure."

"I don't doubt it." Garland glanced around the studio. "Have you ever made witch balls? With a web of color? Streaks and loops around an orb?"

"That's tourist work," Xan said, shrugging.

"A farmer always knows the date. It's almost the last of the ramps: it's the eve of Beltane when witches take their spring tonics and get frisky. On a few country greens, villagers will be setting a peeled tree trunk in the earth, decking it in ribbons and flowers, and asking young women to dance. You see? Like the ash poles set up to Ashtaroth long ago."

"Why should I make a witch ball because children dance around a maypole?"

"The ball catches the spirits of air! They get lost in the maze, or so it's said. You could try to protect her."

"But there's no such—" The gaffer laughed. What was he saying? He gathered the strands of the girl's hair in one hand, wondering at its fine glassine texture. She was so precious—he would do anything not to lose her. Hadn't she come to him as mysteriously as a gift from another world? "Garland, I'd be a fool not to take your advice," Xan said. "You were the one to tell me about the salamander fire. Help me tote the wood, and I'll make a gaudy sphere for every door, window, and chimney in the house and studio."

The girl persisted in trailing after him. He couldn't make her understand that when he crossed a sill, he hadn't vanished and would return shortly. She seemed to know little except how to kiss, though she had managed to arrange the curtain so that she could move more freely. The glass on the shelves and in the annealers allured her, and she gestured from him to the vessels in what seemed comprehension.

At last satisfied that out of sight did not mean gone, she perched on a stump as the two men ferried split lengths between woodshed and furnace.

Garland paused to look up, squinting.

"What's that?"

Xan's arms were loaded with myrtle and oak. He glanced up to see an enormous sky blue pitcher plummeting from the sky. Astonished, he recognized a copy of the vessel he had made on the first morning of his challenge. When it slammed into the earth near the stump, he let the wood crash to the ground.

The foot sprouted legs; the belly, arms; and with a *thlomp!* a big ugly head popped from the spout.

"No!" Xan flew toward his salamander girl, Garland pounding at his heels, but the demon grinned, snatched her up, and tossed her into the mouth of the pot. As it bounced across the clearing, she learned how to shriek. Her clamor made the demon roar with glee as he leaped toward the top of the mountain opposite the cabin. He hung in the air, the lip and handle

looking like clouds and the body of the pitcher almost invisible, and then plunged to land and vanished.

"I'll find you!" Xan dropped to his knees. The pitcher did
not return to sight.

"Get up." Garland hauled him onto his feet. "The car—"

They were off, whirling away from the studio, headed toward Cullowhee Mountain.

"You saw where they went?" Xan craned out of the window, staring toward the tiptop of the slope.

"Her hair's fire in the sunlight. Near the summit road."

Fifteen minutes later they ducked under branches that
bordered the asphalt, Garland apologizing for the sack flung
over his shoulder. "Might find some late greens."

For an hour they tramped up and down the ridge before
they stumbled on a fissure in the earth.

Wisps of steam and voices filtered up.

The farmer held a finger to his lips.

"Scag, did you see the glass doll? Pretty thing. We'll enjoy
tormenting her!"

"Phew! Nothing but a salamander. I haven't seen one of
those in a coon's age."

"Ignorant spark of pipe-guts! You golleroy! I saw one last
week at a smithy in Central Asia."

"You're lying—"

"I snatched out my tongs and grabbed the thing by the tail
and flew off before anybody noticed me fiddling in the flames.
I'd been having a bask and was roasting my toes when the
salamander trickled from a log—"

"Dottle-pated fool!" There was a crack as of club meeting
skull, a howl, and a stutter of noise like an exploding string of
firecrackers.

The two eavesdroppers moved away from the cleft and squatted by a mound of trillium and trout lily.

Xan caught the older man's wrist. "When I find her, how do I manage to get her a soul?"

The farmer gave a slight shake of his head. "That's not in the encyclopedia, not spelled out for sure. Some of the old fairy tales say to marry. And baptism may work if it doesn't kill. But I don't think anybody knows. What you really need is some fellow with a spare one. But who's got that?"

"I'd give her half of mine if I knew how. I'm going down there. If I'm not back in three hours—"

"I'll wait. You'll be clambering up in a jiffy. Here." He reached in his jacket and pulled out a dark apple. "Fresh from the cellar, an Arkansas Black off our trees. Better take it—you might get hungry. Want to borrow my jacket?"

They had sped away so quickly that Xan still wore nothing but pants and battered clogs slipped on at the door. He stuffed the apple into his pocket.

"You may need it. I have a feeling that I won't be cold," he said.

Garland leaned over the gap to watch him go.

Xan shimmied down the walls of a corkscrewed passage. "So long," he whispered. He could see the other man's silhouette against the sunlight.

Barely had he caught the answering reply when he lost his grip and began sliding. His hand found but couldn't seize hold of slits in the rock. He drew up his knees, rocketing down a chute toward faint blue light until he shot into the air and splashed into an immense pool. He leaped upward, shocked that this was not water but fire that lapped the walls of an underground cave. It tingled all around him, warm but somehow insubstantial—distant, he thought, scooping up handfuls of blue. Looking around, he saw nothing of Scag and his companion.

An immense stone, tilted to one side, made an isle that reflected light like a moon. White splinters and spears of brightness broke the surface of waves, and here and there figures lay underneath or floated on top. Eyes open, they were not looking at him but seemed to gaze at something far off. The bodies were pale or dark, the hair floating, and they appeared as oddly simplified as if they were carved Cycladic dolls. Perhaps their details had been worn down by the tide of fire.

He paused to check each one, in case the salamander girl sailed under waves, her staring copper eyes now coins for payment to the ferryman of the dead. Once, wading near the shallows, he hauled a woman to the surface. Slowly, slowly, her eyes groped toward his face. But he couldn't force her to answer his questions. A mist clouded her eyes; she fell into dream. Others had been skewered by the glowing white darts, and on these a golden flame played where shaft met flesh. Recalling the virtue ascribed to the salamander's blood, he wondered if the waves could be hotter than they appeared.

Exploring the cave lake was harder than he had expected and made him think of crossing a glacial moraine. On a trip to Canada, he and Harold had toiled over rocks, trying to reach the source of a glacial stream, but it was farther than it had seemed. In the end, the old man wearied and turned back. A pang of longing like a white arrow pierced him. He had loved Harold and Russ better than any foster father, and now they were both gone, perhaps floating in some pool of lost time. What would he do if he met their faces here?

His limbs grew drowsy as his mind drifted, anchorless. A

single burning point of pain settled under a shoulder blade. Gusts of wind roiled the waters and howled into distant windings of the cavern. After the last echo died, sheer silence filled up the chamber.

"God," he said. He meant it as a prayer, and perhaps it was.

The journey stretched out like a sheet of hot glass. The white boulder in the lake seemed no nearer. He waded into a dreamlike state, automatically checking faces, swimming sluggishly when the flames grew too deep.

At last a pattering and splashing alerted him—treading fire, he hid behind a thicket of white spears. He was now much closer to the stone.

A shape in a tattered dress shirt, herringbone vest, and wool pants wormed out of the waves and hunched on a rocky ledge where the wall began to slant upward. Crouching, he licked at streaks of a mineral deposit.

"Hey," Xan called, making up his mind to collar the figure if necessary. "Hey!"

The other sat up, nosing the air, and revealing a lean face with moth-eaten tufts circling a bald pate.

"Over here." Xan swam closer to the heap of stones. "Have you seen a pretty girl flying by—have you seen a blue pitcher? Maybe that sounds too—"

"Look! If it's not Adam, the red man!" He barked with laughter. "I haven't seen you in fifty years or more. You ripped through here, searching for some kid you'd misplaced; I'm sure of it."

Xan was confused until he remembered that his skin was stained by blood. Didn't *adam* mean red? Had Adam been made from a mud like the rust of mountain clay?

One corner of the man's mouth drew up. "Don't you recognize me? They call me Attorney—or Atty or Fox-marrow or Sir Greedy Bones. What will you give me, Adam, if I squeal? Hair like copper? Eyes like coins?"

So he had seen her. Xan considered. "A shoe."

"One shoe?" Attorney leered, looking sidelong as his tongue wriggled out. "Just one?"

"Yes, just one." What else did he have to offer but his shoes?

"The shoe of Adam. Let me see."

The gaffer waded nearer and then slipped off a clog.

"Nice, very nice," Attorney cooed, cupping his hands. "Pitch it here."

"Not until you tell me."

"I could squall for the demons." Flinching, he darted a look around the cave.

"Go ahead and squall." Xan tapped the sole of the shoe against his palm.

"All right, be that way. She's just there, on the other side of the boulder. Lashed on with ropes and a rag stuffed in her mouth. Easy! I made faces and her eyes went big." He nodded, pleased. "I canoed over on a fire-bather—one of the silver ones. My favorites. You know them? They can't tell what's happening to them, not until the cocoon breaks up. It's the goddess the girl's tied to—that fat pebble! The demons pinch me, but she never makes a peep, just rocks when the earth quakes. Get it? Rocks!" A high-pitched whinny shook echoes from the walls.

Xan shivered in revulsion, imagining silver-lidded eyes and strange hatchings under the fire. "Here." The shoe slapped onto the ledge. He didn't trust Attorney, though he seemed to be telling the truth—at least his pride in scaring the salaman-der girl could probably be relied on as a true confession.

"Don't get riled, Red Man. I'll tell you how to whisk out of here if you give me the mate." He caressed the clog and licked at a loose thread.

"Tell me a shortcut. If it's good, I'll give you the other shoe."

"Got another, do you? I'd rather have a loafer with tassels."

The young man reached for his other clog and held it up. A trembling under his feet signaled a tremor deep in the earth, but he saw that it must be the usual order of business because Attorney took no notice.

Instead, he gestured toward a slanting fold in the rock face. "See that crease? There's a staircase cut in the stone. Easy as pie. Oh, I used to love pie, pie, pie. Apple, raspberry, peach. Give the shoe now," he said, lowering his voice, "or I'll be forced to serve a writ that neither of us will like." Attorney beamed as he caught the other clog. "Stench-blossom. The shoe stinks like a human."

Xan regarded him with curiosity. "But you're human."

"Not for long. By the time these shoes wear out I'll be growing a tail and proto-wings and be buzzing the fire-bathers for kicks. Baal has promised to make me a pseudo-demon. The goddess, she's one of his three daughters. Either that or there's a demon jailed in the rock like a maggot in a Mexican jumping bean. They lie—even Baal. When I earn my wings, I'll perch on her dome. The demons won't call me Atty-boy anymore! I'll have a new name. I've been thinking about names for the past twenty years. I'm partial to Metacarrious. Do you like it, Adam?" He turned the clog in his hands, inspecting the heel.

"For a demon, maybe."

"Exactly!" Attorney's face brightened. "None of this eternal lolling about in the flame baths for me. Baal says I was half a demon when I came here. If I can only jettison the baggage of my soul—"

"Your soul." A tremor passed through Xan. He had nothing left to trade but his pants. And Attorney already had on a ragged pair.

"You wouldn't like to swap for a pair of pants, would you?"

Attorney sneered. "Why do you ask? You like mine better than yours, don't you? Well, so do I!"

"Fine, fine. Could I take a look at your soul? Maybe you'd like me to relieve you—"

"No! No pro bono, see? It has to be barter. De-sir-a-ble trade. That's rules." He nodded with vigor. "Fair, square, devil's hair," he chanted. "And I don't want those jeans." Attorney scrunched his face in disgust. "But I'll show you. It's come loose—tries to fly away." He turned away, body writhing as he hacked and spat.

When he swung round again, something lay in his hands— a mass of sputum clotted onto a rainbowlike substance, delicate and thready. A portion resembled a dragonfly's damaged wing, partially blackened and crimped.

"I've killed most of it," he said cheerfully. "There's a scrap remaining if you want to haggle. Maybe you'll think of something."

"Would you trade if I did?" Xan scanned the waters around him but saw nothing but the purified face of a woman, her features almost burned away. The pain at his back was making him dizzy, so he splashed blue onto his face before remembering that it was only fire.

"Yes, yes, I'd be busting my seed coat and sprouting a tail-root and wings so quick! But it's funny that you want it and have nothing to swap. Poor Adam! Because I don't want those ugly, ugly pants!" Reeling with laughter, Attorney slapped his shanks. "Ugly pants! Ugly pants!"

Xan wondered if he could climb the stairs, find Garland, and trust the would-be pseudo-demon to wait. Probably the creature would go paddling off. Tired of mocking, Attorney scrambled along the lake's edge and began to lick the walls. The soul was crammed in his fist, though one wisp feebly moved between his fingers. An image of Eva, handkerchief upraised, gathered in his thoughts—held itself whole for an instant and then shattered.

A blessed silence overshadowed the lake. The gaffer listened for the whip of wings but heard nothing; he felt that the hush wanted to tell him something. Slipping hand into pocket, his fingers closed over Garland's apple.

"What kind of pie did you say?"

"Blackberry, gallberry, apricot—no, not a nasty apricot—but I loved my mother's apple pie best of all. She was a cruel old witch, yet she knew how to pinch the pastry and roast the pies in her ovens. Bash my poor fingers with the rolling pin if I tried to snitch a little dangle of crust or a bead of hot syrup." His face crumpled, as if he would cry, but the future Metacarrious shook off the urge with a quiver. He began to sing in a piping falsetto:

> *"Snitch, witch, sulphur pitch—*
> *I'd have pie, if I could fly!*
> *Titch, twitch, bacon flitch—*
> *Ditch my soul for apple pie."*

When he slavered, greenish strings of saliva splashed hissing into the waves, giving off an odor of rotten eggs.

The apple seemed strangely soft. Pulling it forth, Xan real-

ized that the fruit had cooked in his pocket. So the lake's temperature was definitely hotter than it seemed. All at once the
Arkansas Black split, tears of sap sliding down the dark cheek
onto his palm.

"Roasted apple. Would you swap your soul for an apple?"

Attorney blinked. "Adam a pock-picketing magician, is it?
Is that the game? The demons put you up to playing tricks."

"No, nothing like that. I just had the apple in my pocket. I
got it from a friend."

"A friend." Attorney pondered. "Oh, yes, a friend. I remember *friend*. A rack with spikes for the broiler, was it?"

Xan didn't answer. The spear point of pain under his
shoulder blade widened. "I can put it back in my pocket." He
brought the apple to his nose and sniffed its fragrance. Nau-
sea brushed up against him. "Or I can eat it myself. Maybe I
should. Maybe you should keep your soul."

"No, no—never that. I'll trade. An unencumbered exchange
of goods, mind." He thrust the damaged soul into Xan's free
hand and reached for the apple.

"You're sure, absolutely sure?" The gaffer wanted the struggling remnant but felt uneasy; perhaps such a swap might leave
an inward scar.

"Yes, yes. This and not the ugly, ugly pants," he caroled.

Xan let the piece of fruit fall into the long-nailed hands.
Attorney glided onto the steep bank and began worrying the
apple, licking and rolling and biting.

The game was finished. It was time to be gone.

Until the fire lapped neck deep, Xan walked in the waves.
All the time he was tugging at his prize as he might a bit of
glass reheated in the glory hole. As blue fire seared away the
blackened frill, the soul began to expand under his fingers.

The floor of the cave dropped away, and Xan began swimming swiftly toward the stone. When he reached the far side, he found that Attorney had not lied. His salamander girl was lashed to the rock, a torn strip of curtain between her lips. He tugged away the ropes and unstopped her mouth.

"What took you so long?" Hair flooded her pale shoulders; crackles of gold and saffron shone in the penny-colored eyes.

"You can talk!"

"The demon put words in my mouth." Flinging her arms around Xan's neck, she laughed with a sound like glass bells.

"Did he do anything—to hurt you?" He cradled her, the coppery hair spilling over his chest.

"Only the words, so much, all at once . . . that stung me. And Mullygrubbious will come flying back, lickety-cut, with a gang of demons. That's what he said."

They floated in the blue fire, and before he taught her how to swim, Xan gave her one long kiss—and something else.

"Open your mouth," he said. When she did so, he pushed the gauzy soul inside and barred the way out with his fingers.

The first tears pooled in her eyes. She held on tight, and they rolled over the waves and the simple faces of the dead. Afterward Xan swam toward shore, towing the salamander girl while she fluttered her arms and legs to some little effect. When the surface fell to waist level, they began to wade. Soon they were skimming along in the shallows. As they fled up the steps, Attorney bellowed for the demons to come quickly and see his plumule of a tail. Xan flung the girl through the slit at the top of the stairs. They tumbled onto an island of ramps and bellwort, with curled sprouts of black cohosh snapping under their bodies.

"I'll be." There was the farmer, his sack almost full.

"Garland," cried the girl. A single clear note of laughter sprang from her lips.

"Let's go home," Xan said, casting a backward glance at the rocks. "My lovely Salamandra needs a trout from the stream and some just-picked ramps for dinner."

"She can talk!"

"Demon's work. He forced words in her mouth."

"You're barefoot and half-naked." Garland surveyed them and smiled. "The sun's going down, so my wife will be worried. But I've got ramps." He hoisted the fragrant bag to show his pickings. His sleeves were rolled up, the trousers stained green at the knees. With a flick of the wrist, he cast a handful of ramps into the crack in the earth.

"That'll hold your sky blue friend a while—a whiff of the sweet incense of creation. And your Salamandra's got a laugh that's as sweet as a bell. It'll make their ears itch."

More than ever, Xan felt a liking for the older man, seeing him there in the dusk with a ramp tucked behind his ear.

"Garland, take a look at something, will you? Below the left shoulder blade. It feels as if an arrow point struck me there." Ripples from a stone lobbed in a pool of flame, pain washed across his back.

The farmer touched him tentatively. "Hard to make out in this light, but it looks like a raggedy splotch of metal. Or a silver flame."

"Or it might even be a curled salamander," the girl offered, stroking the offending spot.

Xan shivered at the caress. "If that's all," he said, "let's go."

I must've missed a half inch of skin. A chink in the armor. He would find out soon enough whether the hurt was going to stay. *If so, the goal had been worth the price. She was worth it.* He knew how to live with a burn, because he had taken one often enough in his apprenticeship. "Chasing after beauty has a cost," Russ had said, bringing an ice pack to hold against his skin.

Xan and Salamandra followed Garland's footsteps to the road, where all three stopped to peer into the valley. The blue of day had been swallowed up. Night lamps in rural yards were already burning like fallen stars as the sunset flung up veils of persimmon and ruby. Here and there, clusters of silvery tin roofs on houses and country churches softly reflected the colors back. Slowly the sky became shadowy as strands of color altered to purple and green and cobalt with streaks and spatterings of gold. Spires and houses stood like a dream kingdom of glass in the valley.

The pain dimmed like a flame seen through a smoked lens.

"I want to learn the glass and the colors like you, Xan." Salamandra slipped her hand in his. "And I want to see things that go with the words inside."

"You'll make a marvelous gaffer. We'll make glass that no one's ever seen before. Because the salamander's blood is on me and in you."

"I want to live happily ever after," she whispered.

"Did the demon put those words in your mouth? How could that be?"

"With you, Xan. And yes, he did. He put all the words in my mouth, the good and the bad, even the ones made from tears and the blasphemies that should never be spoken." She laid her head on his shoulder.

He saw now that all things could be bent to evil. *The world could be hot glass twisted in the claws of a demon. But it hadn't been meant so at the start, that perfect gather of blue and green glass.*

"She's going to be awfully surprised when she finds out that you're not always dyed cinnabar from head to toe," Garland remarked, slinging the bag of ramps over his shoulder. He eyed the younger man's hair, caked with blood. "Pleasantly so, I reckon."

"These jeans, do you think—"

"What?"

"Nothing." The gaffer let out a spark of laughter. "Not a thing."

The roofs in the valley glimmered and faded, and sparks of stars blew in from the hearth of the sky and made the girl cry out in fear and joy. *She's really only a newborn baby*, Xan thought, *despite the words.* So he would sleep in the studio and yield the cabin to her. He would have to let her grow a while before they could promise to live happily ever after. A year and a day floated into his mind; surely he could wait a year and a day. But it was already in him to love her, as it had been from the moment he had helped her from the glory hole—perhaps even when he had lifted the salamander to his cheek. Her blood on the marble had claimed him as her own as surely as if the marver had been not a glassmaker's tool but some pagan goddess— a boulder of granite stained with the blood of children, set up in a grove of stunted acacia trees, somewhere hot and distant and long ago. But she wasn't of that cruel world. She had been burned in the glory of the glass fire and owned a soul.

He shuddered, remembering the stone in the lake of blue flames and the faces drifting beneath the waves. Glancing down, he saw the girl's bare legs glowing white above a drift of dwarf iris leaves. Oh, he longed to remake the world to be as smooth as glass for her feet! Garland was unlocking the car, tossing the ramps into the trunk. Xan felt that he would never be done thanking the man for telling him about the living creatures born from fire. He and Salamandra would visit Garland's farm; then he would go see Eva and show her what sort of woman he could win for himself. Though the widow might be sad because change is often sad for the old, she would welcome them in. There were strands of color in the bewitching ball of Earth—enough to hold them secure in its web.

"Listen!" Salamandra stepped forward. A spine-tingling sound like a waterfall of crystal swept toward them. "The music of the spheres," she said, her face as naked in delight as an infant's.

An enormous windblown tree blossomed in Xan's imagination, its leaves splashed with raindrops, its twigs and branches hung with an endless number of glass bells. Sweet as a mountain breeze, the sureness came to him that all his life to come would be more radiant than before. He sighed with pleasure, gripping the girl's slender fingers. He had feared the stain of Attorney, but now he was certain: the soul had found a better place to nestle and, like a wing of thinnest glass, would unfold and flash with rainbow colors. She would make it her own. Before they turned toward Garland and home, he and his salamander bride-to-be looked up at the glory of the constellations, now strengthening and shining in the furnace of night, and one or the other spoke.

"Before the stars were made, we were dreamed and meant to be."

MARLY YOUMANS is the author of seven books of fiction and poetry. Her most recent fantasy is *Ingledove*. Her novel *The Wolf Pit* won the Michael Shaara Award for Excellence in Civil War Fiction. *Val/Orson*, a novella set in the California treetops and drawing on the legend of Valentine and his wild twin, Orson, was published in 2008. Her first book of poetry is *Claire*. Her short fiction has appeared in many magazines and anthologies, including *Salon Fantastique*; *Logorrhea*; *Firebirds Soaring*; *We Think, Therefore We Are*; and *Postscripts*, and reprinted in *The Year's Best Fantasy and Horror*, and *Fantasy: The Best of the Year*. Her Web site is www.marlyyoumans.com.

✥✥

Author's Note

When *The Beastly Bride* tugged at my sleeve, I had been day-dreaming about glass and its marvelous transformations. I thought immediately of a girl metamorphosed from the mythical fire-born salamander. Fiery and metamorphic glass led me to the furnace, the underworld, and a mix of earthly and otherworldly beauty.

The history of the Blue Ridge Mountains of North Carolina is one that includes magic and mythic beings. Tiny bones and small tunnels of the Little People had been found during construction in Cullowhee, where I grew up. Cherokee tales mixed in my mind with folk ways and stories handed down by settlers from Scotland and Ireland. Later, the magic of these regional tales tinged *The Curse of the Raven Mocker* and *Ingledove* and crept into some of my other novels, poems, and stories—as in this one.

THE MARGAY'S CHILDREN

Richard Bowes

PART ONE

Not to boast, but I'd say I'm pretty good as a godfather. As an actual parent, I'd doubtless have been a disaster. But I have six godchildren, and I love all of them. Selesta is the second eldest and my secret favorite. When she was real small, three and four years old, I had Mondays off and her mother, my friend Joan Mata, would leave her with me while she kept doctors' appointments and met her design clients in the city.

That was when Selesta and I first talked about cats. At the time, I had an apartment on Second Avenue in the teens, and on the ground floor of the building facing mine was a row of small shops, each of which had a cat. Selesta took a great interest in them. That could just have been because she couldn't have a cat of her own.

The Italian deli had a majestic tricolor cat named Maybelline. As a deli cat she had plenty of food, numerous admirers whom she would allow to pet her as she sat in the sun by the front door, and mice to keep her busy at night.

The Russian cobbler next door had a thin gray cat with a truncated tail that twitched back and forth. A shoe repair shop has no food and probably few mice. The cobbler was thin and gray himself, and when I once asked him the cat's name he just shook his head, like he'd never heard of such a thing. So I decided to call him Hank, and Selesta agreed with me.

The third store was a Vietnamese nail and hair and massage shop with elaborate neon signage. It employed a trio of exotic ladies with elaborate nails, and one very silly man. Their cat was a Siamese named Mimi or something like that. Mimi had a wardrobe of exotic sweaters and collars and even booties.

She was usually carried by one of the ladies. When she passed by, the other cats' noses and ears twitched, as if they could sense a cat nearby but couldn't tell where it was.

To amuse ourselves, Selesta and I made up stories about the three cats and their adventures. Once they all went out to find a pair of red striped socks for Hank on his birthday. Another time they went to the moon, which was run by a bunch of gangster mice.

Maybe there I should have discouraged her interest. However, I believe Joan had asked me to be the godfather of her only child because we went back so far and shared so many secrets.

Eventually Selesta's parents moved to Hoboken, New Jersey, she started school, and our Monday afternoons and the adventures of the store cats were no more.

It was a few years later, when she was eight or nine, that Selesta first asked me how her mother and I had become friends. It was the Wednesday after her birthday and I'd just taken her to see a matinee performance of *Cats* on Broadway.

That had been her wish, and her mother had no objection.

The kick in taking a kid to the theater is seeing and sharing her unbridled wonder. Afterward we discussed the show and let the crowd carry us to the Times Square subway station. I noticed that Selesta now had her mother's green eyes flecked with gold.

"My favorite part was the end where the cat goes up to heaven," she said.

"On the old rubber tire," I replied. "That's the way it always happens with cats."

"My mother says she has allergies so I can't have a cat or dog."

This sudden swerve in our conversation took me by surprise. "She *is* allergic, honey," I said automatically and immediately regretted it. Kids are uncanny. Selesta knew I had lied, just as she suspected that her mother was lying.

She followed it up by saying, "Once when I was little you told me you and Mommy lived in a house with a mystery cat. Like Macavity in the show."

Macavity, the villain of the musical, seemed to me too over-the-top to be very scary. The animal Selesta referred to had been very quiet and quite real.

"That was long before you were born or even thought of," I said as the matinee crowds carried us down the subway stairs.

It bothered me that I had no recollection of ever having told her about the cat or about Anise's Place on East Tenth Street. That was the semi–crash pad where her mother, Joan Mata, and I first met back in those legendary times, the late 1960s.

"What was the cat's name?"

By then we were waiting amid a crowd of commuters at 33rd Street for the PATH train to Hoboken. I began the story, and as I did, she listened with exactly the same rapt expression she'd had at the show.

"He was called Trebizon. That was an ancient city far away on the Black Sea. Anise, his owner, was a lady who had started to get a doctorate in history before she became a hippie and decided to let a bunch of people come live with her."

"You and my mother were hippies!" The idea amused her.

"I guess I was. You'd have to ask your mother if she was." Back then, my foothold in the city had been fragile. A stupid romantic quarrel, the kind a young man has at twenty-one, had put me out of the place where I'd been living and sent me crashing at Anise's. But I didn't go into that.

"What was Trebizon like?"

"He was a big old orange cat who seemed very smart." I didn't tell her that the people living in that neighborhood and in that apartment had achieved a really rarefied degree of psychic awareness and mind expansion. Apparently Trebizon shared this.

"It seemed he always had a favorite. When I first came to stay there, he spent every night on the chest of a very quiet stranger, a kid from the South who slept on the living room couch. Anise joked that the cat had adopted him.

"All of a sudden, every time a newcomer entered the apartment, the cat would get off his chest and sit and watch. The kid would take off all his clothes, kneel down on the floor in front of the new arrival, and kiss his or her feet."

"He kissed your feet?" She was amused.

"It was creepy and embarrassing. But I noticed other people were pleased when it happened. Like they said to themselves, *Finally, people are kissing my feet.* I also saw that Trebizon acted like an owner whose pet had done a clever trick.

"I guess word got back to the kid's family. Because one day his parents appeared and took him home."

"What did Trebizon do?"

"Found someone else who lived there, a dreamy kind of girl who was studying to be a dancer. The cat slept beside her in this bed in a little alcove near the kitchen. We called her the Flower Girl because she brought home the single roses that gypsy ladies sold in bars and little sprays of lilies of the valley, potted geraniums.

"Then it escalated. She began coming in with bridal bouquets, with boxes of red carnations, huge bunches of violets. The crash pad began to look like a funeral parlor. Trebizon prowled among them, chewed the ferns, and batted the petals that fell to the floor.

"The Flower Girl started to look furtive, haunted. One time she came home with two shopping bags full of yellow daffodils. Another time it was orchids. Stuff she'd probably stolen. She'd put them on the floor around her bed, and Trebizon would lie there like it was his altar.

"Eventually the police nabbed her as she was ripping off a bank of tulips from the Macy's garden show. With her gone, Trebizon began to notice me."

The train arrived right then, and we didn't get seats. I held on to a pole, and Selesta held on to me. We sang scraps of the songs from *Cats*. She knew a lot of the lyrics. The other passengers pretended we weren't there.

I hoped my goddaughter would forget what we'd been talking about. Telling the story had reminded me of what it had been like to be young and confused and with no place to hide when a demon closes in.

But as soon as we hit the platform of Hoboken terminal

Selesta asked, "Where was my mother when the cat came after you?"

Hoboken twenty years ago was still such a compact, old-fashioned, working-class city that in my memory it's all black and white like an old newsreel. We walked from the station to Newark Street, where a sign in the shape of a giant hand pointed its finger at the Clam Broth House.

On the way, I told Selesta, "Right when the cat began to stalk me was when your mother appeared. Trebizon sat in the doorway of the room where I slept and stared at me. I had no other place to go and I sat on my bed, wondering what I was going to do.

"Then I looked up and there was this girl a little older than me, wearing the shortest miniskirt in the world. She put her bags in the alcove where the Flower Girl had stayed. Her name was Joan Mata. She looked taller than she was, and she had amazing eyes—green and gold like yours. Your mother had been in Europe for the summer. She and Anise had met at Columbia, and she knew Trebizon from back then.

"I didn't even have to tell her what was happening. She gave one look at Trebizon, and he ran and hid in the kitchen."

What Joan had actually done was let out a low growl. Trebizon's reaction was like that of the cobbler's cat and the deli cat when Mimi was carried past. His nose and ears twitched; he looked around, scared and confused, like he sensed a cat but couldn't see one.

Trebizon never came back out of that kitchen. Anise knew something was wrong, but she and the cat were both a bit afraid of Joan.

"Why didn't Trebizon make my mother allergic?" Selesta asked suddenly.

Before I could think of a reply, a voice said, "The allergies developed later, honey." Joan Mata stood smiling at the front entrance of the sprawling block-long maze of dining rooms that was the Clam Broth House.

Joan was a designer. She was married to Selesta's father, the architect Frank Gallen. He was out of town. Their town house was like a showcase for his work and hers. Some part of it was always being rebuilt or redesigned. That week it was the kitchen.

So we ate at the restaurant, which Selesta always loved. The three of us were seated. When Joan put on her glasses to glance at a menu, they seemed to alight on her face for a moment. Like a butterfly.

Selesta recounted scenes from the musical and chunks of our conversation. "And he said he was a hippie, but he didn't know if you were."

"Your godfather has it backward," said Joan. "Everything I owned was in those suitcases. He had a job. It was so cute, every morning in that madhouse, he'd put on his suit and tie and go off to write fashion copy."

Selesta asked, "What happened to Trebizon?"

Neither of us knew. "I imagine he had a few lives left," Joan said.

Selesta left us briefly, reluctantly for the ladies' room, knowing that in her absence secrets would be discussed.

"She asked and I told her a little bit about Trebizon and East Tenth Street."

"That's perfect. She's getting curious, and I'm glad it happened like this and with you."

"Shouldn't you tell her about your father?"

She sighed. "She'll ask and I'll tell her."

Over twenty years before, we had known we'd be friends from the moment we met. In late night conversations on the front steps and back fire escape on East Tenth Street, we talked about sex and drugs and parents and trauma.

Joan sat on railings and never lost her balance. She was only a year or two older than I was but knew so much more. Her mother was a well-known lawyer; her father was Antonio Mata, the Mexican painter who did surrealistic paintings that looked like cartoons and who signed himself "Margay."

That night, for the first time, I questioned her judgment, but said nothing.

PART TWO

About ten years later, when Selesta was in her late teens, a sophomore studying theater at NYU, there was a Friday afternoon when she drove us both out to Long Island. We were going to spend the weekend with her mother and grandmother in the House That Ate the World. It was early June, and the Island was radiant.

That uncanny light you get on that thin, low strip of land on a long afternoon is sunlight reflected off the Atlantic and Long Island Sound.

Selesta was slim but not as painfully thin as she had been a few years before, when her parents divorced and she became bulimic. She had been cured of that, and in high school had lived a tightly scheduled life the point of which, maybe, was to prevent her pondering too much about who she was.

A couple of times over the years, though, we'd talked about her mother and our adventures when we first met. I'd run through my stories of Joan and me dancing at Ondine with Hendrix in the house and talking to Allen Ginsberg in Tompkins

Square Park. All the baggage of the tiresomely hip older generation got trotted out.

That day, though, she asked, "You know about ocelots?" I nodded and had a good idea where the conversation was going.

"They're small; their bodies are a couple of feet long and with a tail almost that long. They have beautiful coats," she said. "They live all through South America and Mexico. Whenever I go anywhere if they have a zoo I check and see if they have ocelots. San Diego does and Cincinnati.

"Ocelots are shy," she added. "And, of course, they're getting scarce because of their fur and the forest disappearing.

"Obviously, though, what I'm really interested in is the margay, a kind of cousin with the same markings. You know about them."

"They live and hunt in trees," I said. "They're nocturnal, very, very shy, and getting rare."

"You know that because my mother talked to you about this, didn't she? Back when you were kids. She knew about all this, about her father. You know Margay was his nickname? I first got interested in them when I was about twelve and heard about Grandfather Margay from Grandma Ruth.

"Ruth took me to Mexico last summer. We went to the town where Antonio Mata was born and grew up. There were still people who knew him. We made a special visit to Belize because of this amazing zoo they have. It's away from the coast with lots of space. More like a nature park with all animals from Central America," she said.

"I waited outside the margay enclosure, and at dusk I saw one on a high tree branch. Its eyes reflected the light. Other people were there, but it looked at me. Then it was gone."

As we rolled along the flat prairie that is the Island's center, late afternoon sunlight made long shadows and gave a kind of magic to the endless strip malls, the buildings with signboards listing dermatologists' and dentists' offices, the used-car lots.

Selesta said, seemingly out of nowhere, "Trebizon may have been possessed, but the way he acted with my mother is how a domestic cat reacts to a wild one."

I realized that Joan must never have talked to her about any of this. "You're right, honey," I said. "That's what it was like."

Keeping her eyes on the road, she reached over with her left hand and pulled down the shoulder of her blouse. There was a small patch of tawny fur with a touch of black.

"How long have you had that?"

"A few years. It was just a speck, and then it grew. I knew what it was when it appeared. I shaved it at first and was afraid someone would find out. Lately I've let it grow."

I watched her staring at the road, tried to see a cat shape in her head. She glanced my way, and for a moment her eyes did catch the light.

"Your mother had the same thing when I first knew her. She had to get rid of it with electrolysis. Painful stuff."

"My mother never volunteers information about things like this. When I first got this I asked her what it meant. She mentioned her father very briefly—then told me about laser treatment."

"But you didn't want that."

"I want to remember. Maybe understand something."

We drove in silence for a while. Then Selesta said, "She was only a few years older than I am now when you met. How much did she know?"

"She had just figured out what had happened to her and to her brother, Luis. She was mad that your grandmother hadn't been able to tell her more. But I think Ruth must have been in shock herself back then. I think your mother was, too. Maybe that's what made them so dedicated to their work."

"Look in that portfolio," she said and indicated one stuck in between our seats.

It contained photos. The first few were of her grandfather, Antonio Mata. As a young man he was thin and poised. Maybe his head and face seemed a bit streamlined. But I might have been seeing that because of what I knew. He was with a group of young people in one picture at a country house in Mexico. I recognized Frida Kahlo in the crowd. In another picture, Antonio Mata in his shirtsleeves painted on a canvas.

I had seen these before. Joan had shown them to me when I first knew her. There was one of Antonio Mata and Ruth, Joan's mother, which I remembered having seen. They made a handsome couple. Ruth wore shorts and a man's shirt.

After her husband's disappearance, Ruth went to Columbia Law School, married the civil rights lawyer Harry Rosen, and became a legal counsel for Amnesty International.

"Look at the next one," Selesta said.

This one was new to me. Antonio Mata lay stretched out on the branch of a tree, looking at the camera with cat's eyes.

"And the next."

The picture had probably been taken at dusk on a porch. A light was on inside the house. Mata was a bit older than in the other shots. He was poised with his hands on the rails, as if he was going to leap into the gathering dark. He looked like he was trapped. I recognized the porch and the house.

"Your mother gave you these?"

"My grandmother. She took them."

The next picture was of three children standing on the

front porch of the place that Mata had called the House That Ate the World. They ranged in age from nine to maybe three. The oldest was a very serious boy who seemed to be looking at something in the distance. This, I knew was Joan's brother, Luis. The youngest was Joan's sister, Catherina, smiling and holding something up to the camera with both hands. Joan was right in between. She gazed up at her brother.

"I'd never seen a picture of her brother."

"There aren't many. They say he was very shy around strangers. A true Margay. Just look at him! Those eyes!"

"He died very young."

"Eighteen," she said. "Drowned in the Great South Bay a few years after his father disappeared back into Mexico. Water killed the cat. Everyone knew it was suicide."

It's tough when a friend you love and respect is doing something you think may be dumb and wrong. "Your mother was still torn up about that and her father's disappearance when I first knew her," I said, like I was pleading her case. "She really had no one to talk to."

Selesta drove in silence. The sun was going down. I looked in her portfolio at the photos she had of Mata paintings. I found *The House That Ate the World*.

It's the house in the old rural Hamptons in which Antonio Mata had lived for some years with his wife and children. In the painting it's distended, bulging. Through open windows and doors flow furniture and phonographs, tennis shoes and radios, refrigerators and easy chairs.

Out of the house and onto the lawn in front and the meadow in back they tumble: cocktail dresses and ice buckets, strollers and overcoats, the possessions of an American household circa 1948.

"Kind of quaint compared to what's inside an American house today," I said.

"I don't think it's about materialism so much as about wariness and curiosity," Selesta said. "And maybe fear. He's a feline in human territory."

"Are you afraid, honey? Like he was?"

"Sometimes I am. I think it's good to be a little afraid sometimes."

We drove for a while before she asked, "Was my mother ever afraid?"

"Not that I saw when she was your age. She only seemed to get scared after you were born."

We talked a little more about her family. Brief bursts of conversation took place amid stretches of silence.

It was dark when we parked at the entrance to the drive-way of the House That Ate the World. Lamps were on inside, but Joan stood on the unlighted porch and smiled as we approached.

"She can see us in the dark," muttered Selesta. "She just shrugs when I ask her about it."

We all embraced and Joan asked, "How was traffic?"

"No problem," said her daughter stepping past her. "How are you?"

By night, it could almost still be the cottage of fifty years before. I caught the tang and murmur of the ocean. A few hundred yards away the tide was coming in.

Through the open windows I saw the easel in the living room with the half-finished painting. Bulbous circa–1950 American cars bore down on the viewer. Antonio Mata had disappeared without finishing it.

"A cat's-eye view of the highway," I murmured.

Joan looked at me and then at her daughter, who smiled. Neither said anything, but they moved down the hall to the kitchen, not touching but walking together.

When they were alone, Joan would ask her daughter what she and I had talked about on the way out here. I was glad to have given them that opening.

"Hello, Richie," said a familiar voice behind me. I turned, and standing at the back porch door was the woman from the 1950s snapshots. Then Ruth Mata Rosen moved and that illusion disappeared. Now she walked with a cane.

Ruth had called me "Richie" the first time we met many years before. There was no reason for it that I've ever been able to discover. Nobody else in the world has ever used that nickname for me.

"They're alone together?" she asked.

"In the kitchen," I said.

"No yelling? No screams?" she asked. "I don't necessarily hear. Especially things I don't want to hear."

"Quiet so far."

"At first, with my background in negotiation, I tried to arbitrate their dispute," said Ruth. "What I discovered was that when you spent twelve years married to the cat man and never asked some basic questions, you're not dealing from a position of moral authority or common sense."

"We've all done things like that."

"Truly, have you ever done anything quite like that?"

"Well . . ."

"No. I was naïve and bedazzled and just plain stupid. And a lot of misfortune came from that."

"You did something fine with Selesta."

"I'd been back to the place where Antonio was born a

couple of times. There are still people who remember him as a kid. A few of the locals had folktales about tree cats who can take human form. Rumors ran that his grandmother was one.

"Poor Joan," Ruth said. "When she was Selesta's age and wanted so much to find out about her father, there was a travel ban in that area. It was a dangerous place. The government was killing student dissidents. And right then I was busy."

The kitchen door opened. Selesta emerged and then Joan. A kind of truce seemed to have been arranged.

"Is anyone else hungry?" asked Ruth.

"Yes," said Joan. "But the sad thing is none of us can cook."

Selesta narrowed her eyes and flashed her teeth. "I can probably rustle up something fresh and tasty from outside."

Joan winced, but I chuckled. Ruth said, "Suit yourself. But there are take-out menus on the refrigerator door. I thought maybe Thai would be nice."

PART THREE

In the way of the busy lives we lead, it was a few years before I found myself back at the House That Ate the World. This time I drove out there with Joan and again arrived after dark. It was the middle of the week and a bit before Memorial Day. The neighbors weren't yet in residence; the season and the Hamptons traffic jams hadn't begun.

Again by night, with a sea breeze and little sound beside the slow rhythm of the Atlantic, the house could well have been the one in the Mata paintings, the old snapshots of the family.

Adding to that illusion, there were children in the cottage. Joan's younger sister Catherina was taking care of her granddaughters, aged three and four, and had brought them to see Great-Grandmother Ruth.

The next morning, though, I stood on the porch with a mug of tea, and 1950 was gone. The pond had been drained decades ago and a summer mansion had been built on the site. A more recent and even larger vacation home now stood on the meadow. The House That Ate the World, by comparison, now seemed like a charming relic of the past.

Joan came out and sat on the porch swing. Two years before, she'd had a brush with cancer. We'd all held our breaths, but it seemed that it was removed in time and she was free and clear. Joan and I had become close again in ways we hadn't been since we were kids back on East Tenth Street.

She talked on her cell phone with her business partner about a corporate logo they were designing. Then she got a call from Selesta, who was driving out to the Hamptons with her husband, Sam.

They'd gotten married a couple of years before. Sammy was a nice young man with a shaved head. Selesta had a tattoo on her throat that matched the blue of his eyes.

Recently she'd told all of us that she was pregnant and that she and Sam had decided to have the child. That news was always in the background now. Her mother and grandmother discussed obstetricians and hospitals. Selesta didn't understand why she might need a doctor who was discreet.

"Because you don't want to end up on the front page of the *National Enquirer*," Joan said. She shook her head when she got off the phone.

"Selesta told me once that it was good to always be a little scared," I told her.

"She won't know what fear is until she becomes a parent."

Two very busy, very small young ladies returned with Catherina from the beach. Each carried a dripping pail. "We found living clams," they told us. Though the clams looked as dead as could be, we exclaimed over them.

Ruth sat out on the lawn under a large umbrella. Her great-granddaughters went to show her the living clams.

"I married the least catlike man in the world," Joan said. "I didn't really understand that was what I was doing. That was his main qualification. Then Selesta was born, and I saw it hadn't worked. I wasn't used to my plans going awry. Not even my unformulated ones."

"You told Selesta all this?"

"Recently I told her everything. Like you said."

"The vestigial tail?" Joan had to have one removed when she was child.

She nodded.

Later that afternoon I sat with Ruth and the little girls. "Richie, you'd think after I'd made such a mess out of my children's lives they wouldn't trust me with their offspring. But you'd be wrong. Someone always needs to dump their kids."

None of Catherina's three daughters had shown the slightest trace of the margay. This was true also of her oldest daughter's two children.

"It's right out of Mendel," Ruth said. "Poor Luis was at one end. Catherina's at the other. Joan is somewhere in between."

She was scratching one of her great-granddaughters' backs. The child suddenly gave a great yawn and arched her back like a kitten.

Ruth looked at me with an expression that said, You've got to wonder.

Later when Selesta and Sam showed up, I told them, "Selesta, much as I love you, you're grown up. You never want toys, you don't like musicals anymore. I mean, how do I justify going to lousy shows if I can't say I'm taking a kid? I want to be the godfather, maybe the god-grandfather to your kid."

"That's the main reason we decided to have a child," she said, and Sam nodded his agreement.

She looked out at Ruth on her lounge chair with the children around her and said, "I want that for Joan."

POSTSCRIPT

When you visit a maternity ward you scarcely know you're in a hospital. It's about life instead of illness, about bedazzled adults and the tiny, red-faced dictators who are going to run their lives.

Selesta's child was a boy, the first male born into the family since Luis Mata over seventy years before.

I got to hold him. It's nice, but in truth I like kids better when they're standing up and talking. There's a wonderful stuffed ocelot that I'm planning to give him. It could as easily be a margay. Selesta will be good with that.

Ruth was there in a motorized wheelchair with her caregiver.

"A perfectly normal baby," said the very discreet doctor.

"Meaning he doesn't have a tail," said Joan quietly when the doctor left.

"Not yet, anyway," murmured Ruth.

RICHARD BOWES has written five novels, the most recent of which is the Nebula Award–nominated *From the Files of the Time Rangers*. His most recent short fiction collection *Streetcar Dreams and Other Midnight Fancies* was published in 2006. He has won the World Fantasy, Lambda, International Horror Guild, and Million Writers awards.

Recent and forthcoming stories appear in *The Magazine of Fantasy and Science Fiction*, *Electric Velocipede*, *Subterranean*, *Clarkesworld*, and *Fantasy* magazines, and the *Del Rey Book of Science Fiction and Fantasy*, *Year's Best Gay Stories 2008*, *Haunted Legends*, and *Naked City* anthologies. Several of these stories are chapters in his novel in progress, *Dust Devil on a Quiet Street*.

His home page is www.rickbowes.com.

Ⓒ

Author's Note

The great thing about writing for an anthology like this is that I already know the general theme before I start. In *The Beastly Bride*, my story would be about that place where human and animal intersect. Because wild cats have fascinated me since I was small, I knew the animal in question would be a member of the Felidae, the cat family.

The question then was how to handle this, what perspective to bring. Almost from the start I knew my story would be about a young woman, Selesta, who had already appeared in a story of mine called "Dust Devil on a Quiet Street," which was included in *Salon Fantastique*, another anthology edited by Ellen Datlow and Terri Windling.

The narrator in "Dust Devil," who would also be the narrator in "The Margay's Children," was Selesta's godfather. This narrator had no children but many godchildren—a situation I know very well.

In this story we discover that Selesta's grandfather was Mexican and had in his genetic makeup traces of a Latin American animal spirit. I thought first of making it an ocelot before settling on the ocelot's cousin, the nocturnal, tree-dwelling margay. In handling this heritage, Selesta is as smart and resourceful as my godchildren almost always are.

And her godfather is quite wise and wonderful—because this, of course, is a fantasy anthology.

THIMBLERIGGERY AND FLEDGLINGS

Steve Berman

THE SORCERER

Bernhard von Rothbart scratched at a sore on his chin with a snow-white feather, then hurled it as a dart at the chart hanging above the bookshelves. The quill's sharp end stabbed through the buried feet of the dunghill cock, *Gallus gallus faeces*, drawn with a scarab clutched in its beak.

"A noble bird," von Rothbart muttered as he bit clean his fingernails, "begins base and eats noble things."

He expected his daughter to look up from a book and answer, "Yes, Papa," but there was only silence. Above him, in the massive wrought iron cage, the wappentier shifted its dark wings. One beak yawned while the other preened. A musky odor drifted down.

Why wasn't Odile studying the remarkable lineage of doves?

Von Rothbart climbed down the stairs. Peered into room after room of the tower. A sullen chanticleer pecked near the coatrack. Von Rothbart paused a moment to recall whether the red-combed bird had been the gardener who had abandoned his sprouts or the glazier who'd installed murky glass.

He hoped to find her in the kitchen and guilty only of brushing crumbs from the pages of his priceless books. But he saw only the new cook, who shied away. Von Rothbart reached above a simmering cauldron to run his fingers along the hot stones until they came back charred black.

Out the main doors, the sorcerer looked out at the wide and tranquil moat encircling his home, and at the swans drifting over its surface. He knew them to be the most indolent of birds. So much so they barely left the water.

He brushed his fingers together. Ash fell to the earth, and the feathers of one gliding swan turned soot-dark and its beak shone like blood.

"Odile," he called. "Come here!"

The black swan swam to shore and slowly waddled over to stand before von Rothbart. Her neck, as sinuous as any serpent's, bent low until she touched her head to his boots.

THE BLACK SWAN

Odile felt more defeated than annoyed at being discovered. Despite the principle that, while also a swan, she should be able to tell one of the bevy from the other, Odile had been floating much of the afternoon without finding Elster. Or if she had, the maiden—Odile refused to think of them as pens, despite Papa insisting that was the proper terminology—had remained mute.

"What toad would want this swan's flesh?" her papa muttered. "I want to look upon the face of my daughter."

In her head, she spoke a phrase of *rara lingua* that shed the albumen granting her form. The transformation left her weak and famished; while she had seen her papa as a pother owl devour a hare in one swallow, Odile as a swan could not stomach moat grass and cloying water roots. No longer the tips of great wings, her fingers dug at the moss between flagstones.

"There's my plain girl." Smiling, he gently lifted her by the arms. "So plain, so sweet." He stroked her cheek with a thumb.

She could hear the love in his voice, but his familiar cooing over her rough-as-vinegar face and gangly limbs still hurt. A tear escaped along the edge of her nose.

"Why you persist in playing amongst the bevy . . ." He stroked her cheek with a thumb. "Come inside." He guided her toward the door. "There won't only be lessons today. I'll bring a Vorspiel of songbirds to the window to make you smile."

Odile nodded and walked with him back into the tower. But she would rather Papa teach her more of *rara lingua*. Ever since her sixteenth birthday, he had grown reluctant to share invocations. At first, Odile thought she had done something wrong and was being punished, but she now suspected that Papa felt magic, like color, belonged to males. The books he let her read dealt with nesting rather than sorcery.

From his stories, Odile knew he had been only a few years older than sixteen when he left his village, adopted a more impressive name, and traveled the world. He had stepped where the ancient augers had read entrails. He had spoken with a cartouche of ibises along the Nile and fended off the copper claws of the gagana on a lost island in the Caspian Sea.

But he never would reveal the true mark of a great sorcerer: how he captured the wappentier. His secrets both annoyed Odile and made her proud.

§   §   §

THE WAPPENTIER

As the sole surviving offspring of the fabled ziz *of the Hebrews, the wappentier is the rarest of raptors. Having never known another of its ilk, the wappentier cannot speak out of loneliness and rarely preens its dark feathers. Some say the beast's wings can stretch from one horizon to the other, but then it could not find room in the sky to fly. Instead, this* lusus naturae *perches atop desolate crags and ruins.*

The Rashi claimed that the wappentier possesses the attributes of both the male and female. It has the desire to nest and yet the urge to kill. As soon as gore is taken to its gullet, the wappentier lays an egg that will never hatch. Instead, these rudiments are prized by theurgists for their arcane properties. Once cracked, the egg, its gilded shell inscribed with the Tetragrammaton, reveals not a yolk but a quintessence of mutable form, reflected in the disparate nature of the beast. A man may change his physique. A woman may change her fate. But buried, the eggs become foul and blacken like abandoned iron.

THIS SWAN MAY

When Elster was nine, her grandmother brought her to the fairgrounds. The little girl clutched a ten-pfennig piece tight in her palm. A gift from her papa, a sour-smelling man who brewed gose beer all day long. "To buy candy. Or a flower," said her grandmother.

The mayhem called to Elster, who tugged at her grandmother's grip, wanting to fly free. She broke loose and ran into the midst of the first crowd she came upon. Pushing her way to the center, she found there a gaunt man dressed in shades of red. He moved tarnished thimbles about a table covered in a faded swatch of silk.

The man's hands, with thick yellowed warts at every bend and crease, moved with a nimble grace. He lifted up one thimble to reveal a florin. A flip and a swirl and the thimble at his right offered a corroded haller. The coins were presented long enough to draw sighs and gasps from the crowd before disappearing under tin shells.

"I can taste that ten-bit you're palming," said the gaunt man. Thick lips hid his teeth. How Elster heard him over the shouts of the crowd—*"Die linke Hand"*—she could not guess. "Wager for a new life? Iron to gold?" His right hand tipped over a thimble to show a shining mark, a bit of minted sunlight stamped with a young woman's face. Little Elster stood on her toes, nearly tipping over the table, to see the coin's features. Not her mother or her grandmother. Not anyone she knew yet. But the coin itself was the most beautiful of sights; the gold glittered and promised her anything. Everything. Her mouth watered, and she wanted the odd man's coin so badly that spittle leaked past her lips.

When she let go of the table, the iron ten-pfennig piece rolled from her sweaty fingers. The gaunt man captured it with a dropped thimble.

"Now which one, magpie? You want the shiny one, true? Left or right or middle or none at all?"

Elster watched his hands. She could not be sure and so closed her eyes and reached out. She clamped her hand over the gaunt man's grip. His skin felt slick and hard like polished horn. "This one," she said. When she looked, his palm held an empty thimble.

"Maybe later you'll find the prize." When he smiled she saw that his front teeth were metal: the left a dull iron, the right gleamed gold.

A strong arm pulled her away from the table. "Stupid child." Her grandmother cuffed her face. "From now on, a thimble will be your keep."

THE MESSAGE

Down in the cellar, the stones seeped with moisture. Odile sneezed from the stink of mold. She could see how her papa trembled at the chill.

The floor was fresh-turned earth. Crates filled niches in the walls. In the tower's other cage, a weeping man sat on a stool. The king's livery, stained, bunched about his shoulders.

"The prince's latest messenger." Papa gestured at a bejeweled necklace glittering at the man's feet. "Bearing a bribe to end the engagement."

Papa followed this with a grunt as he stooped down and began digging in the dirt with his fingers. Odile helped him brush away what covered a dull, gray egg. "Papa, he's innocent."

He gently pulled the egg loose of the earth. "Dear, there's a tradition of blame. Sophocles wrote that 'No man loves the messenger of ill.'"

He took a pin from his cloak and punched a hole into the ends of the egg while intoning *rara lingua*. Then he approached the captive man, who collapsed, shaking, to his knees. Papa blew into one hole, and a vapor reeking of sulfur drifted out to surround the messenger. Screams turned into the frantic call of a songbird.

"We'll send him back to the prince in a gilded cage with a message. 'We delightedly accept your offer of an engagement ball.' Perhaps I should have turned him into a parrot, and he could have spoken that."

"Papa," Odile chided.

"I'll return his form after the wedding. I promise." He carried the egg to one shelf and pulled out the crate of curse eggs nestled in soil. "What king more wisely cares for his subjects?"

THE PRINCE

The prince would rather muck out every filthy stall in every stable of the kingdom than announce his engagement to the sorcerer's daughter at the ball. His father must have schemed his downfall; why else condemn him to marry a harpy?

"Father, be reasonable. Why not the Duke of Bremen's daughter?" The prince glanced up at the fake sky the guildsmen were painting on the ballroom's ceiling. A cloud appeared with a brushstroke.

"The one so lovely that her parents keep her in a cloister?" asked the king. "Boy, your wife should be faithful only to you. Should she look higher to God, she'll never pay you any respect."

"Then that countess from Schaumberg—"

The king sighed. "Son, there are many fine lands with many fine daughters, but none of them have magic."

"Parlor tricks!"

"Being turned into a turkey is not a trick. Besides, von Rothbart is the most learned man I have ever met. If his daughter has half the mind, half the talent . . ."

"Speaking dead languages and reciting dusty verse won't keep a kingdom."

The king laughed. "Don't tell that to Cardinal Passerine."

THE FLEDGLING

In the silence, Odile looked up from yellowed pages that told how a pelican's brood are stillborn until the mother pecks its chest and resurrects them with her own blood. Odile had no memory of her own mother. Papa would never answer any question she asked about her.

She pinched the flame out in the sconce's candle and opened the shutters. The outside night had so many intriguing sounds. Even if she only listened to the breeze it would be enough to entice her from her room.

She went to her dresser, opened the last drawer, and found underneath old mohair sweaters the last of the golden wappentier eggs she had taken. She could break it now, turn herself into a night bird and fly free. The thought tempted her as she stared at her own weak reflection on the shell. She polished it for a moment against her dressing gown.

But the need to see Elster's face overpowered her.

So, as she had done so many nights, Odile gathered and tied bedsheets and old clothes together as a makeshift rope to climb down the outer walls of her papa's tower.

As she descended, guided only by moonlight, something large flew near her head. Odile became still, with the egg safe in a makeshift sling around her chest, her toes squeezing past crumbling mortar. A *fledermaus*? Her papa called them vermin; he hunted them as the pother owl. If he should spot her . . . But no, she did not hear his voice demand she return to her room. Perhaps it was the wappentier. Still clinging to the wall, she waited for the world to end, as her papa had said would happen if the great bird ever escaped from its cage. But her heartbeat slowly calmed and she became embarrassed by all her fears. The elder von Rothbart would have fallen asleep at his desk, cheek smearing ink on the page. The sad wappentier would be huddled behind strong bars. Perhaps it also dreamed of freedom.

Once on the ground, Odile walked toward the moat. Sleeping swans rested on the bank, their long necks twisted back and their bills tucked into pristine feathers.

She held up the wappentier egg. Words of *rara lingua* altered her fingernail, making it sharp as a knife. She punctured the two holes, and as she blew into the first, her thoughts were full of incantations and her love's name. She had trouble holding the words in her head; as if alive and caged, they wanted release on the tongue. Maybe Papa could not stop from turning men into birds, though Odile suspected he truly enjoyed doing so.

She never tired of watching the albumen sputter out of the shell and drift over the quiet swans like marsh fire before falling like gold rain onto one in their midst.

Elster stretched pale limbs. Odile thought the maid looked like some unearthly flower slipping through the damp bank, unfurling slender arms and long blonde hair. Then she stumbled until Odile took her by the hand and offered calm words while the shock of the transformation diminished.

They fled into the woods. Elster laughed to run again. She stopped to reach for fallen leaves, touch bark, then pull at a loose thread of Odile's dressing gown and smile.

Elster had been brought to the tower to fashion Odile a dress for court. Odile could remember that first afternoon, when she had been standing on a chair while the most beautiful girl she'd ever seen stretched and knelt below her, measuring. Odile had never felt so awkward, sure that she'd topple at any moment, yet so ethereal, confident that had she slipped, she would glide to the floor.

Papa instructed Elster that Odile's gown was to be fashioned from sticks and string, like a proper bird's nest. But, alone together, Elster showed Odile bolts of silk and linen, guiding her hand along the cloth to feel its softness. She would reveal strands of chocolate-colored ribbon and thread them through Odile's hair while whispering how pretty she could be. Her lips had lightly brushed Odile's ears.

When Papa barged into Odile's room and found the rushes and leaves abandoned at their feet and a luxurious gown in Elster's lap, he dragged Elster down to the cellar. A tearful Odile followed, but she could not find the voice to beg him not to use a rotten wappentier egg.

In the woods, they stopped, breathless, against a tree trunk. "I brought you a present," Odile said.

"A coach that will carry us far away from your father?"

Odile shook her head. She unlaced the high top of her dressing gown and allowed the neckline to slip down inches. She wore the prince's bribe but now lifted it off her neck. The thick gold links, the amethysts like frozen drops of wine, seemed to catch the moon's fancy as much as their own.

"This must be worth a fortune." Elster stroked the necklace Odile draped over her long, smooth neck.

"Perhaps. Come morning, I would like to know which swan is you by this."

Elster took a step away from Odile. Then another, until the tree was between them. "Another day trapped. And another. And when you marry the prince, what of me? No one will come for me then."

"Papa says he will release all of you. Besides, I don't want to marry the prince."

"No. I see every morning as a swan. You can't—won't— refuse your father."

Odile sighed. Lately, she found herself daydreaming that

Papa had found her as a chick, fallen from the nest, and turned her into a child. "I've never seen the prince," Odile said as she began climbing the tree.

"He'll be handsome. An expensive uniform with shining medals and epaulets. That will make him handsome."

"I heard his father and mother are siblings. He probably has six fingers on a hand." Odile reached down from the fat branch she sat upon to pull Elster up beside her.

"Better to hold you with."

"The ball is tomorrow night."

"What did he do with the gown I made you?"

"He made me burn it."

Elster frowned. "Pity. It would have been lovely." She sighed. "If I could come along to the ball with you—" Elster threaded her fingers through Odile's hair, sweeping a twig from the ends. "Wouldn't you rather I be there than your father?"

Odile leaned close to Elster and marveled at how soft her skin felt. Her pale cheeks. Her arms, her thighs. Odile wanted music then, for them to dance together dangerously on the branches. Balls and courts and gowns seemed destined for other girls.

THE COACH

On the night of the ball, von Rothbart surprised Odile with a coach and driver. "I returned some lost sons and daughters we had around the tower for the reward." He patted the rosewood sides of the coach. "I imagine you'll be traveling to and from the palace in the days to come. A princess shouldn't be flying."

Odile opened the door and looked inside. The seats were plush and satin.

"You wear the same expression as the last man I put in the cellar cage." He kissed her cheek. "Would a life of means and comfort be so horrible?"

The words in her head failed Odile. They wouldn't arrange themselves in an explanation, in the right order to convey to Papa her worries about leaving the tower, her disgust at having to marry a man she didn't know and could never care for. Instead she pressed herself against him. The bound twigs at her bosom stabbed her chest. The only thing that kept her from crying was the golden egg she secreted in the nest gown she wore.

When the coach reached the woods, Odile shouted for the driver to stop. He looked nervous when she opened the door and stepped out onto the road.

"Fräulein, your father insisted you arrive tonight. He said I'd be eatin' worms for the rest of my days."

"A moment." She had difficulty running, because of the rigid gown. She knew her knees would be scratched raw by the time she reached the swans. Odile guided a transformed Elster to the road. The sight of the magnificent coach roused her from the change's fugue.

"Finally I ride with style." Elster waited for the driver to help her climb the small steps into the coach. "But I have no dress to wear tonight."

Odile sat down beside her and stroked the curtains and the cushions. "There is fabric wasted here to make ten gowns."

When Odile transformed her fingernails to sharp points to rip free satin and gauze, she noticed Elster inch away. The magic frightened her. Odile offered a smile and her hand to use as needles. Elster took hold of her wrist with an almost cautious touch.

The bodice took shape in Elster's lap. "We could stay on the road. Not even go to the ball. You could turn the driver into a red-breasted robin and we could go wherever we want."

"I've never been this far away from home." Odile wondered why she hadn't considered such an escape. But all her thoughts had been filled with the dreaded ball, as if she had no choice but to accept the prince's hand. She glanced out the tiny window at the world rushing past. But Papa would be waiting for her tonight. There would be studies tomorrow and feeding the wappentier, and she couldn't abandon Papa.

It was a relief that she had no black egg with her, that she had no means to turn a man into fowl. She had never done so, could not imagine the need. So she shook her head.

Elster frowned. "Always your father's girl." She reached down and bit free the thread linking Odile's fingers and her gown. "Remember that I offered you a choice."

THE BALL

The palace ballroom had been transformed into an enchanting wood. The rugs from distant Persia had been rolled up to allow space for hundreds of fallen leaves fashioned from silk. The noble attendees slipped on the leaves often. A white-bearded ambassador from Lombardy fell and broke his hip; when carried off he claimed it was no accident but an *atto di guerra*.

Trees, fashioned by carpenters and blacksmiths, spread along the walls. The head cook had sculpted dough songbirds and encrusted them with dyed sugars and marzipan beaks.

The orchestra was instructed not to play any tune not found in nature. This left them perplexed and often silent.

"Fraulein Odile von Rothbart and her guest Fräulein Elster Schwanensee." The herald standing on the landing had an oiled, thick mustache.

Odile cringed beneath the layers of twigs and string that covered her torso and trailed off to sweep the floor. How they all stared at her. She wanted to squeeze Elster's hand for strength but found nothing in her grasp; she paused halfway down the staircase, perplexed by her empty hand. She turned back to the crowd of courtiers but saw no sign of her swan maid.

The courtiers flocked around her. They chattered, so many voices that she had trouble understanding anything they said.

"That frock is so . . . unusual." The elderly man who spoke wore a cardinal's red robes. "How very bold to be so . . . indigenous."

A sharp-nosed matron held a silken pomander beneath her nostrils. "I hope that is imported mud binding those sticks," she muttered.

THE LOVEBIRDS

Elster picked up a crystal glass of chilled Silvaner from a servant's platter. She held the dry wine long in her mouth, wanting to remember its taste when she had to plunge a beak into moat water.

"Fräulein von Rothbart. Our fathers would have us dance."

Elster turned around. She had been right about the uniform. Her heart ached to touch the dark-blue-like-evening wool, the gilded buttons, the medals at the chest, and the thick gold braid on the shoulders. A uniform like that would only be at home in a wardrobe filled with fur-lined coats, jodhpurs for riding with leather boots, silken smoking jackets that smelled of Turkish tobacco. The man who owned such clothes would only be satisfied if his darling matched him in taste.

She lowered her gaze with much flutter and curtsied low.

"I am pleased you wore my gift." The prince had trimmed fingernails that looked so pink as to possibly be polished. He lifted up one section of the necklace she wore. The tip of his pinky slid into the crease between her breasts. "How else would I know you?"

She offered a promissory smile.

He led her near where the musicians sought to emulate the chirp of crickets at dusk. "So, I must remember to commend your father on his most successful enchantment."

"Your Imperial and Royal Highness is too kind."

Three other couples, lavish in expensive fabric and pearls and silver, joined them in a quadrille. As the pairs moved, their feet kicked up plumes of silk leaves. Despite the gold she wore around her neck, Elster felt as if she were a tarnished coin thimblerigged along the dance floor.

"I have an admission to make," she whispered in the prince's ear when next she passed him. "I'm not the sorcerer's daughter."

The prince took hold of her arm, not in a rough grasp, but as if afraid she would vanish. "If this is a trick—"

"Once I shared your life of comfort. Sheets as soft as a sigh. Banquet halls filled with drink and laughter. Never the need for a seamstress, as I never wore a dress twice.

"My parents were vassals in Saxony. Long dead now." She slipped free of his hold and went to the nearest window. She waited for his footsteps, waited to feel him press against her. "Am I looking east? To a lost home?"

She turned around. Her eyes lingered a moment on the plum-colored ribbon sewn to one medal on his chest. "So many years ago—I have lost count—a demonic bird flew into my bedchamber."

"Von Rothbart."

Elster nodded at his disgust. "He stole me away, back to his lonely tower. Every morning I wake to find myself trapped as a swan. Every night he demands I become his bride. I have always refused."

"I have never stood before such virtue." The prince began to tear as he stepped back and then fell to one knee. "Though I can see why even the Devil would promise himself to you."

His eyes looked too shiny, as if he might start crying or raving like a madman. Elster had seen the same sheen in Odile's eyes. Elster squeezed the prince's hand but looked over her shoulder at where she had parted with the sorcerer's daughter. The art of turning someone into a bird would never dress her in cashmere or damask. Feathers were only so soft and comforting.

THE LOST

When Odile was a young girl, her father told her terrible tales every *Abend vor Allerheiligen*. One had been about an insane cook who had trapped over twenty blackbirds and half-cooked them as part of a pie. All for the delight of a royal court. Odile had nightmares about being trapped with screeching chicks, all cramped in the dark, the stink of dough, the rising heat. She would not eat any pastry for years.

Watching Elster dance with the prince filled Odile with

pain. She didn't know whether such hurt needed tears or screams to be freed. She approached them. The pair stopped turning.

"Your warning in the coach? Is this your choice?" asked Odile.

Elster nodded, though her hands released the prince's neck.

The *rara lingua* to tear the swan maid's humanity from her slipped between Odile's lips with one long gasp. Her face felt feverish and damp. Perhaps tears. She called for Papa to take the swan by the legs into the kitchen and return carrying a bulging strudel for the prince.

THE STRYGIAN

As a long-eared pother owl, von Rothbart had hoped to intimidate the nobles with a bloodcurdling shriek as he flew in through a window. An impressive father earned respect, he knew. But with the cacophony in the ballroom—courtiers screaming, guards shouting, the orchestra attempting something cheerful—only three fainted.

Von Rothbart roosted on the high-backed chair at the lead table. He shrugged off the mantle of feathers and seated himself with his legs on the tablecloth and his boots in a dish of poached boar.

"I suppose the venery for your lot would be an inbred of royals."

No one listened.

He considered standing atop the table, but his knees ached after every transformation. As did his back. Instead, he pushed his way through the crowd at the far end, where most of the commotion seemed centered.

He did not expect to find a tearful Odile surrounded by a

ring of lowered muskets. One guard trembled so. The prince shouted at her. The king pulled at his son's arm.

Von Rothbart raised his arms. The faux trees shook with a sudden wind that topped glasses, felled wigs, and swept the tiles free of silk leaves. "Stop," he shouted. "Stop and hear me!"

All eyes turned to him. He tasted fear as all the muskets pointed at him.

"You there, I command you to return Elster to me." The prince's face had become ruddy with ire, his mouth flecked with spittle.

"Who?"

"No lies, Sorcerer. Choose your words carefully."

The king stepped between them. He looked old. As old as von Rothbart felt. "Let us have civil words."

"Papa—" cried Odile.

"If you have hurt my daughter in any way—"

A cardinal standing nearby smoothed out his sanguine robes. "Your daughter bewitched an innocent tonight."

"She flew away from me," said the prince. "My sweet Elster is out there. At night. All alone."

Von Rothbart looked around him. He could not remember ever being so surrounded by men and women, and their expressions of disgust, fear, and hatred left him weak. Weak as an old fool, one who thought he could ingratiate his dear child into their ranks like a cuckoo did with its egg.

Only magpies would care for such shiny trappings, and they were sorrowful birds who envied human speech.

He took a deep breath and held it a moment as the magic began. His lungs hurt as the storm swirled within his body. He winced as a rib cracked. He lost two teeth as the gusts escaped his mouth. The clouds painted on the ceiling became dark and thick and spat lightning and rain down upon the people.

Odile stretched and caught the wind von Rothbart sent her as the crowd fled. He took her out of the palace and into the sky. It pained him to speak, so all he asked her was if she was hurt. The tears that froze on her cheeks answered *Yes, Papa.*

THE BLACK SWAN

"Von Rothbart!"

Odile looked out the window. She had expected the prince. Maybe he'd be waving a sword or a blunderbuss and be standing before a thousand men. But not the king standing by the doors and a regal carriage drawn by snorting stallions. He looked dapper in a wool suit, and she preferred his round fur hat to a crown.

"Von Rothbart, please, I seek an audience with you."

Odile ran down the staircase and then opened the doors.

The king plucked the hat from his head and stepped inside. "Fräulein von Rothbart."

"Your Majesty." She remembered to curtsy.

"Your father—"

"Papa is ill. Ever since . . . well, that night, he's taken to bed."

"I'm sorry to hear that. Your departure was marvelous. The court has been talking of nothing else for days." The king chuckled. "I'd rather be left alone."

She led him to the rarely used sitting room. The dusty upholstery embarrassed her.

"It's quiet here. Except the birds, of course." The king winced. "My apologies."

"Your son—"

"Half-mad they say. Those who have seen him. He's roaming the countryside, hoping to find her. A swan by day and the fairest maiden by night." He tugged at his hat, pulling it out of shape. "Only, she's not turning back to a maiden again, is she?"

Odile sat down in her father's chair. She shook her head.

"Unless, child, your father . . . or you would consent to removing the curse."

"Why should I do that, Your Majesty?"

The king leaned forward. "When I was courting the queen, her father, a powerful duke, sent me two packages. In one was an ancient sword, the iron blade dark and scarred. An heirloom of the duke's family that went back generations, used in countless campaigns—every one a victory." The king made a fist. "When I grasped the hilt, leather salted by sweat, I felt I could lead an army."

"And the second package?" Odile asked.

"That one contained a pillow."

"A pillow?"

The king nodded. "Covered with gold brocade and stuffed with goose down." The king laughed. "The messenger delivered as well a note that said I was to bring one, only one, of the packages with me to dinner at the ducal estate."

"A test."

"That is what my father said. My tutors had been soldiers, not statesmen. The sword meant strength, courage, to my father. What a king should, no, must possess to keep his lands and people safe. To him the choice was clear."

Odile smiled. Did all fathers enjoy telling stories of their youth?

"I thought to myself, if the answer was so clear, then why

the test? What had the duke meant by the pillow? Something soft and light, something womanly . . ."

The notion of a woman being pigeonholed so irritated Odile. Was she any less a woman because she lacked the apparent grace of girls like Elster? She looked down at the breeches she liked to wear, comfortable not only because of the fit but also because they had once been worn by her father. Her hands were not smooth but spotted with ink and rubbed with dirt from where she had begun to dig Papa's grave. Their escape had been too taxing. She worried over each breath he struggled to take.

". . . meant to rest upon, to lie your head when sleeping. Perhaps choosing the pillow would show my devotion to his daughter, that I would be a loving husband before a valiant king—"

"Does he love her?" Odile asked.

The king stammered, as if unwilling to tear himself from the story.

"Your son. Does he love her?"

"What else would drive a man of privilege to the woods? He's forsaken crown for thorn. Besides, a lost princess? Every peasant within miles has been bringing fowl to the palace hoping for a reward."

"A princess." Odile felt a bitter smile curl the edges of her mouth. Would his Royal Highness be roaming the land if he knew his true love was a seamstress? But then Odile remembered Elster's touch, the softness of her lips, her skin.

Perhaps Elster had been meant to be born a princess. She had read in Papa's books of birds that raid neighboring nests, roll out the eggs and lay their own. Perhaps that happened to girls as well. The poor parent never recognized the greedy chick for what it truly was. The prince might never as well.

If her own, unwanted destiny of doting bride had been usurped, then couldn't she choose her future? Why not take the one denied to her?

"The rings on your fingers."

"Worth a small fortune." He removed thick bands set with rubies and pearls. "A bride price then? I could also introduce you to one of the many eligible members of my court."

Odile took the rings, heavy and warm. "These will do," she said and told the king to follow her.

By candlelight, she took him down to the dank cellar. He seemed a bit unnerved by the empty cage. She pulled out a tray of blackened eggs. Then another. "She's here. They're all here. Take them."

The king lifted one egg. He looked it over then shook it by his ear.

"Look through the holes." She held the candle flame high.

The king peered through one end. "My Lord," he sputtered. The egg tumbled from his grasp and struck the floor, where it shattered like ancient pottery.

"There—There's a tiny man sleeping inside."

"I know." She brushed aside the shards with her bare foot. A sharp edge cut her sole and left a bloody streak on the stones. "Don't worry, you freed him."

She left him the light. "Find the princess's egg. Break all of them, if you want. There might be other princesses among them." She started up the staircase.

"She stepped on his toes a great deal."

"What was that?"

The king ran his hands over the curse eggs. "When I watched them dance, I noticed how often she stepped on my son's toes. One would think her parents were quite remiss in not teaching her the proper steps." He looked up at her with a sad smile. "One would think."

Odile climbed to the top of the tower to her papa's laboratory. Inside its cage, the wappentier screeched from both heads when she entered. Since their return, she had neglected it; Papa had been the only one who dared feed the beast.

Its last golden egg rested on a taxonomy book. She held it in her hands a moment before moving to the shutters and pushing them open. She felt the strong breeze. Wearing another shape, she could ride the air far. Perhaps all the way to the mountains. Or the sea.

The wanderlust, so new and strong, left her trembling. Abandoning a life could be cruel.

Still clutching the egg to her chest, she went down to her papa's bedroom. He had trouble opening his eyes when she touched his forehead. He tried to speak but lacked the strength.

He'd never taught Odile about death or grieving, other than to mention the pelican hen shedding blood to revive her children. Odile hoped her devotion would mend him. She devised *rara lingua* with a certainty that surprised her. As she envisioned the illustrated vellum of her lessons, her jaw began to ache. Her mouth tasted like the salt spray of the ocean. She looked down at her arms. Where the albumen dripped, white feathers grew.

She called out, the sound hoarse and new and strange, but so fitting coming from the heavy body she wore. As a pelican, she squatted beside Papa's pillow. Her long beak, so heavy and ungainly as she moved her head, rose high. She plunged it down into her own breast, once, twice, until blood began to spill. Drops fell onto Papa's pale lips. As she hopped about the bed, it spattered onto his bared chest.

She forced her eyes to remain open despite the pain, so she could be assured that the color did return to his face, see the rise and fall of each breath grow higher, stronger.

He raised his hand to her chest, but she nudged his fingers away. Her wound had already begun to close on its own.

When she returned to human form, she touched above her breasts and felt the thick line of a scar. No, she decided it must be a badge, a medal like the prince had worn. She wanted it seen.

"Lear would be envious," Papa said in a voice weak but audible, "to have such a pelican daughter."

She laughed and cried a bit as well. She could not voice how his praise made her feel. So after she helped him sit up in bed, she went to his cluttered wardrobe. "I have to leave." She pushed aside garments until she found a curious outfit, a jacket and breeches, all in shades of red.

"Tell me where you're going."

"Tomorrow's lessons are on the road. I'll learn to talk with ibises and challenge monsters."

"Yes, daughter." Papa smiled. "But help me upstairs before you go."

ೞ   ೞ   ೞ

In the tower library, Papa instructed Odile on how to work the heavy mechanism that lowered the wappentier's cage for feeding or recovering the eggs. The wappentier shuddered, and its musty smell filled the room.

"When the time comes, search the highest peaks." Papa unlocked the latch with a white quill and swung the door open.

The hinges screeched. Or maybe the wappentier cried out.

Her heart trembled inside her ribs, and she pulled at her father even as he stepped back.

The wappentier stretched its wings a moment before taking flight. It flew past them—its plumage, which she had always imagined would feel harsh and rough, was gentle like a whisper. The tower shook. Stones fell from the window's sides and ledge as it broke through the wall.

Odile thought she heard screams below. Horses and men.

Her father hugged her then. He felt frail, as if his bones might be hollow, but he held tight a moment. She could not find the words to assure him that she'd return.

Outside the tower, she found the king's carriage wallowed in the moat. The horses still lived, though they struggled to pull the carriage free. After years of a diet of game meat, the wappentier might have more hungered for rarer fare. There was no sign of a driver.

She waded into the water, empty of any swans, she noticed. The carriage door hung ajar. Inside was empty. As she led the horses to land, Odile looked up in the sky and did not see the wappentier. It must no longer be starved. She hoped the king was still down in the cellar smashing eggs.

She looked back at the tower and thought she saw for a moment her father staring down from the ruined window. She told herself there might be another day for books and fathers. Perhaps even swans. Then she stepped up to the driver's seat and took hold of the reins and chose to take the road.

STEVE BERMAN has gone on several nocturnal owl-watches. He falls asleep before he catches even a glimpse of his favorite bird. His novel, *Vintage*, was a finalist for the Andre Norton Award. He has edited the anthologies *Magic in the Mirrorstone*, *So Fey*, and *Wilde Stories*. He roosts in southern New Jersey.

His Web site is www.steveberman.com.

❧❧

Author's Note

Blame the ballet. I had been asked to review a performance of *Giselle* by the Pennsylvania Ballet. My mother had always wanted to see a live ballet, and so she accompanied me to the old Merriam Theater. We both thought the experience was magical. There were moments when the ballerinas achieved a step that looked as if they floated across the stage. I knew I wanted to write something based on the experience.

Conveniently, I had been researching *Swan Lake* when Ellen and Terri sent me the invitation to submit to this anthology. Sadly, there's no pointe work in "Thimbleriggery and Fledglings." Maybe another day, another tale. But the role of Odile, the infamous Black Swan of the ballet, needed to be revisited. I wondered why she went along with her father's schemes. Not every girl wants a prince or even a crown.

I owe another maternal figure for holding my hand through the writing. Ann Zeddies proved she's a remarkable reader, the best of friends for any writer. Odile's story might have been far more tragic if not for Ann's insight. A debt of thanks to Kelly Link, as well, for one night telling me the secret: sleight of hand is no different from sleight of word.

THE FLOCK

Lucius Shepard

Doyle Mixon and I were hanging out beneath the bleachers at the Crescent Creek High football field, passing a joint, zoning on the katydids and the soft Indian summer air, when a school bus carrying the Taunton Warriors pulled up at the curb. Doyle was holding in a toke, his eyes closed and face lifted to the sky; with his long sideburns, he looked like a hillbilly saint at prayer. When he caught sight of the team piling off the bus, he tried to suppress a chuckle and coughed up smoke. The cause of his amusement—Taunton had three monstrously fat linemen, and as their uniforms were purple with black stripes and numerals, they resembled giant plums with feet.

One lineman waddled over, his pod-brothers following close behind. "You guys got a problem?" he asked.

Doyle was too stoned to straighten out and he kind of laughed when he said, "We're fine, dog."

Standing in a row, staring down at us, they made a bulg-

ing purple fence that sealed us off from the rest of the world.
Their hair had been buzzed down to stubble, and their faces were three lumpy helpings of sunburned vanilla pudding.
Tiny round heads poked up between their shoulder pads. They
might have been some weird fatboy rap act like that old MTV
guy, Bubba Sparxxx.

"What's so fucking funny?" a second one asked, and Doyle
and I both said, "Nothing," at about the same time.

"We got a couple of stoners, is what we got," the first one
said, showing Doyle a fist the size of a Monster Burger. "Want
to trip on this, freak?"

I kept my mouth shut, but Doyle, I guess he figured we
were safe on neutral ground or else he simply didn't give a
damn. "You guys," he said. "If beer farts were people, they'd
look like you guys. All bloated and purple and shit."

The third lineman hadn't said a thing—for all I knew, he
might not have possessed the power of speech; but he could
hear well enough. He yanked Doyle upright and slammed an
elbow into the side of his jaw. All three of them went to beating on us. It couldn't have been more than ten seconds before
their coach dragged them off us; but they had done a job in
that short time. Doyle's eyelid was cut and his lip was bleeding.
They hadn't gotten me nearly as bad, but my cheekbone ached
and my shirt was ripped.

The coach, Coach Cunliffe, was a dumpy little guy with
a torso shaped like a frog's and a weak comb-over hidden
beneath a purple cap. "Son-of-a-buck!" he kept saying, and
pounded on their chests. They didn't even quiver when he hit
them. One said something I was too groggy to catch and the
coach calmed down all of a sudden. He took a stand over us,

his hands on hips, and said, "You boys intend to make a report about this, I expect we got something to report on ourselves. Don't we?"

Doyle was busy nursing his eye, and I didn't have a clue what Cunliffe was going on about.

"I was to search your pockets, what you reckon I'd find?" Cunliffe asked. "Think it might be an illegal substance?"

"You lay a hand on me," Doyle said, "I'll tell the cops you grabbed my johnson."

Cunliffe whipped out a cell phone. "No need for me to search. I'll just call down to the sheriff and get him on the case. How about that?" When neither of us responded, he pocketed the phone. "Well, then. Supposing we call it even, all right?"

Doyle muttered something.

"Is that a no?" Cunliffe reached for his phone again.

"Naw, man. Just keep these fuckwits out of my face."

The fuckwits surged forward. Cunliffe spread his arms to restrain them. "You're number twenty-two for the Pirates," he said to Doyle. "I remember you from last year. Cornerback, right?" He gave us both the eye. "You boys down here doing a little scouting?"

Doyle spat redly, and I said, "Uh-huh."

"That's gonna help!" one of the linemen said, and his buds laughed thickly.

Cunliffe shushed them and locked onto Doyle. "You played some damn good ball against us last year, Twenty-two. You figger marijuana's gonna enhance your performance next month?"

"Not as much as the juice made these assholes' nuts fall off," said Doyle.

The linemen rumbled—Cunliffe pushed them toward the

field, and they moved away through the purpling air. "Better get that eye took care of," he said. "Get it all healed up by next month. My boys are like sharks once they get the smell of blood."

"Those are some fat goddamn sharks," Doyle said.

ᘔ   ᘔ   ᘔ

The towns of Taunton, Crescent Creek, and Edenburg are laid out in a triangle in the northeast corner of Culliver County, none more than fifteen miles apart. My mama calls the area "the Bermuda Triangle of South Carolina," because of the weird things that happened there, ghosts and mysterious lights in the sky and such. Now I've done some traveling, I understand weirdness is a vein that cuts all through the world, but I cling to the belief that it cuts deeper than normal through Culliver County, and I do so in large part because of the chain of events whose first link was forged that evening in Crescent Creek.

Doyle and I hadn't gone to the game to scout Taunton—we knew we had no chance against them. Only ninety-six boys at Edenburg High were eligible for football. Most of our team were the sons of tobacco farmers, many of whom couldn't make half the practices because of responsibilities at home. Taunton, on the other hand, drew its student body from a population of factory workers, and they were a machine. Every year they went to the regional finals, and they'd come close to winning State on a couple of occasions. It was considered a moral victory if we held them to thirty points or under, something we hadn't managed to do for the better part of a decade. So what we were up to, Doyle and I, was looking for two girls we'd met at a party in Crescent Creek the week before. We were only halfheartedly looking—I had a girlfriend, and Doyle was unofficially engaged—and after what the linemen had done to us, with our clothes bloody and faces bruised, we decided to go drinking instead.

We picked up a couple of twelve-packs at Snade's Corners, a general store out on State Road 271 where they never checked ID, and drove along a dead-end dirt road to Warnoch's Pond, a scummy eye of water set among scrub pine and brush, with a leafless live oak that clawed up from the bank beside it like a skeletal three-fingered hand. There was a considerable patch of bare ground between the pond and the brush, littered with flattened beer cans and condom wrappers and busted bottles with sun-bleached labels. Half a dozen stained, chewed-up sofas and easy chairs lined the bank. The black sofa on the far left was a new addition, I thought—at least it looked in better shape than the others.

The pond was where a lot of Edenburg girls, not to mention girls from Taunton and Crescent Creek, lost their cherry, but it was too early for couples to be showing up, and we had the place to ourselves. We sat on the black sofa and drank Blue Ribbon and talked about women and football and getting the hell out of Edenburg, the things we always talked about, the only things there *were* to talk about if you were a teenager in that region, except maybe for tobacco and TV. Doyle fumed over the fight for a time, swearing vengeance, but didn't dwell on it—we'd had our butts kicked before. I told him that big as those linemen were, vengeance might require an elephant gun.

"I hate they kill us every year," Doyle said. "I'd like to win one, you know."

I cracked a beer and chugged down half. "Not gonna happen."

"What the hell do you care? Only reason you play so's you can get a better class of woman."

I belched. "You know I'd lay me down and die for the ol' scarlet and silver."

Annoyed, he gave me a shove. "Well, I would for real. Just one win. That's all I'm asking."

"I'm getting a special feeling here," I said.

"Shut up!"

"I'm getting all tingly and shit . . . like God's listening in. He's heard your voice and even now . . ."

He chucked one of his empties at me.

". . . universal forces are gathering, preparing to weave your heartfelt prayer into His Glorious Design."

"I wish," said Doyle.

Darkness folded down around us, hiding the scrub pine. Though it had been overcast all day, the stars were out in force. Doyle twisted up a joint and we smoked, we drank, we smoked some more, and by the time we'd finished the first twelve-pack, the dead live oak appeared more witchy than ever, the stars close enough to snatch down from the sky, and the pond, serene and shimmering with reflected light, might have been an illustration in a book of fairy tales. I thought about pointing this out to Doyle, but I restrained myself—he would have told me to quit talking like a homo.

Clouds blew in from the east, covering the stars, and we fell silent. All I could hear were dogs barking in the distance and that ambient hum that seems to run throughout the American night. I asked what he was thinking and he said, "Taunton."

"Jesus, Doyle. Here." I flipped him a fresh beer. "Get over it, okay?"

He turned the can over in his hands. "It ticks me off."

"Look, man. The only way we'll ever beat them is if their bus breaks down on the way to the game."

"What do you mean?"

"If they show up late, they'll have to forfeit."

"Oh . . . yeah," he said glumly, as if the notion didn't satisfy him.

"So get over it."

He started to respond but was cut off by a shrill *jee-eep*, a sound like a rusty gate opening; this was followed by a rustling, as of many wings.

I jumped up. "What was that?"

"Just a grackle," Doyle said.

I peered into the darkness. Though it was likely my imagination, the night air looked to have taken on the glossiness of a grackle's wing. I didn't much like grackles. They were nest robbers and often ate fledglings. And there were stories . . . A droplet of ice formed at the tip of my spine.

"City boy," said Doyle disparagingly, referring to the fact that I had spent my first decade in Aiken, which *was* a city compared to Edenburg. "Is Andy scared of the birdies?"

There came a series of *jee-eeps*, more rustling. I thought I detected almost invisible movement in every direction I turned.

"Let's get out of here," I said.

"Want me to hold your hand?"

"Come on! We can drive over to Dawn's and see if she wants to do something."

Doyle made a disgusted noise and stood. "Something's about to poke a hole in my ass, anyway." He touched the back of his jeans and then inspected his finger. "Christ, I'm bleeding. I think something bit me." He kicked at the sofa. "I could get an infection off this damn thing!"

"I bet you can get Dawn to suck out the poison," I said, hurrying toward the car.

As I backed up, the headlights swept across the bank, revealing the row of thrown-away sofas and chairs. I could have sworn one of them was missing, and as I went fishtailing off along the dirt road, the more I thought about it, the more certain I became that it was the one we had been sitting on.

ℑ ℑ ℑ

If it hadn't been for football, I would have been an outsider in high school, angry and fucked-up, a loner whom everyone would have voted the Most Likely to Go Columbine. People said I took after my mama—I had her prominent cheekbones and straight black hair and hazel eyes. She was one-quarter Cherokee, still a beauty as she entered her forties, and she had a clever mind and a sharp tongue that could slice you down to size in no time flat. She was a lot quicker than my daddy (a stoic, uncommunicative sort), way too quick to be stuck in a backwater like Edenburg. Some nights she drank too much and Daddy would have to help her upstairs, and some afternoons she went out alone and didn't return until I was in bed, and I would hear them fighting, arguments in which she always got the last word. When I was in the eighth grade I discovered that she had a reputation. According to gossip, she was often seen in the bars and had slept with half the men in Taunton. I got into a bunch of school-yard fights that usually were started by a comment about her. I felt betrayed, and for a while we didn't have much of a relationship. Then Daddy sat me down and we had a talk, the only real talk we'd had to that point.

"I knew what I was getting when I married your mama," he

said. "She's got a wild streak in her, and sometimes it's bound to come out."

"People laughing behind your back and calling her a slag . . . how do you put up with that?"

"Because she loves us," he said. "She loves us more than anyone. People are gonna say what they gonna say. Your mama's had a few flings, and it hurts—don't get me wrong. But she has to put up with me and with the town, so it all evens out. She don't belong in Edenburg. These women around here don't have nothing to offer her, talking about county fairs and recipes. You're the only person she can talk to, and that's because she raised you to be her friend. The two of you can gab about books and art, stuff that goes right over my head. Now with you giving her the cold shoulder, she's got no outlet for that side of things."

I asked straight out if he had slept with other women, and he told me there was a time he did, but that was just vengeful behavior.

"I never wanted anybody but your mama," he said solemnly, as if taking a vow. "She's the only woman I ever gave a damn about. Took me a while to realize it, is all."

I didn't entirely understand him and kept on fighting until he pushed me into football at the beginning of the ninth grade; though it didn't help me understand any better, the game provided a release for my aggression, and things gradually got easier between me and Mama.

By our senior year, Doyle and I were the best players on the team and football had become for me both a means of attracting girls and a way of distracting attention from the fact that I read poetry for fun and effortlessly received As, while the majority of my class watched *American Idol* and struggled with the concepts of basic algebra. My gangly frame had filled out, and I was a better than adequate wide receiver. Not good enough for college ball, probably not good enough to start for Taunton, but I didn't care about that. I loved the feeling of leaping high, the ball settling into my hands, while faceless midgets clawed ineffectually at it, and then breaking free, running along the sideline—it didn't happen all that often, yet when it did, it was the closest thing I knew to satori.

Doyle was undersized, but he was fast and a vicious tackler. Several colleges had shown interest in him, including the University of South Carolina. Steve Spurrier, the Old Ball Coach himself, had attended one of our games and shook Doyle's hand afterward, saying he was going to keep an eye on him. For his part, Doyle wasn't sure he wanted to go to college.

When he told me this, I said, "Are you insane?"

He shot me a bitter glance but said nothing.

"Damn, Doyle!" I said. "You got a chance to play in the SEC and you're going to turn it down? Football's your way out of this shithole."

"I ain't never getting out of here."

He said this so matter-of-factly, for a moment I believed him; but I told him he was the best corner in our conference and to stop talking shit.

"You don't know your ass!" He chested me, his face cinched into a scowl. "You think you do. You think all those books you read make you smart, but you don't have a clue."

I thought he was going to start throwing, but instead he walked away, shoulders hunched, head down, and his hands shoved in the pockets of his letterman's jacket. The next day he was back to normal, grinning and offering sarcastic comments.

Doyle was a moody kid. He was ashamed of his family—everyone in town looked down on them, and whenever I went to pick him up I'd find him waiting at the end of the driveway, as if hoping I wouldn't notice the meager particulars of his life: a dilapidated house with a tar paper roof; a pack of dogs running free across the untended property; one or another of his sisters pregnant by persons unknown; an old man whose breath reeked of fortified wine. I assumed that his defeatist attitude reflected this circumstance, but I didn't realize how deep it cut, how important trivial victories were to him.

§ § §

The big news in Culliver County that fall had to do with the disappearance of a three-week-old infant, Sally Carlysle. The police arrested the mother, Amy, for murder because the story she told made no sense—she claimed that grackles had carried off her child while she was hanging out the wash to dry, but she had also been reported as having said that she hadn't wanted the baby. People shook their heads and blamed post-partum depression and said things like Amy had always been flighty and she should never have had kids in the first place and weren't her two older kids lucky to survive? I saw her picture in the paper—a drab, pudgy little woman, handcuffed and shackled—but I couldn't recall ever having seen her before, even though she lived a couple of miles outside of town.

During the following week, grackle stories of another sort surfaced. A Crescent Creek man told of seeing an enormous flock crossing the morning sky, taking four or five minutes to pass overhead; three teenage girls said grackles had surrounded their car, blanketing it so thickly that they'd been forced to use a flashlight to see each other.

There were other stories put forward by more unreliable witnesses, the most spectacular and unreliable of them being the testimony of a drunk who'd been sleeping it off in a ditch near Edenburg. He passed out near an old roofless barn, and when he woke, he discovered the barn had miraculously acquired a roof of shiny black shingles. As he scratched his head over this development, the roof disintegrated and went flapping up, separating into thousands upon thousands of black birds, with more coming all the time—the entire volume of the barn must have been filled with them, he said. They formed into a column, thick and dark as a tornado, that ascended into the sky and vanished. The farmer who owned the property testified to finding dozens of dead birds inside the barn, and some appeared to have been crushed; but he sneered at the notion that thousands of grackles had been packed into it. This made me think of the sofa at Warnoch's Pond, but I dismissed what I had seen as the product of too much beer and dope. Other people, however, continued to speculate.

In our corner of South Carolina, grackles were called the Devil's Bird, and not simply because they were nest robbers. They were large birds, about a foot long, with glossy purplish black feathers, lemon-colored eyes, and cruel beaks, and were often mistaken at a distance for crows. A mighty flock was rumored to shelter on one of the Barrier Islands, biding their time until called to do the devil's bidding, and it was said that they had been attracted to the region by Blackbeard and his pirates. According to the legend, Blackbeard himself, Satan's earthly emissary, had controlled the flock, and when he died, they had been each infused with a scrap of his immortal spirit and thus embodied in diluted form his malicious ways. No longer under his direction, the mischief they did was erratic, appearing to follow no rational pattern of cause and effect.

Some claimed they had poison beaks and could imitate human speech and do even more arcane imitations. A librarian sent a letter to the paper citing an eighteenth-century account that spoke of a traveler who had come upon an ancient mill where none had stood before and watched it erode and disappear, dissolving into a flock of grackles that somehow "had contrived its likeness from the resource of their myriad bodies, as though shaped and given the hue of weathered wood by a Great Sculptor." Her account was debunked by a college professor who presented evidence that the author of the piece had been a notorious opium addict.

Jason Coombs's daddy—Jason was our strong-side tackle, a huge African-American kid almost as imposing as the Taunton linemen—preached at the stomp-and-shout church over near Nellie's West Side Café, and each year he delivered a sermon using the Devil's Bird as a metaphor, punctuating it with whoops and grunts, saying that evil was always lurking, waiting for its opportunity to strike, to swoop down like an avenging host and punish the innocent for the failures of the weak, suggesting that evil was a by-product of society's moral laxity, a stratagem frequently employed by evangelists but given an inadvertent Marxist spin by the Reverend Coombs, who halfway through the sermon took to substituting the word "comrade" for "brother" and "sister." He had a field day with the Carlysle murder. Jason broke us up after practice one afternoon with an imitation of his old man ("Satan's got his flock, huh, and Jesus got his angels! Praise Jesus!"), an entertainment that caused Coach Tuttle, a gung-ho Christian fitness freak in his thirties, to rebuke us sharply for making fun of a God-fearing man such as the Reverend. He ordered us to run extra laps and generally worked us like mules thereafter.

"You boys better flush everything out of your heads but football," he told us. "This team has a chance to achieve great things and I'm prepared to kick your tails six ways from Sunday to see that you get the job done."

I wasn't fool enough to believe that we could achieve great things, but it was a heady time for Pirate football. We were assured of having our first winning season in four years. Our record was 6–2 going into the Crescent Creek game, and if we won that, our game with Taunton would actually mean something: win that one and we'd play in the regionals up in Charleston.

I did my best to focus on football, but I was experiencing my first real dose of woman trouble. My girlfriend, Carol Ann Bechtol, was making me crazy, saying that she didn't know anymore if we had a future and, to put it delicately, was withholding her affections. She wanted more of a commitment from me. I envied those city kids who had friends with benefits, who could hang out and have sex and stay commitment free, because in Edenburg we still did things the old-fashioned way—we dated, we went steady, we got all messed up over one girl or one boy. Mama warned me not to let myself get trapped.

"You know that's what Carol Ann's doing," she said. "She knows you'll be off to college next year, and she wants to catch onto your coattails and go with you."

"That's not such a bad thing," I said.

"No, not if you love her. Do you?"

"I don't know."

She sighed. "You can't tell anybody what to do, and I'm not going to try and tell you. You have to work it out on your own. But you should ask yourself how Carol Ann is going to fare away from Edenburg, and whether she's going to be a burden or a partner. Will she try and pull you back home or will she be glad to put this sorry place behind her?"

I knew the answers to her questions but kept silent, not wanting to hear myself speak them. We were sitting at the kitchen table. A steady rain fell and the lights were on and the radio played quietly and I felt distant from the gray light and the barren town outside.

"She's a sweet girl," Mama said. "She loves you, and that's why she's manipulating you. It's not just a matter of desperation. She's convinced you'll be better off here in the long run. Maybe she's right. But you're bound to try your wings and you have to decide if you can get off the ground with Carol Ann along."

"Is that what happened to you?" I asked. "With Daddy, I mean."

"It's some of it. I've had regrets, but I've lived past them and learned to make do."

She flattened her long-fingered hands on the table and stared down at them as if they were evidence of regret and love and something less definable, and I saw for an instant what a wild and lovely creature it was that my daddy had gentled. Then the radio crackled and she was just my mama once again.

"What I wonder, Andy," she said, "is if making do's a lesson you need to learn this early on."

ဌ   ဌ   ဌ

I broke up with Carol Ann the Wednesday before the Crescent Creek game, at lunchtime in a corner of the practice field. She accused me of using her for sex, of ruining her life. I didn't trust myself to speak and stood with my head down, my face hot, taking her abuse, wanting to say something that would make her stop and throw her arms around me and draw me into a kiss that would set a seal on our lives; but I couldn't pull the trigger. She ran off crying, looking for her friends, and I went off to American history, where I listened to Mrs. Kemp tell lies about South Carolina's glorious past and doodled pictures of explosions in my notebook.

Friday night, I played the best game of my career. I played with hate and self-loathing in my heart, throwing my body around, slamming into the Crescent City corners with vicious abandon, screaming at them while they lay on the ground—I scored three times, twice on short passes and once on a fumbled kickoff, threading my way through tacklers and plowing under the last man between me and the goal with a lowered shoulder. In the locker room afterward, Coach Tuttle was inspired to curse, something he rarely did.

"Did you see Andy out there tonight?" he asked the gathered team. "That boy played some damn football! He wanted to win and he did something about it!"

The team roared their approval, sounding like dogs with their mouths full of meat, and pounded me on my pads, doing no good to my bruised and aching shoulder.

"You know what next week is?" he asked, and the team responded on cue, "Taunton Week!"

"If y'all play like Andy did tonight, and I know you can"— he paused for effect—"their mamas are gonna be wiping those Taunton boys' asses for a month!"

Doyle and the others wanted me to party with them, but I begged off, saying I needed to ice my shoulder. At home, I told my parents that we'd won and I'd done all right.

Daddy gave me a funny look. "We listened to the game, son."

"Okay," I said angrily. "So I was the goddamn hero. So what?"

His face clouded, but Mama laid a hand on his arm and said I seemed tired and suggested I get some rest.

I burrowed into my room, clamped on the headphones, and listened to some of the new Green Day album, but it wasn't mean enough to suit my mood, so I got on my computer, intending to check my e-mail—all I did was sit and stare at the blank screen. I understood that I hadn't truly broken up with Carol Ann until that night, and the game, my show of ultra-violence, had been a severing act, a repudiation of sorts. If my shoulder hadn't been sore, I might have hit something. I finally turned on the computer and played video games until the dregs of my anger were exhausted from splattering the blood of giant bugs across the walls of a ruined city.

§   §   §

The next morning I received a call from Dawn Cupertino, Doyle's fiancée. She said she was worried about Doyle and wanted to talk. Could I come over? Dawn had been in the class ahead of ours and dropped out at sixteen to have a baby, which she lost during her first trimester. She had never returned to school, instead taking a waitress job at Frederick's Lounge and an apartment in Crescent City, the second floor of an old frame house. She was thin and blue-eyed, a dirty blonde two years older than Doyle, almost three older than me, and had milky skin, nice legs, and a sharp mountain face that might remain pretty for three or four more years before starting to look dried-up and waspish. That would likely be fine with Dawn. Three or four good years would be about what she expected.

Though Doyle bragged on having an older woman with her own place, I thought the real reason he stuck with her was that she shared his low expectations of life but was cheerful about them. She was given to saying things like, "You better be enjoying this, babe, 'cause it's all we're gonna get," and accompanying her comment with a grin, as if even the pleasure of having a beer or watching a movie was more than she could have hoped for.

That morning she met me at the door in jeans and an old sweatshirt three or four sizes too big; her hair was pulled back into a ponytail. She sat on the living room sofa with her knees tucked under her, while I sat beside her, looking around at her collection of glass and porcelain trinkets, a display of old football pennants on the walls, pictures of cute kittens and cuddly dragons, her high school annual on the coffee table. It was a museum of her life up to the point that the baby had come along. Apparently nothing of note had happened since. I felt ungainly, like I was all elbows and knees, and any move I made would shatter the illusion.

Dawn put on a pot of coffee, we chatted about this and that. She said it was too bad about Carol Ann and asked how she was doing.

"She hates me," I said. "I expect she's finding some strength in that."

Dawn giggled nervously, as if she didn't get my meaning.

"What?" I said.

"It just was funny . . . the way you said it." She brushed loose strands of hair back from her brow, then briefly rested her fingers on my arm and asked with exaggerated concern. "And how're you doing?"

"Fine. What's this about Doyle?"

She heaved a sigh. "I don't know what's got into him. He's been acting all weird and . . ." Her chin quivered. "You think he's getting ready to break up with me?"

"Why would you think that?"

"He don't seem real interested anymore." She knuckled one eye, wiping away a trace of moisture from beside it. "Seeing how you broke up with Carol Ann, I figured he might follow suit. Doyle loves you, Andy. Sometimes I think more than he ever loved me."

"That's bullshit," I said.

"It's true. He's always talking about Andy this and Andy that. If you started putting on lipstick and wearing a dress, I swear he'd do it, too." She squared her shoulders. "Maybe we should break up. I'm almost twenty. It's about time I stopped going out with a kid."

"Is that how you see him?"

"Don't you? In a lot of ways Doyle's the same ten-year-old runt who was always trying to lift up my skirt with a stick. Even after he got it lifted up proper, he treated sex like it was something neat he found behind the barn and he's just busting to tell his friends about."

The coffee was ready, and Dawn brought in a tray with the pot and two cups, cream and sugar. When she bent to set it on the table, the neck of her sweatshirt belled and I could see her breasts. I'd seen them plenty of times before whenever a group of us would go skinny-dipping in Crescent Creek, but they hadn't stirred me like they did now. It had been three weeks since I'd been with Carol Ann, and I was way past horny.

I asked Dawn to fill me in on how Doyle was acting weird. She said he'd been spacey, easy to anger, and I told her it had more to do with the Taunton game than her, how he had been obsessed with Taunton ever since the linemen kicked our butts, and how it had made him extradepressed. That appeared to ease her mind, and she turned the conversation back to Carol Ann and me. I opened up to her and told her everything I'd been feeling. She took my hand and commiserated. I knew what was happening, but I didn't allow myself to know it fully—I kept on talking and talking, confessing my fears and weaknesses, thinking about her breasts, her fresh smell, until she leaned over and kissed my cheek, at the same time guiding my hand up under her sweatshirt. She pulled back an inch or two, letting me decide, her eyes holding mine; but there was really no decision to be made.

Afterward, in her bed, she clung to me, not saying anything. I recalled Doyle's stories about her ways. She was a talker, he said. Being with her, it was like making it with a radio play-by-play announcer. Oh, you're doing that, she'd say, and now you're doing this, as if she were describing things for a nationwide audience who couldn't see the field. But with me Dawn had scarcely said a word—she was fiercely concentrated, and when we had done, there was no game summary, no mention of great moves or big plays. She caressed my face and kissed my neck. This made me feel guilty, but that didn't stop us from compounding the felony and doing it a second time. Only after that, as I sat on the edge of the bed buttoning my shirt, did Dawn speak.

"I suppose you're blaming me for this," she said.

"What gives you that idea?"

"You just sitting there, not talking."

"No," I said. "It was mutual."

"Well, that's refreshing."

She padded into the bathroom. I heard the toilet flush, and she came out belting a robe that bore a design of French words and phrases: *Ooh La La* and *Vive la Difference* and such.

"Don't go whipping yourself for this. Okay?" she said, sitting beside me.

"I'm not."

"Sure you are. You're fretting about what Doyle's gonna say. Don't worry. I won't tell him. Me and him are over . . . mostly, anyway."

I glanced at her and began pulling on my socks. She looked neither happy nor sad, but stoic.

"It was my fault, kinda," she said. "I needed to be close with someone. Doyle hardly ever lets me in close, but I thought you would . . . even though it's a one-time thing." She angled her eyes toward me, awaiting a response; then she nudged me in the ribs. "Cheer up, why don'tcha?"

"I'm all right. I was thinking about my mama. About how I used to scorn her when I was in junior high for sneaking around behind my daddy."

The seconds limped past and she said, "I don't reckon we're much smarter than when we were in junior high, but we're for sure less likely to be judging folks."

She offered to fix me lunch, and not being urged in any direction, I accepted. We sat in her kitchen and ate. It was dead gray out the window. Four or five grackles were perched in a leafless myrtle at the corner of her front yard, flying up and resettling. No pedestrians passed. No cars. It was like after an apocalypse that only grackles had survived. I polished off two BLTs and Dawn fixed me another, humming as she turned the strips of bacon, like a young wife doing for her man. I suddenly, desperately wished that I could fit into her life, that we could sustain the fantasy that had failed my parents.

She slipped the sandwich onto the table and handed me a clean napkin, and sat watching me eat and swill down Coke, smiling in pretty reflex when I glanced up. I asked what she was thinking and she said, "Oh, you know. Stuff."

"What kind of stuff?"

I half-hoped she would mention what was in the air and we could embark on a deluded romance that would of course be a major mistake. I was for the moment in love with the idea of making such a mistake. Getting involved with Dawn was the easy way out. Not the easy way out of Edenburg, not out of anywhere, really; but with Dawn and a couple of squalling kids in a double-wide parked on my folks' acreage, at least my problems would be completely defined. Dawn, however, was too smart for that.

She flashed her cheesy waitress grin, the same one she served with an order of chicken-fried steak and biscuits at Frederick's, and said, "Can't a girl keep none of her thoughts private?"

❦   ❦   ❦

Sundays in Edenburg were deader than Saturday mornings. There was one car in the Piggly Wiggly lot that must have been left overnight, and the store windows gave back dull reflections of parking meters and empty sidewalks. Kids had managed to sling several pairs of sneakers over the cable supporting the traffic light at the corner of Ash and Main—a stiff wind blew, and the shoes kicked and heeled in a spooky gallows dance. It reminded me of a zombie movie where things looked normal, but half-eaten citizens lay on the floors inside the feed store and Walgreens.

Somebody with a strong arm could have heaved a baseball from one end of town to the other in maybe three throws, but it took me a long time to drive from my house on the east side to Doyle's, which lay to the west, a mile beyond the city limits sign. I sat idling at the light by the Sunoco station. Wind snapped the blue-and-yellow flags strung between the pumps, scattering paper trash and grit across the concrete apron. I tried once again to resolve the problem I'd wrestled with most of the night. Sooner or later Dawn or one of her friends would tell Doyle, I figured. If I didn't beat them to the punch, I'd lose his friendship. Yet telling him would be a betrayal of Dawn. The whole mess was so fucking high school, it made me want to puke. The light changed. I gunned the engine but didn't put the car in gear and let it drop back down to an idle, resting my head on the seat and closing my eyes. *Screw Doyle*, I thought. I wasn't going to tell him. We'd drive on over to Snade's and sit on the front stoop with a couple of Buds and talk football.

A dairy van pulled up behind me and I rolled down the window and motioned for it to go around; but it just sat there. I peered back at the van. Its windshield was streaked with bird mess. I couldn't make out the driver, though I detected movement inside the cab. I motioned again, and the van didn't stir. It began to piss me off. I climbed out of the car and gestured like one of those guys who guide planes up to the terminal. Nothing. I was inclined to walk back and pound on the door, but the van looked to have acquired an air of menace. Beneath the streaks and gobs of bird shit, its windows were dark, as if they had been blacked out, and I had again a sense of agitated movement within. Horror movies about haunted vehicles flickered through my head. I got back into the car and peeled out, leaving the van stuck at a red light.

Doyle was standing atop a hillock in the field that adjoined his father's property, wearing his letterman jacket, waist deep in brown weeds and grasses; grackles were circling above his head, a half dozen or so. I pulled onto the shoulder and got out and called to him, but he was facing in the opposite direction from me and the wind snatched my words away. I was about to cross the highway when the dairy van came whispering over the hill, going at a fair rate of speed. I flattened against the car, my heart doing a jab-step, and it rolled past me, continuing toward Taunton, disappearing over the next rise. Shaken, I walked to the edge of the field and called to Doyle again. One by one, the grackles dropped from the leaden sky, secreting themselves among the tall grasses, but Doyle gave no sign of having heard. I found a gap in the rusty wire fencing and went twenty or thirty feet into the field. There I stopped, made uneasy by the birds.

"Doyle!" I yelled.

He turned, his face expressionless and pale, and stared—it was like he didn't recognize me for a second or two. Then he signaled me to come up to where he stood. I took pains to avoid places where I thought the grackles had gone to ground.

"Let's go," I said.

He surveyed the empty field with what seemed a measure of satisfaction, like a man contemplating the big house and swimming pool that he planned to build thereon. "Ain't no rush," he said. "Snade's ain't going nowhere."

We stood for nearly a minute without speaking and then he said, "Think we might get some rain?"

"Who the fuck cares? Let's go!"

"We can go. I just thought you might have something you wanted to get off your chest."

I wasn't afraid of Doyle—I had five inches and thirty pounds on him—but I expected he'd come at me hard. I backed off a pace and set myself. He chuckled and looked out over the field.

Perplexed by this behavior, I said, "What the hell's wrong with you?"

He smiled thinly. "That's a fine question, coming from a guy who poked my girlfriend."

"Did she tell you?"

"It don't matter who told me. You got other business to worry about."

He aimed a punch at my head but pulled it back the last second and laughed as, in avoiding the blow, I tripped on the uneven ground and went sprawling. He bent down, hands on his knees, grinning in my face.

"She's a slut, man," he said. "She puts on a real sweet act, but I'm surprised she hasn't jumped you before now."

I stared at him.

"Seriously," he said.

"I thought you two were getting married?"

He snorted. "I'd sooner marry a toilet seat. All she's ever been to me is a hump."

A storm of grackles whirled above the hill behind which the dairy van had vanished, and that confusion in the sky reflected the confusion in my mind. I remembered how needy and tender Dawn had been. After what Doyle had said, I wanted to doubt her, to accept his view of her . . . and I did doubt her on and off for a while; but his lack of regard for her rubbed me the wrong way. For the first time I realized that we might not be friends forever, and I wondered if all my relationships would be so fragile.

৯ ৯ ৯

Against my better judgment, I got caught up in the frenzy of Taunton Week. It was hard not to, what with the entire population of Edenburg telling us that we could win and offering tactical advice. GO PIRATES GO signs were in every shop window. Pep rallies were exercises in hysteria—one cheerleader broke an ankle going for an unprecedented triple somersault and was carted from the gym, still shaking her pompoms and exhorting the crowd. Even Carol, who'd been spreading lies about me all over school, kissed me on the mouth and told me to kill 'em. But along about midweek, reality set in when I watched a tape on Taunton's All-State outside linebacker, a kid named Simpkins, number fifty-five. Coach Tuttle planned to use me on pass patterns going across the middle of the field, where Fifty-five would be waiting to saw me in half. My shoulder hadn't completely healed, and I actually gave consideration to ramming it into a wall or a door, and knocking myself out of the game. On Thursday, after practice, I took a nap and dreamed about Fifty-five. He was standing over me, wearing a black uniform (Taunton wore special black unis for the Edenburg game), and was holding aloft my bloody left shoulder, arm attached, like a trophy.

After my nap I went downtown, trying to walk off the effects of the dream, and ran into Justin Mayhew, our quarterback, a compact, muscular kid with shoulder-length brown hair. He was sitting on the curb out front of the Tastee-Freeze, looking glum. I joined him and he told me that he was worried about the offensive line holding up.

"That number eighty-seven liked to have killed me last year," he said.

"Tell me about it," I said, and mentioned my concerns about Fifty-five. "If you see him lining me up, throw the ball away . . . because I'm going to protect myself first and think about catching it second."

"If I can see around those fat bastards they got on defense, I will." He hawked and spat. "Tuttle's a damn idiot. He can't game plan for shit."

Conversation lagged and Justin was making noises about going out to Snade's, when Mr. Pepper, the ancient school janitor, came shuffling along. He was moving slower than usual and looked somewhat ragged around the edges. We said, "Hey, how you doing?" Normally a garrulous sort, he kept walking. "Hey!" I said, louder this time. Without turning, in a small, raspy voice, he said, "Go to blazes."

We watched him round the corner.

"Did he say, 'Go to blazes?'" I asked.

"He must be drinking again." Justin got to his feet. "Want to run out to Snade's with me?"

"What the hell," I said.

⚶　⚶　⚶

The arc lights were on and the bleachers at Pirate Field were half-full when I arrived for the game. The crowd was mainly Taunton boosters, and they were celebrating early, hooting and carrying on; they were cordoned off from Edenburg supporters by a chain that didn't serve much purpose when passions started to run high. They always brought more people than the bleachers could hold, the overflow spilling onto the sideline behind the Warrior bench. It was like a home game for them. The image of a black-bearded pirate brandishing a saber adorned the scoreboard, and following each victory, they would paint over his jolly grin with an expression of comical fright.

We dressed in a bunkerlike structure in back of the bleachers and the atmosphere inside it was similar, I imagined, to the mood on death row prior to an execution: guys sitting in front of their lockers, wearing doomed expressions. Only Doyle seemed in good spirits, whistling under his breath and briskly strapping on his pads. His locker was next to mine, and when I asked what made him so cheerful, he leaned over and whispered, "I did what you said to."

I looked at him, bewildered. "Huh?"

He glanced around the room, as if checking for eavesdroppers, and said, "I fixed their bus."

I had a vision of bodies scattered across a highway and Doyle in handcuffs telling the police, "I just did what Andy told me." I pushed him against the locker and asked what exactly he had done.

"Ease off, dog!" He barred his elbow under my chin and slipped away. "I nicked their fuel line, okay?"

"They'll just call for another bus."

"They can call," he said. "But all their backups got their tires slashed . . . or so I hear." He winked broadly. "Relax, man. It's in the bag."

It was like someone spiked my paranoia with relief, and I began to feel pretty good. We went out for warm-ups. Taunton had not yet arrived, and an uneasy buzz issued from the bleachers. Coach Tuttle conferred with the game officials while we did our stretches. I ran a few patterns, caught some of Justin's wobbly passes. The field was a brilliant green under the lights; the grass was soft and smelled new mown, the chalked lines glowed white and precise; the specter of Number Fifty-five diminished. The chirpy voices of our cheerleaders sounded distant: . . . *the Edenburg Pirates are hard to beat. They got pads on their shoulders and wings on their feet.* Tuttle sent us back inside and went to talk more with the officials.

In the locker room guys were asking, *What happened? They gonna forfeit?* Doyle just smiled. An air of hopeful expectation possessed the team as it dawned on everyone that we might be going to regionals. Then Tuttle came back in, put his hands on his hips, and said, "They're here." That let the air out of things.

"They're here," Tuttle repeated grimly. "And they don't want no warm-up. Do you hear that? They think they can beat us without even warming up." He searched our faces. "Prove 'em wrong."

I suppose he was going for a General Patton effect, trying to motivate with a few well-chosen words in place of his typical rant; but it fell flat. Everybody was stunned—Doyle, in particular—and we could have used some exhortation. The locker room prayer was especially fervent. As we jogged onto the field, Taunton jeers drowned out the Edenburg cheers and dominated the puny sound of our pep band. The Taunton bus was parked behind the west end zone, and their tri-captains waited at midfield with the referee. In their black uniforms and helmets, they looked like massive chunks of shadow. Justin Coombs and I walked out to meet them for the coin toss. Number Fifty-five centered the Taunton quarterback and one of the linemen, Eighty-seven, who had jumped us in Crescent Creek. He appeared to have grown uglier since last year.

"Gentlemen," the ref said to the tri-captains. "You're the visitors. Call it in the air."

He flipped the silver dollar and Fifty-five said in a feeble, raspy voice, "Tails."

"Tails it is," said the ref, scooping up the coin.

"We'll kii-iick." Fifty-five barely got the words out.

They didn't shake our hands—Edenburg and Taunton never shook hands.

"Did Fifty-five seem weird to you?" I asked Jason as we headed to the sideline.

"I don't know," Jason said, absorbed in his own thoughts.

Things moved quickly after that, the way they always did in the last minutes before the game whistle blew. I knew Daddy and Mama would be home listening to the game—watching me play made Mama anxious—but I searched the crowd for them anyway. Noise and color blurred together. I smelled an odd sourness on the heavy air. Tuttle ran up and down the sideline, slapping us on the ass; then he gathered the return team, yelling, "Right return! Right return!" They trotted out to their positions.

Taunton was already lined up along the forty-yard line, a string of eleven black monsters. I expected them to operate with their characteristic machinelike efficiency, but the kicker approached the tee with a herky-jerky step and the ball dribbled off his foot; the others just stood there. One of our guys recovered the onside kick at the Taunton forty-six.

"They're pissing in our faces!" Coach Tuttle said, incensed. "Disrespecting us!"

He told Justin to run a short-passing series, but when

Justin got us huddled up, he called for a long pass to me off a flea-flicker.

"That ain't what Coach called," said Tick Robbins, our tail-back.

"Fuck him!" Justin said. "This is my last game and I'm calling what I want. That retard's done telling me what to do."

Tick complained and Justin said, "We throw short passes over the middle, it's gonna get Andy dead. Now run the damn play! On two."

We broke the huddle and I lined up opposite a Taunton cornerback. He was looking up into the sky, like he was receiving instruction from God. On two, I faked toward the center of the field and then took off along the sideline. Nobody covered me, and as the ball descended out of the lights, I thought this might be a satori moment. I made the catch, but the pass was a little overthrown and my momentum carried me stumbling out of bounds inside the twenty, where I fell.

That didn't stop the Taunton defenders. They had scarcely moved a muscle when the ball was snapped, yet now they came at what seemed an impossibly fast clip. Their outlines blurred, and it looked as if they weren't running but were skimming over the grass. Three of them piled onto me, but the impact didn't have much effect. I felt something jabbing at me and fought to get clear. As I did, I thought I saw a lemony eye open in the chest of the guy lying atop me—just a flicker, then it was gone—and heard above the noise of the crowd a single, unmistakable *jee-eep*. I scrambled up, confused and frightened. My jersey was covered with tiny rips.

The ref had thrown a flag for unnecessary roughness, and he was chewing out the Taunton players, threatening ejections.

They appeared unconcerned, picking themselves up and walking stiffly, laboriously away. I showed the ref my jersey, but he was mad at the world and told me to shut up and play football. In the huddle I said that something funny was going on, but Justin was all afire to score and paid no attention. After the penalty, we had possession on the Taunton nine-yard line—he dismissed the play Tuttle had sent in and called a quarterback draw. And then Tony Budgen, our right tackle, said "Holy shit!"

The Taunton Warriors, the players on the field and on the sideline, were disintegrating, dissolving into flights of grackles. Their uniforms, their bodies . . . their every particular had been composed of birds, compressed into ungainly shapes, and now those shapes were breaking apart. A helmet appeared to open into a bloom of glossy wings; the numbers 3 and 6 lifted from a jersey, assuming plumper forms, becoming two birds that flew at me, creating a gap from which others emerged; a headless Warrior winnowed to nothing, deconstructing from the neck down like one of those speeded-up time-lapse films detailing the building of a skyscraper, only this one ran backward; the defensive front four exploded into a shrapnel of birds.

Alarmed yet fascinated by the display, we backed toward midfield as the grackles flapped up from the last remaining relics of our opponents, some to perch on the Taunton bus, lining its fenders and roof, a row of hunched, silent spectators, while the rest ascended beyond the lights to join a vast, indistinct disturbance in the sky. Screams issued from the bleachers. Portions of the crowd were disintegrating, too, leaving patches of empty seats, and people pushed and clawed at one another, desperately trying to flee. I had in mind to do the same but was rooted to the spot, staring up into the toiling darkness above the field. It began to get close, stuffy, like when you pull a blanket over your head, and the reason for this soon came clear.

The disturbance above the field was a host of grackles, an unthinkable tonnage of feathers and hollow bones and stringy flesh—as they descended to the level of the lights, the air thickened with their sour smell. They descended farther, whirling and whirling, obscuring the lights so that they showed as dim, flickering suns through a water of black wings.

I could no longer see the sign on the Toddle House beyond the east end of the field, and this led me to believe that the flock had sealed us off from the world. Everyone in the bleachers had poured onto the grass. The pep band's instruments were scattered about. Somebody had stepped on a French horn, crushing the bell. A cheerleader, Beth Pugh, crawled past, black hair striping her face, encaging her demented eyes—when I tried to help her, she slapped my arm away and screamed. People were on their knees, weeping and praying; some shielded their eyes and mouths against the droppings that fell, intermittently peeking at the grackles.

There must have been millions. They must have been stacked to the top of the sky in order to bring such a stench, such an oppressive presence. The great seething of their wings and the rusty chaos of their cries reduced the sounds of human terror to barely audible interruptions in an ocean of white noise. They descended lower yet, roofing the field with their swarming, swirling bodies, darkening the light, and I lay flat, my face buried in the grass, certain that I would be torn apart or crushed or carried off like Amy Carlysle's daughter and dropped from a height.

But when I looked again—after no more than a minute or two, I think—the flock had retreated beyond the tops of the light poles, and they continued their retreat, going beyond the range of sight and hearing until a mere handful were left swooping and curvetting overhead, and those few still perched atop the Taunton bus. Then the bus itself exploded, vanishing in a flurry of the purplish black wings and lemony eyes and cruel beaks that had composed its shape, and we were alone, less than a thousand of us, splattered with bird shit, terrified, wandering the field and searching for our loved ones. I had no one to look for other than Doyle, but I could find him no-where.

ⓢ ⓢ ⓢ

We won the game by way of forfeit and lost in the regionals the week after by the same means. No one wanted to play, and despite some *blah blah blah* spouted by Coach Tuttle about how the dead would want us to soldier on in the face of trag-edy, how events like this could define our lives, the team voted unanimously to accept a painless defeat.

Actually, our losses were not so severe as they had been at first assessed. Coach Cunliffe and the entire Taunton team were found unharmed, albeit bewildered, in a field three miles from Edenburg, their bus intact, and those missing—fourteen, when all was said and done—were peripheral figures like Mr. Pepper and Sally Carlysle, the aged and the unwanted.

And Doyle. I attended his funeral, received a sloppy kiss from one of his gravid sisters and a hug from his daddy, who had made of his death a newly righteous excuse for his drink-ing; yet I was not terribly surprised some months later when I heard he had been spotted in Crawford, a mill town less than a hundred miles away. I drove over there one evening, intending to question him about his involvement with the flock, whether it had been conscious, coerced, or otherwise—I knew he must have had something to do with them or else he wouldn't have run away.

I tracked him down in a roadhouse on the outskirts of Crawford and stood watching him from a noisy corner. He had his arm around a depressed-looking blonde—she was perhaps a decade older than him—and the meanness that now and then had come into his face seemed to have settled in permanently. I left without confronting him, doubting that he would have anything to tell me and realizing that I wouldn't believe him even if he did.

Football, as Coach Tuttle and others of his mentality are fond of saying, is a lot like life. By this I take them to mean that the game seeks to order chaos by means of a system of rules and demarcations. Even if you accept the metaphor as true, it begs the question, what is life like?

In the weeks following the Taunton game, those who could afford to leave Edenburg did so. Dawn Cupertino, for instance, hooked up with a paper towel salesman, and after a whirlwind courtship, they got engaged and moved to his home in Falls Church, Virginia. Most people, my parents included, could not afford to leave and thus suffered through the fumblings of the police, an FBI investigation, an inquiry conducted by the State Bureau of Wildlife and Fisheries, and questioning by countless investigators of the paranormal (they continue to trickle through town). None of this yielded a result that could explain the advent of the flock, but talking and talking about it, and then talking more, it helped dial down our temperature and we began settling into our old routines, both good and bad.

School started up again. Carol Ann and I made a stab at getting back together, but the fizz had gone out of that bottle and we drifted apart. Mama had another of her flings and fought with Daddy until all hours. When you think about it, with its lack of plan or purpose, its stretches of sameness and boredom, its explosive griefs and joys that either last too long or abandon us too quickly, life's not a thing like football, not as Coach Tuttle meant it, anyway . . . though maybe it's a little bit like Edenburg football.

One morning in April, I got a call from Dawn. She had been daydreaming about home and couldn't think of anyone she wanted to talk to except me. I told her I'd received early acceptance into the University of Virginia and that I was doing okay after, you know, all the weirdness. She asked if there had been any grackle sightings, and I said that Culliver County was basically a grackle-free zone, what with everyone declaring open season on the Devil's Bird, blowing them away on sight.

The conversation began to drag and Dawn said she should probably be going, yet showed no real inclination to hang up. I asked what she was doing, and she said that Jim, the salesman, wanted her to have a baby.

"It's a big thing with him," she said. "I'm scared if I don't go along, he's gonna kick me out. I'm not ready to have babies. I don't know as I'll ever be ready."

"I'm not going to be much help with this one, Dawn."

"I know. It's just . . . Oh, hell!"

I thought she might be crying.

After a spell of silence, she said, "Remember when you

and me and Doyle and Carol Ann drove up to the Outer Banks that time, and we were dancing to the car radio on top of the dunes?"

"Uh-huh, yeah."

"I wish I was there now." She sighed. "It all seems so damn ordinary, but when you think back on it, you see it's really not."

"I was thinking just the opposite. You know. How things that seem great, they turn out to be nothing in the long run."

"Yeah," she said. "That, too."

LUCIUS SHEPARD was born in Lynchburg, Virginia, grew up in Daytona Beach, Florida, and currently lives in Portland, Oregon. His fiction has won the Nebula Award, the Hugo Award, the International Horror Writers Award, the National Magazine Award, the *Locus* Award, the Theodore Sturgeon Award, the Shirley Jackson Award, and the World Fantasy Award.

His latest books are the massive career retrospective *The Best of Lucius Shepard*, and a collection of short fiction called *Viator Plus*. Forthcoming in 2010 is a collection of five novellas, tentatively called *Extras*. He is finishing work on a longish novel about which he will not speak.

His Web site is www.lucius-shepard.com.

Author's Note

Half of my sophomore year was spent in a place similar to the one described in "The Flock," a tiny rural high school with barely enough boys to field a varsity football team. When I first came there, I thought the kids were total hicks; after I went back to school in the city, I had a feeling they were smarter than I'd thought. I always wanted to write something that would express their raw innocence and their stubborn rootedness and their bursts of wisdom. I never thought I would, and then I remembered the story about Blackbeard and the Devil's Birds.

THE CHILDREN OF THE
SHARK GOD

Peter S. Beagle

Once there was a village on an island that belonged to
the Shark God. Every man in the village was a fisherman, and the women cooked their catch and mend-
ed their nets and painted their little boats. And because that
island was sacred to him, the Shark God saw to it that there
were always fish to be caught, and seals as well, in the waters
beyond the coral reef, and protected the village from the great
gray typhoons that came every year to flood other lagoons and
blow down the trees and the huts of other islands. Therefore the
children of the village grew fat and strong, and the women were
beautiful and strong, and the fishermen were strong and high-
hearted even when they were old.

In return for his benevolence the Shark God asked little
from his people: only tribute of a single goat at the turn of
each year. To the accompaniment of music and prayers, and
with a wreath of plaited fresh flowers around its neck, it would
be tethered in the lagoon at moonrise. Morning would find it

gone, flower petals floating on the water, and the Shark God never seen—never in *that* form, anyway.

Now the Shark God could alter his shape as he pleased, like any god, but he never showed himself on land more than once in a generation. When he did, he was most often known to appear as a handsome young man, light-footed and charming. Only one woman ever recognized the divinity hiding behind the human mask. Her name was Mirali, and this tale is what is known about her, and about her children.

Mirali's parents were already aging when she was born, and had long since given up the hope of ever having a child— indeed, her name meant *the long-desired one*. Her father had been crippled when the mast of his boat snapped during a storm and crushed his leg, falling on him, and if it had not been for their daughter the old couple's lives would have been hard indeed. Mirali could not go out with the fishing fleet herself, of course—as she greatly wished to do, having loved the sea from her earliest memory—but she did every kind of work for any number of island families, whether cleaning houses, marketing, minding young children, or even assisting the midwife when a birthing was difficult or there were simply too many babies coming at the same time. She was equally known as a seamstress, and also as a cook for special feasts; nor was there anyone who could mend a pandanus-leaf thatching as quickly as she, though this is generally man's work. No drop of rain ever penetrated any pandanus roof that came under Mirali's hands.

Nor did she complain of her labors, for she was very proud of being able to care for her mother and father as a son would have done. Because of this, she was much admired and respected in the village, and young men came courting just as though she were a great beauty. Which she was not, being small and somewhat square-made, with straight brows—considered unlucky by most—and hips that gave no promise of a large family. But she had kind eyes, deep-set under those regrettable brows, and hair as black and thick as that of any woman on the island. Many, indeed, envied her; but of that Mirali knew nothing, She had no time for envy herself, nor for young men, either.

Now it happened that Mirali was often chosen by the village priest to sweep out the temple of the Shark God. This was not only a grand honor for a child barely turned seventeen but a serious responsibility as well, for sharks are cleanly in their habits, and to leave his spiritual dwelling disorderly would surely be to dishonor and anger the god himself. So Mirali was particularly attentive when she cleaned after the worshippers, making certain that no prayer whistle or burned stick of incense was left behind. And in this manner did the Shark God become aware of Mirali.

But he did not actually see her until a day came when, for a wonder, all her work was done, all her tasks out of the way until tomorrow, when they would begin all over again. At such times, rare as they were, Mirali would always wander down to the water, borrow a dugout or an outrigger canoe, and simply let herself drift in the lagoon—or even beyond the reef—reading the clouds for coming weather, or the sea for migrating shoals of fish, or her own young mind for dreams. And if she should chance to see a black or gray or brown dorsal fin cutting the water nearby, she was never frightened, but would drowsily hail the great fish in fellowship, and ask it to convey her most respectful good wishes to the Shark God. For in that time children knew what was expected of them, by parents and gods alike.

She was actually asleep in an uncle's outrigger when the Shark God himself came to Mirali—as a mako, of course, since that is the most beautiful and graceful of all sharks. At the first sight of her, he instantly desired to shed his fishy form and climb into the boat to wake and caress her. But he knew that such behavior would terrify her as no shark could; and so, most reluctantly, he swam three times around her boat, which is magic, and then he sounded and disappeared.

When Mirali woke, it was with equal reluctance, for she had dreamed of a young man who longed for her, and who followed at a respectful distance, just at the edge of her dream, not daring to speak to her. She beached the dugout with a sigh and went home to make dinner for her parents. But that night, and every night thereafter, the same dream came to her, again and again, until she was almost frantic with curiosity to know what it meant.

No priest or wisewoman could offer her any useful counsel, although most suspected that an immortal was concerned in the matter in some way. Some advised praying in a certain way at the temple; others directed her to brew tea out of this or that herb or tree bark to assure herself of a deep, untroubled sleep. But Mirali was not at all sure that she wanted to rid herself of that dream and that shy youth; she only wanted to understand them.

Then one afternoon she heard a man singing in the market, and when she turned to see she knew him immediately as the young man who always followed her in her dream. She went to him, marching straight across the marketplace and facing him boldly to demand, "Who are you? By what right do you come to me as you do?"

The young man smiled at her. He had black eyes, smooth dark-brown skin—with perhaps a touch of blue in it, when he stood in shadow—and fine white teeth, which seemed to Mirali to be just a trifle curved in at the tips. He said gently, "You interrupted my song."

Mirali started to respond, "So? You interrupt my sleep, night on night"—but she never finished saying what she meant to say, because in that moment she knew the Shark God. She bowed her head and bent her right knee, in the respectful manner of the island folk, and she whispered, "*Jalak . . . jalak,*" which means *Lord*.

The young man took her hand and raised her up. "What my own people call me, you could not pronounce," he said to Mirali. "But to you I am no *jalak,* but your own faithful *olohe,*" which is the common word for *servant*. "You must only call me by that name, and no other. Say it now."

Mirali was so frightened, first to be in the presence of the Shark God, and then to be asked to call him her servant, that she had to try the word several times before she could make it come clearly out of her mouth. The Shark God said, "Now, if you wish it, we will go down to the sea and be married. But I promise that I will bear no malice, no vengefulness, against your village or this island if you do not care to marry me. Have no fear, then, but tell me your true desire, Mirali."

The market folk were going about their own business, buying and selling, and more chatting than either. Only a few of them looked toward Mirali where she stood talking with the handsome singer; fewer seemed to take any interest in what the two might be saying to each other. Mirali took heart from this and said, more firmly, "I do wish to marry you, dear *jalak*—I mean, my *olohe*—but how can I live with you under the sea? I do not think I would even be able to hold my breath through the wedding, unless it was a very short ceremony."

Then the Shark God laughed aloud, which he had truly never done in all his long life, and the sound was so full and so joyous that flowers fell from the trees and, unbidden, wove themselves into Mirali's hair, and into a wreath around her neck. The waves of the sea echoed his laughter, and the Shark God lifted Mirali in his arms and raced down to the shore, where sharks and dolphins, tuna and black marlin and barracuda, and whole schools of shimmering wrasse and clownfish and angelfish that swim as one had crowded into the lagoon together, until the water itself turned golden as the morning and green as sunset. The great deep-water octopus, whom no one ever sees except the sperm whale, came also; and it has been said—by people who were not present, nor even born then—that there were mermaids and merrows as well, and even the terrible Paikea, vast as an island, the Master of All Sea Monsters, though he prudently stayed far outside the reef. And all these were there for the wedding of Mirali and the Shark God.

The Shark God lifted Mirali high above his head—she was startled, but no longer frightened—and he spoke out, first in the language of Mirali's people, so that she would understand, and then in the tongue known by everything that swims in every sea and every river. "This is Mirali, whom I take now to wife, and whom you will love and protect from this day forth, and honor as you do me, and as you will honor our children, and their children, always." And the sound that came up from the waters in answer is not a sound that can be told.

In time, when the lagoon was at last empty again, and when husband and wife had sworn and proved their love in the shadows of the mangroves, she said to him, very quietly, "Beloved, my own *olohe*, now that we are wed, shall I ever see you again? For I may be only an ignorant island woman, but I know what too often comes of marriages between gods and mortals. Your children will have been born—I can feel this already—by the time you come again for your tribute. I will nurse them, and bring them up to respect their lineage, as is right . . . but meanwhile you will swim far away, and perhaps father others, and forget us, as is also your right. You are a god, and gods do not raise families. I am not such a fool that I do not know this."

But the Shark God put his finger under Mirali's chin, lifting her face to his and saying, "My wife, I could no more forget that you *are* my wife than forget what I am. Understand that we may not live together on your island, as others do, for my life is in the sea, and of the sea, and this form that you hold in your arms is but a shadow, little more than a dream, compared to my true self. Yet I will come to you every year, without fail, when my tribute is due—every year, here, where we lie together. Remember, Mirali."

Then he closed his eyes, which were black, as all sharks' eyes are, and fell asleep in her arms, and there is no woman who can say what Mirali felt, lying there under the mangroves with her own eyes wide in the moonlight.

When morning came, she walked back to her parents' house alone.

In time it became plain that Mirali was with child, but no one challenged or mocked her to her face, for she was much loved in the village, and her family greatly esteemed. Yet even so it was considered a misfortune by most, and a disgrace by some, as is not the case on certain other islands. If the talk was not public, it was night talk, talk around the cooking fire, talk at the stream over the slapping of wash on stone. Mirali was perfectly aware of this.

She carried herself well and proudly, and it was agreed, even by those who murmured ill of her, that she looked more beautiful every day, even as her belly swelled out like the fishermen's sails. But she shocked the midwife, who was concerned for her narrow hips, and for the chance of twins, by insisting on going off by herself to give birth. Her mother and father were likewise troubled; and the old priest himself took a hand, arguing powerfully that the birth should take place in the very temple of the Shark God. Such a thing had never been allowed, or even considered, but the old priest had his own suspicions about Mirali's unknown lover.

Mirali smiled and nodded respectfully to anyone who had anything to say about the matter, as was always her way. But on the night when her time came she went to the lagoon where she had been wed, as she knew that she must; and in the gentle breath of its shallows her children were born without undue difficulty. For they were indeed twins, a boy and a girl.

Mirali named the boy Keawe, after her father, and the girl Kokinja, which means *born in moonlight*. And as she looked fondly upon the two tiny, noisy, hungry creatures she and the Shark God had made together, she remembered his last words to her and smiled.

Keawe and Kokinja grew up the pets of their family, being not only beautiful but strong and quick and naturally kindly. This was a remarkable thing, considering the barely veiled scorn with which most of the other village children viewed them, taking their cue from the remarks passed between their parents. On the other hand, while there was notice taken of the very slight bluish tinge to Keawe's skin, and the fact that Kokinja's perfect teeth curved just the least bit inward, nothing was ever said concerning these particular traits.

They both swam before they could walk properly; and the creatures of the sea guarded them closely, as they had sworn. More than once little Keawe, who at two and three years regarded the waves and tides as his own servants, was brought safely back to shore clinging to the tail of a dolphin, the flipper of a seal, or even the dorsal, fin of a reef shark. Kokinja had an octopus as her favorite playmate, and would fall as trustingly asleep wrapped in its eight arms as in those of her mother. And Mirali herself learned to put her faith in the wildest sea as completely as did her children. That was the gift of her husband.

Her greatest joy lay in seeing them grow into his image (though she always thought that Keawe resembled her father more than his own), and come to their full strength and beauty in a kind of innocence that kept them free of any vanity. Being twins, they understood each other in a wordless way that even Mirali could not share. This pleased her, for she thought, watching them playing silently together, *they will still have one another when I am gone.*

The Shark God saw the children when he came every year for his tribute, but only while they were asleep. In human form he would stand silently between their floor mats, studying them out of his black, expressionless eyes for a long time, before he finally turned away. Once he said quietly to Mirali, "It is good that I see them no more often than this. A good thing."

Another time she heard him murmur to himself, *"Simpler for sharks . . ."*

As for Mirali herself, the love of the Shark God warded off the cruelty of the passing years, so that she continued to appear little older than her own children. They teased her about this, saying that she embarrassed them, but they were proud, and likewise aware that their mother remained attractive to the men of the village. A number of those came shyly courting, but all were turned away with such civility that they hardly knew they had been rejected; and certainly not by a married woman who saw her husband only once in a twelvemonth.

When Keawe and Kokinja were little younger than she had been when she heard a youth singing in the marketplace, she called them from the lagoon, where they spent most of their playtime, and told them simply, "Your father is the Shark God himself. It is time you knew this."

In all the years that she had imagined this moment, she had guessed—so she thought—every possible reaction that her children might have to these words. Wonder . . . awe . . . pride . . . fear (there are many tales of gods eating their children) . . . even laughing disbelief—she was long prepared for each of these. But it had never occurred to her that both Keawe and Kokinja might be immediately furious at their father for— as they saw it—abandoning his family and graciously condescending to spare a glance over them while passing through the lagoon to gobble his annual goat. Keawe shouted into the wind, "I would rather the lowest palm-wine drunkard on the island had sired us than this—this *god* who cannot be bothered with his wife and children but once a year. Yes, I would prefer that by far!"

"That one day has always lighted my way to the next," his

mother said quietly. She turned to Kokinja. "And as for you, child—"

But Kokinja interrupted her, saying firmly, "The Shark God may have a daughter, but I have no more father today than I had yesterday. But if I *am* the Shark God's daughter, then I will set out tomorrow and swim the sea until I find him. And when I find him, I will ask questions—oh, indeed, I will ask him questions. And he *will* answer me." She tossed her black hair, which was the image of Mirali's hair, as her eyes were those of her father's people. Mirali's own eyes filled with tears as she looked at her nearly grown daughter, remembering a small girl stamping one tiny foot and shouting, "Yes, I will! Yes, I will!" *Oh, there is this much truth in what they say,* she thought to her husband. *You have truly no idea what you have sired.*

In the morning, as she had sworn, Kokinja kissed Mirali and Keawe farewell and set forth into the sea to find the Shark God. Her brother, *being* her brother, was astonished to realize that she meant to keep her vow, and actually begged her to reconsider, when he was not ordering her to do so. But Mirali knew that Kokinja was as much at home in the deep as anything with gills and a tail; and she further knew that no harm would come to Kokinja from any sea creature, because of their promise on her own wedding day. So she said nothing to her daughter, except to remind her, "If any creature can tell you exactly where the Shark God will be at any given moment, it will be the great Paikea, who came to our wedding. Go well, then, and keep warm."

Kokinja had swum out many a time beyond the curving coral reef that had created the lagoon a thousand or more years before, and she had no more fear of the open sea than of the stream where she had drawn water all her life. But this time, when she paused among the little scarlet-and-black fish that swarmed about a gap in the reef, and turned to see her brother Keawe waving after her, then a hand seemed to close on her heart, and she could not see anything clearly for a while. All the same, the moment her vision cleared, she waved once to Keawe and plunged on past the reef out to sea. The next time she looked back, both reef and island were long lost to her sight.

Now it must be understood that Kokinja did not swim as humans do, being whom she was. From her first day splashing in the shallows of the lagoon, she had truly swum like a fish, or perhaps a dolphin. Swimming in this manner she outsped sailfish, marlin, tunny and tuna alike; even had the barracuda not been bound by his oath to the Shark God, he could never have come within snapping distance of the Shark God's daughter. Only the seagull and the great white wandering albatross, borne on the wind, kept even with the small figure far below, utterly alone between horizon and horizon, racing on and on under the darkening sky.

The favor of the waters applied to Kokinja in other ways. The fish themselves always seemed to know when she grew hungry, for then schools of salmon or mackerel would materialize out of the depths to accompany her, and she would express proper gratitude and devour one or another as she swam, as a shark would do. When she tired, she either curled up in a slow-rocking swell and slept, like a seal, or clung to the first sea turtle she encountered and drowsed peacefully on its shell—the leatherbacks were the most comfortable— while it courteously paddled along on the surface, so that she could breathe. Should she arrive at an island, she would haul out on the beach—again, like a seal—and sleep fully for a day; then bathe as she might, and be on her way once more.

Only a storm could overtake her, and those did frighten her at first, striking from the east or the north to tear fiercely at the sea. Not being a fish herself, she could not stay below the vast waves that played with her, Shark God's daughter or no, tossing her back and forth as an orca will toss its prey, then suddenly dropping out from under her, so that she floundered in their hollows, choking and gasping desperately, aware as she so rarely was of her own human weakness and fragility. But she was determined that she would not die without letting her father know what she thought of him; and by and by she learned to laugh at the lightning overhead, even when it struck the water, as though *something* knew she was near and alone. She would laugh, and she would call out, not caring that her voice was lost in wind and thunder, "Missed me again—so sorry, you missed me again!" For if she was the Shark God's daughter, who could swim the sea, she was Mirali's stubborn little girl too.

ဿ   ဿ   ဿ

Keawe, Mirali's son, was of a different nature from his sister. While he shared her anger at the Shark God's neglect, he simply decided to go on living as though he had no father, which was, after all, what he had always believed. And while he feared for Kokinja in the deep sea, and sometimes yearned to follow her, he was even more concerned about their mother. Like most grown children, he believed, despite the evidence of his eyes, that Mirali would dwindle away, starve, pine and die should both he and Kokinja be gone. Therefore he stayed at home and apprenticed himself to Uhila, the master builder of outrigger canoes, telling his mother that he would build the finest boat ever made, and in it he would one day bring Kokinja home. Mirali smiled gently and said nothing.

Uhila was known as a hard, impatient master, but Keawe studied well and swiftly learned everything the old man could teach him, which was not merely about the choosing of woods, nor about the weaving of all manner of sails and ropes, nor about the designing of different boats for different uses; nor how to warp the bamboo float, the *ama*, just so, and bind the long spars, the *iaka*, so that the connection to the hull would hold even in the worst storms. Uhila taught him, more importantly, the understanding of wood, and of water, and of the ancient relationship between them: half alliance, half war. At the end of Keawe's apprenticeship, gruff Uhila blessed him and gave him his own set of tools, which he had never done before in the memory of even the oldest villagers.

But he said also to the boy, "You do not love the boats as I do, for their own sake, for the joy of the making. I could tell that the first day you came to me. You are bound by a purpose—you need a certain boat, and in order to achieve it you needed to achieve every other boat. Tell me, have I spoken truly?"

Then Keawe bowed his head and answered, "I never meant to deceive you, wise Uhila. But my sister is far away, gone farther than an ordinary sailing canoe could find her, and it was on me to build the one boat that could bring her back. For that I needed all your knowledge, and all your wisdom. Forgive me if I have done wrong."

But Uhila looked out at the lagoon, where a new sailing canoe, more beautiful and splendid than any other in the harbor danced like a butterfly at anchor, and he said, "It is too big for any one person to paddle, too big to sail. What will you do for a crew?"

"He will have a crew," a calm voice answered. Both men turned to see Mirali smiling at them. She said to Keawe, "You will not want anyone else. You know that."

And Keawe did know, which was why he had never considered setting out with a crew at all. So he said only, "There is a comfortable seat near the bow for you, and you will be our lookout as you paddle. But I must sit in the rear and take charge of the tiller and the sails."

"For now," replied Mirali gravely, and she winked just a little at Uhila, who was deeply shocked by the notion of a woman steering any boat at all, let alone winking at him.

So Keawe and his mother went searching for Kokinja, and thus—though neither of them spoke of it—for the Shark God. They were, as they had been from Keawe's birth, pleasant company for one another. Keawe often sang the songs Mirali had taught him and his sister as children, and she herself would in turn tell old tales from older times, when all the gods were young, and all was possible. At other times, with a following sea and the handsome yellow sail up, they gave the canoe its head and sat in perfectly companionable silence, thinking thoughts that neither of them ever asked about. When they were hungry, Keawe plunged into the sea and returned swiftly with as much fish as they could eat; when it rained, although they had brought more water than food with them, still they caught the rain in the sail, since one can never have too much fresh water at sea. They slept by turns, warmly, guiding themselves by the stars and the turning of the earth, in the manner of birds, though their only real concern was to keep on straight toward the sunset, as Kokinja had done.

At times, watching his mother regard a couple of flying fish barely missing the sail, or turn her head to laugh at the dolphins accompanying the boat, with her still-black hair blowing across her cheek, Keawe would think, *god or no god, my father was a fool.* But unlike Kokinja, he thought it in pity more than anger. And if a shark should escort them for a little, cruising lazily along with the boat, he would joke with it in his mind—*Are you my aunt? Are you my cousin?*—for he had always had more humor than his sister. Once, when a great blue mako traveled with them for a full day, dawn to dark, now and then circling or sounding, but always near, rolling one black eye back to study them, he whispered, "Father? Is it you?" But it was only once, and the mako vanished at sunset anyway.

ṩ   ṩ   ṩ

On her journey Kokinja met no one who could—or would— tell her where the Shark God might be found. She asked every shark she came upon, sensibly enough; but sharks are a close-mouthed lot, and not one hammerhead, not one whitetip, not one mako or tiger or reef shark ever offered her so much as a hint as to her father's whereabouts. Manta rays and sawfishes were more forthcoming, but mantas, while beautiful, are extremely stupid, and taking a sawfish's advice is always risky: ugly as they know themselves to be, they will say anything to appear wise. As for cod, they travel in great schools and shoals, and think as one, so that to ask a single cod a question is to receive an answer—right or wrong—from a thousand, ten thousand, a hundred thousand. Kokinja found this unnerving.

So she swam on, day after day: a little weary, a little lonely, a good deal older, but as determined as ever not to turn back without confronting the Shark God and demanding the truth of him. *Who are you, that my mother should have accepted you under such terms as you offered? How could you yourself have*

endured to see her—to see us, your children—only once in every
year? Is that a god's idea of love?

One night, the water having turned warm and silkily calm, she was drifting in a half dream of her own lagoon when she woke with a soft bump against what she at first thought an island. It loomed darkly over her, hiding the moon and half the stars, yet she saw no trees, even in silhouette, nor did she hear any birds or smell any sort of vegetation. What she did smell awakened her completely and set her scrambling backward into deeper water, like a frightened crab. It was a fish smell, in part, cold and clear and salty, but there was something of the reptilian about it: equally cold, but dry as well, for all that it emanated from an island—or *not* an island?—sitting in the middle of the sea. It was not a smell she knew, and yet somehow she felt that she should.

Kokinja went on backing into moonlight, which calmed her, and had just begun to swim cautiously around the island when it moved. Eyes as big and yellow-white as lighthouse lamps turned slowly to keep her in view, while an enormous, seemingly formless body lost any resemblance to an island, heaving itself over to reveal limbs ending in grotesquely huge claws. Centered between the foremost of them were two moon white pincers, big enough, clearly, to twist the skull off a sperm whale. The sound it uttered was too low for Kokinja to catch, but she felt it plainly in the sea.

She knew what it was then, and could only hope that her voice would reach whatever the creature used for ears. She said, "Great Paikea, I am Kokinja. I am very small, and I mean no one any harm. Please, can you tell me where I may find my father, the Shark God?"

The lighthouse eyes truly terrified her then, swooping toward her from different directions, with no head or face behind them. She realized that they were on long whiplike stalks, and that Paikea's diamond-shaped head was sheltered under a scarlet carapace studded with scores of small, sharp spines. Kokinja was too frightened to move, which was as well, for Paikea spoke to her in the water, saying against her skin, "Be still, child, that I may see you more clearly, and not bite you in two by mistake. It has happened so." Then Kokinja, who had already swum half an ocean, thought that she might never again move from where she was.

She waited a long time for the great creature to speak again, but was not at all prepared for Paikea's words when they did come. "I could direct you to your father—I could even take you to him—but I will not. You are not ready."

When Kokinja could at last find words to respond, she demanded, "Not *ready*? Who are *you* to say that I am not ready to see my own father?" Mirali and Keawe would have known her best then: she was Kokinja, and anything she feared she challenged.

"What your father has to say to you, you are not yet prepared to hear," came the voice in the sea. "Stay with me a little, Shark God's daughter. I am not what your father is, but I may perhaps be a better teacher for you." When Kokinja hesitated, and clearly seemed about to refuse, Paikea continued, "Child, you have nowhere else to go but home—and I think you are not ready for that, either. Climb on my back now, and come with me." Even for Kokinja, that was an order.

Paikea took her—once she had managed the arduous and tiring journey from claw to leg to mountainside shoulder to a deep, hard hollow in the carapace that might have been made for a frightened rider—to an island (a real one this time, though well smaller than her own) bright with birds and flowers and wild fruit. When the birds' cries and chatter ceased for a moment, she could hear the softer swirl of running water farther inland, and the occasional thump of a falling coconut from one of the palms that dotted the beach. It was a lonely island, being completely uninhabited, but very beautiful.

There Paikea left her to swim ashore, saying only, "Rest," and nothing more. She did as she was bidden, sleeping under bamboo trees, waking to eat and drink, and sleeping again, dreaming always of her mother and brother at home. Each dream seemed more real than the one before, bringing Mirali and Keawe closer to her, until she wept in her sleep, struggling to keep from waking. Yet when Paikea came again, after three days, she demanded audaciously, "What wisdom do you think you have for me that I would not hear if it came from my father? I have no fear of anything he may say to me."

"You have very little fear at all, or you would not be here," Paikea answered her. "You feared me when we first met, I think—but two nights' good sleep, and you are plainly past *that*." Kokinja thought she discerned something like a chuckle in the wavelets lapping against her feet where she sat, but she could not be sure. Paikea said, "But courage and attention are not the same thing. Listening is not the same as hearing. You may be sure I am correct in this, because I know everything."

It was said in such a matter-of-fact manner that Kokinja had to battle back the impulse to laugh. She said, with all the innocence she could muster, "I thought it was my father who was supposed to know everything."

"Oh, no," Paikea replied quite seriously. "The only thing the Shark God has ever known is how to be the Shark God. It is the one thing he is supposed to be—not a teacher, not a wise master, and certainly not a father or a husband. But they *will* take human form, the gods will, and that is where the trouble begins, because they none of them know how to be human— how can they, tell me that?" The eye-stalks abruptly plunged closer, as though Paikea were truly waiting for an enlightening answer. "I have always been grateful for my ugliness; for the fact that there is no way for me to disguise it, no temptation to hide in a more comely shape and pretend to believe that I am what I pretend. Because I am certain I would do just that, if I could. It is lonely sometimes, knowing everything."

Again Kokinja felt the need to laugh; but this time it was somehow easier not to, because Paikea was obviously anxious for her to understand his words. But she fought off sympathy as well, and confronted Paikea defiantly, saying, "You really think that we should never have been born, don't you, my brother and I?"

Paikea appeared to be neither surprised nor offended by her bold words. "Child, what I know is important—what I *think* is not important at all. It is the same way with the Shark God." Kokinja opened her mouth to respond hotly, but the great crab-monster moved slightly closer to shore, and she closed it again. Paikea said, "He is fully aware that he should never have taken a human wife, created a human family in the human world. And he knows also, as he was never meant to know, that when your mother dies—as she will—when you and your brother in time die, his heart will break. No god is supposed to know such a thing; they are simply not equipped to deal with it. Do you understand me, brave and foolish girl?"

Kokinja was not sure whether she understood, and less sure of whether she even wanted to understand. She said slowly, "So he thinks that he should never see us, to preserve his poor heart from injury and grief? Perhaps he thinks it will be for our own good? Parents always say that, don't they, when they really mean for their own convenience. Isn't that what they say, wise Paikea?"

"I never knew my parents," Paikea answered thoughtfully.

"And *I* have never known *him*," snapped Kokinja. "Once a year he comes to lie with his wife, to snap up his goat, to look at his children as we sleep. But what is that to a wife who longs for her husband, to children aching for a real father? God or no god, the very least he could have done would have been to tell us himself what he was, and not leave us to imagine him, telling ourselves stories about why he left our beautiful mother . . . why he didn't want to be with us. . . ." She realized, to her horror, that she was very close to tears and gulped them back as she had done with laughter. "I will never forgive him," she said. "Never."

"Then why have you swum the sea to find him?" asked Paikea. It snapped its horrid pale claws as a human will snap his fingers, waiting for her answer with real interest.

"To *tell* him that I will never forgive him," Kokinja answered. "So there is something even Paikea did not know." She felt triumphant, and stopped wanting to cry.

"You are still not ready," said Paikea, and was abruptly gone, slipping beneath the waves without a ripple, as though its vast body had never been there. It did not return for another three days, during which Kokinja explored the island, sampling every fruit that grew there, fishing as she had done at sea when she desired a change of diet, sleeping when she chose, and continuing to nurse her sullen anger at her father.

Finally, she sat on the beach with her feet in the water, and she called out, "Great Paikea, of your kindness, come to me,

I have a riddle to ask you." None of the sea creatures among whom she had been raised could ever resist a riddle, and she did not see why it should be any different even for the Master of All Sea Monsters.

Presently she heard the mighty creature's voice saying, "You yourself are as much a riddle to me as any you may ask." Paikea surfaced close enough to shore that Kokinja felt she could have reached out and touched its head. It said, "Here I am, Shark God's daughter."

"This is my riddle," Kokinja said. "If you cannot answer it, you who know everything, will you take me to my father?"

"A most human question," Paikea replied, "since the riddle has nothing to do with the reward. Ask, then."

Kokinja took a long breath. "Why would any god ever choose to sire sons and daughters with a mortal woman? Half-divine, yet we die—half-supreme, yet we are vulnerable, breakable—half-perfect, still we are forever crippled by our human hearts. What cruelty could compel an immortal to desire such unnatural children?"

Paikea considered. It closed its huge, glowing eyes on their stalks; it waved its claws this way and that; it even rumbled thoughtfully to itself, as a man might when pondering serious matters. Finally Paikea's eyes opened, and there was a curious amusement in them as it regarded Kokinja. She did not notice this, being young.

"Well riddled," Paikea said. "For I know the answer, but have not the right to tell you. So I cannot." The great claws snapped shut on the last word, with a grinding clash that hinted to Kokinja how fearsome an enemy Paikea could be.

"Then you will keep your word?" Kokinja asked eagerly. "You *will* take me where my father is?"

"I always keep my word," answered Paikea, and sank from sight. Kokinja never saw him again.

But that evening, as the red sun was melting into the green horizon, and the birds and fish that feed at night were setting about their business, a young man came walking out of the water toward Kokinja. She knew him immediately, and her first instinct was to embrace him. Then her heart surged fiercely within her, and she leaped to her feet, challenging him. "So! At last you have found the courage to face your own daughter. Look well, sea-king, for I have no fear of you, and no worship." She started to add, "Nor any love, either," but that last caught in her throat, just as had happened to her mother Mirali when she scolded a singing boy for invading her dreams.

The Shark God spoke the words for her. "You have no reason in the world to love me." His voice was deep and quiet, and woke strange echoes in her memory of such a voice overheard in candlelight in the sweet, safe place between sleep and waking. "Except, perhaps, that I have loved your mother from the moment I first saw her. That will have to serve as my defense, and my apology as well. I have no other."

"And a pitiful enough defense it is," Kokinja jeered. "I asked Paikea why a god should ever choose to father a child with a mortal, and he would not answer me. Will you?" The Shark God did not reply at once, and Kokinja stormed on. "My mother never once complained of your neglect, but I am not my mother. I am grateful for my half heritage only in that it enabled me to seek you out, hide as you would. For the rest, I spit on my ancestry, my birthright, and all else that connects me to you. I just came to tell you that."

Having said this, she began to weep, which infuriated her even more, so that she actually clenched her fists and pounded the Shark God's shoulders while he stood still, making no response. Shamed as she was, she ceased both activities soon enough, and stood silently facing her father with her head high and her wet eyes defiant. For his part, the Shark God studied her out of his own unreadable black eyes, moving neither to caress nor to punish her, but only—as it seemed to Kokinja—to understand the whole of what she was. And to do her justice, she stared straight back, trying to do the same.

When the Shark God spoke at last, Mirali herself might not have known his voice, for the weariness and grief in it. He said, "Believe as you will, but until your mother came into my life, I had no smallest desire for children, neither with beings like myself nor with any mortal, however beautiful she might be. We do find humans dangerously appealing, all of us, as is well known—perhaps precisely because of their short lives and the delicacy of their construction—and many a deity, unable to resist such haunting vulnerability, has scattered half-divine descendants all over your world. Not I; there was nothing I could imagine more contemptible than deliberately to create such a child, one who would share fully in neither inheritance, and live to curse me for it, as you have done." Kokinja flushed and looked down but offered no contrition for anything she had said. The Shark God said mildly, "As well you made no apology. Your mother has never once lied to me, nor should you."

"Why should I ever apologize to you?" Kokinja flared up again. "If you had no wish for children, what are my brother and I doing here?" Tears threatened again, but she bit them savagely back. "You are a god—you could always have kept us from being born! *Why are we here?*"

To her horror, her legs gave way under her then, and she

sank to her knees, still not weeping, but finding herself shame-
fully weak with rage and confusion. Yet when she looked up,
the Shark God was kneeling beside her, for all the world like
a playmate helping her to build a sand castle. It was she who
stared at him without expression now, while he regarded her
with the terrifying pity that belongs to the gods alone. Kokinja
could not bear it for more than a moment; but every time she
turned her face away, her father gently turned her toward him
once more. He said, "Daughter of mine, do you know how old
I am?"

Kokinja shook her head silently. The Shark God said, "I
cannot tell you in years, because there were no such things at
my beginning. Time was very new then, and Those who were
already here had not yet decided whether this was . . . *suitable*,
can you understand me, dear one?" The last two words, heard
for the first time in her life, caused Kokinja to shiver like a
small animal in the rain. Her father did not appear to notice.

"I had no parents, and no childhood, such as you and your
brother have had—I simply *was*, and always had been, beyond
all memory, even my own. All true enough, to my knowledge—
and then a leaky outrigger canoe bearing a sleeping brown girl
drifted across my endless life, and I, who can never change . . .
I changed. Do you hear what I am telling you, daughter of that
girl, daughter who hates me?"

The Shark God's voice was soft and uncertain. "I told your
mother that it was good that I saw her and you and Keawe
only once in a year—that if I allowed myself that wonder even
a day more often I might lose myself in you, and never be able
to find myself again, nor ever wish to. Was that cowardly of
me, Kokinja? Perhaps so, quite likely unforgivably so." It was
he who looked away now, rising and turning to face the dark-

ening scarlet sea. He said, after a time, "But one day—one day that *will* come—when you find yourself loving as helplessly, and as certainly wrongly, as I, loving against all you know, against all you are . . . remember me then."

To this Kokinja made no response; but by and by she rose herself and stood silently beside her father, watching the first stars waken, one with each heartbeat of hers. She could not have said when she at last took his hand.

"I cannot stay," she said. "It is a long way home, and seems longer now."

The Shark God touched her hair lightly. "You will go back more swiftly than you arrived, I promise you that. But if you could remain with me a little time . . ." He left the words unfinished.

"A little time," Kokinja agreed. "But in return . . ." She hesitated, and her father did not press her, but only waited for her to continue. She said presently, "I know that my mother never wished to see you in your true form, and for herself she was undoubtedly right. But I . . . I am not my mother." She had no courage to say more than that.

The Shark God did not reply for some while, and when he did his tone was deep and somber. "Even if I granted it, even if you could bear it, you could never see all of what I am. Human eyes cannot"—he struggled for the exact word—"they do not *bend* in the right way. It was meant as a kindness, I think, just as was the human gift of forgetfulness. You have no idea how the gods envy you that, the forgetting."

"Even so," Kokinja insisted. "Even so, I would not be afraid. If you do not know *that* by now . . ."

"Well, we will see," answered the Shark God, exactly as all human parents have replied to importunate children at one time or another. And with that, even Kokinja knew to content herself.

In the morning, she plunged into the waves to seek her breakfast, as did her father on the other side of the island. She never knew where he slept—or if he slept at all—but he returned in time to see her emerging from the water with a fish in her mouth and another in her hand. She tore them both to pieces, like any shark, and finished the meal before noticing him. Abashed, she said earnestly, "When I am at home, I cook my food as my mother taught me—but in the sea . . ."

"Your mother always cooks dinner for me," the Shark God answered quietly. "We wait until you two are asleep, or away, and then she will come down to the water and call. It has been so from the first."

"Then she *has* seen you—"

"No. I take my tribute afterward, when I leave her, and she never follows then." The Shark God smiled and sighed at the same time, studying his daughter's puzzled face. He said, "What is between us is hard to explain, even to you. Especially to you."

The Shark God lifted his head to taste the morning air, which was cool and cloudless over water so still that Kokinja could hear a dolphin breathing too far away for her to see. He frowned slightly, saying, "Storm. Not now, but in three days' time. It will be hard."

Kokinja did not show her alarm. She said grimly, "I came here through storms. I survived those."

"Child," her father said, and it was the first time he had called her that, "you will be with me." But his eyes were troubled, and his voice strangely distant. For the rest of that day, while Kokinja roamed the island, dozed in the sun, and swam for no reason but pleasure, he hardly spoke but continued watching the horizon, long after both sunset and moonset. When she woke the next morning, he was still pacing the shore, though she could see no change at all in the sky, but only in his face. Now and then he would strike a balled fist against his thigh and whisper to himself through tight pale lips. Kokinja, walking beside him and sharing his silence, could not help noticing how human he seemed in those moments—how mortal, and how mortally afraid. But she could not imagine the reason for it, not until she woke on the following day and felt the sand cold under her.

Since her arrival on the little island, the weather had been so clement that the sand she slept on remained perfectly warm through the night. Now its chill woke her well before dawn, and even in the darkness she could see the mist on the horizon, and the lightning beyond the mist. The sun, orange as the harvest moon, was never more than a sliver between the mounting thunderheads all day. The wind was from the northeast, and there was ice in it.

Kokinja stood alone on the shore, watching the first rain marching toward her across the waves. She had no longer any fear of storms, and was preparing to wait out the tempest in the water, rather than take refuge under the trees. But the Shark God came to her then and led her away to a small cave, where they sat together, listening to the rising wind. When she was hungry, he fished for her, saying, "They seek shelter too, like anyone else in such conditions—but they will come for me." When she became downhearted, he hummed nursery songs that she recalled Mirali singing to her and Keawe very long ago, far away on the other side of any storm. He even sang her oldest favorite, which began:

When a raindrop leaves the sky,
it turns and turns to say good-bye.
Good-bye, dear clouds, so far away,
I'll come again another day. . . .

"Keawe never really liked that one," she said softly. "It made him sad. How do you know all our songs?"

"I listened," the Shark God said, and nothing more.

"I wish . . . I *wish* . . ." Kokinja's voice was almost lost in the pounding of the rain. She thought she heard her father answer, "I, too," but in that moment he was on his feet, striding out of the cave into the storm, as heedless of the weather as though it were flowers sluicing down his body, summer-morning breezes greeting his face. Kokinja hurried to keep up with him. The wind snatched the breath from her lungs, and knocked her down more than once, but she matched his pace to the shore, even so. It seemed to her that the tranquil island had come malevolently alive with the rain; that the vines slapping at her shoulders and entangling her ankles had not been there yesterday, nor had the harsh branches that caught at her hair. All the same, when he turned at the water's edge, she was beside him.

"*Mirali.*" He said the one word, and pointed out into the flying, whipping spindrift and the solid mass of sea-wrack being driven toward land by the howling grayness beyond. Kokinja strained her eyes and finally made out the tiny flicker that was not water, the broken chip of wood sometimes bobbing helplessly on its side, sometimes hurled forward or sideways from one comber crest to another. Staring through the rain, shaking with cold and fear, it took her a moment to realize that her father was gone. Taller than the wavetops, taller than any ship's masts, taller than the wind, she saw the deep blue dorsal and tail fins, so distant from each other, gliding toward the wreck, on which she could see no hint of life. Then she plunged into the sea—shockingly, almost alarmingly warm, by comparison with the air—and followed the Shark God.

It was the first and only glimpse she ever had of the thing her father was. As he had warned her, she never saw him fully: both her eyesight and the sea itself seemed too small to contain him. Her mind could take in a magnificent and terrible fish; her soul knew that that was the least part of what she was seeing; her body knew that it could bear no more than that smallest vision. The mark of his passage was a ripple of beaten silver across the wild water, and although the storm seethed and roared to left and right of her, she swam in his wake as effortlessly as he made the way for her. And whether he actually uttered it or not, she heard his fearful cry in her head, over and over—"*Mirali!* Mirali!"

The mast was in two pieces, the sail a yellow rag, the rudder split and the tiller broken off altogether. The Shark God regained the human form so swiftly that Kokinja was never entirely sure that she had truly seen what she knew she had seen, and the two of them righted the sailing canoe together. Keawe lay in the bottom of the boat, barely conscious, unable to speak, only to point over the side. There was no sign of Mirali.

"Stay with him," her father ordered Kokinja, and he sounded as a shark would have done, vanishing instantly into the darkness below the ruined keel. Kokinja crouched by Keawe, lifting his head to her lap and noticing a deep gash on his forehead and another on his cheekbone. "Tiller," he whispered. "Snapped . . . flew straight at me . . ." His right hand was clenched around some small object; when Kokinja pried it gently open—for he seemed unable to release it himself—she recognized a favorite bangle of their mother's. Keawe began to cry.

"Couldn't hold her . . . *couldn't hold* . . ." Kokinja could not hear a word, for the wind, but she read his eyes and she held him to her breast and rocked him, hardly noticing that she was weeping herself.

The Shark God was a long time finding his wife, but he brought her up in his arms at last, her eyes closed and her face as quiet as always. He placed her gently in the canoe with her children, brought the boat safely to shore, and bore Mirali's body to the cave where he had taken Kokinja for shelter. And while the storm still lashed the island, and his son and daughter sang the proper songs, he dug out a grave and buried her there, with no marker at her head, there being no need. "I will know," he said, "and you will know. And so will Paikea, who knows everything."

Then he mourned.

Kokinja ministered to her brother as she could, and they slept for a long time. When they woke, with the storm passed over and all the sky and sea looking like the first morning of the world, they walked the shore to study the sailing canoe that had been all Keawe's pride. After considering it from all sides, he said at last, "I can make it seaworthy again. Well enough to get us home, at least."

"Father can help," Kokinja said, realizing as she spoke that she had never said the word in that manner before. Keawe shook his head, looking away.

"I can do it myself," he said sharply. "I built it myself."

They did not see the Shark God for three days. When he finally emerged from Mirali's cave—as her children had already begun to call it—he called them to him, saying, "I will see you home, as soon as you will. But I will not come there again."

Keawe, already busy about his boat, looked up but said nothing. Kokinja asked, "Why? You have always been faithfully worshipped there—and it was our mother's home all her life."

The Shark God was slow to answer. "From the harbor to her house, from the market to the beach where the nets are mended, to my own temple, there is no place that does not speak to me of Mirali. Forgive me—I have not the strength to deal with those memories, and I never will."

Kokinja did not reply; but Keawe turned from his boat to face his father openly for the first time since his rescue from the storm. He said, clearly and strongly, "And so, once again, you make a liar out of our mother. As I knew you would."

Kokinja gasped audibly, and the Shark God took a step toward his son without speaking. Keawe said, "She defended you so fiercely, so proudly, when I told her that you were always a coward, god or no god. You abandoned a woman who loved you, a family that belonged to you—and now you will do the same with the island that depends on you for protection and loyalty, that has never failed you, done you no disservice, but only been foolish enough to keep its old bargain with you, and expect you to do the same. And this in our mother's name, because you lack the courage to confront the little handful of memories you two shared. You shame her!"

He never flinched from his father's advance, but stood his ground even when the Shark God loomed above him like a storm in mortal shape, his eyes no longer unreadable but alive with fury. For a moment Kokinja saw human and shark as one, flowing in and out of each other, blurring and bleeding together and separating again, in and out, until she became dazed with it and had to close her eyes. She only opened them again when she heard the Shark God's quiet, toneless voice, "We made fine children, my Mirali and I. It is my loss that I never knew them. My loss alone."

Without speaking further he turned toward the harbor, looking as young as he had on the day Mirali challenged him in the marketplace, but moving now almost like an old human man. He had gone some little way when Keawe spoke again, saying simply, "Not only yours."

The Shark God turned back to look long at his children once again. Keawe did not move, but Kokinja reached out her arms, whispering, "Come back." And the Shark God nodded, and went on to the sea.

PETER S. BEAGLE was born in Manhattan in 1939, on the same night that Billie Holiday was recording "Strange Fruit" and "Fine and Mellow" just a few blocks away. Raised in the Bronx, Peter originally proclaimed when he was ten years old that he would be a writer. Today he is acknowledged as an American fantasy icon, and to the delight of his millions of fans around the world he is now publishing more than ever.

In addition to being an acclaimed novelist and writer of short stories and nonfiction, Peter has also written numerous plays, teleplays, and screenplays; and is a gifted poet, librettist, lyricist, and singer/songwriter. To learn more about *The Last Unicorn*, *A Fine and Private Place*, *I See By My Outfit*, "Two Hearts," and all the rest of his extraordinary body of work, please visit www.peterbeagle.com.

꙳Ɔ Cⱬ

Author's Note

I've always been fascinated by the stories and folktales of the South Seas—just like my friend, the singer-songwriter Marty Atkinson, who hasn't spent any time there either. It's probably due to a Bronx childhood spent reading Robert Louis Stevenson's Samoan tales like "The Bottle Imp" and "The Beach of Falesá," along with a lot of Jack London and my father's beloved Joseph Conrad. I cherished visions out of Herman Melville's haunting classic *Typee*, and fantasies of running off to Tahiti, like Gauguin. I did make it to Fiji once, but it was for a week's vacation on a private island: not at all the same thing as arriving on a whaler and jumping ship forever. Not at all the same.

"The Children of the Shark God" is, both in story and style, very much my attempt at a tale in the manner of Stevenson. All these years and miles away from the Bronx he is still one of my literary heroes, for lots of reasons.

ROSINA

Nan Fry

I.

It began with the turnips.
Sent to get some for supper,
she pulled one up, and underneath crouched
three toads, bright as emeralds.
She picked them up to admire, but one
fell from her hand. Gently, she put
the others down, saying, "Oh, I'm sorry."
Just then the sun sank behind the hill,
and the toads grew into large, gray shadows.
Thinking it a trick of the fading light, she blinked,
and when she opened her eyes, three stout
men in moss green garb and caps the color
of rust stood before her, with sacks
on their backs from which spilled a green light.

One of the men bowed to her and said,
"Thank you for putting us down so gently."
"I thank you, too," said another, crinkling

his face in a smile. "And for your kindness,
we'll make you radiant as the sun."

"Harrumph," croaked the third, glowering at her.
"You've hurt my leg with your carelessness,
maybe broken it. If the sun ever shines on you,
you'll turn into a serpent!"

"Oh, please," she begged, "I didn't mean
to hurt you. Maybe I could set your leg.
Let me see." She reached for him,
but he limped away, his leg dragging.

The other two waved to her and said,
"Stay out of the sun, and all will be well,"
as they disappeared into the shadows.

She ran home and lived in the shade
and the dark, giving forth her own light.
Because she shone with a rosy glow,
she was called Rosina,
but her sister Lydia called her lazy.
"I have to work in the field in the sun,"
said Lydia. "Why won't she?
This story of toads and little old men
is just an excuse."

"But look how she shines,"
said their mother. "There must be something to it."
"Humph," said Lydia. "You always liked her best."
To keep peace in the family, Rosina worked

in the field at night, planting and weeding
by moon and starlight.

Early one morning, before sunup, a prince
who was out hunting saw her in the field
and was drawn by the light that spilled from her.
When they talked, her radiance lit fires
within him, and he asked her to marry him.

Rosina wanted to wait until she knew him better,
but Lydia jeered, "He's a prince. Do you think
he'll wait for you to make up your mind?"
Her mother said, "It's been such a struggle
since your father died, but do what you think best,"
so Rosina accepted, provided
she could live in the dark.

On her wedding day, she was taken,
under veils and parasols, to a royal carriage
whose windows were draped with black cloth.
Her mother and sister climbed in,
and they set off. "It's stuffy in here,"
said Lydia, and she opened the window a crack.
A sliver of sunlight streamed in.
When it struck Rosina, her limbs
shriveled up, her skin grew scales,
and she slithered out the window,
hissing.

At first she longed for all she had lost.
She crept to the edge of her family's field,

and waited for a glimpse of her mother or sister.
When Lydia saw her, she threw a stone,
screaming, "Ugh—a snake!"

Rosina fled to the woods, where she learned
to crawl without feet, to reach with the whole
of herself, to smell the air
with her flickering tongue.

Then she went to the prince's palace,
and climbed the castle wall, peering
in windows, her tongue seeking his scent,
until she found the room where he sat
longing for his lost bride.
She slithered over the sill, and when he saw her,
he jumped up and slammed the window.

Rosina drew back just in time and fell
to the ground. Bruised and sore,
she crawled off and hid in a cave.

The prince sent fifty knights on horseback,
fifty huntsmen, and a hundred hounds
to search for her. The woods rang
with the blowing of bugles and the baying of dogs.
Rosina heard it all and stayed in her cave,
safe from spears, hooves, and teeth.

She came to love the grasses, the mud,
and her strong, sinuous body.
And she loved the sun!

She would coil on the rocks
and bask until she was warm,
supple, and moved like water.

II.

When the fifty knights and fifty huntsmen
returned with their hundred hounds,
they reported they couldn't find Rosina.

The prince moped around the palace
until his parents lost patience. "She was just
a farmer's daughter," they said, and convinced him
to marry a foreign princess.

She came reluctantly from a land she loved
where she'd run barefoot in field and forest.
She used to slip away from the court
and climb a tall pine at the edge
of the woods. She'd feel its rough bark
under her hands, and its pitch would stick
to her feet and fingers. From its top
she could see the nests of hawks
and watch them soaring, swooping
down on their prey, and bringing it back
to feed their babies.

She longed for their wings
when she was told she'd be wed
to a stranger. She ran
to the woods, but her father's guards
caught her and brought her back.

She was hustled on board a ship
and wept as she stood on deck
watching her homeland grow small
in the distance.

III.

As the palace prepared for the wedding feast,
Rosina, coiled around a tree branch,
saw the carts rumble in,
laden with food and finery,
and something in her stirred.
She crept to the edge of a meadow
and hid in a woodpile where she could watch
the comings and goings at the castle.

She fell asleep there,
and when she awoke, she was being thrust,
along with the kindling, into the oven.
It was like diving into the sun.
The heat crackled
around her, and she grew
so warm she flowed,
molten, into a new shape.

The oven door opened.
She heard a scream and stepped,
naked and radiant, a woman
again, from the fire.
The prince, hearing the cook shriek,
came running. "Rosina!" he cried

and embraced her, but she stood,
cool in his arms,
and said, "Who are you?"

He told her how she'd disappeared
on their wedding day, how his men had searched
for her and never found her, how his parents
had urged him to marry a foreign princess,
how he'd finally given in, how today
was the wedding, how the oven
she'd stepped out of was to cook
the marriage feast, and how,
now she was here, rosy and
sweet in his arms, he'd
call it off
and marry her.

"Wait," she said. "Don't you even want
to know where I've been?"
"Uh, yes," he said. "Where *have* you been?"

"I've slithered under rocks, nestled
in the earth's belly, basked in the sun.
I'm not sure. . . ." Just then the princess
who'd been waiting, stiff in brocade,
to meet the stranger she was to marry,
walked in. She saw the prince talking
to a naked, radiant woman.
"Who are you?" she gasped.
"Are you an angel?"

          ✿   ✿   ✿

"No," said Rosina. "I'm a woman, but
I've been a snake."

"You have?" said the princess.
"What was it like?"
"It was cold," said Rosina,
"cold and dark in the cave at night,
but in the morning the sun would heat the rocks
and I'd lie there soaking up warmth through my skin,
and when I was limber and loose and warm,
I'd move over the earth like a wave."

The two women walked off, talking,
and the prince stood there,
looking after them.

There was no wedding that day.
The princess and Rosina left the palace together.
No one knows where they went,
but there are rumors
of two shining women
who live in the heart
of the forest.

NAN FRY is the author of two collections of poetry, *Relearning the Dark*, and *Say What I Am Called*, a selection of riddles she translated from the Anglo-Saxon. Her poems have appeared in a number of magazines, including *Lady Churchill's Rosebud Wristlet*; in anthologies such as *The Year's Best Fantasy and Horror* and *The Faery Reel*, both edited by Ellen Datlow and Terri Windling; and in *The Best of Lady Churchill's Rosebud Wristlet*, edited by Kelly Link and Gavin J. Grant. Some of her other poems can be found online in the poetry archives of the *Journal of Mythic Arts* (www.endicott-studio.com) and in *The Innisfree Poetry Journal.* (www.innisfreepoetry.org). Her first published story appeared in *Gravity Dancers*, edited by Richard Peabody.

She teaches at The Writer's Center in Bethesda, Maryland.

ᴐ ᴄ

Author's Note

Since my favorite animals are dogs and their wild cousins—foxes, coyotes, and wolves—I was surprised to find myself writing about a snake-woman. This poem is a reworking of "Rosina in the Oven" from Italo Calvino's *Italian Folktales*. At the time I discovered that story, I had been reading a lot of fairy tales and had learned that some of them, such as "The Frog Prince," were often used to reassure young women about marriage, often to an older man not of their choosing. That inspired me to try to write an original fairy tale that did not end in marriage. As you can see, I both did and did not succeed.

As I wrote, I had fun imagining what it would feel like to be a snake and realized, by the end of the poem, that Rosina would be transformed—and strengthened—by her experience even after she had returned to human form. As my friend and fellow writer Robert Hiett said, she still had "scales beneath her soft skin."

FURTHER READING

FICTION

NOVELS

Daughter of the Bear King by Eleanor Arnason

Lives of the Monster Dogs by Kirsten Bakis

Sharp Teeth by Toby Barlow

The Innkeeper's Song by Peter S. Beagle

The Jaguar Princess by Clare Bell

Swim the Moon by Paul Brandon

St. Peter's Wolf by Michael Cadnum

The Bloody Chamber by Angela Carter

In a Dark Wood by Amanda Craig

Wilderness by Dennis Danvers

The Dreaming Place by Charles de Lint

Forests of the Heart by Charles de Lint

Greenmantle by Charles de Lint

Medicine Road by Charles de Lint

Someplace to be Flying by Charles de Lint

The Bad Blood Series by Debra Doyle and James Macdonald

Murkmere by Patricia Elliot

The Antelope Wife by Louise Erdrich

Sun and Moon, Ice and Snow by Jessica Day George

The Seventh Swan by Nicholas Stuart Gray

Bearskin by Gareth Hinds

Second Nature by Alice Hoffman

The Silent Strength of Stones by Nina Kiriki Hoffman

Blood Trail by Tanya Huff

The Fox Woman by Kij Johnson

Fudoki by Kij Johnson

Dogsbody by Diana Wynne Jones

The Limits of Enchantment by Graham Joyce

Owl in Love by Patrice Kindl

Blood and Chocolate by Annette Curtis Klause

The Fall of the Kings by Ellen Kushner and Delia Sherman

When Fox Was a Thousand by Larissa Lai

The Wandering Unicorn by Manuel Mujica Lainez

The Earthsea Books by Ursula K. Le Guin

The Claidi Journals by Tanith Lee

The Dragon Hoard by Tanith Lee

Brother to Dragons, Companion to Owls by Jane Lindskold

Through Wolf's Eyes by Jane Lindskold

The Gray Horse by R. A. McAvoy

Once Upon a Winter's Night by Dennis McKiernan

The Book of Atrix Wolfe by Patricia A. McKillip

The Riddlemaster Trilogy by Patricia A. McKillip

Something Rich and Strange by Patricia A. McKillip

Stepping from the Shadows by Patricia A. McKillip

Beauty by Robin McKinley

Deerskin by Robin McKinley

Rose Daughter by Robin McKinley

Coyote Blue by Christopher Moore

Nadya by Pat Murphy

Beast by Donna Jo Napoli

Fur Magic by Andre Norton

East by Edith Pattou

Through a Brazen Mirror by Delia Sherman

The Minotaur Takes a Cigarette Break by Steven Sherrill

The Shape-Changer's Wife by Sharon Shinn

Hannah's Garden by Midori Snyder

Soulstring by Midori Snyder

A Rumor of Gems by Ellen Steiber

A Walk in Wolf Wood by Mary Stewart

Swan's Wing by Ursula Synge

The Baker's Daughter by Margaret Tabor

Wilding by Melanie Tem

The Mavin Manyshaped Trilogy by Sheri S. Tepper

The Animal Wife by Elizabeth Marshall Thomas

Swan Maiden by Heather Tomlinson

The Once and Future King by T. H. White

Benighted by Kit Whitfield

The Wood Wife by Terri Windling

Snow White and Rose Red by Patricia C. Wrede

ANTHOLOGIES

Half Human, edited by Bruce Coville

Through the Eye of the Deer, edited by Carolyn Dunn and
Carol Comfort

GRAPHIC NOVELS

The Dream Hunters, by Neil Gaiman, illustrated by Yoshitaka Amano

Blue, by Elizabeth Genco, illustrated by Sami Makkonen

MYTH, FOLKLORE, AND NONFICTION

The Beast Within: A History of the Werewolf by Douglas Adams

"Where the White Stag Runs: Boundary and Transformation in Deer Myths,
Legends, and Songs" by Ari Berk (*The Journal of Mythic Arts*, Autumn 2003)

The Way of the Animal Powers by Joseph Campbell

A Dictionary of Sacred Myth by Tom Chetwynd

Symbolic and Mythological Animals by J. C. Cooper

"Deer Woman and the Living Myth of the Dreamtime" by Carolyn Dunn
(*The Journal of Mythic Arts*, Autumn 2003)

Shamanism: Archaic Techniques of Ecstasy by Mircea Eliade

"Fox Wives and Other Dangerous Women" by Heinz Insu Fenkl (*The Journal of Mythic Arts*, Winter 2000)

The Mabinogion translated and edited by Jeffrey Ganz

Raven Tales: Traditional Stories of Native Peoples by Peter Goodchild

Beauties and Beasts by Betsy Hearne

Birds in Legend, Fable and Folklore by E. Ingersoll

Deerdancer: The Shapeshifter Archetype in Story and Trance by Michele Jamal

Lady of the Beasts: The Goddess and her Sacred Animals by Buffie Johnson

In Search of the Swan Maiden by Barbara Fass Leavy

Deer Women and Elk Men: The Lakota Narratives of Ella Deloria by Julian Rice

The Frog King: On Legends, Fables, Fairy Tales, and Anecdotes of Animals by Boria Sax

The Serpent and the Swan: The Animal Bride in Folklore and Literature by Boria Sax

"The Monkey Girl" by Midori Snyder (in *Mirror, Mirror on the Wall: Women Writers Explore Their Favorite Fairy Tales* edited by Kate Bernheimer)

"Brother and Sister: A Matter of Seeing" by Ellen Steiber (*The Journal of Mythic Arts*, Spring 2007)

From the Beast to the Blonde: On Fairy Tales and Their Tellers by Marina Warner

Folklore in the English and Scottish Ballads by Charles Lowry Wimberly

"The Symbolism of Rabbits and Hares" by Terri Windling
(*The Journal of Mythic Arts*, Summer 2005)

Favorite Folktales from Around the World edited by Jane Yolen

Beauties, Beasts and Enchantment edited by Jack Zipes

ABOUT THE EDITOR

ELLEN DATLOW was editor of SCI FICTION, the multi award–winning fiction area of SCIFI.COM, for almost six years. She was fiction editor of *OMNI* for over seventeen years and has worked with an array of writers in and outside the science fiction/fantasy/horror genres. Her most recent anthologies include *Inferno*, *The Del Rey Book of Science Fiction and Fantasy*, *Poe: 19 New Tales Inspired by Edgar Allan Poe*, *Lovecraft Unbound* (M Press), *The Green Man*, *The Faery Reel*, *The Coyote Road*, and *Troll's-Eye View* (the latter four with Terri Windling). Forthcoming in 2010 are *Naked City: New Tales of Urban Fantasy* (St. Martin's), *Darkness: Two Decades of Modern Horror* (Tachyon Press), *Digital Domains* (Prime), and *Haunted Legends* (coedited with Nick Mamatas; Tor). She coedited *The Year's Best Fantasy and Horror* for twenty-one years, and now edits *Best Horror of the Year* (Night Shade Books). Datlow has won nine World Fantasy Awards, two Bram Stoker Awards, three Hugo Awards, five Locus Awards, two International Horror Guild Awards, and the Shirley Jackson Award for her editing. She was the recipient of the 2007 Karl Edward Wagner Award, given at the British Fantasy Society Convention for "outstanding contribution to the genre." She lives in New York City with two opinionated cats.

Her Web site is at www.datlow.com and she blogs at ellen-datlow.livejournal.com.

ABOUT THE EDITOR

TERRI WINDLING is an editor, artist, essayist, and the author of books for both children and adults. She has won nine World Fantasy Awards, the Mythopoeic Award, and the Bram Stoker Award, and placed on the short list for the Tiptree. She has edited over thirty anthologies of magical fiction, many of them in collaboration with Ellen Datlow. She was the fantasy editor of *The Year's Best Fantasy and Horror* annual volumes for sixteen years, edited (and often wrote) a regular column on myth for *Realms of Fantasy* magazine for fourteen years, and coedited the online *Journal of Mythic Arts* for eleven years. As a writer, Windling has published mythic novels for adults and young adults, picture books for children, poetry, and numerous essays on subjects ranging from fairy-tale history to profiles of J. M. Barrie and William Morris. As an artist, her paintings have been exhibited at museums and galleries across the United States and Europe. She is also the founder and codirector of The Endicott Studio, a transatlantic organization dedicated to mythic arts. Terri and her husband live in a small arts community on the edge of Dartmoor in Devon, England.

Please visit her Web site (www.terriwindling.com), her blog (windling.typepad.com/blog), and the Endicott Studio's Web site (www.endicott-studio.com).

ABOUT THE ILLUSTRATOR

CHARLES VESS's award-winning work has graced the pages of numerous comic book publishers and has been featured in several gallery and museum exhibitions across the nation, including the first major exhibition of Science Fiction and Fantasy Art (New Britain Museum of American Art, 1980). In 1991, Charles shared the prestigious World Fantasy Award for Best Short Story with Neil Gaiman for their collaboration on *Sandman* #19 (DC Comics)—the first and only time a comic book has held this honor. More recently, they have collaborated on the picture book *Blueberry Girl*.

In the summer of 1997, Vess won the Will Eisner Comic Industry Award for best penciler/inker for his work on *The Book of Ballads and Sagas* (since published as a hardcover collection) as well as *Sandman* #75. In 1999, he received the World Fantasy Award for Best Artist for his work on Neil Gaiman's *Stardust*.

He worked with Jeff Smith on *Rose*, the prequel to Smith's *Bone*; his collaborations with his friend Charles de Lint include the picture book *A Circle of Cats* and the illustrated novels *Seven Wild Sisters* and *Medicine Road*. His other work includes the illustrations for Emma Bull's adaptation of the traditional English ballad "The Black Fox" in the anthology *Firebirds*, and the cover and decorations for Ellen Datlow and Terri Windling's *The Green Man: Tales from the Mythic Forest*, *The Faery Reel: Tales from the Twilight Realm*, and *The Coyote Road: Trickster Tales*.

His Web site address is www.greenmanpress.com.